THE CLANSMAN

THE CLANSMAN

AN HISTORICAL ROMANCE
OF THE KU KLUX KLAN

BY

THOMAS DIXON, JR.

INTRODUCTION BY

THOMAS D. CLARK

THE UNIVERSITY PRESS OF KENTUCKY

Introduction copyright © 1970 by The University Press of Kentucky

Scholarly publisher for the Commonwealth,
serving Bellarmine College, Berea College, Centre
College of Kentucky, Eastern Kentucky University,
The Filson Club, Georgetown College, Kentucky
Historical Society, Kentucky State University,
Morehead State University, Murray State University,
Northern Kentucky University, Transylvania University,
University of Kentucky, University of Louisville,
and Western Kentucky University.

Editorial and Sales Offices: The University Press of Kentucky
663 South Limestone Street, Lexington, Kentucky 40508-4008

The Library of Congress has cataloged the first printing
of this title as follows:

Dixon, Thomas, 1864-1946.
    The clansman; an historical romance of the Ku Klux Klan.
    Introd. by Thomas D. Clark.   Lexington, University Press of
    Kentucky, 1970.
        xviii, 374 p.   21 cm.   (The Novel as American social history)
        ISBN 0-8131-0126-3

    1. Ku-Klux-Klan (1866-1869)—Fiction.   I. Title.
PZ3.D646 C 16   813'.5'2   71-104761
[PS3507.I93]   MARC

INTRODUCTION

by Thomas D. Clark

The first thing to be said in discussing Thomas Dixon, Jr.'s novel *The Clansman* is that no person of critical judgment thinks of it as having artistic conception or literary craftsmanship. One can readily agree with the opinion of the reviewer for the *Bookman* in February 1905, when he wrote, "*The Clansman* may be summed up as a very poor novel, a very ridiculous novel, not a novel at all, yet a novel with a great deal to it; a novel that very properly is going to interest many thousands of readers, of all degrees of taste and education, a book which will be discussed from all points of view, voted superlatively good and superlatively bad, but which will be read."

Other reviewers felt that Dixon had lost his sense of perspective. The reviewer for *Outlook* thought he had used such talent as he had only to arouse the worst passions in his readers, and that his novel would kindle unworthy feelings in the nation at a time when harmony between North and South was most vital. There can be no doubt that these and other reviewers were correct in their appraisals. But what they did not say was that the novel opened wider a vein of racial hatred which was to poison further an age already in a social and political upheaval.

The Clansman was published by Doubleday and Page early in 1905, three years after the appearance of Dixon's *The Leopard's Spots* and perhaps partly as a reaction to the praise and condemnation of the earlier book, which some critics found crude. Between the publication of these two books, Dixon refined his writing craftsmanship somewhat, smoothing crudities and softening angers.

Southerners at this time had almost completed the second phase of their political redemption. Beginning with Mississippi in 1890 and finishing with Oklahoma in 1910, all of the Southern states redrafted their constitutions.

Mississippians had set the pattern for throwing off the yoke of radicalism and thwarting the reconstruction amendments to the United States Constitution. They wrote into their new charter the so-called "Mississippi Plan" for disfranchising the Negro. This clause prescribed educational qualifications for voting which large numbers of whites and few Negroes could meet. Even those Negroes who did qualify were disfranchised either by intimidation or by arbitrary voter registrars. In Louisiana, constitution makers went a step further in disfranchisement by adopting a "grandfather clause" which denied registration to persons whose grandfathers could not vote prior to 1867.

The pattern was set. As constitutional revisions took place across the South it became clear that a major objective was barring Negro voters from the polls. In 1901, white Alabama delegates to a constitutional convention copied their Mississippi neighbors and created even more publicity by their actions. Rural editors published a stream of stories about the convention's activities, chortling over the fact that the Negro was being denied access to the polls. In ringing pronouncements these editors declared that Alabama was white man's country and that the Negro had no social or political claim on the state. White supremacy as an official policy was firmly planted in the South.

The United States Supreme Court established the principle of political discrimination based on race when in 1898 it upheld the Mississippi Plan in *Williams* v. *Mississippi,* although in 1915 the court struck down the grandfather clause in state constitutions in *Guinn and Beal* v. *U. S.*

In a much broader spectrum, Jim Crowism developed in other ways. In 1896 the Supreme Court enunciated the principle of "separate but equal" in *Plessy* v. *Ferguson,* a case arising out of discriminatory practices by a public carrier. At the Atlanta Cotton Exposition on September 19, 1895, Booker T. Washington, addressing a large white audience, reviewed the place of the Negro in Southern economics and society. In a dramatic gesture with his hand he too enunciated a philosophy of "separate and equal."

All of these incidents were in fact a culmination of the white supremacy struggle begun in 1865. Since 1876 Southern editors had carried on an active campaign against Negro participation in politics. From the publisher of the most insignificant little "patent sides" country weekly to Henry W. Grady of the *Atlanta Constitution* there was a rising crescendo of editorial clamor against political equality for Negroes. In a stirring speech in Dallas at the Texas State Fair in October 1887, Grady stated as forcibly as anyone could the position of Southern whites on racial matters: "I deliver to the young men of the South, I declare that the truth above all others to be worn unsullied and sacred in your hearts, to be surrendered to no force, sold for no price, compromised in no necessity, but cherished and defended as the covenant of your prosperity, and the pledge of peace to your children, is that the white race must dominate forever in the South, because it is the white race, and superior to that race by which its supremacy is threatened."

Two years before, Grady had engaged in an angry exchange of views on the Southern race problem with the novelist and short-story writer George W. Cable of

New Orleans. Cable had published an article in the *Century Magazine* entitled "The Freedman's Case in Equity." He had expressed the opinion that Southerners had been unfair to the Negro and needed to revise both their attitudes and their approaches. The Negro deserved a fairer deal at the polls, equal access to transportation facilities and schools, and greater economic opportunity. This article came as a thunderclap to most Southerners. While it did not advocate social equality, it implied, however vaguely, that such would become the case.

Grady prepared an immediate reply in which he set forth the white Southerners' position, and questioned both the attitudes of Negroes toward the issues Cable had raised and the capability of the Negro in many areas. Pettishly, he questioned whether or not Cable was a true Southerner, expressing doubt that any other white Southerner could be found who subscribed to such contentions. He introduced his essay "Plain Black and White" by asserting, "Let it be understood in the beginning, then, that the South will never adopt Mr. Cable's suggestion of intermingling of the races. It can never be driven into accepting it. So far from there being a growing sentiment in the South in favor of the indiscriminate mixing of the races, the intelligence of both races is moving farther from that proposition day by day." In an eloquent peroration he concluded, "And with the South the matter may be left. There it can be left with the fullest confidence that the honor of the Republic will be maintained, the rights of humanity guarded, and the problem worked out in such exact justice as the finite mind can measure or finite agencies administer."

Two major regional issues stirred both Cable and Grady in the 1880s. The first was the rising number of lynchings committed yearly. Again, the columns of weekly and daily newspapers carried literally hundreds of stories about either impending racial uprisings or lynchings. From 1880 until late 1904, when Dixon submitted the manuscript of *The Clansman* for publication, the stain of communal murder by lynching spread across the South, and continued to do so for many years. Even the most illiterate Southerner realized his region's honor was being sullied by the practice. So prevalent was the crime, however, and so bitter was criticism of the practice from outside the region that Southerners all but developed an obsession with the subject. In 1902, the year in which *The Leopard's Spots* was published, the Reverend John Carlisle Kilgo of Trinity College published an essay on lynching in the *South Atlantic Quarterly*. Kilgo suggested that the crime might be eliminated if Southerners were made less socially sensitive. He acknowledged, "A tedious task it is, but it is the cure. In proposing this solution it is not intended to criticise the standards of southern society. These standards of home life, purity, and liberty, are not too high, nor are they poetic dreams. But sensitiveness in social dispositions is no requisite to high ideals. It does not necessarily represent a moral fidelity to high ideals. A standard of conduct and the type of attitude toward it are different things. Poise is the surest mark of strength; excitability is the mark of weakness."

The second issue of the age in which Thomas Dixon, Jr., came to maturity was the economic plight of the South and especially of the Piedmont. It was clear by 1900 that the region's long devotion to staple agriculture had been a serious mistake. Since 1870 the cotton planting industry had suffered a gradual decline. The dream that cotton would finally be enthroned as economic king of Southern farming was the one idea Southerners had brought out of the Civil War virtually untarnished. Competition from abroad, a shifting of regional economies, overproduction, failure to diversify farming practices, and failure to balance agriculture with industry all played havoc with the rural Southern economy.

Both Negro and white farmers had become the victims of a ruinous system of credit and production. The dream of "forty acres and a mule," if in fact it had ever had any foundation, vanished quickly for the Negro after 1870. So did freedom in the classical sense as he and his friends had conceived it at the dawn of emancipation from slavery. A worse form of economic enslavement awaited both races in the sun-scorched cotton fields. Built into postwar tenant farming were elements of certain economic self-destruction.

By the mid-1880s newspaper editors, travelers, and other commentators actively criticized Southern agricultural failures. Even Southern farmers themselves, made desperate by their poverty, were stimulated to revolt against the system. They sought out "whipping boys" in merchants, bankers, railroad managers, state legislators, and congressmen. The resulting populist revolt was a rebellion against an economic system, which became also a conflict within Southern social and political ranks. It fostered the advent of political progressivism in the region, and at the same time denoted a sharp reaction in racial relations. It drove more deeply the wedge of separation between embattled white yeoman farmers and Negroes, and to a lesser extent, between white yeoman farmers and privileged Southern oligarchical leadership. Reflected in the revisionary constitutional conventions was the desire of the poor Southern white to snatch political control from the remaining pockets of plantation dominance and to vest it in the hands of the red-necked farmer and his demagogic leaders.

This was the South which was emerging at the time Thomas Dixon, Jr., graduated from Wake Forest College in 1883. Both Wake County and the area around Dixon's birthplace in Shelby, North Carolina, were disturbed by the changes which were coming to the South. In fact, since his birth on January 11, 1864, Dixon had known little else than crisis. For the most part his people had failed to make a success of farming on the thin soils of the great pine-covered crescent. The economic struggles of the farmers in this area had far deeper implications than those in the lower Southern cotton belt, deeper than the race problem itself. Farmers of the Piedmont were dependent upon the production of cotton, tobacco, and grains. Their farms were too small ever to permit expansion or the development of an efficient agricultural system of credit. Only one avenue for economic betterment was open to them—development of some kind of industrial employment which would relieve them of their dependence upon the land.

The years of Thomas Dixon's youth were a period in which the piedmont South sought with an almost religious fervor to cure its economic ills by developing a textile industry. In *The Clansman* Dixon reflects this *idée fixe* of his age by having the hero, Phil Stoneman, busy himself with the building of a cotton mill at the falls of Broad River. Here Dixon reveals his consciousness of the plight of the modern South.

Young Dixon realized that the people whom he had been taught by his Presbyterian family from infancy to regard as the chosen people of God, were now sinking hopelessly into economic chaos. To his shame and sense of outrage, he realized that it took more than blood and pride in old-world origins to cope with the realities of the late nineteenth century; even so, he could never fully accept the blow of poverty and economic defeat for his people. Thus it was that he wrote into his novels an almost fierce pride in Scotch ancestry and Calvinistic religion. He dedicated *The Clansman* to the memory of "A Scotch-Irish leader of the South, My Uncle, Colonel Leroy McAtee, Grand Titan of the Ku Klux Klan."

Despite his stout Presbyterian background, Dixon enrolled in the Baptist college of Wake Forest. When he left this institution in 1883 with an A. B. degree he went directly to the graduate seminar in history at Johns Hopkins University. On September 16 of that year, Woodrow Wilson went from Asheville, North Carolina, to enter that same university. The two young Southerners quickly became friends. In Herbert Baxter Adams's classroom they were introduced to the processes of scientific historical research and to the literature of history. Unlike Wilson, however, Dixon remained only one year at The Hopkins. In the fall of 1884 he returned to North Carolina and entered a private law school at Greensboro from which he was graduated the following spring with a bachelor's degree in law. That same year he was elected a member of the North Carolina legislature. On February 15, 1886, he wrote Wilson that he had just read a favorable review of Wilson's book *Congressional Government* and wished he were nearby to shake his hand. He himself, however, was now actively participating in the process of making government work.

He informed his Hopkins classmate that he was trying to get through the legislature a bill to revise the North Carolina assessment laws so as to increase the valuation on real property from $200,000,000 to $400,000,000 and at the same time to reduce the tax rate by 50 percent. Clearly he had his sights set on a more exciting future than a mere legislative career. He was also endeavoring, he told Wilson, to get a department of history and political science organized at the University of North Carolina, and hoped that it would be made "a most attractive feature of the University in a short time—you know the temper of our boys." He assured Wilson that the legislature was going "to make a large increase in the annual appropriation to the University, which is now on a genuine boom." Dixon not only envisioned his former classmate in the role of professor of history in the University of North Carolina, but helped secure for him the adornment of an honorary degree from Wake Forest College. On June 7, 1887, he wrote Wilson, "I today proposed your name to the Trustees of this institution for the degree of LL.D & I'm sure you will get it. And you will be the only one too though several have been proposed I understand & some of them backed by the Gov. of N. C. too. . . ." The degree was conferred on Wilson *in absentia*.

If the eager young legislator had a dream of moving into an academic career himself, it was indeed of short duration. In that year, 1886, he entered the Baptist ministry as pastor of a Raleigh church. He preached in Boston from 1888 to 1889, and then for a decade, 1889-1899, in New York City, where he attracted the attention of John D. Rockefeller. While serving the northern pastorates he also lectured around the lyceum circuit, and between 1899 and 1903 lecturing and writing were his chief occupations. It was during these years that he wrote *The Leopard's Spots* (1902), and *The One Woman* (1903), and no doubt made a beginning on *The Clansman*.

The turn of the century brought reassessment of the Reconstruction era. In these years, there began to appear the special state studies on radical rule: James W. Garner published his *Reconstruction in Mississippi* in 1901; William A. Dunning's *Essays on Civil War and Reconstruction* appeared in 1904; and Walter Lynwood Fleming's *Civil War and Reconstruction in Alabama,* in 1905. Numerous articles on the subject were being published by the periodical press, and young college professors just out of the classrooms of Dunning and Adams were organizing departments of history and initiating new courses in the Civil War and Reconstruction.

Thus it was that Dixon, writing between lyceum engagements, turned to the story of radical Reconstruction as a source for his third novel. *The Leopard's Spots* had treated the political redemption of the South from the viewpoint of white radicals, and now Dixon turned to the fount of the evil. His new novel, dealing with radicals and

Negroes, reflected at least a cursory knowledge of a fairly wide range of historical sources. Dixon revealed a familiarity with the biographies of Abraham Lincoln, Andrew Johnson, Thaddeus Stevens, Edwin Stanton, and Charles Sumner. He was so informed on the legislative history of Reconstruction that, as one reviewer stated, Dixon's novel seemed almost to consist of strung-together sections of the *Congressional Record*. Clearly he relied on J. S. Pike's *The Prostrate State* for information on Reconstruction in South Carolina. Possibly he had read the annual essays which appeared in the *American Annual Encyclopedia* and he also may have seen the voluminous reports of the special congressional committees which went south to investigate the activities of the Klan. It is doubtful, however, that he had read J. C. Lester's and D. L. Wilson's *Ku Klux Klan* (1905). His dedication of *The Clansman* to his uncle, grand titan of the Klan for the Shelby area, indicated his firsthand knowledge of that organization from childhood.

Certainly, Dixon knew at firsthand of the intense prejudice of Southern whites against the Negro. Grassroots Southerners were being swayed by the demogogic and racist harangues of Benjamin R. Tillman, Tom Watson, James Kimball Vardaman, and scores of their lesser imitators. Every incident involving racial relations was exaggerated out of all proportion to the actual facts. In 1901 Booker T. Washington of Tuskegee Institute called at the White House to see President Theodore Roosevelt. While he was in the president's office a waiter brought in a luncheon tray for the president, and Roosevelt invited his visitor to share it with him, as any decent Southerner would have. But Vardaman and Tillman and their newspaper supporters raised a great hullabaloo. Not stopping to get the facts nor really wanting to know them, they exaggerated the story into a formal affair where Negroes and whites danced together in the

Executive Mansion. When Roosevelt did later entertain Booker T. Washington at a White House dinner the hullabaloo over race-mixing grew even louder. Vardaman in all of his racy transilliteration described the incident as if it were some horrendous affair drawn out of the depths of a Miltonian castastrophe. He described the mixed dancing of Negroes and whites, and made much of the fact that Booker T. Washington's daughter had come down from an Eastern college to grace the occasion as belle of the ball. Hardly had the shouting over these affairs subsided when Mississippians raised a hue and cry over Roosevelt's appointment of Effie Cox, a Negro, as postmistress at Indianola, Mississippi. Actually, she had originally been appointed to the office by Benjamin Harrison and no one had objected.

While Mississippians were storming over the Indianola postmistress, the president appointed Dr. William D. Crum, a Negro physician, to be collector of customs in the port of Charleston, an act which prompted a similar reaction. Thus between 1900 and 1909 the race issue was continually raised in the South and in Congress. It was in this feverish moment in American social history that *The Clansman* was written and published.

There is no way of determining with any degree of accuracy the influence Dixon's novel exerted on public opinion. The book was popular and apparently had a wide readership in the South. It renewed in bruising, raw fiction the old hurts and animosities suffered after the war by a generation of Southerners then disappearing.

The Clansman is a novel in three parts: the first, an appraisal of the role of Abraham Lincoln in the war; then the grasp for power, after Andrew Johnson's succession to the presidency, by the radicals led by Thaddeus Stevens; and finally the Ku Klux Klan's redemption of the South from Negro and carpetbagger domination.

Dixon wrote of the South and its whites in the most

pronounced "moonlight and roses" vein. Every Southerner who had worn the Confederate gray was a knight wrapped in the armor of virtue, and every Southern woman was the epitome of gentility, humanitarianism, and feminine charm. He set his main stage in Piedmont, South Carolina. The precise place he had in mind can be located only by guess—perhaps the towns of Gaffney, York, or Lockhart— but clearly it was somewhere on the upper reaches of the Broad River and close to the North Carolina state line, just south of Dixon's own birthplace of Shelby.

Although it is not my purpose here to deal with the romantic aspects of this book nor to discuss its literary value as a work of fiction, certain features are too tempting to pass over without comment. One is that Dixon warped his facts, or rather fabricated them, to suit his purpose. He gave Thaddeus Stevens a chivalrous son and daughter of unspecified maternal ancestry, and moved the dying old reprobate to South Carolina to recuperate from a near-fatal illness. In Piedmont, and virtually from his deathbed, the Pennsylvania radical took an active hand in organizing the local freedmen under the binding oath of the Union League. He was determined to the end to throttle the white South with black hands.

Dixon came near turning himself into a writer of comic fiction at the point when Stevens's mythical son Phil has been saved from the radicals and the horrors of the Columbia torture chambers and maybe the wall. "Old Thad" shouts, "The Klan!—The Klan! No? Yes! It's true— glory to God, they've saved my boy! Phil! Phil!"

There is no comedy, however, in Dixon's characterizations of the Negro. He recited every scurrilous thing that had been said about the race. In one passage after another he portrayed the Negro as a sensuous brute whose every physical feature was the mark of the jungle and the untamed animal. He gave wide publicity to the images which the contemporary country editors, Tillman and

Vardaman, and even the Mississippi author Harris Dickson had created. Howling mobs of lynchers were doubtless placated by these same images when they attempted to rationalize their bloody acts. Dixon does not even suggest that white Southerners themselves had made serious mistakes in the Reconstruction era or later in their history. Nor is there any recognition of the constructive aspects of Reconstruction.

The Clansman might have fallen by the wayside as another third-rate novel, even though it was for a while widely read, had it not been for its subsequent history. In 1915 Dixon helped to convert the novel into a motion picture script for *The Birth of a Nation*. This was not only one of the first great motion picture spectaculars; it was one of the earliest attempts by the motion picture industry to deal with a social issue. *The Birth of a Nation* was popular and had a long run in both the North and South. In fact, it is still being shown on occasion. Again, no one can assess with accuracy the film's influence on the public mind. It is clear that the picture presented a dramatic visual image to hundreds of thousands of people who knew nothing of the book. The film version not only included some of the drama of *The Leopard's Spots* and all that of *The Clansman,* but added some of its own. No scholarly historian of Reconstruction was ever able to reach so wide or impressionable an audience as did Thomas Dixon. For every one person who knew of Pike's *Prostrate State,* or the books and articles which were then appearing on the subject, thousands got the message of the movie.

Between 1902 and 1939, Dixon wrote twenty-two novels none of which enjoyed success. During most of this period he also lectured throughout the country. In the late 1920s and 1930s he sought lecture engagements on his own. He interested himself in politics as an ardent Democrat, and in 1938 was rewarded by Franklin D.

Roosevelt with an appointment as clerk of the United States Court, Eastern District of North Carolina. Three years after he retired from this office he died at his home in Raleigh on April 3, 1946.

Already the South he had known and presented in his novels was crumbling. Once again the race problem was a pressing one. In nearby Durham a group of Negro leaders had drafted the "Durham Manifesto" which sought a liberalization of Southern white attitudes toward their Negro neighbors. In Chapel Hill, site of the University where Dixon had hoped to establish an outstanding history and political science department, Howard W. Odum published his "Racial Credo" which rejected and refuted almost every prejudice that Dixon had exhibited in *The Clansman.* Even more damaging to the old prejudices, a new generation of historians was industriously and dispassionately revising the whole story of Reconstruction. Pike's *Prostrate State* had been completely invalidated by a more searching and objective study of South Carolina during Reconstruction.

Time, however, was not to end with the publication of *The Clansman* and the production of *The Birth of a Nation.* The sentiments expressed by Dixon were the universal ones of the white supremacists, and were to be voiced in hundreds of different forms within the first half of the twentieth century. In the Southern irritation with the policies of Franklin D. Roosevelt, and especially with those of Harry S. Truman, the spirit of *The Clansman* was renewed. It was not until the Supreme Court decision in *Brown* v. *Board of Education of Topeka* in 1954, however, that the full force of racial hatred and unrest was unleashed in the extremist newspapers, pamphlets, and orations of the white citizens councils, the Ku Klux Klan, and other racist organizations. Thomas Dixon, Jr., had in fact given voice in his novel to one of the most powerful latent forces in the social and political mind of the South.

TO THE READER

"THE CLANSMAN" is the second book of a series of historical novels planned on the Race Conflict. "The Leopard's Spots" was the statement in historical outline of the conditions from the enfranchisement of the Negro to his disfranchisement.

"The Clansman" develops the true story of the "Ku Klux Klan Conspiracy," which overturned the Reconstruction régime.

The organisation was governed by the Grand Wizard Commander-in-Chief, who lived at Memphis, Tennessee. The Grand Dragon commanded a State, the Grand Titan a Congressional District, the Grand Giant a County, and the Grand Cyclops a Township Den. The twelve volumes of Government reports on the famous Klan refer chiefly to events which occurred after 1870, the date of its dissolution.

The chaos of blind passion that followed Lincoln's assassination is inconceivable to-day. The Revolution it produced in our Government, and the bold attempt of Thaddeus Stevens to Africanise ten great states of the American Union, read now like tales from "The Arabian Nights."

I have sought to preserve in this romance both the letter and the spirit of this remarkable period. The men who enact the drama of fierce revenge into which

To the Reader

I have woven a double love-story are historical figures. I have merely changed their names without taking a liberty with any essential historic fact.

In the darkest hour of the life of the South, when her wounded people lay helpless amid rags and ashes under the beak and talon of the Vulture, suddenly from the mists of the mountains appeared a white cloud the size of a man's hand. It grew until its mantle of mystery enfolded the stricken earth and sky. An "Invisible Empire" had risen from the field of Death and challenged the Visible to mortal combat.

How the young South, led by the reincarnated souls of the Clansmen of Old Scotland, went forth under this cover and against overwhelming odds, daring exile, imprisonment, and a felon's death, and saved the life of a people, forms one of the most dramatic chapters in the history of the Aryan race.

THOMAS DIXON, jr.

DIXONDALE, Va., December 14, 1904.

THE CLANSMAN

Book I—The Assassination

CHAPTER I

THE BRUISED REED

THE fair girl who was playing a banjo and singing to the wounded soldiers suddenly stopped, and, turning to the surgeon, whispered :

"What's that?"

"It sounds like a mob——"

With a common impulse they moved to the open window of the hospital and listened.

On the soft spring air came the roar of excited thousands sweeping down the avenue from the Capitol toward the White House. Above all rang the cries of struggling newsboys screaming an "Extra." One of them darted around the corner, his shrill voice quivering with excitement:

"*Extra! Extra! Peace! Victory!*"

Windows were suddenly raised, women thrust their heads out, and others rushed into the street and crowded around the boy, struggling to get his papers. He threw them right and left and snatched the money—no one asked for change. Without ceasing rose his cry:

3

"Extra! Peace! Victory! Lee has surrendered!"
At last the end had come.

The great North, with its millions of sturdy people and their exhaustless resources, had greeted the first shot on Sumter with contempt and incredulity. A few regiments went forward for a month's outing to settle the trouble. The Thirteenth Brooklyn marched gayly Southward on a thirty days' jaunt, with pieces of rope conspicuously tied to their muskets with which to bring back each man a Southern prisoner to be led in a noose through the streets on their early triumphant return! It would be unkind to tell what became of those ropes when they suddenly started back home ahead of the scheduled time from the first battle of Bull Run.

People from the South, equally wise, marched gayly North, to whip five Yankees each before breakfast, and encountered unforeseen difficulties.

Both sides had things to learn, and learned them in a school whose logic is final—a four years' course in the University of Hell—the scream of eagles, the howl of wolves, the bay of tigers, the roar of lions—all locked in Death's embrace, and each mad scene lit by the glare of volcanoes of savage passions!

But the long agony was over.

The city bells began to ring. The guns of the forts joined the chorus, and their deep steel throats roared until the earth trembled

Just across the street a mother who was reading the fateful news turned and suddenly clasped a boy to her heart, crying for joy. The last draft of half a million had called for him.

The Capital of the Nation was shaking off the long nightmare of horror and suspense. More than once the city had shivered at the mercy of those daring men in gray, and the reveille of their drums had startled even the President at his desk.

Again and again had the destiny of the Republic hung on the turning of a hair, and in every crisis, Luck, Fate, God, had tipped the scale for the Union.

A procession of more than five hundred Confederate deserters, who had crossed the lines in groups, swung into view, marching past the hospital, indifferent to the tumult. Only a nominal guard flanked them as they shuffled along, tired, ragged, and dirty. The gray in their uniforms was now the colour of clay. Some had on blue pantaloons, some blue vests, others blue coats captured on the field of blood. Some had pieces of carpet, and others old bags around their shoulders. They had been passing thus for weeks. Nobody paid any attention to them.

"One of the secrets of the surrender!" exclaimed Doctor Barnes. "Mr. Lincoln has been at the front for the past weeks with offers of peace and mercy, if they would lay down their arms. The great soul of the President, even the genius of Lee could not resist. His smile began to melt those gray ranks as the sun is warming the earth to-day."

"You are a great admirer of the President," said the girl, with a curious smile.

"Yes, Miss Elsie, and so are all who know him."

She turned from the window without reply. A shadow crossed her face as she looked past the long rows of cots, on which rested the men in blue, until her eyes found one on which lay, alone among his enemies, a young Confederate officer.

The surgeon turned with her toward the man.

"Will he live?" she asked.

"Yes, only to be hung."

"For what?" she cried.

"Sentenced by court-martial as a guerilla. It's a lie, but there's some powerful hand back of it—some mysterious influence in high authority. The boy wasn't fully conscious at the trial."

"We must appeal to Mr. Stanton."

"As well appeal to the Devil. They say the order came from his office."

"A boy of nineteen!" she exclaimed. "It's a shame. I'm looking for his mother. You told me to telegraph to Richmond for her."

"Yes, I'll never forget his cries that night, so utterly pitiful and childlike. I've heard many a cry of pain, but in all my life nothing so heart-breaking as that boy in fevered delirium talking to his mother. His voice is one of peculiar tenderness, penetrating and musical. It goes quivering into your soul, and compels you to listen until you swear it's your brother or sweetheart or sister or mother calling you. You should have seen him the day he fell. God of mercies, the pity and the glory of it!"

"Phil wrote me that he was a hero and asked me to look after him. Were you there?"

"Yes, with the battery your brother was supporting. He was the colonel of a shattered rebel regiment lying just in front of us before Petersburg. Richmond was doomed, resistance was madness, but there they were, ragged and half-starved, a handful of men not more than four hundred, but their bayonets gleamed and flashed in the sunlight. In the face of a murderous fire, he charged and actually drove our men out of an entrenchment. We concentrated our guns on him as he crouched behind this earthwork. Our own men lay outside in scores, dead, dying, and wounded. When the fire slacked, we could hear their cries for water.

"Suddenly this boy sprang on the breastwork. He was dressed in a new gray colonel's uniform that mother of his, in the pride of her soul, had sent him.

"He was a handsome figure—tall, slender, straight, a gorgeous yellow sash tasselled with gold around his waist, his sword flashing in the sun, his slouch hat cocked on one side and an eagle's feather in it.

"We thought he was going to lead another charge, but just as the battery was making ready to fire, he deliberately walked down the embankment in a hail of musketry and began to give water to our wounded men.

"Every gun ceased firing, and we watched him. He walked back to the trench, his naked sword flashed suddenly above that eagle's feather, and his grizzled ragamuffins sprang forward and charged us like so many demons.

"There were not more than three hundred of them now, but on they came, giving that hellish rebel yell at every jump—the cry of the hunter from the hilltop at the sight of his game! All Southern men are hunters, and that cry was transformed in war into something unearthly when it came from a hundred throats in chorus and the game was human.

"Of course, it was madness. We blew them down that hill like chaff before a hurricane. When the last man had staggered back or fallen, on came this boy alone, carrying the colours he had snatched from a falling soldier, as if he were leading a million men to victory.

"A bullet had blown his hat from his head, and we could see the blood streaming down the side of his face. He charged straight into the jaws of one of our guns. And then, with a smile on his lips and a dare to Death in his big brown eyes, he rammed that flag into the cannon's mouth, reeled, and fell! A cheer broke from our men.

"Your brother sprang forward and caught him in his arms, and as we bent over the unconscious form, he exclaimed: 'My God, doctor, look at him! He is so much like me I feel as if I had been shot myself!' They were as much alike as twins—only his hair was darker. I tell you, Miss Elsie, it's a sin to kill men like that. One such man is worth more to this Nation than every negro that ever set his flat foot on this continent!"

The girl's eyes had grown dim as she listened to the story.

"I will appeal to the President," she said, firmly.

"It's the only chance. And just now, he is under

tremendous pressure. His friendly order to the Virginia Legislature to return to Richmond, Stanton forced him to cancel. A master hand has organised a conspiracy in Congress to crush the President. They curse his policy of mercy as imbecility, and swear to make the South a second Poland. Their watchwords are vengeance and confiscation. Four-fifths of his party in Congress are in this plot. The President has less than a dozen real friends in either House on whom he can depend. They say that Stanton is to be given a free hand, and that the gallows will be busy. This cancelled order of the President looks like it."

"I'll try my hand with Mr. Stanton," she said with slow emphasis.

"Good luck, Little Sister—let me know if I can help," the surgeon answered cheerily as he passed on his round of work.

Elsie Stoneman took her seat beside the cot of the wounded Confederate and began softly to sing and play.

A little farther along the same row a soldier was dying, a faint choking just audible in his throat. An attendant sat beside him and would not leave till the last. The ordinary chat and hum of the ward went on indifferent to peace, victory, life, or death. Before the finality of the hospital, all other events of earth fade. Some were playing cards or checkers, some laughing and joking, and others reading.

At the first soft note from the singer, the games ceased, and the reader put down his book.

The banjo had come to Washington with the negroes

following the wake of the army. She had laid aside her guitar and learned to play all the stirring camp-songs of the South. Her voice was low, soothing, and tender. It held every silent listener in a spell.

As she played and sang the songs the wounded man loved, her eyes lingered in pity on his sun-bronzed face, pinched and drawn with fever. He was sleeping the stupid sleep that gives no rest. She could count the irregular pounding of his heart in the throb of the big vein on his neck. His lips were dry and burnt, and the little boyish moustache curled upward from the row of white teeth as if scorched by the fiery breath.

He began to talk in flighty sentences, and she listened—his mother—his sister—and yes, she was sure as she bent nearer—a little sweetheart who lived next door. They all had sweethearts—these Southern boys. Again he was teasing his dog—and then back in battle.

At length he opened his eyes, great dark-brown eyes, unnaturally bright, with a strange yearning look in their depths as they rested on Elsie. He tried to smile and feebly said:

"Here's—a—fly—on—my—left—ear—my—guns—can't—somehow—reach—him—won't—you——"

She sprang forward and brushed the fly away.

Again he opened his eyes.

"Excuse—me—for—asking—but am I alive?"

"Yes, indeed," was the cheerful answer.

"Well, now, then, is this me, or is it not me, or has a cannon shot me, or has the Devil got me?"

"It's you. The cannon didn't shoot you, but three

muskets did. The Devil hasn't got you yet, but he will, unless you're good."

"I'll be good if you won't leave me——"

Elsie turned her head away smiling, and he went on slowly:

"But I'm dead, I know. I'm sleeping on a cot with a canopy over it. I ain't hungry any more, and an angel has been hovering over me playing on a harp of gold——"

"Only a little Yankee girl playing the banjo."

"Can't fool me—I'm in heaven."

"You're in the hospital."

"Funny hospital—look at that harp and that big trumpet hanging close by it—that's Gabriel's trumpet——"

"No," she laughed. "This is the Patent Office building, that covers two blocks, now a temporary hospital. There are seventy thousand wounded soldiers in town, and more coming on every train. The thirty-five hospitals are overcrowded."

He closed his eyes a moment in silence, and then spoke with a feeble tremor:

"I'm afraid you don't know who I am—I can't impose on you—I'm a rebel——"

"Yes, I know. You are Colonel Ben Cameron. It makes no difference to me now which side you fought on."

"Well, I'm in heaven—been dead a long time. I can prove it, if you'll play again."

"What shall I play?"

"First, '*O Jonny Booker Help Dis Nigger*.'"

She played and sang it beautifully.

"Now, '*Wake Up In the Morning.*'"

Again he listened with wide, staring eyes, that saw nothing except visions within.

"Now, then, '*The Ole Gray Hoss.*'"

As the last notes died away, he tried to smile again:

"One more—'*Hard Times an' Wuss er Comin'.*'"

With deft, sure touch and soft negro dialect she sang it through.

"Now, didn't I tell you that you couldn't fool me? No Yankee girl could play and sing these songs. I'm in heaven, and you're an angel."

"Aren't you ashamed of yourself to flirt with me, with one foot in the grave?"

"That's the time to get on good terms with the angels— but I'm done dead——"

Elsie laughed in spite of herself.

"I know it," he went on, "because you have shining golden hair and amber eyes, instead of blue ones. I never saw a girl in my life before with such eyes and hair."

"But you're young yet."

"Never — was — such — a — girl — on — earth — you're—an——"

She lifted her finger in warning, and his eyelids drooped in exhausted stupor.

"You mustn't talk any more," she whispered, shaking her head.

A commotion at the door caused Elsie to turn from the cot. A sweet motherly woman of fifty, in an old faded black dress, was pleading with the guard to be allowed to pass.

"Can't do it, M'um. It's agin the rules."

"But I must go in. I've tramped for four days through a wilderness of hospitals, and I know he must be here."

"Special orders, M'um—wounded rebels in here that belong in prison."

"Very well, young man," said the pleading voice. "My baby boy's in this place, wounded and about to die. I'm going in there. You can shoot me if you like, or you can turn your head the other way."

She stepped quickly past the soldier, who merely stared with dim eyes out the door and saw nothing.

She stood for a moment with a look of helpless bewilderment. The vast area of the second story of the great monolithic pile was crowded with rows of sick, wounded, and dying men—a strange, solemn, and curious sight. Against the walls were ponderous glass cases, filled with models of every kind of invention the genius of man had dreamed. Between these cases were deep lateral openings, eight feet wide, crowded with the sick, and long rows of them were stretched through the centre of the hall. A gallery ran around above the cases, and this was filled with cots. The clatter of the feet of passing surgeons and nurses over the marble floor added to the weird impression.

Elsie saw the look of helpless appeal in the mother's face and hurried forward to meet her:

"Is this Mrs. Cameron, of South Carolina?"

The trembling figure in black grasped her hand eagerly:

"Yes, yes, my dear, and I'm looking for my boy, who is wounded unto death. Can you help me?"

"I thought I recognised you from a miniature I've seen,'
she answered softly.   "I'll lead you direct to his cot."

"Thank you, thank you!" came the low reply.

In a moment she was beside him, and Elsie walked away
to the open window through which came the chirp of
sparrows from the lilac-bushes in full bloom below.

The mother threw one look of infinite tenderness
on the drawn face, and her hands suddenly clasped in
prayer:

"I thank Thee, Lord Jesus, for this hour! Thou hast
heard the cry of my soul and led my feet!" She gently
knelt, kissed the hot lips, smoothed the dark tangled hair
back from his forehead, and her hand rested over his eyes.

A faint flush tinged his face.

"It's you, Mama—I—know—you—that's—your—hand
—or—else—it's—God's!"

She slipped her arms about him.

"My hero, my darling, my baby!"

"I'll get well now, Mama, never fear.   You see, I had
whipped them that day as I had many a time before.   I
don't know how it happened—my men seemed all to go
down at once.   You know—I couldn't surrender in
that new uniform of a colonel you sent me—we made a
gallant fight, and—now—I'm—just—a—little—tired—but
you are here, and it's all right."

"Yes, yes, dear.   It's all over now.   General Lee has
surrendered, and when you are better I'll take you home,
where the sunshine and flowers will give you strength
again."

"How's my little Sis?"

"Hunting in another part of the city for you. She's grown so tall and stately you'll hardly know her. Your Papa is at home, and don't know yet that you are wounded."

"And my sweetheart, Marion Lenoir?"

"The most beautiful little girl in Piedmont—as sweet and mischievous as ever. Mr. Lenoir is very ill, but he has written a glorious poem about one of your charges. I'll show it to you to-morrow. He is our greatest poet. The South worships him. Marion sent her love to you and a kiss for the young hero of Piedmont. I'll give it to you now."

She bent again and kissed him.

"And my dogs?"

"General Sherman left them, at least."

"Well, I'm glad of that—my mare all right?"

"Yes, but we had a time to save her—Jake hid her in the woods till the army passed."

"Bully for Jake."

"I don't know what we should have done without him."

"Old Aleck still at home, and getting drunk as usual?"

"No, he ran away with the army and persuaded every negro on the Lenoir place to go, except his wife, Aunt Cindy."

"The old rascal, when Mrs. Lenoir's mother saved him from burning to death when he was a boy!"

"Yes, and he told the Yankees those fire scars were made with the lash, and led a squad to the house one night to burn the barns. Jake headed them off and told on him. The soldiers were so mad they strung him up and thrashed him nearly to death. We haven't seen him since."

"Well, I'll take care of you, Mama, when I get home. Of course I'll get well. It's absurd to die at nineteen. You know I never believed the bullet had been moulded that could hit me. In three years of battle, I lived a charmed life and never got a scratch."

His voice had grown feeble and laboured, and his face flushed. His mother placed her hand on his lips.

"Just one more," he pleaded feebly. "Did you see the little angel who has been playing and singing for me? You must thank her."

"Yes, I see her coming now. I must go and tell Margaret, and we will get a pass and come every day."

She kissed him, and went to meet Elsie.

"And you are the dear girl who has been playing and singing for my boy, a wounded stranger here alone among his foes?"

"Yes, and for all the others, too."

Mrs. Cameron seized both of her hands and looked at her tenderly.

"You will let me kiss you? I shall always love you."

She pressed Elsie to her heart. In spite of the girl's reserve, a sob caught her breath at the touch of the warm lips. Her own mother had died when she was a baby, and a shy, hungry heart, long hidden from the world, leaped in tenderness and pain to meet that embrace.

Elsie walked with her to the door, wondering how the terrible truth of her boy's doom could be told.

She tried to speak, looked into Mrs. Cameron's face,

radiant with grateful joy, and the words froze on her lips. She decided to walk a little way with her. But the task became all the harder.

At the corner she stopped abruptly and bade her good-bye:

"I must leave you now, Mrs. Cameron. I will call for you in the morning and help you secure the passes to enter the hospital."

The mother stroked the girl's hand and held it lingeringly.

"How good you are," she said, softly. "And you have not told me your name?"

Elsie hesitated and said:

"That's a little secret. They call me Sister Elsie, the Banjo Maid, in the hospitals. My father is a man of distinction. I should be annoyed if my full name were known. I'm Elsie Stoneman. My father is the leader of the House. I live with my aunt."

"Thank you," she whispered, pressing her hand.

Elsie watched the dark figure disappear in the crowd with a strange tumult of feeling.

The mention of her father had revived the suspicion that he was the mysterious power threatening the policy of the President and planning a reign of terror for the South. Next to the President, he was the most powerful man in Washington, and the unrelenting foe of Mr. Lincoln, although the leader of his party in Congress, which he ruled with a rod of iron. He was a man of fierce and terrible resentments. And yet, in his personal life, to those he knew he was generous and considerate.

"Old Austin Stoneman, the Great Commoner," he was called, and his name was one to conjure with in the world of deeds. To this fair girl he was the noblest Roman of them all, her ideal of greatness. He was an indulgent father, and, while not demonstrative, loved his children with passionate devotion.

She paused and looked up at the huge marble columns that seemed each a sentinel beckoning her to return within to the cot that held a wounded foe. The twilight had deepened, and the soft light of the rising moon had clothed the solemn majesty of the building with shimmering tenderness and beauty.

"Why should I be distressed for one, an enemy, among these thousands who have fallen?" she asked herself. Every detail of the scene she had passed through with him and his mother stood out in her soul with startling distinctness—and the horror of his doom cut with the deep sense of personal anguish.

"He shall not die," she said, with sudden resolution. "I'll take his mother to the President. He can't resist her. I'll send for Phil to help me."

She hurried to the telegraph office and summoned her brother.

CHAPTER II

The Great Heart

THE next morning, when Elsie reached the obscure boarding-house at which Mrs. Cameron stopped, the mother had gone to the market to buy a bunch of roses to place beside her boy's cot.

As Elsie awaited her return, the practical little Yankee maid thought with a pang of the tenderness and folly of such people. She knew this mother had scarcely enough to eat, but to her bread was of small importance, flowers necessary to life. After all, it was very sweet, this foolishness of these Southern people, and it somehow made her homesick.

"How can I tell her!" she sighed. "And yet I must."

She had only waited a moment when Mrs. Cameron suddenly entered with her daughter. She threw her flowers on the table, sprang forward to meet Elsie, seized her hands and called to Margaret.

"How good of you to come so soon! This, Margaret, is our dear little friend who has been so good to Ben and to me."

Margaret took Elsie's hand and longed to throw her arms around her neck, but something in the quiet dignity of the Northern girl's manner held her back. She only

19

smiled tenderly through her big dark eyes, and softly
said:

"We love you! Ben was my last brother. We were
playmates and chums. My heart broke when he ran
away to the front. How can we thank you and your
brother!"

"I'm sure we've done nothing more than you would
have done for us," said Elsie, as Mrs. Cameron left the
room.

"Yes, I know, but we can never tell you how grateful
we are to you. We feel that you have saved Ben's life
and ours. The war has been one long horror to us since
my first brother was killed. But now it's over, and we
have Ben left, and our hearts have been crying for joy
all night."

"I hoped my brother, Captain Phil Stoneman, would
be here to-day to meet you and help me, but he can't
reach Washington before Friday."

"He caught Ben in his arms!" cried Margaret. "I
know he's brave, and you must be proud of him."

"Doctor Barnes says they are as much alike as twins—
only Phil is not quite so tall and has blond hair like mine."

"You will let me see him and thank him the moment
he comes?"

"Hurry, Margaret!" cheerily cried Mrs. Cameron,
re-entering the parlour. "Get ready; we must go at
once to the hospital."

Margaret turned and with stately grace hurried from
the room. The old dress she wore as unconscious of
its shabbiness as though it were a royal robe.

"And now, my dear, what must I do to get the passes?" asked the mother eagerly.

Elsie's warm amber eyes grew misty for a moment, and the fair skin with its gorgeous rose-tints of the North paled. She hesitated, tried to speak, and was silent.

The sensitive soul of the Southern woman read the message of sorrow words had not framed.

"Tell me, quickly! The doctor—has—not—concealed —his—true—condition—from—me?"

"No, he is certain to recover."

"What then?"

"Worse—he is condemned to death by court-martial."

"Condemned to death—a—wounded—prisoner—of— war!" she whispered slowly, with blanched face.

"Yes, he was accused of violating the rules of war as a guerilla raider in the invasion of Pennsylvania."

"Absurd and monstrous! He was on General Jeb Stuart's staff and could have acted only under his orders. He joined the infantry after Stuart's death, and rose to be a colonel, though but a boy. There's some terrible mistake!"

"Unless we can obtain his pardon," Elsie went on in even, restrained tones, "there is no hope. We must appeal to the President."

The mother's lips trembled, and she seemed about to faint.

"Could I see the President?" she asked, recovering herself with an effort.

"He has just reached Washington from the front, and is thronged by thousands. It will be difficult."

The mother's lips were moving in silent prayer, and her eyes were tightly closed to keep back the tears.

"Can you help me, dear?" she asked, piteously.

"Yes," was the quick response.

"You see," she went on, "I feel so helpless. I have never been to the White House or seen the President, and I don't know how to go about seeing him or how to ask him—and—I am afraid of Mr. Lincoln! I have heard so many harsh things said of him."

"I'll do my best, Mrs. Cameron. We must go at once to the White House and try to see him."

The mother lifted the girl's hand and stroked it gently.

"We will not tell Margaret. Poor child! she could not endure this. When we return, we may have better news. It can't be worse. I'll send her on an errand."

She took up the bouquet of gorgeous roses with a sigh, buried her face in the fresh perfume, as if to gain strength in their beauty and fragrance, and left the room.

In a few moments she had returned and was on her way with Elsie to the White House.

It was a beautiful spring morning, this eleventh day of April, 1865. The glorious sunshine, the shimmering green of the grass, the warm breezes, and the shouts of victory mocked the mother's anguish.

At the White House gates they passed the blue sentry pacing silently back and forth, who merely glanced at them with keen eyes and said nothing. In the steady beat of his feet the mother could hear the tramp of soldiers leading her boy to the place of death!

A great lump rose in her throat as she caught the first
view of the Executive Mansion gleaming white and silent
and ghostlike among the budding trees. The tall
columns of the great façade, spotless as snow, the spray
of the fountain, the marble walls, pure, dazzling and cold,
seemed to her the gateway to some great tomb in which
her own dead and the dead of all the people lay! To
her the fair white palace, basking there in the sunlight
and budding grass, shrub and tree, was the Judgment
House of Fate. She thought of all the weary feet that
had climbed its fateful steps in hope to return in despair,
of its fierce dramas on which the lives of millions had
hung, and her heart grew sick.

A long line of people already stretched from the entrance
under the portico far out across the park, awaiting their
turn to see the President.

Mrs. Cameron placed her hand falteringly on Elsie's
shoulder.

"Look, my dear, what a crowd already! Must we
wait in line?"

"No, I can get you past the throng with my father's
name."

"Will it be very difficult to reach the President?"

"No, it's very easy. Guards and sentinels annoy
him. He frets until they are removed. An assassin or
maniac could kill him almost any hour of the day or
night. The doors are open at all hours, very late at
night. I have often walked up to the rooms of his
secretaries as late as nine o'clock without being challenged by a soul."

"What must I call him? Must I say 'Your Excellency'?"

"By no means—he hates titles and forms. You should say 'Mr. President' in addressing him. But you will please him best if, in your sweet, homelike way, you will just call him by his name. You can rely on his sympathy. Read this letter of his to a widow. I brought it to show you."

She handed Mrs. Cameron a newspaper clipping on which was printed Mr. Lincoln's letter to Mrs. Bixby, of Boston, who had lost five sons in the war.

Over and over she read its sentences until they echoed as solemn music in her soul:

"I feel how weak and fruitless must be any words of mine which should attempt to beguile you from the grief of a loss so overwhelming. But I cannot refrain from tendering you the consolation that may be found in the thanks of the republic they died to save. I pray that our Heavenly Father may assuage the anguish of your bereavement, and leave you only the cherished memory of the loved and lost, and the solemn pride that must be yours to have laid so costly a sacrifice upon the altar of freedom.

"Yours very sincerely and respectfully,
"ABRAHAM LINCOLN."

"And the President paused amid a thousand cares to write that letter to a broken-hearted woman?" the mother asked.

"Yes."

"Then he is good down to the last secret depths of a great heart! Only a Christian father could have written that letter. I shall not be afraid to speak to him. And they told me he was an infidel!"

Elsie led her by a private way past the crowd and

into the office of Major Hay, the President's private secretary. A word from the Great Commoner's daughter admitted them at once to the President's room.

"Just take a seat on one side, Miss Elsie," said Major Hay; "watch your first opportunity and introduce your friend."

On entering the room, Mrs. Cameron could not see the President, who was seated at his desk surrounded by three men in deep consultation over a mass of official documents.

She looked about the room nervously and felt reassured by its plain aspect. It was a medium-sized, office-like place, with no signs of elegance or ceremony. Mr. Lincoln was seated in an arm-chair beside a high writing-desk and table combined. She noticed that his feet were large and that they rested on a piece of simple straw matting. Around the room were sofas and chairs covered with green worsted.

When the group about the chair parted a moment, she caught the first glimpse of the man who held her life in the hollow of his hand. She studied him with breathless interest. His back was still turned. Even while seated, she saw that he was a man of enormous stature, fully six feet four inches tall, legs and arms abnormally long, and huge broad shoulders slightly stooped. His head was powerful and crowned with a mass of heavy brown hair, tinged with silver.

He turned his head slightly and she saw his profile set in its short dark beard—the broad intellectual brow, half covered by unmanageable hair, his face marked with deep-cut lines of life and death, with great hollows in the cheeks and under the eyes. In the lines which marked the corners of his mouth she could see firmness, and his beetling brows and unusually heavy eyelids looked stern and formidable. Her heart sank. She looked again and saw goodness, tenderness, sorrow, canny shrewdness, and a strange lurking smile all haunting his mouth and eye.

Suddenly he threw himself forward in his chair, wheeled and faced one of his tormentors with a curious and comical expression. With one hand patting the other, and a funny look overspreading his face, he said:

"My friend, let me tell you something——"

The man again stepped before him, and she could hear nothing. When the story was finished, the man tried to laugh. It died in a feeble effort. But the President laughed heartily, laughed all over, and laughed his visitors out of the room.

Mrs. Cameron turned toward Elsie with a mute look of appeal to give her this moment of good-humour in which to plead her cause, but before she could move a man of military bearing suddenly stepped before the President.

He began to speak, but, seeing the look of stern decision in Mr. Lincoln's face, turned abruptly and said:

"Mr. President, I see you are fully determined not to do me justice!"

Mr. Lincoln slightly compressed his lips, rose quietly, seized the intruder by the arm, and led him toward the door.

"This is the third time you have forced your presence on me. sir, asking that I reverse the just sentence of a court-martial, dismissing you from the service. I told you my decision was carefully made and was final. Now I give you fair warning never to show yourself in this room again. I can bear censure, but I will not endure insult!"

In whining tones, the man begged for his papers he had dropped.

"Begone, sir," said the President, as he thrust him through the door. "Your papers will be sent to you."

The poor mother trembled at this startling act and sank back limp in her seat.

With quick, swinging stride the President walked back to his desk, accompanied by Major Hay and a young German girl, whose simple dress told that she was from the Western plains.

He handed the Secretary an official paper.

"Give this pardon to the boy's mother when she comes this morning," he said kindly to the Secretary, his eyes suddenly full of gentleness.

"How could I consent to shoot a boy raised on a farm, in the habit of going to bed at dark, for falling asleep at his post when required to watch all night? I'll never go into eternity with the blood of such a boy on my skirts."

Again the mother's heart rose.

"You remember the young man I pardoned for a similar offence in '62, about which Stanton made such a fuss?" he went on in softly reminiscent tones. "Well, here is that pardon."

He drew from the lining of his silk hat a photograph, around which was wrapped an executive pardon. Through the lower end of it was a bullet-hole stained with blood.

"I got this in Richmond. They found him dead on the field. He fell in the front ranks with my photograph in his pocket next to his heart, this pardon wrapped around it, and on the back of it in his boy's scrawl, '*God bless Abraham Lincoln.*' I love to invest in bonds like that."

The Secretary returned to his room, the girl who was waiting stepped forward, and the President rose to receive her.

The mother's quick eye noted, with surprise, the simple dignity and chivalry of manner with which he received this humble woman of the people.

With straightforward eloquence the girl poured out her story, begging for the pardon of her young brother who had been sentenced to death as a deserter. He listened in silence.

How pathetic the deep melancholy of his sad face! Yes, she was sure, the saddest face that God ever made in all the world! Her own stricken heart for a moment went out to him in sympathy.

The President took off his spectacles, wiped his forehead with the large red silk handkerchief he carried, and his eyes twinkled kindly down into the good German face.

"You seem an honest, truthful, sweet girl," he said, "and"—he smiled—"you don't wear hoop-skirts! I may be whipped for this, but I'll trust you and your brother, too. He shall be pardoned."

Elsie rose to introduce Mrs. Cameron, when a Congressman from Massachusetts suddenly stepped before her and pressed for the pardon of a slave-trader whose ship had been confiscated. He had spent five years in prison, but could not pay the heavy fine in money imposed.

The President had taken his seat again, and read the eloquent appeal for mercy. He looked up over his spectacles, fixed his eyes piercingly on the Congressman and said:

"This is a moving appeal, sir, expressed with great eloquence. I might pardon a murderer under the spell of such words, but a man who can make a business of going to Africa and robbing her of her helpless children and selling them into bondage—no, sir—he may rot in jail before he shall have liberty by any act of mine!"

Again the mother's heart sank.

Her hour had come. She must put the issue of life or death to the test, and, as Elsie rose and stepped quickly forward, she followed, nerving herself for the ordeal.

The President took Elsie's hand familiarly and smiled without rising. Evidently she was well-known to him.

"Will you hear the prayer of a broken-hearted mother of the South, who has lost four sons in General Lee's army?" she asked.

Looking quietly past the girl, he caught sight, for the first time, of the faded dress and the sorrow-shadowed face.

He was on his feet in a moment, extended his hand and led her to a chair.

"Take this seat, Madam, and then tell me in your own way what I can do for you."

In simple words, mighty with the eloquence of a mother's heart, she told her story and asked for the pardon of her boy, promising his word of honour and her own that he would never again take up arms against the Union.

"The war is over now, Mr. Lincoln," she said, "and we have lost all. Can you conceive the desolation of *my* heart? My four boys were noble men. They may have been wrong, but they fought for what they believed to be right. You, too, have lost a boy."

The President's eyes grew dim.

"Yes, a beautiful boy——" he said, simply.

"Well, mine are all gone but this baby. One of them sleeps in an unmarked grave at Gettysburg. One died in a Northern prison. One fell at Chancellorsville, one in the Wilderness, and this, my baby, before Petersburg. Perhaps I've loved him too much, this last one—he's only a child yet——"

"You shall have your boy, my dear Madam," the President said, simply, seating himself and writing a brief order to the Secretary of War.

The mother drew near his desk, softly crying. Through her tears she said:

"My heart is heavy, Mr. Lincoln, when I think of all the hard and bitter things we have heard of you."

"Well, give my love to the people of South Carolina, when you go home, and tell them that I am their President, and that I have never forgotten this fact in the darkest hours of this awful war; and I am going to do everything in my power to help them."

"You will never regret this generous act," the mother cried with gratitude.

"I reckon not," he answered. "I'll tell you something,

Madam, if you won't tell anybody. It's a secret of my administration. I'm only too glad of an excuse to save a life when I can. Every drop of blood shed in this war North and South has been as if it were wrung out of my heart. A strange fate decreed that the bloodiest war in human history should be fought under my direction. And I, to whom the sight of blood is a sickening horror —I have been compelled to look on in silent anguish because I could not stop it! Now that the Union is saved, not another drop of blood shall be spilled if I can prevent it."

"May God bless you!" the mother cried, as she received from him the order.

She held his hand an instant as she took her leave, laughing and sobbing in her great joy.

"I must tell you, Mr. President," she said, "how surprised and how pleased I am to find you are a Southern man."

"Why, didn't you know that my parents were Virginians, and that I was born in Kentucky?"

"Very few people in the South know it. I am ashamed to say I did not."

"Then, how did you know I am a Southerner?"

"By your looks, your manner of speech, your easy, kindly ways, your tenderness and humour, your firmness in the right as you see it, and, above all, the way you rose and bowed to a woman in an old, faded black dress, whom you knew to be an enemy."

"No, Madam, not an enemy now," he said, softly. "That word is out of date."

"If we had only known you in time——"

The President accompanied her to the door with a deference of manner that showed he had been deeply touched.

"Take this letter to Mr. Stanton at once," he said. "Some folks complain of my pardons, but it rests me after a hard day's work if I can save some poor boy's life. I go to bed happy, thinking of the joy I have given to those who love him."

As the last words were spoken, a peculiar dreaminess of expression stole over his care-worn face, as if a throng of gracious memories had lifted for a moment the burden of his life.

CHAPTER III

THE MAN OF WAR

ELSIE led Mrs. Cameron direct from the White House to the War Department.

"Well, Mrs. Cameron, what did you think of the President?" she asked.

"I hardly know," was the thoughtful answer. "He is the greatest man I ever met. One feels this instinctively."

When Mrs. Cameron was ushered into the Secretary's Office, Mr. Stanton was seated at his desk writing.

She handed the order of the President to a clerk, who gave it to the Secretary.

He was a man in the full prime of life, intellectual and physical, low and heavy set, about five feet eight inches in height and inclined to fat. His movements, however, were quick, and as he swung in his chair the keenest vigour marked every movement of body and every change of his countenance.

His face was swarthy and covered with a long, dark beard touched with gray. He turned a pair of little black piercing eyes on her and without rising said:

"So you are the woman who has a wounded son under sentence of death as a guerilla?"

"I am so unfortunate," she answered.

"Well, I have nothing to say to you," he went on in

33

a louder and sterner tone, "and no time to waste on you. If you have raised up men to rebel against the best government under the sun, you can take the consequences——"

"But, my dear sir," broke in the mother, "he is a mere boy of nineteen, who ran away three years ago and entered the service——"

"I don't want to hear another word from you!" he yelled in rage. "I have no time to waste—go at once. I'll do nothing for you."

"But I bring you an order from the President," protested the mother.

"Yes, I know it," he answered, with a sneer, "and I'll do with it what I've done with many others—see that it is not executed—now go."

"But the President told me you would give me a pass to the hospital, and that a full pardon would be issued to my boy!"

"Yes, I see. But let me give you some information. The President is a fool—a d—— fool! Now, will you go?"

With a sinking sense of horror, Mrs. Cameron withdrew and reported to Elsie the unexpected encounter.

"The brute!" cried the girl. "We'll go back immediately and report this insult to the President."

"Why are such men intrusted with power?" the mother sighed.

"It's a mystery to me, I'm sure. They say he is the greatest Secretary of War in our history. I don't believe it. Phil hates the sight of him, and so does every army

officer I know, from General Grant down.   I hope Mr.
Lincoln will expel him from the Cabinet for this insult."

When they were again ushered into the President's
office, Elsie hastened to inform him of the outrageous
reply the Secretary of War had made to his order.

"Did Stanton say that I was a fool?" he asked, with a
quizzical look out of his kindly eyes.

"Yes, he did," snapped Elsie.   "And he repeated it
with a blankety prefix."

The President looked good-humouredly out of the
window toward the War Office and musingly said:

"Well, if Stanton says that I am a blankety fool, it
must be so, for I have found out that he is nearly always
right, and generally means what he says.   I'll just step
over and see Stanton."

As he spoke the last sentence, the humour slowly faded
from his face, and the anxious mother saw back of those
patient gray eyes the sudden gleam of the courage and
conscious power of a lion.

He dismissed them with instructions to return the next
day for his final orders and walked over to the War
Department alone.

The Secretary of War was in one of his ugliest moods,
and made no effort to conceal it when asked his reasons
for the refusal to execute the order.

"The grounds for my action are very simple," he said,
with bitter emphasis.   "The execution of this traitor is
part of a carefully considered policy of justice on which
the future security of the Nation depends.   If I am to
administer this office, I will not be hamstrung by constant

Executive interference. Besides, in this particular case, I was urged that justice be promptly executed by the most powerful man in Congress. I advise you to avoid a quarrel with old Stoneman at this crisis in our history."

The President sat on a sofa with his legs crossed, relapsed into an attitude of resignation, and listened in silence until the last sentence, when suddenly he sat bolt upright, fixed his deep gray eyes intently on Stanton and said:

"Mr. Secretary, I reckon you will have to execute that order."

"I cannot do it," came the firm answer. "It is an interference with justice, and I will not execute it."

Mr. Lincoln held his eyes steadily on Stanton and slowly said:

"Mr. Secretary, it will have to be done."

Stanton wheeled in his chair, seized a pen and wrote very rapidly a few lines to which he fixed his signature. He rose with the paper in his hand, walked to his chief, and, with deep emotion, said:

"Mr. President, I wish to thank you for your constant friendship during the trying years I have held this office. The war is ended, and my work is done. I hand you my resignation."

Mr. Lincoln's lips came suddenly together, he slowly rose, and looked down with surprise into the flushed angry face.

He took the paper, tore it into pieces, slipped one of his long arms around the Secretary and said in low accents:

"Stanton, you have been a faithful public servant, and it is not for you to say when you will be no longer needed. Go on with your work. I will have my way in this matter; but I will attend to it personally."

Stanton resumed his seat, and the President returned to the White House.

CHAPTER IV

A CLASH OF GIANTS

ELSIE secured from the Surgeon-General temporary passes for the day, and sent her friends to the hospital with the promise that she would not leave the White House until she had secured the pardon.

The President greeted her with unusual warmth. The smile that had only haunted his sad face during four years of struggle, defeat, and uncertainty had now burst into joy that made his powerful head radiate light. Victory had lifted the veil from his soul, and he was girding himself for the task of healing the Nation's wounds.

"I'll have it ready for you in a moment, Miss Elsie," he said, touching with his sinewy hand a paper which lay on his desk, bearing on its face the red seal of the Republic. "I am only waiting to receive the passes."

"I am very grateful to you, Mr. President," the girl said, feelingly.

"But tell me," he said, with quaint, fatherly humour, "why you, of all our girls, the brightest, fiercest little Yankee in town, take so to heart a rebel boy's sorrows?"

Elsie blushed, and then looked at him frankly with a saucy smile.

"I am fulfilling the Commandments."

"Love your enemies?"

"Certainly. How could one help loving the sweet, motherly face you saw yesterday."

The President laughed heartily. "I see—of course, of course!"

"The Honourable Austin Stoneman," suddenly announced a clerk at his elbow.

Elsie started in surprise and whispered:

"Do not let my father know I am here. I will wait in the next room. You'll let nothing delay the pardon, will you, Mr. President?"

Mr. Lincoln warmly pressed her hand as she disappeared through the door leading into Major Hay's room, and turned to meet the Great Commoner who hobbled slowly in, leaning on his crooked cane.

At this moment he was a startling and portentous figure in the drama of the Nation, the most powerful parliamentary leader in American history, not excepting Henry Clay.

No stranger ever passed this man without a second look. His clean-shaven face, the massive chiselled features, his grim eagle look and cold, colourless eyes, with the frosts of his native Vermont sparkling in their depths, compelled attention.

His walk was a painful hobble. He was lame in both feet, and one of them was deformed. The left leg ended in a mere bunch of flesh, resembling more closely an elephant's hoof than the foot of a man.

He was absolutely bald, and wore a heavy brown wig that seemed too small to reach to the edge of his enormous forehead.

He rarely visited the White House. He was the able, bold, unscrupulous leader of leaders, and men came to see him. He rarely smiled, and when he did it was the smile of the cynic and misanthrope. His tongue had the lash of a scorpion. He was a greater terror to the trimmers and time-servers of his own party than to his political foes. He had hated the President with sullen, consistent, and unyielding venom from his first nomination at Chicago down to the last rumour of his new proclamation.

In temperament a fanatic, in impulse a born revolutionist, the word conservatism was to him as a red rag to a bull. The first clash of arms was music to his soul. He laughed at the call for 75,000 volunteers, and demanded the immediate equipment of an army of a million men. He saw it grow to 2,000,000. From the first, his eagle eye had seen the end and all the long, blood-marked way between. And from the first, he began to plot the most cruel and awful vengeance in human history.

And now his time had come.

The giant figure in the White House alone had dared to brook his anger and block the way; for old Stoneman was the Congress of the United States. The opposition was too weak even for his contempt. Cool, deliberate, and venomous, alike in victory or defeat, the fascination of his positive faith and revolutionary programme had drawn the rank and file of his party in Congress to him as charmed satellites.

The President greeted him cordially, and with his habitual deference to age and physical infirmity hastened to place for him an easy chair near his desk.

He was breathing heavily and evidently labouring under great emotion. He brought his cane to the floor with violence, placed both hands on its crook, leaned his massive jaws on his hands for a moment, and then said:

"Mr. President, I have not annoyed you with many requests during the past four years, nor am I here to-day to ask any favours. I have come to warn you that, in the course you have mapped out, the executive and legislative branches have come to the parting of the ways, and that your encroachments on the functions of Congress will be tolerated, now that the Rebellion is crushed, not for a single moment!"

Mr. Lincoln listened with dignity, and a ripple of fun played about his eyes as he looked at his grim visitor. The two men were face to face at last,—the two men above all others who had built and were to build the foundations of the New Nation,—Lincoln's in love and wisdom to endure forever, the Great Commoner's in hate and madness, to bear its harvest of tragedy and death for generations yet unborn.

"Well, now, Stoneman," began the good-humoured voice, "that puts me in mind——"

The old Commoner lifted his hand with a gesture of angry impatience:

"Save your fables for fools. Is it true that you have prepared a proclamation restoring the conquered province of North Carolina to its place as a state in the Union with no provision for Negro suffrage or the exile and disfranchisement of its rebels?"

The President rose and walked back and forth with his hands folded behind him, before answering.

"I have. The Constitution grants to the National Government no power to regulate suffrage, and makes no provision for the control of 'conquered provinces.'"

"Constitution!" thundered Stoneman. "I have a hundred constitutions in the pigeon-holes of my desk!"

"I have sworn to support but one."

"A worn-out rag——"

"Rag or silk, I've sworn to execute it, and I'll do it, so help me God!" said the quiet voice.

"You've been doing it for the past four years, haven't you!" sneered the Commoner. "What right had you under the Constitution to declare war against a 'sovereign' state? To invade one for coercion? To blockade a port? To declare slaves free? To suspend the writ of *habeas corpus?* To create the state of West Virginia by the consent of two states, one of which was dead, and the other one of which lived in Ohio? By what authority have you appointed military governors in the 'sovereign' states of Virginia, Tennessee, and Louisiana? Why trim the hedge and lie about it? We, too, are revolutionists, and you are our executive. The Constitution sustained and protected slavery. It *was* 'a league with death and a covenant with hell,' and our flag 'a polluted rag'!"

"In the stress of war," said the President, with a far-away look, "it was necessary that I do things as Commander-in-Chief of the Army and Navy to save the Union which I have no right to do now that the Union is saved and its Constitution preserved. My first duty is to re-establish the Constitution as our supreme law over every inch of our soil."

"The Constitution be d——d!" hissed the old man. "It was the creation, both in letter and spirit, of the slave-holders of the South."

"Then the world is their debtor, and their work is a monument of imperishable glory to them and to their children. I have sworn to preserve it!"

"We have outgrown the swaddling clothes of a babe. We will make new constitutions!"

"'Fools rush in where angels fear to tread,'" softly spoke the tall, self-contained man.

For the first time the old leader winced. He had long ago exhausted the vocabulary of contempt on the President, his character, ability, and policy. He felt as a shock the first impression of supreme authority with which he spoke. The man he had despised had grown into the great constructive statesman who would dispute with him every inch of ground in the attainment of his sinister life-purpose.

His hatred grew more intense as he realised the prestige and power with which he was clothed by his mighty office.

With an effort he restrained his anger, and assumed an argumentative tone.

"Can't you see that your so-called states are now but conquered provinces? That North Carolina and other waste territories of the United States are unfit to associate with civilised communities?"

"We fought no war of conquest," quietly urged the President, "but one of self-preservation as an indissoluble Union. No state ever got out of it, by the grace of God and the power of our arms. Now that we have won, and established for all time its unity, shall we stultify ourselves by declaring we were wrong? These states must be immediately restored to their rights, or we shall betray the blood we have shed. There are no 'conquered provinces' for us to spoil. A nation cannot make conquest of its own territory."

"But we are acting outside the Constitution," interrupted Stoneman.

"Congress has no existence outside the Constitution," was the quick answer.

The old Commoner scowled, and his beetling brows hid for a moment his eyes. His keen intellect was catching its first glimpse of the intellectual grandeur of the man with whom he was grappling. The facility with which he could see all sides of a question, and the vivid imagination which lit his mental processes, were a revelation. We always underestimate the men we despise.

"Why not out with it?" cried Stoneman, suddenly changing his tack. "You are determined to oppose Negro suffrage?"

"I have suggested to Governor Hahn of Louisiana to consider the policy of admitting the more intelligent and those who served in the war. It is only a suggestion. The state alone has the power to confer the ballot."

"But the truth is this little 'suggestion' of yours is only a bone thrown to radical dogs to satisfy our howlings for the moment! In your soul of souls, you don't believe in the equality of man if the man under comparison be a negro?"

"I believe that there is a physical difference between the white and black races which will forever forbid their living together on terms of political and social equality. If such be attempted, one must go to the wall."

"Very well, pin the Southern white man to the wall. Our party and the Nation will then be safe."

"That is to say, destroy African slavery and establish white slavery under Negro masters! That would be progress with a vengeance."

A grim smile twitched the old man's lips as he said:

"Yes, your prim conservative snobs and male waiting-maids in Congress went into hysterics when I armed the negroes. Yet the heavens have not fallen."

"True. Yet no more insane blunder could now be made than any further attempt to use these Negro troops. There can be no such thing as restoring this Union to its basis of fraternal peace with armed negroes, wearing the uniform of this Nation, tramping over the South, and rousing the basest passions of the freedmen and their former masters. General Butler, their old commander, is now making plans for their removal, at my request. He expects to dig the Panama Canal with these black troops.

"Fine scheme that—on a par with your messages to Congress asking for the colonisation of the whole Negro race!"

"It will come to that ultimately," said the President,

firmly. "The Negro has cost us $5,000,000,000, the deso-
lation of ten great states, and rivers of blood. We can
well afford a few million dollars more to effect a permanent
settlement of the issue. This is the only policy on which
Seward and I have differed——"

"Then Seward was not an utterly hopeless fool. I'm
glad to hear something to his credit," growled the old
Commoner.

"I have urged the colonisation of the negroes, and I
shall continue until it is accomplished. My emancipation proclamation was linked with this plan. Thousands
of them have lived in the North for a hundred years, yet
not one is the pastor of a white church, a judge, a governor,
a mayor, or a college president. There is no room for two
distinct races of white men in America, much less for two
distinct races of whites and blacks. We can have no inferior servile class, peon or peasant. We must assimilate
or expel. The American is a citizen king or nothing. I
can conceive of no greater calamity than the assimilation
of the Negro into our social and political life as our equal.
A mulatto citizenship would be too dear a price to pay
even for emancipation."

"Words have no power to express my loathing for such
twaddle!" cried Stoneman, snapping his great jaws together and pursing his lips with contempt.

"If the Negro were not here would we allow him to
land?" the President went on, as if talking to himself. "The duty to exclude carries the right to expel.
Within twenty years, we can peacefully colonise the Negro
in the tropics, and give him our language, literature,

religion, and system of government under conditions in which he can rise to the full measure of manhood. This he can never do here. It was the fear of the black tragedy behind emancipation that led the South into the insanity of secession. We can never attain the ideal Union our fathers dreamed, with millions of an alien, inferior race among us, whose assimilation is neither possible nor desirable. The Nation cannot now exist half white and half black, any more than it could exist half slave and half free."

"Yet 'God hath made of one blood all races,'" quoted the cynic with a sneer.

"Yes—but finish the sentence—'and fixed the bounds of their habitation.' God never meant that the Negro should leave his habitat or the white man invade his home. Our violation of this law is written in two centuries of shame and blood. And the tragedy will not be closed until the black man is restored to his home."

"I marvel that the minions of slavery elected Jeff. Davis their chief with so much better material at hand!"

"His election was a tragic and superfluous blunder. I am the President of the United States, North and South," was the firm reply.

"Particularly the South!" hissed Stoneman. "During all this hideous war, they have been your pets—these rebel savages who have been murdering our sons. You have been the ever-ready champion of traitors. And you now dare to bend this high office to their defence——"

"My God, Stoneman, are you a man or a savage!" cried the President. "Is not the North equally respon-

sible for slavery? Has not the South lost all? Have
not the Southern people paid the full penalty of all the
crimes of war? Are our skirts free? Was Sherman's
march a picnic? This war has been a giant conflict of
principles to decide whether we are a bundle of petty
sovereignties held by a rope of sand or a mighty nation of
freemen. But for the loyalty of four border Southern
states—but for Farragut and Thomas and their two
hundred thousand heroic Southern brethren who fought
for the Union against their own flesh and blood, we should
have lost. You cannot indict a people——"

"I do indict them!" muttered the old man.

"Surely," went on the even, throbbing voice, "surely,
the vastness of this war, its titanic battles, its heroism,
its sublime earnestness, should sink into oblivion all low
schemes of vengeance! Before the sheer grandeur of its
history, our children will walk with silent lips and uncovered heads."

"And forget the prison-pen at Andersonville!"

"Yes. We refused, as a policy of war, to exchange
those prisoners, blockaded their ports, made medicine
contrabrand, and brought the Southern Army itself to
starvation. The prison records, when made at last for
history, will show as many deaths on our side as on theirs."

"The murderer on the gallows always wins more sympathy than his forgotten victim," interrupted the cynic.

"The sin of vengeance is an easy one under the subtle
plea of justice," said the sorrowful voice. "Have we not
had enough of bloodshed? Is not God's vengeance
enough? When Sherman's army swept to the sea, be-

fore him lay the Garden of Eden, behind him stretched a
desert! A hundred years cannot give back to the wasted
South her wealth, or two hundred years restore to her the
lost seed treasures of her young manhood——"

"The imbecility of a policy of mercy in this crisis can
only mean the reign of treason and violence," persisted
the old man, ignoring the President's words.

"I leave my policy before the judgment bar of time,
content with its verdict. In my place, radicalism would
have driven the border states into the Confederacy, every
Southern man back to his kinsmen, and divided the North
itself into civil conflict. I have sought to guide and
control public opinion into the ways on which depended
our life. This rational flexibility of policy you and your
fellow radicals have been pleased to call my vacillating
imbecility."

"And what is your message for the South?"

"Simply this: 'Abolish slavery, come back home, and
behave yourself.' Lee surrendered to our offers of peace
and amnesty. In my last message to Congress, I told
the Southern people they could have peace at any moment
by simply laying down their arms and submitting to
National authority. Now that they have taken me at
my word, shall I betray them by an ignoble revenge?
Vengeance cannot heal and purify; it can only brutalise
and destroy."

Stoneman shuffled to his feet with impatience.

"I see it is useless to argue with you. I'll not waste
my breath. I give you an ultimatum. The South is
conquered soil. I mean to blot it from the map. Rather

than admit one traitor to the halls of Congress from these so-called states, I will shatter the Union itself into ten thousand fragments! I will not sit beside men whose clothes smell of the blood of my kindred. At least dry them before they come in. Four years ago, with yells and curses, these traitors left the halls of Congress to join the armies of Catiline. Shall they return to rule?"

"I repeat," said the President, "you cannot indict a people. Treason is an easy word to speak. A traitor is one who fights and loses. Washington was a traitor to George III. Treason won, and Washington is immortal. Treason is a word that victors hurl at those who fail."

"Listen to me," Stoneman interrupted with vehemence. "The life of our party demands that the Negro be given the ballot and made the ruler of the South. This can be done only by the extermination of its landed aristocracy, that their mothers shall not breed another race of traitors. This is not vengeance. It is justice, it is patriotism, it is the highest wisdom and humanity. Nature, at times, blots out whole communities and races that obstruct progress. Such is the political genius of these people that, unless you make the Negro the ruler, the South will yet reconquer the North and undo the work of this war."

"If the South in poverty and ruin can do this, we deserve to be ruled! The North is rich and powerful—the South, a land of wreck and tomb. I greet with wonder, shame, and scorn such ignoble fear! The Nation cannot be healed until the South is healed. Let the gulf be closed in which we bury slavery, sectional animosity, and all strifes and hatreds. The good sense of our people will never consent to your scheme of insane vengeance."

"The people have no sense. A new fool is born every second. They are ruled by impulse and passion."

"I have trusted them before, and they have not failed me. The day I left for Gettysburg to dedicate the battle-field, you were so sure of my defeat in the approaching convention that you shouted across the street to a friend as I passed, 'Let the dead bury the dead!' It was a brilliant sally of wit. I laughed at it myself. And yet the people unanimously called me again to lead them to victory."

"Yes, in the past," said Stoneman, bitterly, "you have triumphed, but mark my word: from this hour your star grows dim. The slumbering fires of passion will be kindled. In the fight we join to-day, I'll break your back and wring the neck of every dastard and time-server who fawns at your feet."

The President broke into a laugh that only increased the old man's wrath.

"I protest against the insult of your buffoonery!"

"Excuse me, Stoneman; I have to laugh or die beneath the burdens I bear, surrounded by such supporters!"

"Mark my word," growled the old leader, "from the moment you publish that North Carolina proclamation, your name will be a by-word in Congress."

"There are higher powers."

"You will need them."

"I'll have help," was the calm reply, as the dreaminess of the poet and mystic stole over the rugged face. "I

would be a presumptuous fool, indeed, if I thought that
for a day I could discharge the duties of this great office
without the aid of One who is wiser and stronger than
all others."

"You'll need the help of Almighty God in the course
you've mapped out!"

"Some ships come into port that are not steered," went
on the dreamy voice. "Suppose Pickett had charged
one hour earlier at Gettysburg? Suppose the *Monitor*
had arrived one hour later at Hampton Roads? I had
a dream last night that always presages great events.
I saw a white ship passing swiftly under full sail. I have
often seen her before. I have never known her port of
entry or her destination, but I have always known her
Pilot!"

The cynic's lips curled with scorn. He leaned heavily
on his cane, and took a shambling step toward the door.

"You refuse to heed the wishes of Congress?"

"If your words voice them, yes. Force your scheme
of revenge on the South, and you sow the wind to reap the
whirlwind."

"Indeed! and from what secret cave will this whirlwind come?"

"The despair of a mighty race of world-conquering
men, even in defeat, is still a force that statesmen reckon
with."

"I defy them," growled the old Commoner.

Again the dreamy look returned to Lincoln's face, and
he spoke as if repeating a message of the soul caught in the
clouds in an hour of transfiguration:

"And I'll trust the honour of Lee and his people. The mystic chords of memory, stretching from every battlefield and patriot grave to every living heart and hearthstone all over this broad land, will yet swell the chorus of the Union, when touchęd again, as they surely will be, by the better angels of our nature."

"You'll be lucky to live to hear that chorus."

"To dream it is enough. If I fall by the hand of an assassin now, he will not come from the South. · I was safer in Richmond, this week, than I am in Washington, to-day."

The cynic grunted and shuffled another step toward the door.

The President came closer.

"Look here, Stoneman; have you some deep personal motive in this vengeance on the South? Come, now, I've never in my life known you to tell a lie."

The answer was silence and a scowl.

"Am I right?"

"Yes and no. I hate the South because I hate the Satanic Institution of Slavery with consuming fury. It has long ago rotted the heart out of the Southern people. Humanity cannot live in its tainted air, and its children are doomed. If my personal wrongs have ordained me for a mighty task, no matter; I am simply the chosen instrument of Justice!"

Again the mystic light clothed the rugged face, calm and patient as Destiny, as the President slowly repeated:

"With malice toward none, with charity for all, with firmness in the right, as God gives me to see the right, I shall strive to finish the work we are in, and bind up the Nation's wounds."

"I've given you fair warning," cried the old Commoner, trembling with rage, as he hobbled nearer the door. "From this hour your administration is doomed."

"Stoneman," said the kindly voice, "I can't tell you how your venomous philanthropy sickens me. You have misunderstood and abused me at every step during the past four years. I bear you no ill will. If I have said anything to-day to hurt your feelings, forgive me. The earnestness with which you pressed the war was an invaluable service to me and to the Nation. I'd rather work with you than fight you. But now that we have to fight, I'd as well tell you I'm not afraid of you. I'll suffer my right arm to be severed from my body before I'll sign one measure of ignoble revenge on a brave, fallen foe, and I'll keep up this fight until I win, die, or my country forsakes me."

"I have always known you had a sneaking admiration for the South," came the sullen sneer.

"I love the South! It is a part of this Union. I love every foot of its soil, every hill and valley, mountain, lake, and sea, and every man, woman, and child that breathes beneath its skies. I am an American."

As the burning words leaped from the heart of the President, the broad shoulders of his tall form lifted, and his massive head rose in unconscious heroic pose.

"I marvel that you ever made war upon your loved ones!" cried the cynic.

"We fought the South because we loved her and would

not let her go.   Now that she is crushed and lies bleeding at our feet—you shall not make war on the wounded, the dying, and the dead!"

Again the lion gleamed in the calm gray eyes.

CHAPTER V

THE BATTLE OF LOVE

ELSIE carried Ben Cameron's pardon to the anxious mother and sister with her mind in a tumult. The name on these fateful papers fascinated her. She read it again and again with a curious personal joy that she had saved a life!

She had entered on her work among the hospitals a bitter partisan of her father's school, with the simple idea that all Southerners were savage brutes. Yet as she had seen the wounded boys from the South among the men in blue, more and more she had forgotten the difference between them. They were so young, these slender, dark-haired ones from Dixie—so pitifully young! Some of them were only fifteen, and hundreds not over sixteen. A lad of fourteen she had kissed one day in sheer agony of pity for his loneliness.

The part her father was playing in the drama on which Ben Cameron's life had hung puzzled her. Was his the mysterious arm back of Stanton? Echoes of the fierce struggle with the President had floated through the half-open door.

She had implicit faith in her father's patriotism and pride in his giant intellect. She knew that he was a king among men by divine right of inherent power. His sen-

56

sitive spirit, brooding over a pitiful lameness, had hidden from the world behind a frowning brow like a wounded animal. Yet her hand in hours of love, when no eye save God's could see, had led his great soul out of its dark lair. She loved him with brooding tenderness, knowing that she had gotten closer to his inner life than any other human being—closer than her own mother, who had died while she was a babe. Her aunt, with whom she and Phil now lived, had told her the mother's life was not a happy one. Their natures had not proved congenial, and her gentle Quaker spirit had died of grief in the quiet home in southern Pennsylvania.

Yet there were times when he was a stranger even to her. Some secret, dark and cold, stood between them. Once she had tenderly asked him what it meant. He merely pressed her hand, smiled wearily, and said:

"Nothing, my dear, only the Blue Devils after me again."

He had always lived in Washington in a little house with black shutters, near the Capitol, while the children had lived with his sister, near the White House, where they had grown from babyhood.

A curious fact about this place on the Capitol hill was that his housekeeper, Lydia Brown, was a mulatto, a woman of extraordinary animal beauty and the fiery temper of a leopardess. Elsie had ventured there once and got such a welcome she would never return. All sorts of gossip could be heard in Washington about this woman, her jewels, her dresses, her airs, her assumption of the dignity of the presiding genius of National legislation and her domination of the old Commoner and his life. It gradually crept into the newspapers and magazines, but he never once condescended to notice it.

Elsie begged her father to close this house and live with them.

His reply was short and emphatic:

"Impossible, my child. This club-foot must live next door to the Capitol. My house is simply an executive office at which I sleep. Half the business of the Nation is transacted there. Don't mention this subject again."

Elsie choked back a sob at the cold menace in the tones of this command, and never repeated her request. It was the only wish he had ever denied her, and, somehow, her heart would come back to it with persistence and brood and wonder over his motive.

The nearer she drew, this morning, to the hospital door, the closer the wounded boy's life and loved ones seemed to hers. She thought with anguish of the storm about to break between her father and the President— the one demanding the desolation of their land, wasted, harried, and unarmed!—the President firm in his policy of mercy, generosity, and healing.

Her father would not mince words. His scorpion tongue, set on fires of hell, might start a conflagration that would light the Nation with its glare. Would not his name be a terror for every man and woman born under Southern skies? The sickening feeling stole over her that he was wrong, and his policy cruel and unjust.

She had never before admired the President. It was fashionable to speak with contempt of him in Washington.

He had little following in Congress. Nine-tenths of the politicians hated or feared him, and she knew her father had been the soul of a conspiracy at the Capitol to prevent his second nomination and create a dictatorship, under which to carry out an iron policy of reconstruction in the South. And now she found herself heart and soul the champion of the President.

She was ashamed of her disloyalty, and felt a rush of impetuous anger against Ben and his people for thrusting themselves between her and her own. Yet how absurd to feel thus against the innocent victims of a great tragedy! She put the thought from her. Still she must part from them now before the brewing storm burst. It would be best for her and best for them. This pardon delivered would end their relations. She would send the papers by a messenger and not see them again. And then she thought with a throb of girlish pride of the hour to come in the future when Ben's big brown eyes would be softened with a tear when he would learn that she had saved his life. They had concealed all from him as yet.

She was afraid to question too closely in her own heart the shadowy motive that lay back of her joy. She read again with a lingering smile the name "Ben Cameron" on the paper with its big red Seal of Life. She had laughed at boys who had made love to her, dreaming a wider, nobler life of heroic service. And she felt that she was fulfilling her ideal in the generous hand she had extended to these who were friendless. Were they not the children of her soul in that larger, finer world of which she had dreamed and sung? Why should she give them up now for brutal politics? Their sorrow had been hers, their joy should be hers too. She would take the papers herself and then say good-bye.

She found the mother and sister beside the cot. Ben was sleeping with Margaret holding one of his hands. The mother was busy sewing for the wounded Confederate boys she had found scattered through the hospital.

At the sight of Elsie holding aloft the message of life, she sprang to meet her with a cry of joy.

She clasped the girl to her breast, unable to speak. At last she released her and said with a sob:

"My child, through good report and through evil report, my love will enfold you!"

Elsie stammered, looked away, and tried to hide her emotion. Margaret had knelt and bowed her head on Ben's cot. She rose at length, threw her arms around Elsie in a resistless impulse, kissed her and whispered:

"My sweet sister!"

Elsie's heart leaped at the words, as her eyes rested on the face of the sleeping soldier.

CHAPTER VI

THE ASSASSINATION

ELSIE called in the afternoon at the Camerons'
lodgings, radiant with pride, accompanied by her
brother.

Captain Phil Stoneman, athletic, bronzed, a veteran of
two years' service, dressed in his full uniform, was the
ideal soldier, and yet he had never loved war. He was
bubbling over with quiet joy that the end had come and he
could soon return to a rational life. Inheriting his mother's
temperament, he was generous, enterprising, quick, intelligent, modest, and ambitious. War had seemed to him
a horrible tragedy from the first. He had early learned to
respect a brave foe, and bitterness had long since melted
out of his heart.

He had laughed at his father's harsh ideas of Southern
life gained as a politician, and, while loyal to him after
a boy's fashion, he took no stock in his Radical programme.

The father, colossal egotist that he was, heard Phil's
protests with mild amusement and quiet pride in his
independence, for he loved this boy with deep tenderness.

Phil had been touched by the story of Ben's narrow
escape, and was anxious to show his mother and sister
every courtesy possible in part atonement for the wrong
he felt had been done them. He was timid with girls,

and yet he wished to give Margaret a cordial greeting for Elsie's sake. He was not prepared for the shock the first appearance of the Southern girl gave him.

When the stately figure swept through the door to greet him, her black eyes sparkling with welcome, her voice low and tender with genuine feeling, he caught his breath in surprise.

Elsie noted his confusion with amusement and said:

"I must go to the hospital for a little work. Now, Phil, I'll meet you at the door at eight o'clock."

"I'll not forget," he answered abstractedly, watching Margaret intently as she walked with Elsie to the door.

He saw that her dress was of coarse, unbleached cotton, dyed with the juice of walnut hulls and set with wooden hand-made buttons. The story these things told of war and want was eloquent, yet she wore them with unconscious dignity. She had not a pin or brooch or piece of jewelry. Everything about her was plain and smooth, graceful and gracious. Her face was large—the lovely oval type—and her luxuriant hair, parted in the middle, fell downward in two great waves. Tall, stately, handsome, her dark rare Southern beauty full of subtle languor and indolent grace, she was to Phil a revelation.

The coarse black dress that clung closely to her figure seemed alive when she moved, vital with her beauty. The musical cadences of her voice were vibrant with feeling, sweet, tender, and homelike. And the odour of the rose she wore pinned low on her breast he could swear was the perfume of her breath.

Lingering in her eyes and echoing in the tones of her

voice, he caught the shadowy memory of tears for the loved and lost that gave a strange pathos and haunting charm to her youth.

She had returned quickly and was talking at ease with him.

"I'm not going to tell you, Captain Stoneman, that I hope to be a sister to you. You have already made yourself my brother in what you did for Ben."

"Nothing, I assure you, Miss Cameron, that any soldier wouldn't do for a brave foe."

"Perhaps; but when the foe happens to be an only brother, my chum and playmate, brave and generous, whom I've worshipped as my beau-ideal man—why, you know I must thank you for taking him in your arms that day. May I, again?"

Phil felt the soft warm hand clasp his, while the black eyes sparkled and glowed their friendly message.

He murmured something incoherently, looked at Margaret as if in a spell, and forgot to let her hand go.

She laughed at last, and he blushed and dropped it as though it were a live coal.

"I was about to forget, Miss Cameron. I wish to take you to the theatre to-night, if you will go?"

"To the theatre?"

"Yes. It's to be an occasion, Elsie tells me. Laura Keene's last appearance in 'Our American Cousin,' and her one-thousandth performance of the play. She played it in Chicago at McVicker's, when the President was first nominated, to hundreds of the delegates who voted for him. He is to be present to-night, so the *Evening Star* has announced, and General and Mrs. Grant with him. It will be the opportunity of your life to see these famous men—besides, I wish you to see the city illuminated on the way."

Margaret hesitated.

"I should like to go," she said with some confusion. "But you see we are old-fashioned Scotch Presbyterians down in our village in South Carolina. I never was in a theatre—and this is Good Friday——"

"That's a fact, sure," said Phil, thoughtfully. "It never occurred to me. War is not exactly a spiritual stimulant, and it blurs the calendar. I believe we fight on Sundays oftener than on any other day."

"But I'm crazy to see the President since Ben's pardon. Mama will be here in a moment, and I'll ask her."

"You see, it's really an occasion," Phil went on. "The people are all going there to see President Lincoln in the hour of his triumph, and his great General fresh from the field of victory. Grant has just arrived in town."

Mrs. Cameron entered and greeted Phil with motherly tenderness.

"Captain, you're so much like my boy! Had you noticed it, Margaret?"

"Of course, Mama, but I was afraid I'd tire him with flattery if I tried to tell him."

"Only his hair is light and wavy, and Ben's straight and black, or you'd call them twins. Ben's a little taller—excuse us, Captain Stoneman, but we've fallen so in love with your little sister we feel we've known you all our lives."

"I assure you, Mrs. Cameron, your flattery is very sweet. Elsie and I do not remember our mother, and all this friendly criticism is more than welcome."

"Mama, Captain Stoneman asks me to go with him and his sister to-night to see the President at the theatre. May I go?"

"Will the President be there, Captain?" asked Mrs. Cameron.

"Yes, Madam, with General and Mrs. Grant—it's really a great public function in celebration of peace and victory. To-day the flag was raised over Ft. Sumter, the anniversary of its surrender four years ago. The city will be illuminated."

"Then, of course, you can go. I will sit with Ben. I wish you to see the President."

At seven o'clock Phil called for Margaret. They walked to the Capitol hill and down Pennsylvania Avenue.

The city was in a ferment. Vast crowds thronged the streets. In front of the hotel where General Grant stopped, the throng was so dense the streets were completely blocked. Soldiers, soldiers, soldiers, at every turn, in squads, in companies, in regimental crowds, shouting cries of victory.

The display of lights was dazzling in its splendour. Every building in every street in every nook and corner of the city was lighted from attic to cellar. The public buildings and churches vied with each other in the magnificence of their decorations and splendour of illuminations.

They turned a corner, and suddenly the Capitol on the throne of its imperial hill loomed a grand constellation in the heavens! Another look, and it seemed a huge bonfire against the background of the dark skies. Every window in its labyrinths of marble, from the massive base to its crowning statue of Freedom, gleamed and flashed with light—more than ten thousand jets poured their rays through its windows, besides the innumerable lights that circled the mighty dome within and without.

Margaret stopped, and Phil felt her soft hand grip his arm with sudden emotion.

"Isn't it sublime!" she whispered.

"Glorious!" he echoed.

But he was thinking of the pressure of her hand on his arm and the subtle tones of her voice. Somehow he felt that the light came from her eyes. He forgot the Capitol and the surging crowds before the sweeter creative wonder silently growing in his soul.

"And yet," she faltered, "when I think of what all this means for our people at home—their sorrow and poverty and ruin—you know it makes me faint."

Phil's hand timidly sought the soft one resting on his arm and touched it reverently.

"Believe me, Miss Margaret, it will be all for the best in the end. The South will yet rise to a nobler life than she has ever lived in the past. This is her victory as well as ours."

"I wish I could think so," she answered.

They passed the City Hall and saw across its front, in giant letters of fire thirty feet deep, the words:

"UNION, SHERMAN AND GRANT"

On Pennsylvania Avenue, the hotels and stores had hung every window, awning, cornice and swaying tree-top with lanterns. The grand avenue was bridged by tri-coloured balloons floating and shimmering ghost-like far up in the dark sky. Above these, in the blacker zone toward the stars, the heavens were flashing sheets of chameleon flames from bursting rockets.

Margaret had never dreamed such a spectacle. She walked in awed silence, now and then suppressing a sob for the memory of those she had loved and lost. A moment of bitterness would cloud her heart, and then with the sense of Phil's nearness, his generous nature, the beauty and goodness of his sister, and all they owed to her for Ben's life, the cloud would pass.

At every public building, and in front of every great hotel, bands were playing. The wild war strains, floating skyward, seemed part of the changing scheme of light. The odour of burnt powder and smouldering rockets filled the warm spring air.

The deep bay of the great fort guns now began to echo from every hill-top commanding the city, while a thousand smaller guns barked and growled from every square and park and crossing.

Jay Cooke & Co.'s banking-house had stretched across its front, in enormous blazing letters, the words:

"THE BUSY B'S—BALLS, BALLOTS AND BONDS"

Every telegraph and newspaper office was a roaring whirlpool of excitement, for the same scenes were being enacted in every centre of the North. The whole city was now a fairy dream, its dirt and sin, shame and crime, all wrapped in glorious light.

But above all other impressions was the contagion of the thunder shouts of hosts of men surging through the streets—the human roar with its animal and spiritual magnetism, wild, resistless, unlike any other force in the universe!

Margaret's hand again and again unconsciously tightened its hold on Phil's arm, and he felt that the whole celebration had been gotten up for his benefit.

They passed through a little park on their way to Ford's Theatre on 10th Street, and the eye of the Southern girl was quick to note the budding flowers and full-blown lilacs.

"See what an early spring!" she cried. "I know the flowers at home are gorgeous now."

"I shall hope to see you among them some day, when all the clouds have lifted," he said.

She smiled and replied with simple earnestness:

"A warm welcome will await your coming."

And Phil resolved to lose no time in testing it.

They turned into 10th Street, and in the middle of the block stood the plain three-story brick structure of Ford's Theatre, an enormous crowd surging about its five doorways and spreading out on the sidewalk and half across the driveway.

"Is that the theatre?" asked Margaret.

"Yes."

"Why, it looks like a church without a steeple."

"Exactly what it really is, Miss Margaret. It was a Baptist church. They turned it into a playhouse, by remodelling its gallery into a dress-circle and balcony and adding another gallery above. My grandmother Stoneman is a devoted Baptist, and was an attendant at this church. My father never goes to church, but he used to go here occasionally to please her. Elsie and I frequently came."

Phil pushed his way rapidly through the crowd with a peculiar sense of pleasure in making a way for Margaret and in defending her from the jostling throng.

They found Elsie at the door, stamping her foot with impatience.

"Well, I must say, Phil, this is prompt for a soldier who had positive orders," she cried. "I've been here an hour."

"Nonsense, Sis, I'm ahead of time," he protested.

Elsie held up her watch.

"It's a quarter past eight. Every seat is filled, and they've stopped selling standing-room. I hope you have good seats."

"The best in the house to-night, the first row in the balcony dress-circle, opposite the President's box. We can see everything on the stage, in the box, and every nook and corner of the house."

"Then, I'll forgive you for keeping me waiting."

They ascended the stairs, pushed through the throng standing, and at last reached the seats.

What a crowd! The building was a mass of throbbing humanity, and, over all, the hum of the thrilling wonder of peace and victory!

The women in magnificent costumes, officers in uniforms flashing with gold, the show of wealth and power, the perfume of flowers and the music of violin and flutes gave Margaret the impression of a dream, so sharp was the contrast with her own life and people in the South.

The interior of the house was a billow of red, white, and blue. The President's box was wrapped in two enormous silk flags with gold-fringed edges gracefully draped and hanging in festoons.

Withers, the leader of the orchestra, was in high feather. He raised his baton with quick, inspired movement. It was for him a personal triumph, too. He had composed the music of a song for the occasion. It was dedicated to the President, and the programme announced that it would be rendered during the evening between the acts by a famous quartet, assisted by the whole company in chorus. The National flag would be draped about each singer, worn as the togas of ancient Greece and Rome.

It was already known by the crowd that General and Mrs. Grant had left the city for the North and could not be present, but every eye was fixed on the door through which the President and Mrs. Lincoln would enter. It was the hour of his supreme triumph.

What a romance his life! The thought of it thrilled the crowd as they waited. A few years ago this tall, sad-faced man had floated down the Sangamon River into a rough Illinois town, ragged, penniless, friendless, alone, begging for work. Four years before, he had entered

Washington as President of the United States—but he came under cover of the night with a handful of personal friends, amid universal contempt for his ability and the loud expressed conviction of his failure from within and without his party. He faced a divided Nation and the most awful civil convulsion in history. Through it all he had led the Nation in safety, growing each day in power and fame, until to-night, amid the victorious shouts of millions of a Union fixed in eternal granite, he stood forth the idol of the people, the first great American, the foremost man of the world.

There was a stir at the door, and the tall figure suddenly loomed in view of the crowd. With one impulse they leaped to their feet, and shout after shout shook the building. The orchestra was playing "Hail to the Chief!" but nobody heard it. They saw the Chief! They were crying their own welcome in music that came from the rhythmic beat of human hearts.

As the President walked along the aisle with Mrs. Lincoln, accompanied by Senator Harris' daughter and Major Rathbone, cheer after cheer burst from the crowd. He turned, his face beaming with pleasure, and bowed as he passed.

The answer of the crowd shook the building to its foundations, and the President paused. His dark face flashed with emotion as he looked over the sea of cheering humanity. It was a moment of supreme exaltation. The people had grown to know and love and trust him, and it was sweet. His face, lit with the responsive fires of emotion, was transfigured. The soul seemed to separate

itself from its dreamy, rugged dwelling-place and flash
its inspiration from the spirit world.

As around this man's personality had gathered the
agony and horror of war, so now about his head glowed
and gleamed in imagination the splendours of victory.

Margaret impulsively put her hand on Phil's arm:

"Why, how Southern he looks! How tall and dark and
typical his whole figure!"

"Yes, and his traits of character even more typical,"
said Phil. "On the surface, easy friendly ways and the
tenderness of a woman—beneath, an iron will and lion
heart. I like him. And what always amazes me is his
universality. A Southerner finds in him the South, the
Western man the West, even Charles Sumner, from
Boston, almost loves him. You know I think he is the
first great all-round American who ever lived in the
White House."

The President's party had now entered the box, and as
Mr. Lincoln took the arm-chair nearest the audience,
in full view of every eye in the house, again the cheers
rent the air. In vain Withers' baton flew, and the
orchestra did its best. The music was drowned as in the
roar of the sea. Again he rose and bowed and smiled,
his face radiant with pleasure. The soul beneath those
deep-cut lines had long pined for the sunlight. His
love of the theatre and the humorous story were the
protest of his heart against pain and tragedy. He stood
there bowing to the people, the grandest, gentlest figure
of the fiercest war of human history—a man who was
always doing merciful things stealthily as others do

crimes. Little sunlight had come into his life, yet to-
night he felt that the sun of a new day in his history and
the history of the people was already tingeing the horizon
with glory.

Back of those smiles what a story! Many a night he
had paced back and forth in the telegraph office of the
War Department, read its awful news of defeat, and
alone sat down and cried over the list of the dead. Many
a black hour his soul had seen when the honours of
earth were forgotten and his great heart throbbed on his
sleeve. His character had grown so evenly and silently
with the burdens he had borne, working mighty deeds
with such little friction, he could not know, nor could the
crowd to whom he bowed, how deep into the core of the
people's life the love of him had grown.

As he looked again over the surging crowd, his tall
figure seemed to straighten, erect and buoyant, with the
new dignity of conscious triumphant leadership. He
knew that he had come unto his own at last, and his
brain was teeming with dreams of mercy and healing.

The President resumed his seat, the tumult died away,
and the play began amid a low hum of whispered comment
directed at the flag-draped box. The actors struggled in
vain to hold the attention of the audience, until finally
Hawk, the actor playing Dundreary, determined to
catch their ear, paused and said:

"Now, that reminds me of a little story, as Mr. Lincoln
says——"

Instantly the crowd burst into a storm of applause, the
President laughed, leaned over and spoke to his wife, and

the electric connection was made between the stage, the box, and the people.

After this, the play ran its smooth course, and the audience settled into its accustomed humour of sympathetic attention.

In spite of the novelty of this her first view of a theatre, the President fascinated Margaret. She watched the changing lights and shadows of his sensitive face with untiring interest, and the wonder of his life grew upon her imagination. This man who was the idol of the North and yet to her so purely Southern, who had come out of the West and yet was greater than the West or the North, and yet always supremely human—this man who sprang to his feet from the chair of State and bowed to a sorrowing woman with the deference of a knight, every man's friend, good-natured, sensible, masterful and clear in intellect, strong, yet modest, kind and gentle—yes, he was more interesting than all the drama and romance of the stage!

He held her imagination in a spell. Elsie, divining her abstraction, looked toward the President's box and saw approaching it along the balcony aisle the figure of John Wilkes Booth.

"Look," she cried, touching Margaret's arm. "There's John Wilkes Booth, the actor! Isn't he handsome? They say he's in love with my chum, a senator's daughter whose father hates Mr. Lincoln with perfect fury."

"He is handsome," Margaret answered. "But I'd be afraid of him, with that raven hair and eyes shining like something wild."

"They say he is wild and dissipated, yet half the silly girls in town are in love with him. He's as vain as a peacock."

Booth, accustomed to free access to the theatre, paused near the entrance to the box and looked deliberately over the great crowd, his magnetic face flushed with deep emotion, while his fiery inspiring eyes glittered with excitement.

Dressed in a suit of black broadcloth of faultless fit, from the crown of his head to the soles of his feet he was physically without blemish. A figure of perfect symmetry and proportion, his dark eyes flashing, his marble forehead crowned with curling black hair, agility and grace stamped on every line of his being—beyond a doubt he was the handsomest man in America. A flutter of feminine excitement rippled the surface of the crowd in the balcony as his well-known figure caught the wandering eyes of the women.

He turned and entered the door leading to the President's box, and Margaret once more gave her attention to the stage.

Hawk, as Dundreary, was speaking his lines and looking directly at the President, instead of at the audience:

"Society, eh? Well, I guess I know enough to turn you inside out, old woman, you darned old sockdologing man-trap!"

Margaret winced at the coarse words, but the galleries burst into shouts of laughter that lingered in ripples and murmurs and the shuffling of feet.

The muffled crack of a pistol in the President's box hushed the laughter for an instant.

No one realised what had happened, and when the assassin suddenly leaped from the box, with a blood-marked knife flashing in his right hand, caught his foot in the flags and fell to his knees on the stage, many thought it a part of the programme, and a boy, leaning over the gallery rail, giggled. When Booth turned his face of statuesque beauty lit by eyes flashing with insane desperation and cried, "*Sic semper tyrannis,*" they were only confirmed in this impression.

A sudden, piercing scream from Mrs. Lincoln, quivering, soul-harrowing! Leaning far out of the box, from ashen cheeks and lips leaped the piteous cry of appeal, her hand pointing to the retreating figure:

"The President is shot! He has killed the President!"

Every heart stood still for one awful moment. The brain refused to record the message—and then the storm burst!

A wild roar of helpless fury and despair! Men hurled themselves over the footlights in vain pursuit of the assassin. Already the clatter of his horse's feet could be heard in the distance. A surgeon threw himself against the door of the box, but it had been barred within by the cunning hand. Another leaped on the stage, and the people lifted him up in their arms and over the fatal railing.

Women began to faint, and strong men trampled down the weak in mad rushes from side to side.

The stage in a moment was a seething mass of crazed

men, among them the actors and actresses in costumes and painted faces, their mortal terror shining through the rouge. They passed water up to the box, and some tried to climb up and enter it.

The two hundred soldiers of the President's guard suddenly burst in, and, amid screams and groans of the weak and injured, stormed the house with fixed bayonets, cursing, yelling, and shouting at the top of their voices:

"Clear out! Clear out! You sons of Hell!"

One of them suddenly bore down with fixed bayonet toward Phil.

Margaret shrank in terror close to his side and tremblingly held his arm.

Elsie sprang forward, her face aflame, her eyes flashing fire, her little figure tense, erect, and quivering with rage:

"How dare you, idiot, brute!"

The soldier, brought to his senses, saw Phil in full captain's uniform before him, and suddenly drew himself up, saluting. Phil ordered him to guard Margaret and Elsie for a moment, drew his sword, leaped between the crazed soldiers and their victims and stopped their insane rush.

Within the box, the great head lay in the surgeon's arms, the blood slowly dripping down, and the tiny death bubbles forming on the kindly lips. They carried him tenderly out, and another group bore after him the unconscious wife. The people tore the seats from their fastenings and heaped them in piles to make way for the precious burdens.

As Phil pressed forward with Margaret and Elsie,

through the open door came the roar of the mob without, shouting its cries:

"The President is shot!"

"Seward is murdered!"

"Where is Grant?"

"Where is Stanton?"

"To arms! To arms!"

The peal of signal guns could now be heard, the roll of drums and the hurried tramp of soldiers' feet. They marched none too soon. The mob had attacked the stockade holding ten thousand unarmed Confederate prisoners.

At the corner of the block in which the theatre stood, they seized a man who looked like a Southerner and hung him to the lamp-post. Two heroic policemen fought their way to his side and rescued him.

If the temper of the people during the war had been convulsive, now it was insane—with one mad impulse and one thought—vengeance! Horror, anger, terror, uncertainty, each passion fanned the one animal instinct into fury.

Through this awful night, with the lights still gleaming as if to mock the celebration of victory, the crowds swayed in impotent rage through the streets, while the telegraph bore on the wings of lightning the awe-inspiring news. Men caught it from the wires, and stood in silent groups weeping, and their wrath against the fallen South began to rise as the moaning of the sea under a coming storm.

At dawn, black clouds hung threatening on the eastern horizon. As the sun rose, tingeing them for a moment with scarlet and purple glory, Abraham Lincoln breathed his last.

Even grim Stanton, the iron-hearted, stood by his bedside and through blinding tears exclaimed:

"Now he belongs to the ages!"

The deed was done. The wheel of things had moved. Vice-President Johnson took the oath of office, and men hailed him Chief; but the seat of Empire had moved from the White House to a little dark house on the Capitol hill, where dwelt an old club-footed man, alone, attended by a strange brown woman of sinister animal beauty and the restless eyes of a leopardess.

CHAPTER VII

The Frenzy of a Nation

PHIL hurried through the excited crowds with Margaret and Elsie, left them at the hospital door, and ran to the War Department to report for duty. Already the tramp of regiments echoed down every great avenue.

Even as he ran, his heart beat with a strange new stroke when he recalled the look of appeal in Margaret's dark eyes as she nestled close to his side and clung to his arm for protection. He remembered with a smile the almost resistless impulse of the moment to slip his arm around her and assure her of safety. If he had only dared!

Elsie begged Mrs. Cameron and Margaret to go home with her until the city was quiet.

"No," said the mother. "I am not afraid. Death has no terrors for me any longer. We will not leave Ben a moment now, day or night. My soul is sick with dread for what this awful tragedy will mean for the South! I can't think of my own safety. Can any one undo this pardon now?" she asked anxiously.

"I am sure they can not. The name on that paper should be mightier dead than living."

"Ah, but will it be? Do you know Mr. Johnson?

Can he control Stanton? He seemed to be more powerful than the President himself. What will that man do now with those who fall into his hands!"

"He can do nothing with your son, rest assured."

"I wish I knew it," said the mother, wistfully.

.   .   .   .

A few moments after the President died on Saturday morning, the rain began to pour in torrents. The flags that flew from a thousand gilt-tipped peaks in celebration of victory drooped to half-mast and hung weeping around their staffs. The litter of burnt fireworks, limp and crumbling, strewed the streets, and the tri-coloured lanterns and balloons, hanging pathetically from their wires, began to fall to pieces.

Never in all the history of man had such a conjunction of events befallen a nation. From the heights of heaven's rejoicing to be suddenly hurled to the depths of hell in piteous, helpless grief! Noon to midnight without a moment between. A pall of voiceless horror spread its shadows over the land. Nothing short of an earthquake or the sound of the archangel's trumpet could have produced the sense of helpless consternation, the black and speechless despair. The people read their papers in tears. The morning meal was untouched. By no other single feat could Death have carried such peculiar horror to every home. Around this giant figure, the heart-strings of the people had been unconsciously knit. Even his political enemies had come to love him.

Above all, in just this moment he was the incarnation of the Triumphant Union on the altar of whose life every house had laid the offering of its first-born. The tragedy was stupefying—it was unthinkable—it was the mockery of Fate!

Men walked the streets of the cities, dazed with the sense of blind grief. Every note of music and rejoicing became a dirge. All business ceased. Every wheel in every mill stopped. The roar of the great city was hushed, and Greed for a moment forgot his cunning.

The army only moved with swifter spring, tightening its mighty grip on the throat of the bleeding prostrate South.

As the day wore on its gloomy hours, and men began to find speech, they spoke to each other at first in low tones of Fate, of Life, of Death, of Immortality, of God—and then as grief found words the measureless rage of baffled strength grew slowly to madness.

On every breeze from the North came the deep-muttered curses.

Easter Sunday dawned after the storm, clear and beautiful in a flood of glorious sunshine. The churches were thronged as never in their history. All had been decorated for the double celebration of Easter and the triumph of the Union. The preachers had prepared sermons pitched in the highest anthem key of victory— victory over Death and the grave of Calvary, and victory for the Nation opening a future of boundless glory. The churches were labyrinths of flowers, and around every pulpit and from every gothic arch hung the red, white, and blue flags of the Republic.

And now, as if to mock this gorgeous pageant, Death had

in the night flung a black mantle over every flag and wound a strangling web of crape round every Easter flower.

When the preachers faced the silent crowds before them, looking into the faces of fathers, mothers, brothers, sisters, and lovers whose dear ones had been slain in battle or died in prison pens, the tide of grief and rage rose and swept them from their feet! The Easter sermon was laid aside. Fifty thousand Christian ministers, stunned and crazed by insane passion, standing before the altars of God, hurled into the broken hearts before them the wildest cries of vengeance — cries incoherent, chaotic, unreasoning, blind in their awful fury!

The pulpits of New York and Brooklyn led in the madness.

Next morning old Stoneman read his paper with a cold smile playing about his big stern mouth, while his furrowed brow flushed with triumph, as again and again he exclaimed: "At last! At last!"

Even Beecher, who had just spoken his generous words at Fort Sumter, declared:

"Never while time lasts, while heaven lasts, while hell rocks and groans, will it be forgotten that Slavery, by its minions, slew him, and slaying him made manifest its whole nature. A man can not be bred in its tainted air. I shall find saints in hell sooner than I shall find true manhood under its accursed influences. The breeding-ground of such monsters must be utterly and forever destroyed."

Dr. Stephen Tyng said:

"The leaders of this rebellion deserve no pity from any human being. Now let them go. Some other land must be their home. Their property is justly forfeited to the Nation they have attempted to destroy!"

In big black-faced type stood Dr. Charles S. Robinson's bitter words:

"This is the earliest reply which chivalry makes to our forbearance. Talk to me no more of the same race, of the same blood. He is no brother of mine and of no race of mine who crowns the barbarism of Treason with the murder of an unarmed husband in the sight of his wife. On the villains who led this Rebellion let justice fall swift and relentless. Death to every traitor of the South! Pursue them one by one! Let every door be closed upon them and judgment follow swift and implacable as death!"

Dr. Theodore Cuyler exclaimed:

"This is no time to talk of leniency and conciliation! I say before God, make no terms with rebellion short of extinction. Booth wielding the assassin's weapon is but the embodiment of the bowie-knife barbarism of a slaveholding oligarchy."

Dr. J. P. Thompson said:

"Blot every Southern state from the map. Strip every rebel of property and citizenship, and send them into exile beggared and infamous outcasts."

Bishop Littlejohn, in his impassioned appeal, declared:

"The deed is worthy of the Southern cause which was conceived in sin, brought forth in iniquity, and consummated in crime. This murderous hand is the same hand which lashed the slave's bared back, struck down New England's Senator for daring to speak, lifted the torch of rebellion, slaughtered in cold blood its thousands, and starved our helpless prisoners. Its end is not martyrdom, but dishonour."

Bishop Simpson said:

"Let every man who was a member of Congress and aided this rebellion be brought to speedy punishment. Let every officer educated at public expense, who turned his sword against his country, be doomed to a traitor's death!"

With the last note of this wild music lingering in the old Commoner's soul, he sat as if dreaming, laughed cynically, turned to the brown woman and said:

"My speeches have not been lost after all! Prepare dinner for six. My cabinet will meet here to-night."

While the press was re-echoing these sermons, gathering strength as they were caught and repeated in every town, village, and hamlet in the North, the funeral procession started westward. It passed in grandeur through the great cities on its journey of one thousand six hundred miles to the tomb. By day, by night, by dawn, by sunlight, by twilight, and lit by solemn torches, millions of silent men and women looked on his dead face. Around the person of this tall, lonely man, rugged, yet full of sombre dignity and spiritual beauty, the thoughts, hopes, dreams, and ideals of the people had gathered in four years of agony and death, until they had come to feel their own hearts beat in his breast and their own life throb in his life. The assassin's bullet had crashed into their own brains, and torn their souls and bodies asunder.

The masses were swept from their moorings, and reason destroyed. All historic perspective was lost. Our first assassination, there was no precedent for comparison. It had been over two hundred years in the world's history since the last murder of a great ruler, when William of Orange fell.

On the day set for the public funeral, twenty million people bowed at the same hour.

When the procession reached New York, the streets were lined with a million people. Not a sound could be heard save the tramp of soldiers' feet and the muffled cry of the dirge. Though on every foot of earth stood a human being, the silence of the desert and of Death! The Nation's living heroes rode in that procession, and passed without a sign from the people.

Four years ago he drove down Broadway as President-elect, unnoticed and with soldiers in disguise attending him lest the mob should stone him.

To-day, at the mention of his name in the churches, the preachers' voices in prayer wavered and broke into silence, while strong men among the crowd burst into sobs. Flags flew at half-mast from their steeples, and their bells tolled in grief.

Every house that flew but yesterday its banner of victory was shrouded in mourning. The flags and pennants of a thousand ships in the harbour drooped at half-mast, and from every staff in the city streamed across the sky the black mists of crape like strange meteors in the troubled heavens.

For three days every theatre, school, court, bank, shop, and mill was closed.

And with muttered curses men looked Southward.

Across Broadway the cortege passed under a huge transparency on which appeared the words:

"A Nation bowed in grief
Will rise in might to exterminate
The leaders of this accursed Rebellion."

Farther along swung the black-draped banner:

"Justice to Traitors
is
Mercy to the People."

Another flapped its grim message:

"The Barbarism of Slavery.
Can Barbarism go Further?"

Across the Ninth Regiment Armory, in gigantic letters, were the words:

"A Time for Weeping
But Vengeance is not Sleeping!"

When the procession reached Buffalo, the house of Millard Fillmore was mobbed because the ex-President, stricken on a bed of illness, had neglected to drape his house in mourning. The procession passed to Springfield through miles of bowed heads dumb with grief. The plough stopped in the furrow, the smith dropped his hammer, the carpenter his plane, the merchant closed his door, the clink of coin ceased, and over all hung brooding silence with low-muttered curses, fierce and incoherent.

No man who walked the earth ever passed to his tomb through such a storm of human tears. The pageants of Alexander, Cæsar, and Wellington were tinsel to this. Nor did the spirit of Napoleon, the Corsican Lieutenant of Artillery who once presided over a congress of kings whom he had conquered, look down on its like even in France.

And now that its pomp was done and its memory but bitterness and ashes, but one man knew exactly what he wanted and what he meant to do. Others were stunned by the blow. But the cold eyes of the Great Commoner, leader of leaders, sparkled, and his grim lips smiled. From him not a word of praise or fawning sorrow for the dead. Whatever he might be, he was not a liar : when he hated, he hated.

The drooping flags, the city's black shrouds, processions, torches, silent seas of faces and bared heads, the dirges and the bells, the dim-lit churches, wailing organs, fierce invectives from the altar, and the perfume of flowers piled in heaps by silent hearts—to all these was he heir.

And more—the fierce unwritten, unspoken, and unspeakable horrors of the war itself, its passions, its cruelties, its hideous crimes and sufferings, the wailing of its women, the graves of its men—all these now were his.

The new President bowed to the storm. In one breath he promised to fulfil the plans of Lincoln. In the next he, too, breathed threats of vengeance.

The edict went forth for the arrest of General Lee.

Would Grant, the Commanding General of the Army, dare protest? There were those who said that if Lee were arrested and Grant's plighted word at Appomattox smirched, the silent soldier would not only protest, but draw his sword, if need be, to defend his honour and the honour of the Nation. Yet—would he dare? It remained to be seen.

The jails were now packed with Southern men, taken unarmed from their homes. The old Capitol Prison was full, and every cell of every grated building in the city, and they were filling the rooms of the Capitol itself.

Margaret, hurrying from the market in the early morning with her flowers, was startled to find her mother bowed in anguish over a paragraph in the morning paper.

She rose and handed it to the daughter, who read:

"Dr. Richard Cameron, of South Carolina, arrived in Washington and was placed in jail last night, charged with complicity in the murder of President Lincoln. It was discovered that Jeff. Davis spent the night at his home in Piedmont, under the pretence of needing medical attention. Beyond all doubt, Booth, the assassin, merely acted under orders from the Arch Traitor. May the gallows have a rich and early harvest!"

Margaret tremblingly wound her arms around her mother's neck. No words broke the pitiful silence—only blinding tears and broken sobs.

Book II—The Revolution

CHAPTER I

THE FIRST LADY OF THE LAND

THE little house on the Capitol hill now became the centre of fevered activity. This house, selected by its grim master to become the executive mansion of the Nation, was perhaps the most modest structure ever chosen for such high uses.

It stood, a small, two-story brick building, in an unpretentious street. Seven windows opened on the front with black solid-panelled shutters. The front parlour was scantily furnished. A huge mirror covered one wall, and on the other hung a life-size oil portrait of Stoneman, and between the windows were a portrait of Washington Irving and a picture of a nun. Among his many charities he had always given liberally to an orphanage conducted by a Roman Catholic sisterhood.

The back parlour, whose single window looked out on a small garden, he had fitted up as a library, with leather-upholstered furniture, a large desk and table, and scattered on the mantel and about its walls were the photographs of his personal ιriends and a few costly prints. This room he used as his executive office, and no person was allowed to enter it without first stating his business or

presenting a petition to the tawny brown woman with restless eyes who sat in state in the front parlour and received
his visitors.   The books in their cases gave evidence of
little use for many years, although their character indicated the tastes of a man of culture.   His Pliny, Cæsar,
Cicero, Tacitus, Sophocles, and Homer had evidently been
read by a man who knew their beauties and loved them
for their own sake.

This house was now the Mecca of the party in power
and the storm-centre of the forces destined to shape the
Nation's life.   Senators, Representatives, politicians of
low and high degree, artists, correspondents, foreign ministers, and cabinet officers hurried to acknowledge their
fealty to the uncrowned king, and hail the strange brown
woman who held the keys of his house as the first lady of
the land.

When Charles Sumner called, a curious thing happened.
By a code agreed on between them, Lydia Brown touched
an electric signal which informed the old Commoner of
his appearance.   Stoneman hobbled to the folding-doors
and watched through the slight opening the manner in
which the icy Senator greeted the negress whom he was
compelled to meet thus as his social equal, though she was
always particular to pose as the superior of all who bowed
the knee to the old man whose house she kept.

Sumner at this time was supposed to be the most powerful man in Congress.   It was a harmless fiction which
pleased him, and at which Stoneman loved to laugh.

The Senator from Massachusetts had just made a speech
in Boston expounding the "Equality of Man," yet he

could not endure personal contact with a negro. He would go secretly miles out of the way to avoid it.

Stoneman watched him slowly and daintily approach this negress and touch her jewelled hand gingerly with the tips of his classic fingers as if she were a toad. Convulsed, he scrambled back to his desk and hugged himself while he listened to the flow of Lydia's condescending patronage in the next room.

"This world's too good a thing to lose!" he chuckled. "I think I'll live always."

When Sumner left, the hour for dinner had arrived, and by special invitation two men dined with him.

On his right sat an army officer who had been dismissed from the service, a victim of the mania for gambling. His ruddy face, iron-gray hair, and jovial mien indicated that he enjoyed life in spite of troubles.

There were no clubs in Washington at this time except the regular gambling-houses, of which there were more than one hundred in full blast.

Stoneman was himself a gambler, and spent a part of almost every night at Hall & Pemberton's Faro Palace on Pennsylvania Avenue, a place noted for its famous restaurant. It was here that he met Colonel Howle and learned to like him. He was a man of talent, cool and audacious, and a liar of such singular fluency that he quite captivated the old Commoner's imagination.

"Upon my soul, Howle," he declared soon after they met, "you made the mistake of your life going into the army. You're a born politician. You're what I call a natural liar, just as a horse is a pacer, a dog a setter. You lie without effort, with an ease and grace that excels all art. Had you gone into politics, you could easily have been Secretary of State, to say nothing of the vice-presidency. I would say President but for the fact that men of the highest genius never attain it."

From that moment Colonel Howle had become his charmed henchman. Stoneman owned this man body and soul, not merely because he had befriended him when he was in trouble and friendless, but because the Colonel recognised the power of the leader's daring spirit and revolutionary genius.

On his left sat a negro of perhaps forty years, a man of charming features for a mulatto, who had evidently inherited the full physical characteristics of the Aryan race, while his dark yellowish eyes beneath his heavy brows glowed with the brightness of the African jungle. It was impossible to look at his superb face, with its large, finely chiselled lips and massive nose, his big neck and broad shoulders, and watch his eyes gleam beneath the projecting forehead, without seeing pictures of the primeval forest. "The head of a Cæsar and the eyes of the jungle" was the phrase coined by an artist who painted his portrait.

His hair was black and glossy and stood in dishevelled profusion on his head between a kink and a curl. He was an orator of great power, and stirred a Negro audience as by magic.

Lydia Brown had called Stoneman's attention to this man, Silas Lynch, and induced the statesman to send him to college. He had graduated with credit and had entered

the Methodist ministry.   In his preaching to the freedmen
he had already become a marked man.   No house could
hold his audiences.

As he stepped briskly into the dining-room and passed
the brown woman, a close observer might have seen him
suddenly press her hand and caught her sly answering
smile, but the old man waiting at the head of the table
saw nothing.

The woman took her seat opposite Stoneman and presided over this curious group with the easy assurance of
conscious power.   Whatever her real position, she knew
how to play the rôle she had chosen to assume.

No more curious or sinister figure ever cast a shadow
across the history of a great nation than did this mulatto
woman in the most corrupt hour of American life.   The
grim old man who looked into her sleek tawny face and
followed her catlike eyes was steadily gripping the Nation
by the throat.   Did he aim to make this woman the
arbiter of its social life, and her ethics the limit of its
moral laws?

Even the white satellite who sat opposite Lynch flushed
for a moment as the thought flashed through his brain.

The old cynic, who alone knew his real purpose, was
in his most genial mood to-night, and the grim lines of his
powerful face relaxed into something like a smile as they
ate and chatted and told good stories.

Lynch watched him with keen interest.   He knew his
history and character, and had built on his genius a brilliant
scheme of life.

This man who meant to become the dictator of the

Republic had come from the humblest early conditions. His father was a worthless character, from whom he had learned the trade of a shoemaker, but his mother, a woman of vigorous intellect and indomitable will, had succeeded in giving her lame boy a college education. He had early sworn to be a man of wealth, and to this purpose he had throttled the dreams and ideals of a wayward imagination.

His hope of great wealth had not been realised. His iron mills in Pennsylvania had been destroyed by Lee's army. He had developed the habit of gambling, which brought its train of extravagant habits, tastes, and inevitable debts. In his vigorous manhood, in spite of his lameness, he had kept a pack of hounds and a stable of fine horses. He had used his skill in shoemaking to construct a set of stirrups to fit his lame feet, and had become an expert hunter to hounds.

One thing he never neglected—to be in his seat in the House of Representatives and wear its royal crown of leadership, sick or well, day or night. The love of power was the breath of his nostrils, and his ambitions had at one time been boundless. His enormous power to-day was due to the fact that he had given up all hope of office beyond the robes of the king of his party. He had been offered a cabinet position by the elder Harrison and for some reason it had been withdrawn. He had been promised a place in Lincoln's cabinet, but some mysterious power had snatched it away. He was the one great man who had now no ambition for which to trim and fawn and lie, and for the very reason that he had abolished himself he was the most powerful leader who ever walked the halls of Congress.

His contempt for public opinion was boundless. Bold, original, scornful of advice, of all the men who ever lived in our history he was the one man born to rule in the chaos which followed the assassination of the chief magistrate.

Audacity was stamped in every line of his magnificent head. His choicest curses were for the cowards of his own party before whose blanched faces he shouted out the hidden things until they sank back in helpless silence and dismay. His speech was curt, his humour sardonic, his wit biting, cruel and coarse.

The incarnate soul of revolution, he despised convention and ridiculed respectability.

There was but one weak spot in his armour—and the world never suspected it: the consuming passion with which he loved his two children. This was the side of his nature he had hidden from the eyes of man. A refined egotism, this passion, perhaps—for he meant to live his own life over in them—yet it was the one utterly human and lovable thing about him. And if his public policy was one of stupendous avarice, this dream of millions of confiscated wealth he meant to seize, it was not for himself but for his children.

As he looked at Howle and Lynch seated in his library after dinner, with his great plans seething in his brain, his eyes were flashing, intense and fiery, yet without colour —simply two centres of cold light.

"Gentlemen," he said at length. "I am going to ask

you to undertake for the Government, the Nation, and yourselves a dangerous and important mission. I say yourselves, because, in spite of all our beautiful lies, self is the centre of all human action. Mr. Lincoln has fortunately gone to his reward—fortunately for him and for his country. His death was necessary to save his life. He was a useful man living, more useful dead. Our party has lost its first President, but gained a god—why mourn?"

"We will recover from our grief," said Howle.

The old man went on, ignoring the interruption:

"Things have somehow come my way. I am almost persuaded late in life that the gods love me. The insane fury of the North against the South for a crime which they were the last people on earth to dream of committing is, of course, a power to be used—but with caution. The first execution of a Southern leader on such an idiotic charge would produce a revolution of sentiment. The people are an aggregation of hysterical fools."

"I thought you favoured the execution of the leaders of the Rebellion?" said Lynch with surprise.

"I did, but it is too late. Had they been tried by drumhead court-martial and shot dead red-handed as they stood on the field in their uniforms, all would have been well. Now sentiment is too strong. Grant showed his teeth to Stanton and he backed down from Lee's arrest. Sherman refused to shake hands with Stanton on the grandstand the day his army passed in review, and it's a wonder he didn't knock him down. Sherman was denounced as a renegade and traitor for giving Joseph E. Johnston the terms Lincoln ordered him to give. Lincoln dead,

his terms are treason! Yet had he lived, we should have
been called upon to applaud his mercy and patriotism.
How can a man live in this world and keep his face
straight?"

"I believe God permitted Mr. Lincoln's death to give
the great Commoner, the Leader of Leaders, the right of
way," cried Lynch with enthusiasm.

The old man smiled. With all his fierce spirit
he was as susceptible to flattery as a woman—far
more so than the sleek brown woman who carried the
keys of his house.

"The man at the other end of the Avenue, who pretends
to be President, in reality an alien of the conquered province of Tennessee, is pressing Lincoln's plan of 'restoring'
the Union. He has organised state governments in the
South, and their Senators and Representatives will appear
at the Capitol in December for admission to Congress.
He thinks they will enter——"

The old man broke into a low laugh and rubbed his
hands.

"My full plans are not for discussion at this juncture.
Suffice it to say, I mean to secure the future of our party
and the safety of this Nation. The one thing on which
the success of my plan absolutely depends is the
confiscation of the millions of acres of land owned
by the white people of the South and its division among
the negroes and those who fought and suffered in this
war——"

The old Commoner paused, pursed his lips, and fumbled his hands a moment, the nostrils of his eagle-

beaked nose breathing rapacity, sensuality throbbing in his massive jaws, and despotism frowning from his heavy brows.

"Stanton will probably add to the hilarity of nations, and amuse himself by hanging a few rebels," he went on, "but we will address ourselves to serious work. All men have their price, including the present company, with due apologies to the speaker——"

Howle's eyes danced, and he licked his lips.

"If I haven't suffered in this war, who has?"

"Your reward will not be in accordance with your sufferings. It will be based on the efficiency with which you obey my orders. Read that——"

He handed to him a piece of paper on which he had scrawled his secret instructions.

Another he gave to Lynch.

"Hand them back to me when you read them, and I will burn them. These instructions are not to pass the lips of any man until the time is ripe—four bare walls are not to hear them whispered."

Both men handed to the leader the slips of paper simultaneously.

"Are we agreed, gentlemen?"

"Perfectly," answered Howle.

"Your word is law to me, sir," said Lynch.

"Then you will draw on me personally for your expenses, and leave for the South within forty-eight hours. I wish your reports delivered to me two weeks before the meeting of Congress."

As Lynch passed through the hall on his way to the door,

the brown woman bade him good-night and pressed into his hand a letter.

As his yellow fingers closed on the missive, his eyes flashed for a moment with catlike humour.

The woman's face wore the mask of a sphinx.

CHAPTER II

WHEN the first shock of horror at her husband's peril passed, it left a strange new light in Mrs. Cameron's eyes.

The heritage of centuries of heroic blood from the martyrs of old Scotland began to flash its inspiration from the past. Her heart beat with the unconscious life of men and women who had stood in the stocks, and walked in chains to the stake with songs on their lips.

The threat against the life of Doctor Cameron had not only stirred her martyr blood: it had roused the latent heroism of a beautiful girlhood. To her he had ever been the lover and the undimmed hero of her girlish dreams. She spent whole hours locked in her room alone. Margaret knew that she was on her knees. She always came forth with shining face and with soft words on her lips.

She struggled for two months in vain efforts to obtain a single interview with him, or to obtain a copy of the charges. Doctor Cameron had been placed in the old Capitol Prison, already crowded to the utmost. He was in delicate health, and so ill when she had left home he could not accompany her to Richmond.

Not a written or spoken word was allowed to pass

those prison doors. She could communicate with him only through the officers in charge. Every message from him was the same. "I love you always. Do not worry. Go home the moment you can leave Ben. I fear the worst at Piedmont."

When he had sent this message, he would sit down and write the truth in a little diary he kept:

"Another day of anguish. How long, O Lord? Just one touch of her hand, one last pressure of her lips, and I am content. I have no desire to live—I am tired."

The officers repeated the verbal messages, but they made no impression on Mrs. Cameron. By a mental telepathy which had always linked her life with his her soul had passed those prison bars. If he had written the pitiful record with a dagger's point on her heart, she could not have felt it more keenly.

At times overwhelmed, she lay prostrate and sobbed in half-articulate cries. And then from the silence and mystery of the spirit world in which she felt the beat of the heart of Eternal Love would come again the strange peace that passeth understanding. She would rise and go forth to her task with a smile.

In July she saw Mrs. Surratt taken from this old Capitol Prison to be hung with Payne, Herold, and Atzerodt for complicity in the assassination. The military commission before whom this farce of justice was enacted, suspicious of the testimony of the perjured wretches who had sworn her life away, had filed a memorandum with their verdict asking the President for mercy.

President Johnson never saw this memorandum. It

was secretly removed in the War Department, and only replaced after he had signed the death-warrant.

In vain Annie Surratt, the weeping daughter, flung herself on the steps of the White House on the fatal day, begging and praying to see the President. She could not believe they would allow her mother to be murdered in the face of a recommendation of mercy. The fatal hour struck at last, and the girl left the White House with set eyes and blanched face, muttering incoherent curses.

The Chief Magistrate sat within, unconscious of the hideous tragedy that was being enacted in his name. When he discovered the infamy by which he had been made the executioner of an innocent woman, he made his first demand that Edwin M. Stanton resign from his cabinet as Secretary of War. And, for the first time in the history of America, a cabinet officer waived the question of honour and refused to resign.

With a shudder and blush of shame, strong men saw that day the executioner gather the ropes tightly three times around the dress of an innocent American mother and bind her ankles with cords. She fainted and sank backward upon the attendants, the poor limbs yielding at last to the mortal terror of death. But they propped her up and sprung the fatal trap.

A feeling of uncertainty and horror crept over the city and the Nation, as rumours of the strange doings of the "Bureau of Military Justice," with its secret factory of testimony and powers of tampering with verdicts, began to find their way in whispered stories among the people.

Public opinion, however, had as yet no power of ad-

justment. It was an hour of lapse to tribal insanity.
Things had gone wrong. The demand for a scapegoat,
blind, savage and unreasoning, had not spent itself. The
Government could do anything as yet, and the people
would applaud.

Mrs. Cameron had tried in vain to gain a hearing before the President. Each time she was directed to apply
to Mr. Stanton. She refused to attempt to see him, and
again turned to Elsie for help. She had learned that the
same witnesses who had testified against Mrs. Surratt
were being used to convict Doctor Cameron, and her
heart was sick with fear.

"Ask your father," she pleaded, "to write President
Johnson a letter in my behalf. Whatever his politics,
he can't be *your* father and not be good at heart."

Elsie paled for a moment. It was the one request she
had dreaded. She thought of her father and Stanton
with dread. How far he was supporting the Secretary
of War she could only vaguely guess. He rarely spoke of
politics to her, much as he loved her.

"I'll try, Mrs. Cameron," she faltered. "My father
is in town to-day and takes dinner with us before he leaves
for Pennsylvania to-night. I'll go at once."

With fear, and yet boldly, she went straight home to
present her request. She knew he was a man who
never cherished small resentments, however cruel and
implacable might be his public policies. And yet she
dreaded to put it to the test.

"Father, I've a very important request to make of you,"
she said, gravely.

"Very well, my child, you need not be so solemn. What is it?"

"I've some friends in great distress—Mrs. Cameron, of South Carolina, and her daughter Margaret."

"Friends of yours?" he asked with an incredulous smile. "Where on earth did you find them?"

"In the hospital, of course. Mrs. Cameron is not allowed to see her husband, who has been here in jail for over two months. He can not write to her, nor can she receive a letter from her. He is on trial for his life, is ill and helpless, and is not allowed to know the charges against him, while hired witnesses and detectives have broken open his house, searched his papers, and are ransacking heaven and earth to convict him of a crime of which he never dreamed. It's a shame. You don't approve of such things, I know?"

"What's the use of my expressing an opinion when you have already settled it?" he answered, good-humouredly.

"You *don't* approve of such injustice?"

"Certainly not, my child. Stanton's frantic efforts to hang a lot of prominent Southern men for complicity in Booth's crime is sheer insanity. Nobody who has any sense believes them guilty. As a politician I use popular clamour for my purposes, but I am not an idiot. When I go gunning, I never use a pop-gun or hunt small game."

"Then you will write the President a letter asking that they be allowed to see Doctor Cameron?"

The old man frowned.

"Think, father, if you were in jail and friendless, and I were trying to see you——"

"Tut, tut, my dear, it's not that I am unwilling—I was only thinking of the unconscious humour of *my* making a request of the man who at present accidentally occupies the White House. Of all the men on earth, this alien from the province of Tennessee! But I'll do it for you. When did you ever know me to deny my help to a weak man or woman in distress?"

"Never, father. I was sure you would do it," she answered, warmly.

He wrote the letter at once and handed it to her.

She bent and kissed him.

"I can't tell you how glad I am to know that you have no part in such injustice."

"You should not have believed me such a fool, but I'll forgive you for the kiss. Run now with this letter to your rebel friends, you little traitor! Wait a minute——"

He shuffled to his feet, placed his hand tenderly on her head, and stooped and kissed the shining hair.

"I wonder if you know how I love you? How I've dreamed of your future? I may not see you every day as I wish; I'm absorbed in great affairs. But more and more I think of you and Phil. I'll have a big surprise for you both some day."

"Your love is all I ask," she answered, simply.

Within an hour, Mrs. Cameron found herself before the new President. The letter had opened the door as by magic. She poured out her story with impetuous eloquence while Mr. Johnson listened in uneasy silence. His ruddy face, his hesitating manner and restless eyes were in striking contrast to the conscious power of the tall dark man who had listened so tenderly and sympathetically to her story of Ben but a few weeks before.

The President asked:

"Have you seen Mr. Stanton?"

"I have seen him once," she cried with sudden passion. "It is enough. If that man were God on His throne, I would swear allegiance to the Devil and fight him!"

The President lifted his eyebrows and his lips twitched with a smile:

"I shouldn't say that your spirits are exactly drooping! I'd like to be near and hear you make that remark to the distinguished Secretary of War."

"Will you grant my prayer?" she pleaded.

"I will consider the matter," he promised, evasively.

Mrs. Cameron's heart sank.

"Mr. President," she cried, bitterly, "I have felt sure that I had but to see you face to face and you could not deny me. Surely, it is but justice that he have the right to see his loved ones, to consult with counsel, to know the charges against him, and defend his life when attacked in his poverty and ruin by all the power of a mighty government? He is feeble and broken in health and suffering from wounds received carrying the flag of the Union to victory in Mexico. Whatever his errors of judgment in this war, it is a shame that a Nation for which he once bared his breast in battle should treat him as an outlaw without a trial."

"You must remember, Madam," interrupted the President, "that these are extraordinary times, and that popular clamour, however unjust, will make itself felt and must be heeded by those in power. I am sorry for you, and I trust it may be possible for me to grant your request."

"But I wish it now," she urged. "He sends me word I must go home. I can't leave without seeing him. I will die first."

She drew closer and continued in throbbing tones:

"Mr. President, you are a native Carolinian—you are of Scotch Covenanter blood. You are of my own people of the great past, whose tears and sufferings are our common glory and birthright. Come, you must hear me— I will take no denial. Give me now the order to see my husband!"

The President hesitated, struggling with deep emotion, called his secretary and gave the order.

As she hurried away with Elsie, who insisted on accompanying her to the jail door, the girl said:

"Mrs. Cameron, I fear you are without money. You must let me help you until you can return it."

"You are the dearest little heart I've met in all the world, I think sometimes," said the older woman, looking at her tenderly. "I wonder how I can ever pay you for half you've done already."

"The doing of it has been its own reward," was the soft reply. "May I help you?"

"If I need it, yes. But I trust it will not be necessary. I still have a little store of gold Doctor Cameron was wise enough to hoard during the war. I brought half of it with me when I left home, and we buried the rest. I hope to find it on my return. And if we can save the twenty bales of cotton we have hidden we shall be relieved of want."

"I'm ashamed of my country when I think of such ignoble methods as have been used against Doctor Cameron. My father is indignant too."

The last sentence Elsie spoke with eager girlish pride.

"I am very grateful to your father for his letter. I am sorry he has left the city before I could meet and thank him personally. You must tell him for me."

At the jail the order of the President was not honoured for three hours, and Mrs. Cameron paced the street in angry impatience at first and then in dull despair.

"Do you think that man Stanton would dare defy the President?" she asked, anxiously.

"No," said Elsie, "but he is delaying as long as possible as an act of petty tyranny."

At last the messenger arrived from the War Department permitting an order of the Chief Magistrate of the Nation, the Commander-in-Chief of its Army and Navy, to be executed.

The grated door swung on its heavy hinges, and the wife and mother lay sobbing in the arms of the lover of her youth.

For two hours they poured into each other's hearts the story of their sorrows and struggles during the six fateful months that had passed. When she would return from every theme back to his danger, he would laugh her fears to scorn.

"Nonsense, my dear, I'm as innocent as a babe. Mr. Davis was suffering from erysipelas, and I kept him in

my house that night to relieve his pain. It will all blow
over. I'm happy now that I have seen you. Ben will
be up in a few days. You must return at once. You
have no idea of the wild chaos at home. I left Jake in
charge. I have implicit faith in him, but there's no telling what may happen. I will not spend another moment
in peace until you go."

The proud old man spoke of his own danger with easy
assurance. He was absolutely certain, since the day of
Mrs. Surratt's execution, that he would be railroaded to
the gallows by the same methods. He had long looked
on the end with indifference, and had ceased to desire to
live except to see his loved ones again.

In vain she warned him of danger.

"My peril is nothing, my love," he answered, quietly.
"At home, the horrors of a servile reign of terror have become a reality. These prison walls do not interest me.
My heart is with our stricken people. You must go home.
Our neighbour, Mr. Lenoir, is slowly dying. His wife will
always be a child. Little Marion is older and more self-
reliant. I feel as if they are our own children. There
are so many who need us. They have always looked
to me for guidance and help. You can do more
for them than any one else. My calling is to heal
others. You have always helped me. Do now as I
ask you."

At last she consented to leave for Piedmont on the following day, and he smiled.

"Kiss Ben and Margaret for me and tell them that I'll
be with them soon," he said, cheerily. He meant in the

spirit, not the flesh. Not the faintest hope of life even flickered in his mind.

In the last farewell embrace a faint tremor of the soul, half-sigh, half-groan, escaped his lips, and he drew her again to his breast, whispering:

"Always my sweetheart, good, beautiful, brave and true!"

CHAPTER III

THE JOY OF LIVING

WITHIN two weeks after the departure of Mrs.
Cameron and Margaret, the wounded soldier
had left the hospital with Elsie's hand resting
on his arm and her keen eyes watching his faltering steps.
She had promised Margaret to take her place until he
was strong again. She was afraid to ask herself the
meaning of the songs that were welling up from the depth
of her own soul. She told herself again and again that
she was fulfilling her ideal of unselfish human service.

Ben's recovery was rapid, and he soon began to give
evidence of his boundless joy in the mere fact of life.

He utterly refused to believe his father in danger.

"What, my dad a conspirator, an assassin!" he cried,
with a laugh. "Why, he wouldn't kill a flea without
apologising to it. And as for plots and dark secrets,
he never had a secret in his life and couldn't keep one
if he had it. My mother keeps all the family secrets.
Crime couldn't stick to him any more than dirty water
to a duck's back!"

"But we must secure his release on parole, that he may
defend himself."

"Of course. But we won't cross any bridges till we
come to them. I never saw things so bad they couldn't

be worse. Just think what I've been through. The war's over. Don't worry."

He looked at her tenderly.

"Get that banjo and play 'Get Out of the Wilderness!'"

His spirit was contagious and his good-humour resistless. Elsie spent the days of his convalescence in an unconscious glow of pleasure in his companionship. His handsome boyish face, his bearing, his whole personality, invited frankness and intimacy. It was a divine gift, this magnetism, the subtle meeting of quick intelligence, tact, and sympathy. His voice was tender and penetrating, with soft caresses in its tones. His vision of life was large and generous, with a splendid carelessness about little things that didn't count. Each day Elsie saw new and striking traits of his character which drew her.

"What will we do if Stanton arrests you one of these fine days?" she asked him one day.

"Afraid they'll nab me for something!" he exclaimed. "Well, that is a joke! Don't you worry. The Yankees know who to fool with. I licked 'em too many times for them to bother me any more."

"I was under the impression that you got licked," Elsie observed.

"Don't you believe it. We wore ourselves out whipping the other fellows."

Elsie smiled, took up the banjo, and asked him to sing while she played.

She had no idea that he could sing, yet to her surprise he sang his camp-songs boldly, tenderly, and with deep, expressive feeling.

As the girl listened, the memory of the horrible hours of suspense she had spent with his mother when his unconscious life hung on a thread came trooping back into her heart and a tear dimmed her eyes.

And he began to look at her with a new wonder and joy slowly growing in his soul.

CHAPTER IV

HIDDEN TREASURE

BEN had spent a month of vain effort to secure his father's release. He had succeeded in obtaining for him a removal to more comfortable quarters, books to read, and the privilege of a daily walk under guard and parole. The doctor's genial temper, the wide range of his knowledge, the charm of his personality, and his heroism in suffering had captivated the surgeons who attended him and made friends of every jailer and guard.

Elsie was now using all her woman's wit to secure a copy of the charges against him as formulated by the Judge Advocate General, who, in defiance of civil law, still claimed control of these cases.

To the boy's sanguine temperament the whole proceeding had been a huge farce from the beginning, and at the last interview with his father he had literally laughed him into a good humour.

"Look here, Pa," he cried. "I believe you're trying to slip off and leave us in this mess. It's not fair. It's easy to die."

"Who said I was going to die?"

"I heard you were trying to crawl out that way."

"Well, it's a mistake. I'm going to live just for the fun of disappointing my enemies and to keep you company. But you'd better get hold of a copy of these charges against me—if you don't want me to escape."

"It's a funny world if a man can be condemned to death without any information on the subject."

"My son, we are now in the hands of the revolutionists, army sutlers, contractors, and adventurers. The Nation will touch the lowest tide-mud of its degradation within the next few years. No man can predict the end."

"Oh, go' long!" said Ben. "You've got jail cobwebs in your eyes."

"I'm depending on you."

"I'll pull you through if you don't lie down on me and die to get out of trouble. You know you *can* die if you try hard enough."

"I promise you, my boy," he said with a laugh.

"Then I'll let you read this letter from home," Ben said, suddenly thrusting it before him.

The doctor's hand trembled a little as he put on his glasses and read:

My Dear Boy: I cannot tell you how much good your bright letters have done us. It's like opening the window and letting in the sunlight while fresh breezes blow through one's soul.

Margaret and I have had stirring times. I send you inclosed an order for the last dollar of money we have left. You must hoard it. Make it last until your father is safe at home. I dare not leave it here. Nothing is safe. Every piece of silver and everything that could be carried has been stolen since we returned.

Uncle Aleck betrayed the place Jake had hidden our twenty precious bales of cotton. The war is long since over, but the "Treasury Agent" declared them confiscated, and then offered to relieve us of his order if we gave him five bales, each worth three hundred dollars in gold. I agreed, and within a week another thief came and declared the other fifteen bales confiscated. They steal it, and the Government never gets a cent. We dared not try to sell it in open market, as every bale exposed for sale is "confiscated" at once.

No crop was planted this summer. The negroes are all drawing rations at the Freedman's Bureau.

We have turned our house into a hotel, and our table has become famous. Margaret is a treasure. She has learned to do everything. We tried to raise a crop on the farm when we came home, but the negroes stopped work. The Agent of the Bureau came to us and said he could send them back for a fee of $50. We paid it, and they worked a week. We found it easier to run a hotel. We hope to start the farm next year.

Our new minister at the Presbyterian Church is young, handsome, and eloquent—Rev. Hugh McAlpin.

Mr. Lenoir died last week—but his end was so beautiful, our tears were half joy. He talked incessantly of your father and how the country missed him. He seemed much better the day before the end came, and we took him for a little drive to Lovers' Leap. It was there, sixteen years ago, he made love to Jeannie. When we propped him up on the rustic seat, and he looked out over the cliff and the river below, I have never seen a face so transfigured with peace and joy.

"What a beautiful world it is, my dears!" he exclaimed, taking Jeannie and Marion both by the hand.

They began to cry, and he said with a smile:

"Come now—do you love me?"

And they covered his hands with kisses.

"Well, then you must promise me two things faithfully here, with Mrs. Cameron to witness!"

"We promise," they both said in a breath.

"That when I fall asleep, not one thread of black shall ever cloud the sunlight of our little home, that you will never wear it, and that you will show your love for me by making my flowers grow richer, that you will keep my memory green by always being as beautiful as you are to-day, and make this old world a sweeter place to live in. I wish you, Jeannie, my mate, to keep on making the young people glad. Don't let their joys be less even for a month because I have laid down to rest. Let them sing and dance——"

"Oh, Papa!" cried Marion.

"Certainly, my little serious beauty—I'll not be far away.

I'll be near and breathe my songs into their hearts, and into yours—you both promise?"

"Yes, yes!" they both cried.

As we drove back through the woods, he smiled tenderly and said to me:

"My neighbour, Doctor Cameron, pays taxes on these woods, but I own them! Their sighing boughs, stirred by the breezes, have played for me oratorios grander than all the scores of human genius. I'll hear the Choir Invisible play them when I sleep."

He died that night suddenly. With his last breath he sighed: "Draw the curtains and let me see again the moonlit woods!"

They are trying to carry out his wishes. I found they had nothing to eat, and that he had really died from insufficient nourishment—a polite expression meaning starvation. I've divided half our little store with them and send the rest to you. I think Marion more and more the incarnate soul of her father. I feel as if they are both my children.

My little grandchick, Hugh, is the sweetest youngster alive. He was a wee thing when you left. Mrs. Lenoir kept him when they arrested your father. He is so much like your brother Hugh I feel as if he has come to life again. You should hear him say grace, so solemnly and tenderly, we can't help crying. He made it up himself. This is what he says at every meal:

"God, please give my grandpa something good to eat in jail, keep him well, don't let the pains hurt him any more, and bring him home to me quick, for Jesus' sake. Amen."

I never knew before how the people loved the doctor, nor how dependent they were on him for help and guidance. Men, both white and coloured, come here every day to ask about him. Some of them come from far up in the mountains.

God alone knows how lonely our home and the world has seemed without him. They say that those who love and live the close sweet home-life for years grow alike in soul and body, in tastes, ways, and habits. I find it so. People have told me that your father and I are more alike than brother and sister of the same blood. In spirit I'm sure it's true. I know you love him and that you will leave nothing undone for his health and safety. Tell him that my only cure for loneliness in his absence is my fight to keep the wolf from the door, and save our home against his coming.   Lovingly, your MOTHER.

When the Doctor had finished the reading, he looked out the window of the jail at the shining dome of the Capitol for a moment in silence.

"Do you know, my boy, that you have the heritage of royal blood? You are the child of a wonderful mother. I'm ashamed when I think of the helpless stupor under which I have given up, and then remember the deathless courage with which she has braved it all—the loss of her boys, her property, your troubles and mine. She has faced the world alone like a wounded lioness standing over her cubs. And now she turns her home into a hotel, and begins life in a strange new world without one doubt of her success. The South is yet rich even in its ruin."

"Then you'll fight and go back to her with me?"

"Yes, never fear."

"Good! You see, we're so poor now, Pa, you're lucky to be saving a board bill here. I'd 'conspire' myself and come in with you but for the fact it would hamper me a little in helping you."

CHAPTER V

ACROSS THE CHASM

WHEN Ben had fully recovered and his father's case looked hopeful, Elsie turned to her study of music, and the Southern boy suddenly waked to the fact that the great mystery of life was upon him. He was in love at last—genuinely, deeply, without one reservation. He had from habit flirted in a harmless way with every girl he knew. He left home with little Marion Lenoir's girlish kiss warm on his lips. He had made love to many a pretty girl in old Virginia as the red tide of war had ebbed and flowed around Stuart's magic camps.

But now the great hour of the soul had struck. No sooner had he dropped the first tender words that might have their double meaning, feeling his way cautiously toward her, than she had placed a gulf of dignity between them, and attempted to cut every tie that bound her life to his.

It had been so sudden it took his breath away. Could he win her? The word "fail" had never been in his vocabulary. It had never run in the speech of his people.

Yes, he would win if it was the only thing he did in this world. And forthwith he set about it. Life took on new meaning and new glory. What mattered war or wounds, pain or poverty, jails and revolutions—it was the dawn of life!

He sent her a flower every day and pinned one just like it on his coat. And every night found him seated by her side. She greeted him cordially, but the gulf yawned between them. His courtesy and self-control struck her with surprise and admiration. In the face of her coldness he carried about him an air of smiling deference and gallantry.

She finally told him of her determination to go to New York to pursue her studies until Phil had finished the term of his enlistment in his regiment, which had been ordered on permanent duty in the West.

He laughed with his eyes at this announcement, blinking the lashes rapidly without moving his lips. It was a peculiar habit of his when deeply moved by a sudden thought. It had flashed over him like lightning that she was trying to get away from him. She would not do that unless she cared.

"When are you going?" he asked, quietly.

"Day after to-morrow."

"Then you will give me one afternoon for a sail on the river to say good-bye and thank you for what you have done for me and mine?"

She hesitated, laughed, and refused.

"To-morrow at four o'clock I'll call for you," he said firmly. "If there's no wind, we can drift with the tide."

"I will not have time to go."

"Promptly at four," he repeated as he left.

Ben spent hours that night weighing the question of
how far he should dare to speak his love.   It had been
such an easy thing before.   Now it seemed a question of
life and death.   Twice the magic words had been on his
lips, and each time something in her manner chilled him
into silence.

Was she cold and incapable of love?   No; this
manner of the North was on the surface.   He knew that
deep down within her nature lay banked and smouldering
fires of passion for the one man whose breath could stir
it into flame.   He felt this all the keener now that the
spell of her companionship and the sweet intimacy of her
daily ministry to him had been broken.   The memory
of little movements of her petite figure, the glance of her
warm amber eyes, and the touch of her hand—all had their
tongues of revelation to his eager spirit.

He found her ready at four o'clock.

"You see I decided to go after all," she said.

"Yes, I knew you would," he answered.

She was dressed in a simple suit of navy-blue cloth cut
V-shaped at the throat, showing the graceful lines of her
exquisite neck as it melted into the plump shoulders.
She had scorned hoop-skirts.

He admired her for this, and yet it made him uneasy.
A woman who could defy an edict of fashion was a new
thing under the sun, and it scared him.

They were seated in the little sail-boat now, drifting
out with the tide.   It was a perfect day in October, one
of those matchless days of Indian summer in the Virginia
climate when an infinite peace and vast brooding silence

fill the earth and sky until one feels that words are a sacrilege.

Neither of them spoke for minutes, and his heart grew bold in the stillness. No girl could be still who was unmoved.

She was seated just in front of him on the left, with her hand idly rippling the surface of the silvery waters, gazing at the wooded cliff on the river banks clothed now in their gorgeous robes of yellow, purple, scarlet, and gold.

The soft strains of distant music came from a band in the fort, and her hand in the rippling water seemed its accompaniment.

Ben was conscious only of her presence. Every sight and sound of nature seemed to be blended in her presence. Never in all his life had he seen anything so delicately beautiful as the ripe rose colour of her cheeks, and all the tints of autumn's glory seemed to melt into the gold of her hair.

And those eyes he felt that God had never set in such a face before—rich amber, warm and glowing, big and candid, courageous and truthful.

"Are you dead again?" she asked, demurely.

"Well, as the Irishman said in answer to his mate's question when he fell off the house, 'not dead—but spacheless.'"

He was quick to see the opening her question with its memories had made, and took advantage of it.

"Look here, Miss Elsie, you're too honest, independent, and candid to play hide-and-seek with me. I want to ask you a plain question. You've been trying to pick a quarrel of late. What have I done?"

"Nothing. It has simply come to me that our lives are far apart. The gulf between us is real and very deep. Your father was but yesterday a slaveholder——"

Ben grinned:

"Yes, your slave-trading grandfather sold them to us the day before."

Elsie blushed and bristled for a fight.

"You won't mind if I give you a few lessons in history, will you?" Ben asked, softly.

"Not in the least. I didn't know that Southerners studied history," she answered, with a toss of her head.

"We made a specialty of the history of slavery, at least. I had a dear old teacher at home who fairly blazed with light on this subject. He is one of the best-read men in America. He happens to be in jail just now. But I haven't forgotten—I know it by heart."

"I am waiting for light," she interrupted, cynically.

"The South is no more to blame for Negro slavery than the North. Our slaves were stolen from Africa by Yankee skippers. When a slaver arrived at Boston, your pious Puritan clergyman offered public prayer of thanks that 'A gracious and overruling Providence had been pleased to bring to this land of freedom another cargo of benighted heathen to enjoy the blessings of a gospel dispensation——'"

She looked at him with angry incredulity and cried:

"Go on."

"Twenty-three times the Legislature of Virginia passed

acts against the importation of slaves, which the King vetoed on petition of the Massachusetts slave - traders. Jefferson made these acts of the King one of the grievances of the Declaration of Independence, but a Massachusetts member succeeded in striking it out. The Southern men in the convention which framed the Constitution put into it a clause abolishing the slave-trade, but the Massachusetts men succeeded in adding a clause extending the trade twenty years——"

He smiled and paused.

"Go on," she said, with impatience.

"In Colonial days a negro woman was publicly burned to death in Boston. The first Abolition paper was published in Tennessee by Embree. Benjamin Lundy, his successor, could not find a single Abolitionist in Boston. In 1828 over half the people of Tennessee favoured Abolition. At this time there were one hundred and forty Abolition Societies in America—one hundred and three in the South, and not one in Massachusetts. It was not until 1836 that Massachusetts led in Abolition—not until all her own slaves had been sold to us at a profit and the slave-trade had been destroyed——"

She looked at Ben with anger for a moment and met his tantalising look of good-humour.

"Can you stand any more?"

"Certainly, I enjoy it."

"I'm just breaking down the barriers—so to speak," he said, with the laughter still lurking in his eyes, as he looked steadily ahead.

"By all means, go on," she said, soberly. "I thought

at first you were trying to tease me. I see that you are in earnest."

"Never more so. This is about the only little path of history I'm at home in—I love to show off in it. I heard a cheerful idiot say the other day that your father meant to carry the civilisation of Massachusetts to the Rio Grande until we had a Democracy in America. I smiled. While Massachusetts was enforcing laws about the dress of the rich and the poor, founding a church with a whipping-post, jail, and gibbet, and limiting the right to vote to a church membership fixed by pew-rents, Carolina was the home of freedom where first the equal rights of men were proclaimed. New England people worth less than one thousand dollars were prohibited by law from wearing the garb of a gentleman, gold or silver lace, buttons on the knees, or to walk in great boots, or their women to wear silk or scarfs, while the Quakers, Maryland Catholics, Baptists, and Scotch-Irish Presbyterians were everywhere in the South the heralds of man's equality before the law."

"But barring our ancestors, I have some things against the men of this generation."

"Have I too sinned and come short?" he asked, with mock gravity.

"Our ideals of life are far apart," she firmly declared.

"What ails my ideal?"

"Your egotism, for one thing. The air with which you calmly select what pleases your fancy. Northern men are bad enough—the insolence of a Southerner is beyond words!"

"You don't say so!" cried Ben, bursting into a hearty laugh. "Isn't your aunt, Mrs. Farnham, the president of a club?"

"Yes, and she is a very brilliant woman."

"Enlighten me further."

"I deny your heaven-born male kingship. The lord of creation is after all a very inferior animal—nearer the brute creation, weaker in infancy, shorter lived, more imperfectly developed, given to fighting, and addicted to idiocy. I never saw a female idiot in my life—did you?"

"Come to think of it, I never did," acknowledged Ben with comic gravity. "What else?"

"Isn't that enough?"

"It's nothing. I agree with everything you say, but it is irrelevant. I'm studying law, you know."

"I have a personality of my own. You and your kind assume the right to absorb all lesser lights."

"Certainly; I'm a man."

"I don't care to be absorbed by a mere man."

"Don't wish to be protected, sheltered, and cared for?"

"I dream of a life that shall be larger than the four walls of a home. I have never gone into hysterics over the idea of becoming a cook and housekeeper without wages, and snuffing my life out while another grows, expands, and claims the lordship of the world. I can sing. My voice is to me what eloquence is to man. My ideal is an intellectual companion who will inspire and lead me to develop all that I feel within to its highest reach."

She paused a moment and looked defiantly into Ben's brown eyes, about which a smile was constantly playing.

He looked away, and again the river echoed with his contagious laughter. She had to join in spite of herself. He laughed with boyish gaiety. It danced in his eyes, and gave spring to every movement of his slender wiry body. She felt its contagion infold her.

His laughter melted into a song. In a voice vibrant with joy he sang, "If you get there before I do, tell 'em I'm comin' too!"

As Elsie listened, her anger grew as she recalled the amazing folly that had induced her to tell the secret feelings of her inmost soul to this man almost a stranger. Whence came this miracle of influence about him, this gift of intimacy? She felt a shock as if she had been immodest. She was in an agony of doubt as to what he was thinking of her, and dreaded to meet his gaze.

And yet, when he turned toward her, his whole being a smiling compound of dark Southern blood and bone and fire, at the sound of his voice all doubt and questioning melted.

"Do you know," he said earnestly, "that you are the funniest, most charming girl I ever met?"

"Thanks. I've heard your experience has been large for one of your age."

Ben's eyes danced.

"Perhaps, yes. You appeal to things in me that I didn't know were there—to all the senses of body and soul at once. Your strength of mind, with its conceits, and your quick little temper seem so odd and out of place, ciothed in the gentleness of your beauty."

"I was never more serious in my life. There are other things more personal about you that I do not like."

"What?"

"Your cavalier habits."

"Cavalier fiddlesticks. There are no Cavaliers in my country. We are all Covenanter and Huguenot folks. The idea that Southern boys are lazy loafing dreamers is a myth. I was raised on the catechism."

"You love to fish and hunt and frolic—you flirt with every girl you meet, and you drink sometimes. I often feel that you are cruel and that I do not know you."

Ben's face grew serious, and the red scar in the edge of his hair suddenly became livid with the rush of blood.

"Perhaps I don't mean that you shall know all yet," he said, slowly. "My ideal of a man is one that leads, charms, dominates, and yet eludes. I confess that I'm close kin to an angel and a devil, and that I await a woman's hand to lead me into the ways of peace and life."

The spiritual earnestness of the girl was quick to catch the subtle appeal of his last words. His broad, high forehead, straight, masterly nose, with its mobile nostrils, seemed to her very manly at just that moment and very appealing. A soft answer was on her lips.

He saw it, and leaned toward her in impulsive tenderness. A timid look on her face caused him to sink back in silence.

They had now drifted near the city. The sun was slowly sinking in a smother of fiery splendour that mirrored its changing hues in the still water. The hush of the harvest fullness of autumn life was over all nature.

They passed a camp of soldiers and then a big hospital on the banks above. A gun flashed from the hill, and the flag dropped from its staff.

The girl's eyes lingered on the flower in his coat a moment and then on the red scar in the edge of his dark hair, and somehow the difference between them seemed to melt into the falling twilight. Only his nearness was real. Again a strange joy held her.

He threw her a look of tenderness, and she began to tremble. A sea-gull poised a moment above them and broke into a laugh.

Bending nearer, he gently took her hand, and said:

"I love you!"

A sob caught her breath and she buried her face on her arm.

"I am for you, and you are for me. Why beat your wings against the thing that is and must be? What else matters? With all my sins and faults my land is yours—a land of sunshine, eternal harvests, and everlasting song, old-fashioned and provincial perhaps, but kind and hospitable. Around its humblest cottage song-birds live and mate and nest and never leave. The winged ones of your own cold fields have heard their call, and the sky to-night will echo with their chatter as they hurry Southward. Elsie, my own, I too have called—come; I love you!"

She lifted her face to him full of tender spiritual charm, her eyes burning their passionate answer.

He bent and kissed her.

"Say it! Say it!" he whispered.

"I love you!" she sighed.

CHAPTER VI

THE GAUGE OF BATTLE

THE day of the first meeting of the National Congress after the war was one of intense excitement. The galleries of the House were packed. Elsie was there with Ben in a fever of secret anxiety lest the stirring drama should cloud her own life. She watched her father limp to his seat with every eye fixed on him.

The President had pursued with persistence the plan of Lincoln for the immediate restoration of the Union. Would Congress follow the lead of the President or challenge him to mortal combat?

Civil governments had been restored in all the Southern states, with men of the highest ability chosen as governors and lawmakers. Their legislatures had unanimously voted for the Thirteenth Amendment to the Constitution abolishing slavery, and elected Senators and Representatives to Congress. Mr. Seward, the Secretary of State had declared the new amendment a part of the organic law of the Nation by the vote of these states.

General Grant went to the South to report its condition and boldly declared:

"I am satisfied that the mass of thinking people of the South accept the situation in good faith. Slavery and secession they regard as settled forever by the highest

131

known tribunal, and consider this decision a fortunate one for the whole country."

Would the Southerners be allowed to enter?

Amid breathless silence the clerk rose to call the roll of members-elect. Every ear was bent to hear the name of the first Southern man. Not one was called! The master had spoken. His clerk knew how to play his part.

The next business of the House was to receive the message of the Chief Magistrate of the Nation.

The message came, but not from the White House. It came from the seat of the Great Commoner.

As the first thrill of excitement over the challenge to the President slowly subsided, Stoneman rose, planted his big club foot in the middle of the aisle, and delivered to Congress the word of its new master.

It was Ben's first view of the man of all the world just now of most interest. From his position he could see his full face and figure.

He began speaking in a careless, desultory way. His tone was loud yet not declamatory, at first in a grumbling, grandfatherly, half - humourous, querulous accent that riveted every ear instantly. A sort of drollery of a contagious kind haunted it. Here and there a member tittered in expectation of a flash of wit.

His figure was taller than the average, slightly bent with a dignity which suggested reserve power and contempt for his audience. One knew instinctively that back of the boldest word this man might say there was a bolder unspoken word he had chosen not to speak.

His limbs were long, and their movements slow, yet

nervous as from some internal fiery force. His hands were big and ugly, and always in ungraceful fumbling motion as though a separate soul dwelt within them.

The heaped-up curly profusion of his brown wig gave a weird impression to the spread of his mobile features. His eagle-beaked nose had three distinct lines and angles. His chin was broad and bold, and his brows beetling and projecting. His mouth was wide, marked and grim; when opened, deep and cavernous; when closed, it seemed to snap so tightly that the lower lip protruded.

Of all his make-up, his eye was the most fascinating, and it held Ben spellbound. It could thrill to the deepest fibre of the soul that looked into it, yet it did not gleam. It could dominate, awe, and confound, yet it seemed to have no colour or fire. He could easily see it across the vast hall from the galleries, yet it was not large. Two bold, colourless dagger-points of light they seemed. As he grew excited, they darkened as if passing under a cloud.

A sudden sweep of his huge ape-like arm in an angular gesture, and the drollery and carelessness of his voice were riven from it as by a bolt of lightning.

He was driving home his message now in brutal frankness. Yet in the height of his fiercest invective he never seemed to strengthen himself or call on his resources. In its climax he was careless, conscious of power, and contemptuous of results, as though as a gambler he had staked and lost all and in the moment of losing suddenly become the master of those who had beaten him.

His speech never once bent to persuade or convince. He meant to brain the opposition with a single blow, and he did it. For he suddenly took the breath from his foes by shouting in their faces the hidden motive of which they were hoping to accuse him!

"Admit these Southern Representatives," he cried, "and with the Democrats elected from the North, within one term they will have a majority in Congress and the Electoral College. The supremacy of our party's life is at stake. The man who dares palter with such a measure is a rebel, a traitor to his party and his people."

A cheer burst from his henchmen, and his foes sat in dazed stupor at his audacity. He moved the appointment of a "Committee on Reconstruction" to whom the entire government of the "conquered provinces of the South" should be committed, and to whom all credentials of their pretended representatives should be referred.

He sat down as the Speaker put his motion, declared it carried, and quickly announced the names of this Imperial Committee with the Hon. Austin Stoneman as its chairman.

He then permitted the message of the President of the United States to be read by his clerk.

"Well, upon my soul," said Ben, taking a deep breath and looking at Elsie, "he's the whole thing, isn't he?"

The girl smiled with pride.

"Yes; he is a genius. He was born to command and yet never could resist the cry of a child or the plea of a woman. He hates, but he hates ideas and systems. He makes threats, yet when he meets the man who stands for all he hates he falls in love with his enemy."

"Then there's hope for me?"

"Yes, but I must be the judge of the time to speak."

"Well, if he looks at me as he did once to-day, you may have to do the speaking also."

"You will like him when you know him. He is one of the greatest men in America."

"At least he's the father of the greatest girl in the world, which is far more important."

"I wonder if you know how important?" she asked, seriously. "He is the apple of my eye. His bitter words, his cynicism and sarcasm, are all on the surface—masks that hide a great sensitive spirit. You can't know with what brooding tenderness I have always loved and worshipped him. I will never marry against his wishes."

"I hope he and I will always be good friends," said Ben, doubtfully.

"You must," she replied, eagerly pressing his hand.

CHAPTER VII

A Woman Laughs

EACH day the conflict waxed warmer between the President and the Commoner.

The first bill sent to the White House to Africanise the "conquered provinces" the President vetoed in a message of such logic, dignity, and power, the old leader found to his amazement it was impossible to rally the two-thirds majority to pass it over his head.

At first, all had gone as planned. Lynch and Howle brought to him a report on "Southern Atrocities," secured through the councils of the secret oath-bound Union League, which had destroyed the impression of General Grant's words and prepared his followers for blind submission to his Committee.

Yet the rally of a group of men in defence of the Constitution had given the President unexpected strength.

Stoneman saw that he must hold his hand on the throat of the South and fight another campaign. Howle and Lynch furnished the publication committee of the Union League the matter, and they printed four million five hundred thousand pamphlets on "Southern Atrocities."

The Northern states were hostile to Negro suffrage, the first step of his revolutionary programme, and not a dozen men in Congress had yet dared to favour it. Ohio, Michigan, New York, and Kansas had rejected it by overwhelming majorities. But he could appeal to their passions and prejudices against the "Barbarism" of the South. It would work like magic. When he had the South where he wanted it, he would turn and ram Negro suffrage and Negro equality down the throats of the reluctant North.

His energies were now bent to prevent any effective legislation in Congress until his strength should be omnipotent.

A cloud disturbed the sky for a moment in the Senate. John Sherman, of Ohio, began to loom on the horizon as a constructive statesman, and without consulting him was quietly forcing over Sumner's classic oratory a Reconstruction Bill restoring the Southern states to the Union on the basis of Lincoln's plan, with no provision for interference with the suffrage. It had gone to its last reading, and the final vote was pending.

The house was in session at 3 A. M., waiting in feverish anxiety the outcome of this struggle in the Senate.

Old Stoneman was in his seat, fast asleep from the exhaustion of an unbroken session of forty hours. His meals he had sent to his desk from the Capitol restaurant. He was seventy-four years old and not in good health, yet his energy was tireless, his resources inexhaustible, and his audacity matchless.

Sunset Cox, the wag of the House, an opponent but personal friend of the old Commoner, passing his seat and seeing the great head sunk on his breast in sleep, laughed softly and said:

"Mr. Speaker!"

The presiding officer recognised the young Democrat with a nod of answering humour and responded:

"The gentleman from New York."

"I move you, sir," said Cox, "that, in view of the advanced age and eminent services of the distinguished gentleman from Pennsylvania, the Sergeant-at-Arms be instructed to furnish him with enough poker-chips to last till morning!"

The scattered members who were awake roared with laughter, the Speaker pounded furiously with his gavel, the sleepy little pages jumped up, rubbing their eyes, and ran here and there answering imaginary calls, and the whole House waked to its usual noise and confusion.

The old man raised his massive head and looked to the door leading toward the Senate just as Sumner rushed through. He had slept for a moment, but his keen intellect had taken up the fight at precisely the point at which he left it.

Sumner approached his desk rapidly, leaned over, and reported his defeat and Sherman's triumph.

"For God's sake throttle this measure in the House or we are ruined!" he exclaimed.

"Don't be alarmed" replied the cynic. "I'll be here with stronger weapons than articulated wind."

"You have not a moment to lose. The bill is on its way to the Speaker's desk, and Sherman's men are going to force its passage to-night."

The Senator returned to the other end of the Capitol wrapped in the mantle of his outraged dignity, and in thirty minutes the bill was defeated, and the House adjourned.

As the old Commoner hobbled through the door, his crooked cane thumping the marble floor, Sumner seized and pressed his hand:

"How did you do it?"

Stoneman's huge jaws snapped together and his lower lip protruded:

"I sent for Cox and summoned the leader of the Democrats. I told them if they would join with me and defeat this bill, I'd give them a better one the next session. And I will—Negro suffrage! The gudgeons swallowed it whole!"

Sumner lifted his eyebrows and wrapped his cloak a little closer.

The great Commoner laughed, as he departed:

"He is yet too good for this world, but he'll forget it before we're done this fight."

On the steps a beggar asked him for a night's lodging, and he tossed him a gold eagle.

.   .   .   .

The North, which had rejected Negro suffrage for itself with scorn, answered Stoneman's fierce appeal to their passions against the South, and sent him a delegation of radicals eager to do his will.

So fierce had waxed the combat between the President and Congress that the very existence of Stanton's prisoners languishing in jail was forgotten, and the Secretary of War himself became a football to be kicked back and forth in this conflict of giants. The fact that Andrew

Johnson was from Tennessee, and had been an old-line Democrat before his election as a Unionist with Lincoln, was now a fatal weakness in his position. Under Stoneman's assaults he became at once an executive without a party, and every word of amnesty and pardon he proclaimed for the South in accordance with Lincoln's plan was denounced as the act of a renegade courting the favour of traitors and rebels.

Stanton remained in his cabinet against his wishes to insult and defy him, and Stoneman, quick to see the way by which the President of the Nation could be degraded and made ridiculous, introduced a bill depriving him of the power to remove his own cabinet officers. The act was not only meant to degrade the President; it was a trap set for his ruin. The penalties were so fixed that its violation would give specific ground for his trial, impeachment, and removal from office.

Again Stoneman passed his first act to reduce the "conquered provinces" of the South to Negro rule.

President Johnson vetoed it with a message of such logic in defence of the constitutional rights of the states that it failed by one vote to find the two-thirds majority needed to become a law without his approval.

The old Commoner's eyes froze into two dagger-points of icy light when this vote was announced.

With fury he cursed the President, but above all he cursed the men of his own party who had faltered.

As he fumbled his big hands nervously, he growled:

"If I only had five men of genuine courage in Congress, I'd hang the man at the other end of the Avenue from the

porch of the White House! But I haven't got them—
cowards, dastards, dolts, and snivelling fools——"

His decision was instantly made. He would expel
enough Democrats from the Senate and the House to
place his two-thirds majority beyond question. The
name of the President never passed his lips. He referred
to him always, even in public debate, as "the man at the
other end of the Avenue," or "the former Governor of
Tennessee who once threatened rebels—the late lamented
Andrew Johnson, of blessed memory."

He ordered the expulsion of the new member of
the House from Indiana, Daniel W. Voorhees, and
the new Senator from New Jersey, John P. Stockton. This would give him a majority of two-thirds
composed of men who would obey his word without a
question.

Voorhees heard of the edict with indignant wrath. He
had met Stoneman in the lobbies, where he was often the
centre of admiring groups of friends. His wit and audacity, and, above all, his brutal frankness, had won the
admiration of the "Tall Sycamore of the Wabash."
He could not believe such a man would be a party
to a palpable fraud. He appealed to him personally:

"Look here, Stoneman," the young orator cried with
wrath, "I appeal to your sense of honour and decency.
My credentials have been accepted by your own committee, and my seat been awarded me. My majority is
unquestioned. This is a high-handed outrage. You
cannot permit this crime."

The old man thrust his deformed foot out before him, struck it meditatively with his cane, and, looking Voorhees straight in the eye, boldly said:

"There's nothing the matter with your majority, young man. I've no doubt it's all right. Unfortunately, you are a Democrat, and happen to be the odd man in the way of the two-thirds majority on which the supremacy of my party depends. You will have to go. Come back some other time." And he did.

In the Senate there was a hitch. When the vote was taken on the expulsion of Stockton, to the amazement of the leader it was a tie.

He hobbled into the Senate Chamber, with the steel point of his cane ringing on the marble flags as though he were thrusting it through the vitals of the weakling who had sneaked and hedged and trimmed at the crucial moment.

He met Howle at the door.

"What's the matter in there?" he asked.

"They're trying to compromise."

"Compromise—the Devil of American politics," he muttered. "But how did the vote fail—it was all fixed before the roll-call?"

"Morrill, of Maine, has trouble with his conscience! He is paired not to vote on this question with Stockton's colleague, who is sick in Trenton. His 'honour' is involved, and he refuses to break his word."

"I see," said Stoneman, pulling his bristling brows down until his eyes were two beads of white light gleaming through them. "Tell Wade to summon every mem-

ber of the party in his room immediately and hold the
Senate in session."

When the group of Senators crowded into the Vice-
president's room, the old man faced them leaning on his
cane and delivered an address of five minutes they never
forgot.

His speech had a nameless fascination. The man
himself with his elemental passions was a wonder. He
left on public record no speech worth reading, and yet
these powerful men shrank under his glance. As the
nostrils of his big three-angled nose dilated, the scream
of an eagle rang in his voice, his huge ugly hand
held the crook of his cane with the clutch of a tiger,
his tongue flew with the hiss of an adder, and his big
deformed foot seemed to grip the floor as the claw
of a beast.

"The life of a political party, gentlemen," he growled
in conclusion, "is maintained by a scheme of subterfuges
in which the moral law cuts no figure. As your leader, I
know but one law—success. The world is full of fools
who must have toys with which to play. A belief in politics is the favourite delusion of shallow American minds.
But you and I have no delusions. Your life depends on
this vote. If any man thinks the abstraction called
'honour' is involved, let him choose between his honour
and his life! I call no names. This issue must be settled
now before the Senate adjourns. There can be no to-
morrow. It is life or death. Let the roll be called again
immediately."

The grave Senators resumed their seats, and Wade, the

acting Vice-president, again put the question of Stockton's expulsion.

The member from New England sat pale and trembling, in his soul the anguish of the mortal combat between his Puritan conscience, the iron heritage of centuries, and the order of his captain.

When the clerk of the Senate called his name, still the battle raged. He sat in silence, the whiteness of death about his lips, while the clerk at a signal from the Chair paused.

And then a scene the like of which was never known in American history! August Senators crowded around his desk, begging, shouting, imploring, and demanding that a fellow Senator break his solemn word of honour!

For a moment pandemonium reigned.

"Vote! Vote! Call his name again!" they shouted.

High above all rang the voice of Charles Sumner leading the wild chorus, crying:

"Vote! Vote! Vote!"

The galleries hissed and cheered—the cheers at last drowning every hiss.

Stoneman pushed his way among the mob which surrounded the badgered Puritan as he attempted to retreat into the cloak-room.

"Will you vote?" he hissed, his eyes flashing poison.

"My conscience will not permit it," he faltered.

"To hell with your conscience!" the old leader thundered. "Go back to your seat, ask the clerk to call your name, and vote, or by the living God I'll read you out of the party to-night and brand you a snivelling coward, a copperhead, a renegade, and traitor!"

Trembling from head to foot, he staggered back to his seat, the cold sweat standing in beads on his forehead, and gasped:

"Call my name!"

The shrill voice of the clerk rang out in the stillness like the peal of a trumpet:

"Mr. Morrill!"

And the deed was done.

A cheer burst from his colleagues, and the roll-call proceeded.

When Stockton's name was reached, he sprang to his feet, voted for himself, and made a second tie!

With blank faces they turned to the leader, who ordered Charles Sumner to move that the Senator from New Jersey be not allowed to answer his name on an issue involving his own seat.

It was carried. Again the roll was called, and Stockton expelled by a majority of one.

In the moment of ominous silence which followed, a yellow woman of sleek animal beauty leaned far over the gallery rail and laughed aloud.

The passage of each act of the Revolutionary programme over the veto of the President was now but a matter of form. The act to degrade his office by forcing him to keep a cabinet officer who daily insulted him, the Civil Rights Bill, and the Freedman's Bureau Bill followed in rapid succession.

Stoneman's crowning Reconstruction Act was passed,

two years after the war had closed, shattering the Union again into fragments, blotting the names of ten great Southern states from its roll, and dividing their territory into five Military Districts under the control of belted satraps.

When this measure was vetoed by the President, it came accompanied by a message whose words will be forever etched in fire on the darkest page of the Nation's life.

Amid hisses, curses, jeers, and cat-calls, the Clerk of the House read its burning words:

"*The power thus given to the commanding officer over the people of each district is that of an absolute monarch. His mere will is to take the place of law. He may make a criminal code of his own; he can make it as bloody as any recorded in history, or he can reserve the privilege of acting on the impulse of his private passions in each case that arises.*

"*Here is a bill of attainder against nine millions of people at once. It is based upon an accusation so vague as to be scarcely intelligible, and found to be true upon no credible evidence. Not one of the nine millions was heard in his own defence. The representatives even of the doomed parties were excluded from all participation in the trial. The conviction is to be followed by the most ignominious punishment ever inflicted on large masses of men. It disfranchises them by hundreds of thousands and degrades them all— even those who are admitted to be guiltless—from the rank of freemen to the condition of slaves.*

"*Such power has not been wielded by any monarch in England for more than five hundred years, and in all that time no people who speak the English tongue have borne such servitude.*"

When the last jeering cat-call which greeted this message of the Chief Magistrate had died away on the floor and in the galleries, old Stoneman rose, with a smile playing about his grim mouth, and introduced his bill to impeach the President of the United States and remove him from office.

CHAPTER VIII

A DREAM

ELSIE spent weeks of happiness in an abandonment
of joy to the spell of her lover. His charm was
resistless. His gift of delicate intimacy, the eloquence with which he expressed his love, and yet the
manly dignity with which he did it, threw a spell no
woman could resist.

Each day's working hours were given to his father's
case and to the study of law. If there was work to do, he
did it, and then struck the word care from his life, giving
himself body and soul to his love. Great events were
moving. The shock of the battle between Congress and
the President began to shake the Republic to its foundations. He heard nothing, felt nothing, save the music of
Elsie's voice.

And she knew it. She had only played with lovers
before. She had never seen one of Ben's kind, and he
took her by storm. His creed was simple. The chief
end of life is to glorify the girl you love. Other things
could wait. And he let them wait. He ignored their
existence.

But one cloud cast its shadow over the girl's heart during
these red-letter days of life—the fear of what her father
would do to her lover's people. Ben had asked her whether

he must speak to him. When she said "No, not yet," he forgot that such a man lived. As for his politics, he knew nothing and cared less.

But the girl knew and thought with sickening dread, until she forgot her fears in the joy of his laughter. Ben laughed so heartily, so insinuatingly, the contagion of his fun could not be resisted.

He would sit for hours and confess to her the secrets of his boyish dreams of glory in war, recount his thrilling adventures and daring deeds with such enthusiasm that his cause seemed her own, and the pity and the anguish of the ruin of his people hurt her with the keen sense of personal pain. His love for his native state was so genuine, his pride in the bravery and goodness of its people so chivalrous, she began to see for the first time how the cords which bound the Southerner to his soil were of the heart's red blood.

She began to understand why the war, which had seemed to her a wicked, cruel, and causeless rebellion, was the one inevitable thing in our growth from a loose group of sovereign states to a United Nation. Love had given her his point of view.

Secret grief over her father's course began to grow into conscious fear. With unerring instinct she felt the fatal day drawing nearer when these two men, now of her inmost life, must clash in mortal enmity.

She saw little of her father. He was absorbed with fevered activity and deadly hate in his struggle with the President.

Brooding over her fears one night, she had tried to

interest Ben in politics. To her surprise she found that
he knew nothing of her father's real position or power as
leader of his party. The stunning tragedy of the war had
for the time crushed out of his consciousness all political
ideas, as it had for most young Southerners. He took her
hand while a dreamy look overspread his swarthy face:

"Don't cross a bridge till you come to it. I learned
that in the war. Politics are a mess. Let me tell you
something that counts——"

He felt her hand's soft pressure and reverently kissed
it. "Listen," he whispered. "I was dreaming last night
after I left you of the home we'll build. Just back of our
place, on the hill overlooking the river, my father and
mother planted trees in exact duplicate of the ones they
placed around our house when they were married. They
set these trees in honour of the first-born of their love, that
he should make his nest there when grown. But it was
not for him. He has pitched his tent on higher ground,
and the others with him. This place will be mine. There
are forty varieties of trees, all grown—elm, maple, oak,
holly, pine, cedar, magnolia, and every fruit and flowering
stem that grows in our friendly soil. A little house, built
near the vacant space reserved for the homestead, is
nicely kept by a farmer, and birds have learned to build
in every shrub and tree. All the year their music rings
its chorus—one long overture awaiting the coming of my
bride——"

Elsie sighed.

"Listen, dear," he went on, eagerly. "Last night I
dreamed the South had risen from her ruins. I saw you

there. I saw our home standing amid a bower of roses your hands had planted. The full moon wrapped it in soft light, while you and I walked hand in hand in silence beneath our trees. But fairer and brighter than the moon was the face of her I loved, and sweeter than all the songs of birds the music of her voice!"

A tear dimmed the girl's warm eyes, and a deeper flush mantled her cheeks, as she lifted her face and whispered:

"Kiss me."

CHAPTER IX

The King Amuses Himself

WITH savage energy the Great Commoner pressed to trial the first impeachment of a President of the United States for high crimes and misdemeanours.

His bill to confiscate the property of the Southern people was already pending on the calendar of the House. This bill was the most remarkable ever written in the English language or introduced into a legislative body of the Aryan race. It provided for the confiscation of ninety per cent. of the land of ten great states of the American Union. To each negro in the South was allotted forty acres from the estate of his former master, and the remaining millions of acres were to be divided among the "loyal who had suffered by reason of the Rebellion."

The execution of this, the most stupendous crime ever conceived by an English law-maker, involving the exile and ruin of millions of innocent men, women, and children, could not be intrusted to Andrew Johnson.

No such measure could be enforced so long as any man was President and Commander-in-chief of the Army and Navy who claimed his title under the Constitution. Hence the absolute necessity of his removal.

The conditions of society were ripe for this daring enterprise.

Not only was the Ship of State in the hands of revolutionists who had boarded her in the storm stress of a civic convulsion, but among them swarmed the pirate captains of the boldest criminals who ever figured in the story of a nation.

The first great Railroad Lobby, with continental empires at stake, thronged the Capitol with its lawyers, agents, barkers, and hired courtesans.

The Cotton Thieves, who operated through a ring of Treasury agents, had confiscated unlawfully three million bales of cotton hidden in the South during the war and at its close, the last resource of a ruined people. The Treasury had received a paltry twenty thousand bales for the use of its name with which to seize alleged "property of the Confederate Government." The value of this cotton, stolen from the widows and orphans, the maimed and crippled, of the South was over $700,000,000 in gold—a capital sufficient to have started an impoverished people again on the road to prosperity. The agents of this ring surrounded the halls of legislation, guarding their booty from envious eyes, and demanding the enactment of vaster schemes of legal confiscation.

The Whiskey Ring had just been formed, and began its system of gigantic frauds by which it scuttled the Treasury.

Above them all towered the figure of Oakes Ames, whose master mind had organised the *Credit Mobilier* steal. This vast infamy had already eaten its way into the heart of Congress and dug the graves of many illustrious men.

So open had become the shame that Stoneman was compelled to increase his committees in the morning, when a corrupt majority had been bought the night before.

He arose one day, and, looking at the distinguished Speaker, who was himself the secret associate of Oakes Ames, said:

"Mr. Speaker: While the House slept, the enemy has sown tares among our wheat. The corporations of this country, having neither bodies to be kicked nor souls to be lost, have, *perhaps* by the power of argument alone, beguiled from the majority of my Committee the member from Connecticut. The enemy have now a majority of one. I move to increase the Committee to twelve."

Speaker Colfax, soon to be hurled from the Vice-president's chair for his part with those thieves, increased his Committee.

Everybody knew that "the power of argument alone" meant ten thousand dollars cash for the gentleman from Connecticut, who did not appear on the floor for a week, fearing the scorpion tongue of the old Commoner.

A Congress which found it could make and unmake laws in defiance of the Executive went mad. Taxation soared to undreamed heights, while the currency was depreciated and subject to the wildest fluctuations.

The statute-books were loaded with laws that shackled chains of monopoly on generations yet unborn. Public lands wide as the reach of empires were voted as gifts to private corporations, and subsidies of untold millions fixed as a charge upon the people and their children's children.

The demoralisation incident to a great war, the waste of unheard-of sums of money, the giving of contracts involving millions by which fortunes were made in a night, the riot of speculation and debauchery by those who tried to get rich suddenly without labour, had created a new Capital of the Nation. The vulture army of the base, venal, unpatriotic, and corrupt, which had swept down, a black cloud, in war-time to take advantage of the misfortunes of the Nation, had settled in Washington and gave new tone to its life.

Prior to the Civil War the Capital was ruled, and the standards of its social and political life fixed, by an aristocracy founded on brains, culture, and blood. Power was with few exceptions intrusted to an honourable body of high-spirited public officials. Now a Negro electorate controlled the city government, and gangs of drunken negroes, its sovereign citizens, paraded the streets at night firing their muskets unchallenged and unmolested.

A new mob of onion-laden breath, mixed with perspiring African odour, became the symbol of American Democracy.

A new order of society sprouted in this corruption. The old high-bred ways, tastes, and enthusiasms were driven into the hiding-places of a few families and cherished as relics of the past.

Washington, choked with scrofulous wealth, bowed the knee to the Almighty Dollar. The new altar was covered with a black mould of human blood—but no questions were asked.

A mulatto woman kept the house of the foremost man of the Nation and received his guests with condescension.

In this atmosphere of festering vice and gangrene passions, the struggle between the Great Commoner and the President on which hung the fate of the South approached its climax.

The whole Nation was swept into the whirlpool, and business was paralysed. Two years after the close of a victorious war, the credit of the Republic dropped until its six per cent. bonds sold in the open market for seventy-three cents on the dollar.

The revolutionary junta in control of the Capital was within a single step of the subversion of the Government and the establishment of a Dictator in the White House.

A convention was called in Philadelphia to restore fraternal feeling, heal the wounds of war, preserve the Constitution, and restore the Union of the fathers. It was a grand assemblage representing the heart and brain of the Nation. Members of Lincoln's first Cabinet, protesting Senators and Congressmen, editors of great Republican and Democratic newspapers, heroes of both armies, long estranged, met for a common purpose. When a group of famous Negro worshippers from Boston suddenly entered the hall, arm in arm with ex-slaveholders from South Carolina, the great meeting rose and walls and roof rang with thunder peals of applause.

Their committee, headed by a famous editor, journeyed to Washington to appeal to the Master at the Capitol. They sought him not in the White House, but in the little Black House in an obscure street on the hill.

The brown woman received them with haughty dignity, and said:

"Mr. Stoneman can not be seen at this hour. It is after nine o'clock. I will submit to him your request for an audience to-morrow morning."

"We must see him to-night," replied the editor, with rising anger.

"The king is amusing himself," said the yellow woman, with a touch of malice.

"Where is he?"

Her cat-like eyes rolled from side to side, and a smile played about her full lips as she said:

"You will find him at Hall & Pemberton's gambling hell—you've lived in Washington. You know the way."

With a muttered oath the editor turned on his heel and led his two companions to the old Commoner's favourite haunt. There could be no better time or place to approach him than seated at one of its tables laden with rare wines and savoury dishes.

On reaching the well-known number of Hall & Pemberton's place, the editor entered the unlocked door, passed with his friends along the soft-carpeted hall, and ascended the stairs. Here the door was locked. A sudden pull of the bell, and a pair of bright eyes peeped through a small grating in the centre of the door revealed by the sliding of its panel.

The keen eyes glanced at the proffered card, the door flew open, and a well-dressed mulatto invited them with cordial welcome to enter.

Passing along another hall, they were ushered into a

palatial suite of rooms furnished in princely state. The floors were covered with the richest and softest carpets—so soft and yielding that the tramp of a thousand feet could not make the faintest echo. The walls and ceilings were frescoed by the brush of a great master, and hung with works of art worth a king's ransom. Heavy curtains, in colours of exquisite taste, masked each window, excluding all sound from within or without.

The rooms blazed with light from gorgeous chandeliers of trembling crystals, shimmering and flashing from the ceilings like bouquets of diamonds.

Negro servants, faultlessly dressed, attended the slightest want of every guest with the quiet grace and courtesy of the lost splendours of the old South.

The proprietor, with courtly manners, extended his hand:

"Welcome, gentlemen; you are my guests. The tables and the wines are at your service without price. Eat, drink, and be merry—play or not, as you please."

A smile lighted his dark eyes, but faded out near his mouth, cold and rigid.

At the farther end of the last room hung the huge painting of a leopard, so vivid and real its black and tawny colours, so furtive and wild its restless eyes, it seemed alive and moving behind invisible bars.

Just under it, gorgeously set in its jewel-studded frame, stood the magic green table on which men staked their gold and lost their souls.

The rooms were crowded with Congressmen, government officials, officers of the Army and Navy, clerks, contractors, paymasters, lobbyists, and professional gamblers.

The centre of an admiring group was a Congressman who had during the last session of the House broken the "bank" in a single night, winning more than a hundred thousand dollars. He had lost it all and more in two weeks, and the courteous proprietor now held orders for the lion's share of the total pay and milcage of nearly every member of the House of Representatives.

Over that table thousands of dollars of the people's money had been staked and lost during the war, by quartermasters, paymasters, and agents in charge of public funds. Many a man had approached that green table with a stainless name and left it a perjured thief. Some had been carried out by those handsomely dressed waiters, and the man with the cold mouth could point out, if he would, more than one stain on the soft carpet which marked the end of a tragedy deeper than the pen of romancer has ever sounded.

Stoneman at the moment was playing. He was rarely a heavy player, but he had just staked a twenty-dollar gold-piece and won fourteen hundred dollars.

Howle, always at his elbow, ready for a "sleeper" or a stake, said:

"Put a stack on the ace."

He did so, lost, and repeated it twice.

"Do it again," urged Howle. "I'll stake my reputation that the ace wins this time."

With a doubting glance at Howle, old Stoneman shoved a stack of blue chips, worth fifty dollars, over the ace, playing it to win on Howle's judgment and reputation. It lost.

Without the ghost of a smile, the old statesman said: "Howle, you owe me five cents."

As he turned abruptly on his club-foot from the table, he encountered the editor and his friends, a Western manufacturer and a Wall Street banker. They were soon seated at a table in a private room, over a dinner of choice oysters, diamond-back terrapin, canvas-back duck, and champagne.

They presented their plea for a truce in his fight until popular passion had subsided.

He heard them in silence. His answer was characteristic:

"The will of the people, gentlemen, is supreme," he said, with a sneer. "We are the people. 'The man at the other end of the Avenue' has dared to defy the will of Congress. He must go. If the Supreme Court lifts a finger in this fight, we will reduce that tribunal to one man or increase it to twenty at our pleasure."

"But the Constitution——" broke in the chairman.

"There are higher laws than paper compacts. We are conquerors treading conquered soil. Our will alone is the source of law. The drunken boor who claims to be President is in reality an alien of a conquered province."

"We protest," exclaimed the man of money, "against the use of such epithets in referring to the Chief Magistrate of the Republic!"

"And why, pray?" sneered the Commoner.

"In the name of common decency, law, and order. The

President is a man of inherent power, even if he did learn to read after his marriage. Like many other Americans, he is a self-made man——"

"Glad to hear it," snapped Stoneman. "It relieves Almighty God of a fearful responsibility."

They left him in disgust and dismay.

CHAPTER X

Tossed by the Storm

AS the storm of passion raised by the clash between her father and the President rose steadily to the sweep of a cyclone, Elsie felt her own life but a leaf driven before its fury.

Her only comfort she found in Phil, whose letters to her were full of love for Margaret. He asked Elsie a thousand foolish questions about what she thought of his chances.

To her own confessions he was all sympathy.

"Of father's wild scheme of vengeance against the South," he wrote, "I am heart-sick. I hate it on principle, to say nothing of a girl I know. I am with General Grant for peace and reconciliation. What does your lover think of it all? I can feel your anguish. The bill to rob the Southern people of their land, which I hear is pending, would send your sweetheart and mine, our enemies, into beggared exile. What will happen in the South? Riot and bloodshed, of course—perhaps a guerilla war of such fierce and terrible cruelty humanity sickens at the thought. I fear the Rebellion unhinged our father's reason on some things. He was too old to go to the front. The cannon's breath would have cleared the air and sweetened his temper. But its healing was denied. I believe the tawny leopardess who keeps his house influences him in this cruel madness. I could wring her neck with exquisite pleasure. Why he allows her to stay and cloud his life with her she-devil temper and fog his name with vulgar gossip is beyond me."

Seated in the park on the Capitol hill the day after her father had introduced his Confiscation Bill in the House, pending the impeachment of the President, she again attempted to draw Ben out as to his feelings on politics.

She waited in sickening fear and bristling pride for the first burst of his anger which would mean their separation.

"How do I feel?" he asked. "Don't feel at all. The surrender of General Lee was an event so stunning, my mind has not yet staggered past it. Nothing much can happen after that, so it don't matter."

"Negro suffrage don't matter?"

"No. We can manage the Negro," he said, calmly.

"With thousands of your own people disfranchised?"

" The negroes will vote with us, as they worked for us during the war. If they give them the ballot, they'll wish they hadn't."

Ben looked at her tenderly, bent near, and whispered:

"Don't waste your sweet breath talking about such things. My politics is bounded on the North by a pair of amber eyes, on the South by a dimpled little chin, on the East and West by a rosy cheek. Words do not frame its speech. Its language is a mere sign, a pressure of the lips—yet it thrills body and soul beyond all words."

Elsie leaned closer, and looking at the Capitol, said wistfully:

"I don't believe you know anything that goes on in that big marble building."

"Yes, I do."

"What happened there yesterday?"

"You honoured it by putting your beautiful feet on its steps. I saw the whole huge pile of cold marble suddenly glow with warm sunlight and flash with beauty as you entered it."

The girl nestled still closer to his side, feeling her utter helplessness in the rapids of the Niagara through which they were being whirled by blind and merciless forces. For the moment she forgot all fears in his nearness and the sweet pressure of his hand.

CHAPTER XI

The Supreme Test

IT is the glory of the American Republic that every man who has filled the office of President has grown in stature when clothed with its power and has proved himself worthy of its solemn trust. It is our highest claim to the respect of the world and the vindication of man's capacity to govern himself.

The impeachment of President Andrew Johnson would mark either the lowest tide-mud of degradation to which the Republic could sink, or its end. In this trial our system would be put to its severest strain. If a partisan majority in Congress could remove the Executive, and defy the Supreme Court, stability to civic institutions was at an end, and the breath of a mob would become the sole standard of law.

Congress had thrown to the winds the last shreds of decency in its treatment of the Chief Magistrate. Stoneman led this campaign of insult, not merely from feelings of personal hate, but because he saw that thus the President's conviction before the Senate would become all but inevitable.

When his messages arrived from the White House they were thrown into the waste-basket without being read, amid jeers, hisses, curses, and ribald laughter.

In lieu of their reading, Stoneman would send to the Clerk's desk an obscene tirade from a party newspaper, and the Clerk of the House would read it amid the mocking groans, laughter, and applause of the floor and galleries.

A favourite clipping described the President as "an insolent drunken brute, in comparison with whom Caligula's horse was respectable."

In the Senate, whose members were to sit as sworn judges to decide the question of impeachment, Charles Sumner used language so vulgar that he was called to order. Sustained by the Chair and the Senate, he repeated it with increased violence, concluding with cold venom:

"Andrew Johnson has become the successor of Jefferson Davis. In holding him up to judgment I do not dwell on his beastly intoxication the day he took the oath as Vice-president, nor do I dwell on his maudlin speeches by which he has degraded the country, nor hearken to the reports of pardons sold, or of personal corruption. These things are bad. But he has usurped the powers of Congress."

Conover, the perjured wretch, in prison for his crimes as a professional witness in the assassination trial, now circulated the rumour that he could give evidence that President Johnson was the assassin of Lincoln. Without a moment's hesitation, Stoneman's henchmen sent a petition to the President for the pardon of this villain that he might turn against the man who had pardoned him and swear his life away! This scoundrel was borne in triumph from prison to the Capitol and placed before the Impeachment Committee, to whom he poured out his wondrous tale.

The sewers and prisons were dragged for every scrap of testimony to be found, and the day for the trial approached.

As it drew nearer, excitement grew intense. Swarms of adventurers expecting the overthrow of the Government crowded into Washington. Dreams of honours, profits, and division of spoils held riot. Gamblers thronged the saloons and gaming-houses, betting their gold on the President's head.

Stoneman found the business more serious than even his daring spirit had dreamed. His health suddenly gave way under the strain, and he was put to bed by his physician with the warning that the least excitement would be instantly fatal.

Elsie entered the little Black House on the hill for the first time since her trip at the age of twelve, some eight years before. She installed an army nurse, took charge of the place, and ignored the existence of the brown woman, refusing to speak to her or permit her to enter her father's room.

His illness made it necessary to choose an assistant to conduct the case before the High Court. There was but one member of the House whose character and ability fitted him for the place—General Benj. F. Butler, of Massachusetts, whose name was enough to start a riot in any assembly in America.

His selection precipitated a storm at the Capitol. A

member leaped to his feet on the floor of the House and shouted:

"If I were to characterise all that is pusillanimous in war, inhuman in peace, forbidden in morals, and corrupt in politics, I could name it in one word—Butlerism!"

For this speech he was ordered to apologise, and when he refused with scorn they voted that the Speaker publicly censure him. The Speaker did so, but winked at the offender while uttering the censure.

John A. Bingham, of Ohio, who had been chosen for his powers of oratory to make the principal speech against the President, rose in the House and indignantly refused to serve on the Board of Impeachment with such a man.

General Butler replied with crushing insolence:

"It is true, Mr. Speaker, that I may have made an error of judgment in trying to blow up Fort Fisher with a powder-ship at sea. I did the best I could with the talents God gave me. An angel could have done no more. At least I bared my own breast in my country's defence—a thing the distinguished gentleman who insults me has not ventured to do—his only claim to greatness being that, behind prison walls, on perjured testimony, his fervid eloquence sent an innocent American mother screaming to the gallows."

The fight was ended only by an order from the old Commoner's bed to Bingham to shut his mouth and work with Butler. When the President had been crushed, then they could settle Kilkenny-cat issues. Bingham obeyed.

When the august tribunal assembled in the Senate

Chamber, fifty-five Senators, presided over by Salmon P. Chase, Chief Justice of the Supreme Court, constituted the tribunal. They took their seats in a semicircle in front of the Vice-president's desk at which the Chief Justice sat. Behind them crowded the one hundred and ninety members of the House of Representatives, the accusers of the ruler of the mightiest Republic in human history. Every inch of space in the galleries was crowded with brilliantly dressed men and women, army officers in gorgeous uniforms, and the pomp and splendour of the ministers of every foreign court of the world. In spectacular grandeur no such scene was ever before witnessed in the annals of justice.

The peculiar personal appearance of General Butler, whose bald head shone with insolence while his eye seemed to be winking over his record as a warrior and making fun of his fellow-manager Bingham, added a touch of humour to the solemn scene.

The magnificent head of the Chief Justice suggested strange thoughts to the beholder. He had been summoned but the day before to try Jefferson Davis for the treason of declaring the Southern States out of the Union. To-day he sat down to try the President of the United States for declaring them to be in the Union! He had protested with warmth that he could not conduct both these trials at once.

The Chief Justice took oath to "do impartial justice according to the Constitution and the laws," and to the chagrin of Sumner administered this oath to each Senator in turn. When Benjamin F. Wade's name was called, Hendricks, of Indiana, objected to his sitting as judge.

He could succeed temporarily to the Presidency, as the presiding officer of the Senate, and his own vote might decide the fate of the accused and determine his own succession. The law forbids the Vice-president to sit on such trials. It should apply with more vigour in his case. Besides, he had without a hearing already pronounced the President guilty.

Sumner, forgetting his motion to prevent Stockton's voting against his own expulsion, flew to the defence of Wade. Hendricks smilingly withdrew his objection, and "Bluff Ben Wade" took the oath and sat down to judge his own cause with unruffled front.

When the case was complete, the whole bill of indictment stood forth a tissue of stupid malignity without a shred of evidence to support its charges.

On the last day of the trial, when the closing speeches were being made, there was a stir at the door. The throng of men, packing every inch of floor space, were pushed rudely aside. The crowd craned their necks, Senators turned and looked behind them to see what the disturbance meant, and the Chief Justice rapped for order.

Suddenly through the dense mass appeared the forms of two gigantic negroes carrying an old man. His grim face, white and rigid, and his big club foot hanging pathetically from those black arms, could not be mistaken. A thrill of excitement swept the floor and galleries, and a faint cheer rippled the surface, quickly suppressed by the gavel.

The negroes placed him in an arm-chair facing the semicircle of Senators, and crouched down on their haunches beside him. Their kinky heads, black skin, thick lips, white teeth, and flat noses made for the moment a curious symbolic frame for the chalk-white passion of the old Commoner's face.

No sculptor ever dreamed a more sinister emblem of the corruption of a race of empire-builders than this group. Its black figures, wrapped in the night of four thousand years of barbarism, squatted there the "equal" of their master, grinning at his forms of Justice, the evolution of forty centuries of Aryan genius. To their brute strength the white fanatic in the madness of his hate had appealed, and for their hire he had bartered the birthright of a mighty race of freemen.

The speaker hurried to his conclusion that the half-fainting master might deliver his message. In the meanwhile his eyes, cold and thrilling, sought the secrets of the souls of the judges before him.

He had not come to plead or persuade. He had eluded the vigilance of his daughter and nurse, escaped with the aid of the brown woman and her black allies, and at the peril of his life had come to command. Every energy of his indomitable will he was using now to keep from fainting. He felt that if he could but look those men in the face they would not dare to defy his word.

He shambled painfully to his feet amid a silence that was awful. Again the sheer wonder of the man's personality held the imagination of the audience. His audacity, his fanaticism, and the strange contradictions of his character stirred the mind of friend and foe alike—this man who tottered there before them, holding off Death with his big ugly left hand, while with his right he clutched at the throat of his foe! Honest and dishonest, cruel and tender, great and mean, a party leader who scorned public opinion, a man of conviction, yet the most unscrupulous politician, a philosopher who preached the equality of man, yet a tyrant who hated the world and despised all men!

His very presence before them an open defiance of love and life and death, would not his word ring omnipotent when the verdict was rendered? Every man in the great court-room believed it as he looked on the rows of Senators hanging on his lips.

He spoke at first with unnatural vigour, a faint flush of fever lighting his white face, his voice quivering yet penetrating.

"Upon that man among you who shall dare to acquit the President," he boldly threatened, "I hurl the everlasting curse of a Nation—an infamy that shall rive and blast his children's children until they shrink from their own name as from the touch of pollution!"

He gasped for breath, his restless hands fumbled at his throat, he staggered and would have fallen had not his black guards caught him. He revived, pushed them back on their haunches, and sat down. And then, with his big club foot thrust straight in front of him, his gnarled hands gripping the arms of his chair, the massive head shaking back and forth like a wounded lion, he continued his speech, which grew in fierce intensity with each laboured breath.

The effect was electrical. Every Senator leaned forward to catch the lowest whisper, and so awful was the suspense in the galleries the listeners grew faint.

When his last mad challenge was hurled into the teeth of the judges, the dazed crowd paused for breath and the galleries burst into a storm of applause.

In vain the Chief Justice rose, his lion-like face livid with anger, pounded for order, and commanded the galleries to be cleared.

They laughed at him. Roar after roar was the answer. The Chief Justice in loud angry tones ordered the Sergeant-at-Arms to clear the galleries.

Men leaned over the rail and shouted in his face:

"He can't do it!"

"He hasn't got men enough!"

"Let him try it if he dares!"

The doorkeepers attempted to enforce the order by announcing it in the name of the peace and dignity and sovereign power of the Senate over its sacred chamber. The crowd had now become a howling mob which jeered them.

Senator Grimes, of Iowa, rose and demanded the reason why the Senate was thus insulted and the order had not been enforced.

A volley of hisses greeted his question.

The Chief Justice, evidently quite nervous, declared the order would be enforced.

Senator Trumbull, of Illinois, moved that the offenders be arrested.

In reply the crowd yelled:

"We'd like to see you do it!"

At length the mob began to slowly leave the galleries under the impression that the High Court had adjourned.

Suddenly a man cried out:

"Hold on! They ain't going to adjourn. Let's see it out!"

Hundreds took their seats again. In the corridors a crowd began to sing in wild chorus:

"Old Grimes is dead, that poor old man." The women joined with glee. Between the verses the leader would curse the Iowa Senator as a traitor and copperhead. The singing could be distinctly heard by the Court as its roar floated through the open doors.

When the Senate Chamber had been cleared and the most disgraceful scene that ever occurred within its portals had closed, the High Court of Impeachment went into secret session to consider the evidence and its verdict.

Within an hour from its adjournment it was known to the Managers that seven Republican Senators were doubtful, and that they formed a group under the leadership of two great constitutional lawyers who still believed in the sanctity of a judge's oath—Lyman Trumbull, of Illinois, and William Pitt Fessenden, of Maine. Around them had gathered Senators Grimes, of Iowa, Van Winkle, of Rhode Island, Fowler, of Tennessee, Henderson, of Missouri, and Ross, of Kansas. The Managers were in a panic. If these men dared to hold together with the twelve Democrats, the President would be acquitted by one vote—they could count thirty-four certain for conviction.

The Revolutionists threw to the winds the last scruple of decency, went into caucus and organised a conspiracy for forcing, within the few days which must pass before the verdict, these judges to submit to their decree.

Fessenden and Trumbull were threatened with impeachment and expulsion from the Senate and bombarded by the most furious assaults from the press, which denounced them as infamous traitors, "as mean, repulsive and noxious as hedgehogs in the cages of a travelling menagerie."

A mass-meeting was held in Washington which said:

"Resolved, that we impeach Fessenden, Trumbull, and Grimes at the bar of justice and humanity, as traitors before whose guilt the infamy of Benedict Arnold becomes respectability and decency."

The Managers sent out a circular telegram to every state from which came a doubtful judge:

"Great danger to the peace of the country if impeachment fails. Send your Senators public opinion by resolutions, letters, and delegates."

The man who excited most wrath was Ross, of Kansas. That Kansas of all states should send a "traitor" was more than the spirits of the Revolutionists could bear.

A mass-meeting in Leavenworth accordingly sent him the telegram:

"Kansas has heard the evidence and demands the conviction of the President.

"D. R. ANTHONY and 1,000 others."

To this Ross replied:

"I have taken an oath to do impartial justice. I trust

I shall have the courage and honesty to vote according to the dictates of my judgment and for the highest good of my country."

He got this answer:

"Your motives are Indian contracts and greenbacks. Kansas repudiates you as she does all perjurers and skunks."

The Managers organised an inquisition for the purpose of torturing and badgering Ross into submission. His one vote was all they lacked.

They laid siege to little Vinnie Ream, the sculptress, to whom Congress had awarded a contract for the statue of Lincoln. Her studio was in the crypt of the Capitol. They threatened her with the wrath of Congress, the loss of her contract and ruin of her career unless she found a way to induce Senator Ross, whom she knew, to vote against the President.

Such an attempt to gain by fraud the verdict of a common court of law would have sent its promoters to prison for felony. Yet the Managers of this case, before the highest tribunal of the world, not only did it without a blush of shame, but cursed as a traitor every man who dared to question their motives.

As the day approached for the Court to vote, Senator Ross remained to friend and foe a sealed mystery. Reporters swarmed about him, the target of a thousand eyes. His rooms were besieged by his radical constituents who had been imported from Kansas in droves to browbeat him into a promise to convict. His movements day and night, his breakfast, his dinner, his supper, the clothes he

wore, the colour of his cravat, his friends and companions, were chronicled in hourly bulletins and flashed over
the wires from the delirious Capital.

Chief Justice Chase called the High Court of Impeachment to order, to render its verdict. Old Stoneman had
again been carried to his chair in the arms of two negroes, and sat with his cold eyes searching the faces of
the judges.

The excitement had reached the highest pitch of intensity. A sense of choking solemnity brooded over the
scene. The feeling grew that the hour had struck which
would test the capacity of man to establish an enduring
Republic.

The clerk read the Eleventh Article, drawn by the
Great Commoner as the supreme test.

As its last words died away the Chief Justice rose
amid a silence that was agony, placed his hands on the
sides of the desk as if to steady himself, and said:

"Call the roll."

Each Senator answered "Guilty" or "Not Guilty,"
exactly as they had been counted by the Managers, until
Fessenden's name was called.

A moment of stillness and the great lawyer's voice rang
high, cold, clear, and resonant as a Puritan church bell on
Sunday morning:

"Not Guilty!"

A murmur, half groan and sigh, half cheer and cry,
rippled the great hall.

The other votes were discounted now save that of
Edmund G. Ross, of Kansas. No human being on earth

knew what this man would do save the silent invisible man within his soul.

Over the solemn trembling silence the voice of the Chief Justice rang:

"Senator Ross, how say you? Is the respondent, Andrew Johnson, guilty or not guilty of a high misdemeanor as charged in this article?"

The great Judge bent forward; his brow furrowed as Ross arose.

His fellow Senators watched him spellbound. A thousand men and women, hanging from the galleries, focused their eyes on him. Old Stoneman drew his bristling brows down, watching him like an adder ready to strike, his lower lip protruding, his jaws clinched as a viçe, his hands fumbling the arms of his chair.

Every breath is held, every ear strained, as the answer falls from the sturdy Scotchman like the peal of a trumpet:

"Not Guilty!"

The crowd breathes—a pause, a murmur, the shuffle of a thousand feet——

The President is acquitted, and the Republic lives!

The House assembled and received the report of the verdict. Old Stoneman pulled himself half erect, holding to his desk, addressed the Speaker, introduced his second bill for the impeachment of the President, and fell fainting in the arms of his black attendants.

CHAPTER XII

Triumph in Defeat

UPON the failure to convict the President, Edwin M. Stanton resigned, sank into despair and died, and a soldier Secretary of War opened the prison doors.

Ben Cameron and his father hurried Southward to a home and land passing under a cloud darker than the dust and smoke of blood-soaked battle-fields—the Black Plague of Reconstruction.

For two weeks the old Commoner wrestled in silence with Death. When at last he spoke, it was to the stalwart negroes who had called to see him and were standing by his bedside.

Turning his deep-sunken eyes on them a moment, he said slowly:

"I wonder whom I'll get to carry me when you boys die!"

Elsie hurried to his side and kissed him tenderly. For a week his mind hovered in the twilight that lies between time and eternity. He seemed to forget the passions and fury of his fierce career and live over the memories of his youth, recalling pathetically its bitter poverty and its fair dreams. He would lie for hours and hold Elsie's hand, pressing it gently.

In one of his lucid moments he said:

"How beautiful you are, my child! You shall be a queen. I've dreamed of boundless wealth for you and my boy. My plans are Napoleonic—and I shall not fail—never fear—aye, beyond the dreams of avarice!"

"I wish no wealth save the heart treasure of those I love, father," was the soft answer.

"Of course, little day-dreamer. But the old cynic who has outlived himself and knows the mockery of time and things will be wisdom for your foolishness. You shall keep your toys. What pleases you shall please me. Yet I will be wise for us both."

She laid her hand upon his lips, and he kissed the warm little fingers.

In these days of soul-nearness the iron heart softened as never before in love toward his children. Phil had hurried home from the West and secured his release from the remaining weeks of his term of service.

As the father lay watching them move about the room, the cold light in his deep-set wonderful eyes would melt into a soft glow.

As he grew stronger, the old fierce spirit of the unconquered leader began to assert itself. He would take up the fight where he left it off and carry it to victory.

Elsie and Phil sent the doctor to tell him the truth and beg him to quit politics.

"Your work is done; you have but three months to live unless you go South and find new life," was the verdict.

"In either event I go to a warmer climate, eh, doctor?" said the cynic.

"Perhaps," was the laughing reply.

"Good. It suits me better. I've had the move in mind. I can do more effective work in the South for the next two years. Your decision is fate. I'll go at once."

The doctor was taken aback.

"Come now," he said, persuasively. "Let a disinterested Englishman give you some advice. You've never taken any before. I give it as medicine, and I won't put it on your bill. Slow down on politics. Your recent defeat should teach you a lesson in conservatism."

The old Commoner's powerful mouth became rigid, and the lower lip bulged:

"Conservatism—fossil putrefaction!"

"But defeat?"

"Defeat?" cried the old man. "Who said I was defeated? The South lies in ashes at my feet—the very names of her proud states blotted from history. The Supreme Court awaits my nod. True, there's a man boarding in the White House, and I vote to pay his bills; but the page who answers my beck and call has more power. Every measure on which I've set my heart is law, save one—my Confiscation Act—and this but waits the fulness of time."

The doctor, who was walking back and forth with his hands folded behind him, paused and said:

"I marvel that a man of your personal integrity could conceive such a measure; you, who refused to accept the legal release of your debts until the last farthing was paid—you, whose cruelty of the lip is hideous, and yet beneath it so gentle a personality, I've seen the pages in the House stand at your back and mimic you while speaking, secure in the smile with which you turned to greet their fun. And yet you press this crime upon a brave and generous foe?"

"A wrong can have no rights," said Stoneman, calmly. "Slavery will not be dead until the landed aristocracy on which it rested is destroyed. I am not cruel or unjust. I am but fulfilling the largest vision of universal democracy that ever stirred the soul of man—a democracy that shall know neither rich nor poor, bond nor free, white nor black. If I use the wild pulse-beat of the rage of millions, it is only a means to an end—this grander vision of the soul."

"Then why not begin at home this vision, and give the stricken South a moment to rise?"

"No. The North is impervious to change, rich, proud, and unscathed by war. The South is in chaos and cannot resist. It is but the justice and wisdom of Heaven that the Negro shall rule the land of his bondage. It is the only solution of the race problem. Lincoln's contention that we could not live half white and half black is sound at the core. When we proclaim equality, social, political, and economic for the Negro, we mean always to enforce it in the South. The Negro will never be treated as an equal in the North. We are simply a set of coldblooded liars on that subject, and always have been. To the Yankee the very physical touch of a Negro is pollution."

"Then you don't believe this twaddle about equality?" asked the doctor.

"Yes and no. Mankind in the large is a herd of mer-

cenary gudgeons or fools. As a lawyer in Pennsylvania
I have defended fifty murderers on trial for their lives.
Forty-nine of them were guilty. All these I succeeded in
acquitting. One of them was innocent. This one they
hung. Can a man keep his face straight in such a world?
Could Negro blood degrade such stock? Might not an
ape improve it? I preach equality as a poet and seer
who sees a vision beyond the rim of the horizon of
to-day."

The old man's eyes shone with the set stare of a fanatic.

"And you think the South is ready for this wild vision?"

"Not ready, but helpless to resist. As a cold-blooded
scientific experiment, I mean to give the Black Man one
turn at the Wheel of Life. It is an act of just retribution.
Besides, in my plans I need his vote; and that settles it."

"But will your plans work? Your own reports show
serious trouble in the South already."

Stoneman laughed.

"I never read my own reports. They are printed in
molasses to catch flies. The Southern legislatures played
into my hands by copying the laws of New England relating to Servants, Masters, Apprentices and Vagrants.
But even these were repealed at the first breath of criticism.
Neither the Freedman's Bureau nor the army has ever
loosed its grip on the throat of the South for a moment.
These disturbances and 'atrocities' are dangerous only
when printed on campaign fly-paper."

"And how will you master and control these ten great
Southern states?"

"Through my Reconstruction Acts by means of the

Union League. As a secret between us, I am the soul of
this order. I organised it in 1863 to secure my plan of
confiscation. We pressed it on Lincoln. He repudiated
it. We nominated Frémont at Cleveland against Lincoln
in '64, and tried to split the party or force Lincoln to retire. Frémont, a conceited ass, went back on this plank
in our platform, and we dropped him and helped elect
Lincoln again."

"I thought the Union League a patriotic and social
organisation?" said the doctor, in surprise.

"It has these features, but its sole aim as a secret order
is to confiscate the property of the South. I will perfect
this mighty organisation until every negro stands drilled
in serried line beneath its banners, send a solid delegation
here to do my bidding, and return at the end of two years
with a majority so overwhelming that my word will be
law. I will pass my Confiscation Bill. If Ulysses S.
Grant, the coming idol, falters, my second bill of Impeachment will only need the change of a name."

The doctor shook his head.

"Give up this madness. Your life is hanging by a
thread. The Southern people even in their despair will
never drink this black broth you are pressing to their
lips."

"They've got to drink it."

"Your decision is unalterable?"

"Absolutely. It's the breath I breathe. As my physician you may select the place to which I shall be banished.
It must be reached by rail and wire. I care not its name
or size. I'll make it the capital of the Nation. There'll

be poetic justice in setting up my establishment in a fallen slaveholder's mansion."

The doctor looked intently at the old man:

"The study of men has become a sort of passion with me, but you are the deepest mystery I've yet encountered in this land of surprises."

"And why?" asked the cynic.

"Because the secret of personality resides in motives, and I can't find yours either in your actions or words."

Stoneman glanced at him sharply from beneath his wrinkled brows and snapped·

"Keep on guessing."

"I will. In the meantime I'm going to send you to the village of Piedmont, South Carolina. Your son and daughter both seem enthusiastic over this spot."

"Good; that settles it. And now that mine own have been conspiring against me," said Stoneman, confidentially, "a little guile on my part. Not a word of what has passed between us to my children. Tell them I agree with your plans and give up my work. I'll give the same story to the press—I wish nothing to mar their happiness while in the South. My secret burdens need not cloud their young lives."

Dr. Barnes took the old man by the hand:

"I promise. My assistant has agreed to go with you. I'll say good-bye. It's an inspiration to look into a face like yours, lit by the splendour of an unconquerable will! But I want to say something to you before you set out on this journey."

"Out with it," said the Commoner

"The breed to which the Southern white man belongs has conquered every foot of soil on this earth their feet have pressed for a thousand years. A handful of them hold in subjection three hundred millions in India. Place a dozen of them in the heart of Africa, and they will rule the continent unless you kill them——"

"Wait" cried Stoneman, "until I put a ballot in the hand of every negro and a bayonet at the breast of every white man from the James to the Rio Grande!"

"I'll tell you a little story," said the doctor with a smile. "I once had a half-grown eagle in a cage in my yard. The door was left open one day, and a meddlesome rooster hopped in to pick a fight. The eagle had been sick a week and seemed an easy mark. I watched. The rooster jumped and wheeled and spurred and picked pieces out of his topknot. The young eagle didn't know at first what he meant. He walked around dazed, with a hurt expression. When at last it dawned on him what the chicken was about, he simply reached out one claw, took the rooster by the neck, planted the other claw in his breast, and snatched his head off."

The old man snapped his massive jaws together and grunted contemptuously.

Book III—The Reign of Terror

CHAPTER I

A Fallen Slaveholder's Mansion

PIEDMONT, South Carolina, which Elsie and Phil had selected for reasons best known to themselves as the place of retreat for their father, was a favourite summer resort of Charleston people before the war.

Ulster county, of which this village was the capital, bordered on the North Carolina line, lying alongside the ancient shire of York. It was settled by the Scotch folk who came from the North of Ireland in the great migrations which gave America three hundred thousand people of Covenanter martyr blood, the largest and most important addition to our population, larger in numbers than either the Puritans of New England or the so-called Cavaliers of Virginia and Eastern Carolina; and far more important than either, in the growth of American nationality.

To a man they had hated Great Britain. Not a Tory was found among them. The cries of their martyred dead were still ringing in their souls when George III. started on his career of oppression. The fiery words of Patrick Henry, their spokesman in the valley of Virginia, had swept the aristocracy of the Old Dominion into rebellion against the King and on into triumphant Democracy.

They had made North Carolina the first home of freedom in the New World, issued the first Declaration of Independence in Mecklenburg, and lifted the first banner of rebellion against the tyranny of the Crown.

They grew to the soil wherever they stopped, always home-lovers and home-builders, loyal to their own people, instinctive clan leaders and clan followers. A sturdy, honest, covenant-keeping, God-fearing, fighting people, above all things they hated sham and pretence. They never boasted of their families, though some of them might have quartered the royal arms of Scotland on their shields.

To these sturdy qualities had been added a strain of Huguenot tenderness and vivacity.

The culture of cotton as the sole industry had fixed African slavery as their economic system. With the heritage of the Old World had been blended forces inherent in the earth and air of the new Southland, something of the breath of its unbroken forests, the freedom of its untrod mountains, the temper of its sun, and the sweetness of its tropic perfumes.

When Mrs. Cameron received Elsie's letter, asking her to secure for them six good rooms at the "Palmetto" hotel, she laughed. The big rambling hostelry had been burned by roving negroes, pigs were wallowing in the sulphur springs, and along its walks, where lovers of olden days had strolled, the cows were browsing on the shrubbery.

But she laughed for a more important reason. They had asked for a six-room cottage if accommodations could not be had in the hotel.

She could put them in the Lenoir place. The cotton

crop from their farm had been stolen from the gin—the cotton tax of $200 could not be paid, and a mortgage was about to be foreclosed on both their farm and home. She had been brooding over their troubles in despair. The Stonemans' coming was a godsend.

Mrs. Cameron was helping them set the house in order to receive the new tenants.

"I declare," said Mrs. Lenoir, gratefully. "It seems too good to be true. Just as I was about to give up—the first time in my life—here came those rich Yankees and with enough rent to pay the interest on the mortgages and our board at the hotel. I'll teach Margaret to paint, and she can give Marion lessons on the piano. The darkest hour's just before day. And last week I cried when they told me I must lose the farm."

"I was heart-sick over it for you."

"You know, the farm was my dowry with the dozen slaves Papa gave us on our wedding-day. The negroes did as they pleased, yet we managed to live and were very happy."

Marion entered and placed a bouquet of roses on the table, touching them daintily until they stood each flower apart in careless splendour. Their perfume, the girl's wistful dreamy blue eyes and shy elusive beauty, all seemed a part of the warm sweet air of the June morning. Mrs. Lenoir watched her lovingly.

"Mama, I'm going to put flowers in every room. I'm sure they haven't such lovely ones in Washington," said Marion, eagerly, as she skipped out.

The two women moved to the open window, througn

which came the drone of bees and the distant music of the river falls.

"Marion's greatest charm," whispered her mother, "is in her way of doing things easily and gently without a trace of effort. Watch her bend over to get that rose. Did you ever see anything like the grace and symmetry of her figure—she seems a living flower!"

"Jeannie, you're making an idol of her——"

"Why not? With all our troubles and poverty, I'm rich in her! She's fifteen years old, her head teeming with romance. You know, I was married at fifteen. There'll be a half-dozen boys to see her to-night in our new home—all of them head over heels in love with her."

"Oh, Jeannie, you must not be so silly! We should worship God only."

"Isn't she God's message to me, and to the world?"

"But if anything should happen to her——"

The young mother laughed. "I never think of it. Some things are fixed. Her happiness and beauty are to me the sign of God's presence."

"Well, I'm glad you're coming to live with us in the heart of town. This place is a cosey nest, just such a one as a poet-lover would build here in the edge of these deep woods, but it is too far out for you to be alone. Dr. Cameron has been worrying about you ever since he came home."

"I'm not afraid of the negroes. I don't know one of them who wouldn't go out of his way to do me a favour. Old Aleck is the only rascal I know among them, and he's too busy with politics now even to steal a chicken."

"And Gus, the young scamp we used to own; you haven't forgotten him? He is back here, a member of the company of negro troops, and parades before the house every day to show off his uniform. Dr. Cameron told him yesterday he'd thrash him if he caught him hanging around the place again. He frightened Margaret nearly to death when she went to the barn to feed her horse."

"I've never known the meaning of fear. We used to roam the woods and fields together all hours of the day and night, my lover, Marion and I. This panic seems absurd to me."

"Well, I'll be glad to get you two children under my wing. I was afraid I'd find you in tears over moving from your nest."

"No, where Marion is, I'm at home, and I'll feel I've a mother when I get with you."

"Will you come to the hotel before they arrive?"

"No; I'll welcome and tell them how glad I am they have brought me good luck."

"I'm delighted, Jeannie. I wished you to do this, but I couldn't ask it. I can never do enough for this old man's daughter. We must make their stay happy. They say he's a terrible old Radical politician, but I suppose he's no meaner than the others. He's very ill, and she loves him devotedly. He is coming here to find health, and not to insult us. Besides, he was kind to me. He wrote a letter to the President. Nothing that I have will be too good for him or for his. It's very brave and sweet of you to stay and meet them."

"I'm doing it to please Marion. She suggested it last

night, sitting out on the porch in the twilight. She slipped her arm around me and said:

"'Mama, we must welcome them, and make them feel at home. He is very ill. They will be tired and homesick. Suppose it were you and I, and we were taking my Papa to a strange place.'"

. . . .

When the Stonemans arrived, the old man was too ill and nervous from the fatigue of the long journey to notice his surroundings or to be conscious of the restful beauty of the cottage into which they carried him. His room looked out over the valley of the river for miles, and the glimpse he got of its broad fertile acres only confirmed his ideas of the "slaveholding oligarchy" it was his life-purpose to crush. Over the mantel hung a steel engraving of Calhoun. He fell asleep with his deep, sunken eyes resting on it and a cynical smile playing about his grim mouth.

Margaret and Mrs. Cameron had met the Stonemans and their physician at the train, and taken Elsie and her father in the old weather-beaten family carriage to the Lenoir cottage, apologising for Ben's absence.

"He has gone to Nashville on some important legal business, and the doctor is ailing, but as the head of the clan Cameron he told me to welcome your father to the hospitality of the county, and beg him to let us know if he could be of help."

The old man, who sat in a stupor of exhaustion, made no response, and Elsie hastened to say:

"We appreciate your kindness more than I can tell you,

Mrs. Cameron. I trust father will be better in a day or two, when he will thank you. The trip has been more than he could bear."

"I am expecting Ben home this week," the mother whispered. "I need not tell you that he will be delighted at your coming."

Elsie smiled and blushed.

"And I'll expect Captain Stoneman to see me very soon," said Margaret, softly. "You will not forget to tell him for me?"

"He's a very retiring young man," said Elsie, "and pretends to be busy about our baggage just now. I'm sure he will find the way."

Elsie fell in love at sight with Marion and her mother. Their easy genial manners, the genuineness of their welcome, and the simple kindness with which they sought to make her feel at home put her heart into a warm glow.

Mrs. Lenoir explained the conveniences of the place and apologised for its defects, the results of the war.

"I am sorry about the window-curtains—we have used them all for dresses. Marion is a genius with a needle, and we took the last pair out of the parlour to make a dress for a birthday party. The year before, we used the ones in my room for a costume at a starvation party in a benefit for our rector—you know we're Episcopalians—strayed up here for our health from Charleston among these good Scotch Presbyterians."

"We will soon place curtains at the windows," said Elsie, cheerfully.

"The carpets were sent to the soldiers for blankets during the war. It was all we could do for our poor boys, except to cut my hair and sell it. You see my hair hasn't grown out yet. I sent it to Richmond the last year of the war. I felt I must do something, when my neighbours were giving so much. You know Mrs. Cameron lost four boys."

"I prefer the floors bare," Elsie replied. "We will get a few rugs."

She looked at the girlish hair hanging in ringlets about Mrs. Lenoir's handsome face, smiled pathetically, and asked:

"Did you really make such sacrifices for your cause?"

"Yes, indeed. I was glad when the war was ended for some things. We certainly needed a few pins, needles, and buttons, to say nothing of a cup of coffee or tea."

"I trust you will never lack for anything again," said Elsie, kindly.

"You will bring us good luck," Mrs. Lenoir responded. "Your coming is so fortunate. The cotton tax Congress levied was so heavy this year, we were going to lose everything. Such a tax when we are all about to starve! Dr. Cameron says it was an act of stupid vengeance on the South, and that no other farmers in America have their crops taxed by the National Government. I am so glad your father has come. He is not hunting for an office. He can help us, maybe."

"I am sure he will," answered Elsie, thoughtfully.

Marion ran up the steps, lightly, her hair dishevelled and face flushed.

"Now, Mama, it's almost sundown; you get ready to go. I want her awhile to show her about my things."

She took Elsie shyly by the hand and led her into the lawn, while her mother paid a visit to each room, and made up the last bundle of odds and ends she meant to carry to the hotel.

"I hope you will love the place as we do," said the girl, simply.

"I think it very beautiful and restful," Elsie replied. "This wilderness of flowers looks like fairyland. You have roses running on the porch around the whole length of the house."

"Yes, Papa was crazy over the trailing roses, and kept planting them until the house seems just a frame built to hold them, with a roof on it. But you can see the river through the arches from three sides. Ben Cameron helped me set that big beauty on the south corner the day he ran away to the war——"

"The view is glorious!" Elsie exclaimed, looking in rapture over the river valley.

The village of Piedmont crowned an immense hill on the banks of the Broad River, just where it dashes over the last stone barrier in a series of beautiful falls and spreads out in peaceful glory through the plains toward Columbia and the distant sea. The muffled roar of these falls, rising softly through the trees on its wooded cliff, held the daily life of the people in the spell of distant music. In fair weather it soothed and charmed, and in storm and freshet rose to the deep solemn growl of thunder.

The river made a sharp bend as it emerged from the

hills and flowed westward for six miles before it turned
south again. Beyond this six-mile sweep of its broad
channel loomed the three ranges of the Blue Ridge mountains, the first one dark, rich, distinct, clothed in eternal
green, the last one melting in dim lines into the clouds
and soft azure of the sky.

As the sun began to sink now behind these distant
peaks, each cloud that hung about them burst into a
blazing riot of colour. The silver mirror of the river
caught their shadows, and the water glowed in sympathy.

As Elsie drank the beauty of the scene, the music of the
falls ringing its soft accompaniment, her heart went out
in a throb of love and pity for the land and its people.

"Can you blame us for loving such a spot?" said Marion.
"It's far more beautiful from the cliff at Lover's Leap.
I'll take you there some day. My father used to tell me
that this world was Heaven, and that the spirits would all
come back to live here when sin and shame and strife
were gone."

"Are your father's poems published?" asked Elsie.

"Only in the papers. We have them clipped and
pasted in a scrap-book. I'll show you the one about Ben
Cameron some day. You met him in Washington, didn't
you?"

"Yes," said Elsie, quietly.

"Then I know he made love to you."

"Why?"

"You're so pretty. He couldn't help it."

"Does he make love to every pretty girl?"

"Always. It's his religion. But he does it so beautifully you can't help believing it, until you compare notes with the other girls."

"Did he make love to you?"

"He broke my heart when he ran away. I cried a whole week. But I got over it. He seemed so big and grown when he came home this last time. I was afraid to let him kiss me."

"Did he dare to try?"

"No, and it hurt my feelings. You see, I'm not quite old enough to be serious with the big boys, and he looked so brave and handsome with that ugly scar on the edge of his forehead, and everybody was so proud of him. I was just dying to kiss him, and I thought it downright mean in him not to offer it."

"Would you have let him?"

"I expected him to try."

"He is very popular in Piedmont?"

"Every girl in town is in love with him."

"And he in love with all?"

"He pretends to be—but between us, he's a great flirt. He's gone to Nashville now on some pretended business. Goodness only knows where he got the money to go. I believe there's a girl there."

"Why?"

"Because he was so mysterious about his trip. I'll keep an eye on him at the hotel. You know Margaret, too, don't you?"

"Yes; we met her in Washington."

"Well, she's the slyest flirt in town—it runs in the blood —has a half-dozen beaux to see her every day. She plays the organ in the Presbyterian Sunday school, and the young minister is dead in love with her. They say they are engaged. I don't believe it. I think it's another one. But I must hurry, I've so much to show and tell you. Come here to the honeysuckle——"

Marion drew the vines apart from the top of the fence and revealed a mocking-bird on her nest.

"She's setting. Don't let anything hurt her. I'd push her off and show you her speckled eggs, but it's so late."

"Oh, I wouldn't hurt her for the world!" cried Elsie with delight.

"And right here," said Marion, bending gracefully over a tall bunch of grass, "is a pee-wee's nest, four darling little eggs; look out for that."

Elsie bent and saw the pretty nest perched on stems of grass, and, over it, the taller leaves drawn to a point.

"Isn't it cute!" she murmured.

"Yes; I've six of these and three mocking-bird nests. I'll show them to you. But the most particular one of all is the wren's nest in the fork of the cedar, close to the house."

She led Elsie to the tree, and about two feet from the ground, in the forks of the trunk, was a tiny hole from which peeped the eyes of a wren.

"Whatever you do, don't let anything hurt her. Her mate sings '*Free-nigger! Free-nigger! Free-nigger!*' every morning in this cedar."

"And you think we will specially enjoy that?" asked Elsie, laughing.

"Now, really," cried Marion, taking Elsie's hand, "you know I couldn't think of such a mean joke. I forgot you were from the North. You seem so sweet and homelike. He really does sing that way. You will hear him in the morning, bright and early, '*Free-nigger! Free-nigger! Free-nigger!*' just as plain as I'm saying it."

"And did you learn to find all these birds' nests by yourself?"

"Papa taught me. I've got some jay-birds and some cat-birds so gentle they hop right down at my feet. Some people hate jay-birds. But I like them, they seem to be having such a fine time and enjoy life so. You don't mind jay-birds, do you?"

"I love every bird that flies."

"Except hawks and owls and buzzards——"

"Well, I've seen so few I can't say I've anything particular against them."

"Yes, they eat chickens—except the buzzards, and they're so ugly and filthy. Now, I've a chicken to show you—please don't let Aunt Cindy—she's to be your cook—please don't let her kill him—he's crippled—has something the matter with his foot. He was born that way. Everybody wanted to kill him, but I wouldn't let them. I've had an awful time raising him, but he's all right now."

Marion lifted a box and showed her the lame pet, softly clucking his protest against the disturbance of his rest.

'I'll take good care of *him*, never fear," said Elsie, with a tremor in her voice.

"And I have a queer little black cat I wanted to show you, but he's gone off somewhere. I'd take him with

me—only it's bad luck to move cats. He's awful wild—
won't let anybody pet him but me. Mama says he's an
imp of Satan—but I love him. He runs up a tree when
anybody else tries to get him. But he climbs right up on
my shoulder. I never loved any cat quite as well as this
silly, half-wild one. You don't mind black cats, do you?"

"No, dear; I like cats."

"Then I know you'll be good to him."

"Is that all?" asked Elsie, with amused interest.

"No, I've the funniest yellow dog that comes here at
night to pick up the scraps and things. He isn't my dog—
just a little personal friend of mine—but I like him very
much, and always give him something. He's very cute.
I think he's a nigger dog."

"A nigger dog? What's that?"

"He belongs to some coloured people, who don't give
him enough to eat. I love him because he's so faithful
to his own folks. He comes to see me at night and pretends to love me, but as soon as I feed him he trots back
home. When he first came, I laughed till I cried at his
antics over a carpet—we had a carpet then. He never
saw one before, and barked at the colours and the figures
in the pattern. Then he'd lie down and rub his back
on it and growl. You won't let anybody hurt him?"

"No. Are there any others?"

"Yes, I 'most forgot. If Sam Ross comes—Sam's an
idiot who lives at the poorhouse — if he comes, he'll expect a dinner—my, my, I'm afraid he'll cry when he finds
we're not here! But you can send him to the hotel to me.
Don't let Aunt Cindy speak rough to him. Aunt Cindy's

awfully good to me, but she can't bear Sam. She thinks he brings bad luck."

"How on earth did you meet him?"

"His father was rich. He was a good friend of my Papa's. We came near losing our farm once, because a bank failed. Mr. Ross sent Papa a signed check on his own bank, and told him to write the amount he needed on it, and pay him when he was able. Papa cried over it, and wouldn't use it, and wrote a poem on the back of the check—one of the sweetest of all, I think. In the war Mr. Ross lost his two younger sons, both killed at Gettysburg. His wife died heart-broken, and he only lived a year afterward. He sold his farm for Confederate money, and everything was lost. Sam was sent to the poorhouse. He found out somehow that we loved him and comes to see us. He's as harmless as a kitten, and works the garden beautifully."

"I'll remember," Elsie promised.

"And one thing more," she said, hesitatingly. "Mama asked me to speak to you of this—that's why she slipped away. There's one little room we have locked. It was Papa's study just as he left it, with his papers scattered on the desk, the books and pictures that he loved—you won't mind?"

Elsie slipped her arm about Marion, looked into the blue eyes, dim with tears, drew her close, and said:

"It shall be sacred, my child. You must come every day if possible, and help me."

"I will. I've so many beautiful places to show you in the woods—places he loved, and taught us to see and love.

They won't let me go in the woods any more alone. But you have a big brother. That must be very sweet."

Mrs. Lenoir hurried to Elsie.

"Come, Marion, we must be going now."

"I am very sorry to see you leave the home you love so dearly, Mrs. Lenoir," said the Northern girl, taking her extended hand. "I hope you can soon find a way to have it back."

"Thank you," replied the mother, cheerily. "The longer you stay, the better for us. You don't know how happy I am over your coming. It has lifted a load from our hearts. In the liberal rent you pay us you are our benefactors. We are very grateful and happy."

Elsie watched them walk across the lawn to the street, the daughter leaning on the mother's arm. She followed slowly and stopped behind one of the arbor-vitæ bushes beside the gate. The full moon had risen as the twilight fell and flooded the scene with soft white light. A whippoorwill struck his first plaintive note, his weird song seeming to come from all directions and yet to be under her feet. She heard the rustle of dresses returning along the walk, and Marion and her mother stood at the gate. They looked long and tenderly at the house. Mrs. Lenoir uttered a broken sob, Marion slipped an arm around her, brushed the short curling hair back from her forehead, and softly said:

"Mama, dear, you know it's best. I don't mind. Everybody in town loves us. Every boy and girl in Piedmont worships you. We will be just as happy at the hotel."

In the pauses between the strange bird's cry, Elsie caught the sound of another sob, and then a soothing murmur as of a mother bending over a cradle, and they were gone.

CHAPTER II

THE EYES OF THE JUNGLE

ELSIE stood dreaming for a moment in the shadow of the arbor-vitæ, breathing the sensuous perfumed air and listening to the distant music of the falls, her heart quivering in pity for the anguish of which she had been a witness. Again the spectral cry of the whippoorwill rang near-by, and she noted for the first time the curious cluck with which the bird punctuated each call. A sense of dim foreboding oppressed her.

She wondered if the chatter of Marion about the girl in Nashville were only a child's guess or more. She laughed softly at the absurdity of the idea. Never since she had first looked into Ben Cameron's face did she feel surer of the honesty and earnestness of his love than to-day in this quiet home of his native village. It must be the queer call of the bird which appealed to superstitions she did not know were hidden within her being.

Still dreaming under its spell, she was startled at the tread of two men approaching the gate.

The taller, more powerful-looking man put his hand on the latch and paused.

"Allow no white man to order you around. Remember you are a freeman and as good as any pale-face who walks this earth."

She recognised the voice of Silas Lynch.

"Ben Cameron dare me to come about de house," said the other voice.

"What did he say?"

"He say, wid his eyes batten' des like lightnen', 'Ef I ketch you hangin' 'roun' dis place agin', Gus, I'll jump on you en stomp de life outen ye.'"

"Well, you tell him that your name is Augustus, not 'Gus,' and that the United States troops quartered in this town will be with him soon after the stomping begins. You wear its uniform.   Give the white trash in this town to understand that they are not even citizens of the Nation. As a sovereign voter, you, once their slave, are not only their equal—you are their master."

"Dat I will!" was the firm answer.

The negro to whom Lynch spoke disappeared in the direction taken by Marion and her mother, and the figure of the handsome mulatto passed rapidly up the walk, ascended the steps and knocked at the door.

Elsie followed him.

"My father is too much fatigued with his journey to be seen now; you must call to-morrow," she said.

The negro lifted his hat and bowed:

"Ah, we are delighted to welcome you, Miss Stoneman, to our land!   Your father asked me to call immediately on his arrival.   I have but obeyed his orders."

Elsie shrank from the familiarity of his manner and the tones of authority and patronage with which he spoke.

"He cannot be seen at this hour," she answered, shortly.

"Perhaps you will present my card, then—say that I

am at his service, and let him appoint the time at which I shall return?"

She did not invite him in, but with easy assurance he took his seat on the joggle-board beside the door and awaited her return.

Against her urgent protest, Stoneman ordered Lynch to be shown at once to his bedroom.

When the door was closed, the old Commoner, without turning to greet his visitor or moving his position in bed, asked:

"Are you following my instructions?"

"To the letter, sir."

"You are initiating the negroes into the League and teaching them the new catechism?"

"With remarkable success. Its secrecy and ritual appeal to them. Within six months we shall have the whole race under our control almost to a man."

"*Almost* to a man?"

"We find some so attached to their former masters that reason is impossible with them. Even threats and the promise of forty acres of land have no influence."

The old man snorted with contempt.

"If anything could reconcile me to the Satanic Institution, it is the character of the wretches who submit to it and kiss the hand that strikes. After all, a slave deserves to be a slave. The man who is mean enough to wear chains ought to wear them. You must teach, *teach*, TEACH, these black hounds to know they are men, not brutes!"

The old man paused a moment, and his restless hands fumbled the cover.

"Your first task, as I told you in the beginning, is to teach every negro to stand erect in the presence of his former master and assert his manhood. Unless he does this, the South will bristle with bayonets in vain. The man who believes he is a dog, is one. The man who believes himself a king, may become one. Stop this snivelling and sneaking round the back doors. I can do nothing, God Almighty can do nothing, for a coward. Fix this as the first law of your own life. Lift up your head! The world is yours. Take it. Beat this into the skulls of your people, if you do it with an axe. Teach them the military drill at once. I'll see that Washington sends the guns. The state, when under your control, can furnish the powder."

"It will surprise you to know the thoroughness with which this has been done already by the League," said Lynch. "The white master believed he could vote the Negro as he worked him in the fields during the war. The League, with its blue flaming altar, under the shadows of night, has wrought a miracle. The Negro is the enemy of his former master and will be for all time."

"For the present," said the old man, meditatively, "not a word to a living soul as to my connection with this work. When the time is ripe, I'll show my hand."

Elsie entered, protesting against her father's talking longer, and showed Lynch to the door.

He paused on the moonlit porch and tried to engage her in familiar talk.

She cut him short, and he left reluctantly.

As he bowed his thick neck in pompous courtesy, she

caught with a shiver the odor of pomade on his black half-kinked hair. He stopped on the lower step, looked back with smiling insolence, and gazed intently at her beauty. The girl shrank from the gleam of the jungle in his eyes and hurried within.

She found her father sunk in a stupor. Her cry brought the young surgeon hurrying into the room, and at the end of an hour he said to Elsie and Phil:

"He has had a stroke of paralysis. He may lie in mental darkness for months and then recover. His heart action is perfect. Patience, care, and love will save him. There is no cause for immediate alarm."

CHAPTER III

AUGUSTUS CAESAR

PHIL early found the home of the Camerons the most charming spot in town. As he sat in the old-fashioned parlour beside Margaret, his brain seethed with plans for building a hotel on a large scale on the other side of the Square and restoring her home intact.

The Cameron homestead was a large brick building with an ample porch, looking out directly on the Court House Square, standing in the middle of a lawn full of trees, flowers, shrubbery, and a wilderness of evergreen boxwood planted fifty years before. It was located on the farm from which it had always derived its support. The farm extended up into the village itself, with the great barn easily seen from the street.

Phil was charmed with the doctor's genial personality. He often found the father a decidedly easier person to get along with than his handsome daughter. The Rev. Hugh McAlpin was a daily caller, and Margaret had a tantalising way of showing her deference to his opinions.

Phil hated this preacher from the moment he laid eyes on him. His pugnacious piety he might have endured but for the fact that he was good-looking and eloquent. When he rose in the pulpit in all his sacred dignity, fixed his eyes on Margaret, and began in tenderly modulated voice to tell about the love of God, Phil clinched his fist. He didn't care to join the Presbyterian church, but he quietly made up his mind that, if it came to the worst and she asked him, he would join anything. What made him furious was the air of assurance with which the young divine carried himself about Margaret, as if he had but to say the word and it would be fixed as by a decree issued from before the foundations of the world.

He was pleased and surprised to find that his being a Yankee made no difference in his standing or welcome. The people seemed unconscious of the part his father played at Washington. Stoneman's Confiscation Bill had not yet been discussed in Congress, and the promise of land to the negroes was universally regarded as a hoax of the League to win their followers. The old Commoner was not an orator. Hence his name was scarcely known in the South. The Southern people could not conceive of a great leader except one who expressed his power through the megaphone of oratory. They held Charles Sumner chiefly responsible for Reconstruction.

The fact that Phil was a Yankee who had no axe to grind in the South caused the people to appeal to him in a pathetic way that touched his heart. He had not been in town two weeks before he was on good terms with every youngster, had the entrée to every home, and Ben had taken him, protesting vehemently, to see every pretty girl there. He found that, in spite of war and poverty, troubles present, and troubles to come, the young Southern woman was the divinity that claimed and received the chief worship of man.

The tremendous earnestness with which these young-
sters pursued the work of courting, all of them so poor
they scarcely had enough to eat, amazed and alarmed him
beyond measure. He found in several cases as many as
four making a dead set for one girl, as if heaven and
earth depended on the outcome, while the girl seemed to
receive it all as a matter of course—her just tribute.

Every instinct of his quiet reserved nature revolted at
any such attempt to rush his cause with Margaret, and yet
it made the cold chills run down his spine to see that Presbyterian preacher drive his buggy up to the hotel, take her
to ride, and stay three hours. He knew where they had
gone—to Lover's Leap and along the beautiful road which
led to the North Carolina line. He knew the way—Margaret had showed him. This road was the Way of Romance. Every farm-house, cabin, and shady nook along
its beaten track could tell its tale of lovers fleeing from the
North to find happiness in the haven of matrimony across
the line in South Carolina. Everything seemed to favour
marriage in this climate. The State required no license.
A legal marriage could be celebrated, anywhere, at any
time, by a minister in the presence of two witnesses, with
or without the consent of parent or guardian. Marriage
was the easiest thing in the state—divorce the one thing
impossible. Death alone could grant divorce.

He was now past all reason in love. He followed the
movement of Margaret's queenly figure with pathetic
abandonment. Beneath her beautiful manners he swore
with a shiver that she was laughing at him. Now and
then he caught a funny expression about her eyes, as

if she were consumed with a sly sense of humour in her love-affairs.

What he felt to be his manliest traits, his reserve, dignity, and moral earnestness, she must think cold and slow beside the dash, fire, and assurance of these Southerners. He could tell by the way she encouraged the preacher before his eyes that she was criticising and daring him to let go for once. Instead of doing it, he sank back appalled at the prospect and let the preacher carry her off again.

He sought solace in Dr. Cameron, who was utterly oblivious of his daughter's love-affairs.

Phil was constantly amazed at the variety of his knowledge, the genuineness of his culture, his modesty, and the note of youth and cheer with which he still pursued the study of medicine.

His company was refreshing for its own sake. The slender graceful figure, ruddy face, with piercing, dark-brown eyes in startling contrast to his snow-white hair and beard, had for Phil a perpetual charm. He never tired listening to his talk, and noting the peculiar grace and dignity with which he carried himself, unconscious of the commanding look of his brilliant eyes.

"I hear that you have used Hypnotism in your practice, Doctor," Phil said to him one day, as he watched with fascination the changing play of his mobile features.

"Oh, yes! used it for years. Southern doctors have always been pioneers in the science of medicine. Dr. Crawford Long, of Georgia, you know, was the first practitioner in America to apply anesthesia to surgery."

"But where did you run up against Hypnotism? I thought this a new thing under the sun?"

The doctor laughed.

"It's not a home industry, exactly. I became interested in it in Edinburgh while a medical student, and pursued it with increased interest in Paris."

"Did you study medicine abroad?" Phil asked in surprise.

"Yes; I was poor, but I managed to raise and to borrow enough to take three years on the other side. I put all I had and all my credit in it. I've never regretted the sacrifice. The more I saw of the great world, the better I liked my own world. I've given these farmers and their families the best God gave to me."

"Do you find much use for your powers of hypnosis?" Phil asked.

"Only in an experimental way. Naturally I am endowed with this gift—especially over certain classes who are easily the subjects of extreme fear. I owned a rascally slave named Gus whom I used to watch stealing. Suddenly confronting him, I've thrown him into unconsciousness with a steady gaze of the eye, until he would drop on his face, trembling like a leaf, unable to speak until I allowed him."

"How do you account for such powers?"

"I don't account for them at all. They belong to the world of spiritual phenomena of which we know so little and yet which touch our material lives at a thousand points every day. How do we account for sleep and dreams, or second sight, or the day-dreams which we call visions?"

Phil was silent, and the doctor went on dreamily:

"The day my boy Richard was killed at Gettysburg, I saw him lying dead in a field near a house. I saw some soldiers bury him in the corner of that field, and then an old man go to the grave, dig up his body, cart it away into the woods, and throw it into a ditch. I saw it before I heard of the battle or knew that he was in it. He was reported killed, and his body has never been found. It is the one unspeakable horror of the war to me. I'll never get over it."

"How very strange!" exclaimed Phil.

"And yet the war was nothing, my boy, to the horrors I feel clutching the throat of the South to-day. I'm glad you and your father are down here. Your disinterested view of things may help us at Washington when we need it most. The South seems to have no friend at Court."

"Your younger men, I find, are hopeful, Doctor," said Phil.

"Yes, the young never see danger until it's time to die. I'm not a pessimist, but I was happier in jail. Scores of my old friends have given up in despair and died. Delicate and cultured women are living on cowpeas, corn bread and molasses—and of such quality they would not have fed it to a slave. Children go to bed hungry. Droves of brutal negroes roam at large, stealing, murdering, and threatening blacker crimes. We are under the heel of petty military tyrants, few of whom ever smelled gunpowder in a battle. At the approaching election, not a decent white man in this county can take the infamous test-oath. I am disfranchised because I gave a cup of

water to the lips of one of my dying boys on the battle-field.
My slaves are all voters. There will be a negro majority
of more than one hundred thousand in this state. Des-
peradoes are here teaching these negroes insolence and
crime in their secret societies. The future is a nightmare."

"You have my sympathy, sir," said Phil, warmly extending his hand. "These Reconstruction Acts, conceived in sin and brought forth in iniquity, can bring only
shame and disgrace until the last trace of them is wiped
from our laws. I hope it will not be necessary to do it in
blood."

The doctor was deeply touched. He could not be mistaken in the genuineness of any man's feeling. He never
dreamed this earnest straightforward Yankee youngster
was in love with Margaret, and it would have made no
difference in the accuracy of his judgment.

"Your sentiments do you honour, sir," he said, with
grave courtesy. "And you honour us and our town with
your presence and friendship."

As Phil hurried home in a warm glow of sympathy for
the people whose hospitality had made him their friend
and champion, he encountered a negro trooper standing
on the corner, watching the Cameron house with furtive
glance.

Instinctively he stopped, surveyed the man from head
to foot and asked:

"What's the trouble?"

"None er yo' business," the negro answered, slouching
across to the opposite side of the street.

Phil watched him with disgust. He had the short, heavy-set neck of the lower order of animals. His skin was coal black, his lips so thick they curled both ways up and down with crooked blood-marks across them. His nose was flat, and its enormous nostrils seemed in perpetual dilation. The sinister bead eyes, with brown splotches in their whites, were set wide apart and gleamed ape-like under his scant brows. His enormous cheekbones and jaws seemed to protrude beyond the ears and almost hide them.

"That we should send such soldiers here to flaunt our uniform in the faces of these people!" he exclaimed, with bitterness.

He met Ben hurrying home from a visit to Elsie. The two young soldiers whose prejudices had melted in the white-heat of battle had become fast friends.

Phil laughed and winked:

"I'll meet you to-night around the family altar!"

When he reached home, Ben saw, slouching in front of the house, walking back and forth and glancing furtively behind him, the negro trooper whom his friend had passed.

He walked quickly in front of him, and, blinking his eyes rapidly, said:

"Didn't I tell you, Gus, not to let me catch you hanging around this house again?"

The negro drew himself up, pulling his blue uniform into position as his body stretched out of its habitual slouch, and answered:

"My name ain't 'Gus.'"

Ben gave a quick little chuckle and leaned back against

the palings, his hand resting on one that was loose. He glanced at the negro carelessly and said:

"Well, Augustus Caesar, I give your majesty thirty seconds to move off the block."

Gus' first impulse was to run, but remembering himself he threw back his shoulders and said:

"I reckon de streets is free——"

"Yes, and so is kindling-wood!"

Quick as a flash of lightning the paling suddenly left the fence and broke three times in such bewildering rapidity on the negro's head he forgot everything he ever knew or thought he knew save one thing—the way to run. He didn't fly, but he made remarkable use of the facilities with which he had been endowed.

Ben watched him disappear toward the camp.

He picked up the pieces of paling, pulled a strand of black wool from a splinter, looked at it curiously and said:

"A sprig of his majesty's hair—I'll doubtless remember him without it!"

CHAPTER IV

AT THE POINT OF THE BAYONET

WITHIN an hour from Ben's encounter, he was arrested without warrant by the military commandant, handcuffed, and placed on the train for Columbia, more than a hundred miles distant. The first purpose of sending him in charge of a negro guard was abandoned for fear of a riot. A squad of white troops accompanied him.

Elsie was waiting at the gate, watching for his coming, her heart aglow with happiness.

When Marion and little Hugh ran to tell the exciting news, she thought it a joke and refused to believe it.

"Come, dear, don't tease me; you know it's not true!"

"I wish I may die if 'taint so!" Hugh solemnly declared. "He run Gus away 'cause he scared Aunt Margaret so. They come and put handcuffs on him and took him to Columbia. I tell you Grandpa and Grandma and Aunt Margaret are mad!"

Elsie called Phil and begged him to see what had happened.

When Phil reported Ben's arrest without a warrant, and the indignity to which he had been subjected on the amazing charge of resisting military authority, Elsie hurried with Marion and Hugh to the hotel to express her

indignation, and sent Phil to Columbia on the next train
to fight for his release.

By the use of a bribe Phil discovered that a special
inquisition had been hastily organised to procure perjured
testimony against Ben on the charge of complicity in
the murder of a carpet-bag adventurer named Ashburn,
who had been killed at Columbia in a row in a disrep-
utable resort. This murder had occurred the week Ben
Cameron was in Nashville. The enormous reward of
$25,000 had been offered for the conviction of any man
who could be implicated in the killing. Scores of venal
wretches, eager for this blood-money, were using every
device of military tyranny to secure evidence on which to
convict—no matter who the man might be. Within six
hours of his arrival they had pounced on Ben.

They arrested as a witness an old negro named John
Stapler, noted for his loyalty to the Camerons. The
doctor had saved his life once in a dangerous illness.
They were going to put him to torture and force him to
swear that Ben Cameron had tried to bribe him to kill
Ashburn. General Howle, the commandant of the Columbia district, was in Charleston on a visit to headquarters.

Phil resorted to the ruse of pretending, as a Yankee, the
deepest sympathy for Ashburn, and by the payment of a
fee of twenty dollars to the Captain, was admitted to the
fort to witness the torture.

They led the old man trembling into the presence of the
Captain, who sat on an improvised throne in full uniform.

"Have you ordered a barber to shave this man's head?"
sternly asked the judge.

"Please, Marster, fer de Lawd's sake, I ain' done nuttin'—doan' shave my head. Dat ha'r been wropped lak dat fur ten year! I die sho' ef I lose my ha'r."

"Bring the barber, and take him back until he comes," was the order. In an hour they led him again into the room, blindfolded, and placed him in a chair.

"Have you let him see a preacher before putting him through?" the Captain asked. "I have an order from the General in Charleston to put him through to-day."

"For God's sake, Marster, doan' put me froo—I ain't done nuttin' en I doan' know nuttin'!"

The old negro slipped to his knees, trembling from head to foot.

The guards caught him by the shoulders and threw him back into the chair. The bandage was removed, and just in front of him stood a brass cannon pointed at his head, a soldier beside it holding the string ready to pull. John threw himself backward, yelling:

"Goddermighty!"

When he scrambled to his feet and started to run, another cannon swung on him from the rear. He dropped to his knees and began to pray:

"Yas, Lawd, I'se er comin'. I hain't ready—but, Lawd, I got ter come! Save me!"

"Shave him!" the Captain ordered.

While the old man sat moaning, they lathered his head with two scrubbing-brushes and shaved it clean.

"Now stand him up by the wall and measure him for his coffin," was the order.

They snatched him from the chair, pushed him against

the wall, and measured him.   While they were taking his measure, the man next to him whispered:

"Now's the time to save your hide—tell all about Ben Cameron trying to hire you to kill Ashburn."

"Give him a few minutes," said the Captain, "and maybe we can hear what Mr. Cameron said about Ashburn."

"I doan' know nuttin', General," pleaded the old darkey.   "I ain't heard nuttin'—I ain't seed Marse Ben fer two monts."

"You needn't lie to us.   The rebels have been posting you.   But it's no use.   We'll get it out of you."

"'Fo' Gawd, Marster, I'se er telling de truf!"

"Put him in the dark cell and keep him there the balance of his life unless he tells," was the order.

At the end of four days, Phil was summoned again to witness the show.

John was carried to another part of the fort and shown the sweat-box.

"Now tell all you know or in you go!" said his tormentor.

The negro looked at the engine of torture in abject terror—a closet in the walls of the fort just big enough to admit the body, with an adjustable top to press down too low for the head to be held erect.   The door closed tight against the breast of the victim.   The only air admitted was through an auger-hole in the door.

The old man's lips moved in prayer.

"Will you tell?" growled the Captain.

"I cain't tell ye nuttin' 'cept'n' a lie!" he moaned.

They thrust him in, slammed the door, and in a loud voice the Captain said:

"Keep him there for thirty days unless he tells."

He was left in the agony of the sweat-box for thirty-three hours and taken out. His limbs were swollen, and when he attempted to walk he tottered and fell.

The guard jerked him to his feet, and the Captain said:

"I'm afraid we've taken him out too soon, but if he don't tell he can go back and finish the month out."

The poor old negro dropped in a faint, and they carried him back to his cell.

Phil determined to spare no means, fair or foul, to secure Ben's release from the clutches of these devils. He had as yet been unable to locate his place of confinement.

He continued his ruse of friendly curiosity, kept in touch with the Captain, and the Captain in touch with his pocket-book.

Summoned to witness another interesting ceremony, he hurried to the fort.

The officer winked at him confidentially, and took him out to a row of dungeons built of logs and ceiled inside with heavy boards. A single pane of glass about eight inches square admitted light ten feet from the ground.

There was a commotion inside, curses, groans and cries for mercy mingling in rapid succession.

"What is it?" asked Phil.

"Hell's goin' on in there!" laughed the officer.

"Evidently."

A heavy crash, as though a ton-weight had struck the floor, and then all was still.

"By George, it's too bad we can't see it all!" exclaimed the officer.

"What does it mean?" urged Phil.

Again the Captain laughed immoderately.

"I've got a blue-blood in there taking the bluin' out of his system. He gave me some impudence. I'm teaching him who's running this country!"

"What are you doing to him?" Phil asked with a sudden suspicion.

"Oh, just having a little fun! I put two big white drunks in there with him—half-fighting drunks, you know —and told them to work on his teeth and manicure his face a little to initiate him into the ranks of the common people, so to speak!"

Again he laughed.

Phil, listening at the keyhole, held up his hand:

"Hush, they're talking——"

He could hear Ben Cameron's voice in the softest drawl:

"Say it again."

"Please, Marster!"

"Now both together, and a little louder."

"*Please, Marster!*" came the united chorus.

"Now what kind of a dog did I say you are?"

"The kind as comes when his marster calls."

"Both together—the under dog seems to have too much cover, like his mouth might be full of cotton."

They repeated it louder.

"A common—stump-tailed—cur-dog?"

"Yessir."

"Say it."

"A common—stump-tailed—cur-dog—Marster!"

"A pair of them."

"A pair of 'em."

"No, the whole thing — all together—'we—are—a—pair!'"

"Yes—Marster." They repeated it in chorus.

"With apologies to the dogs——"

"Apologies to the dogs——"

"And why does your master honour the kennel with his presence to-day?"

"He hit a nigger on the head so hard that he strained the nigger's ankle, and he's restin' from his labours."

"That's right, Towser. If I had you and Tige a few hours every day I could make good squirrel-dogs out of you."

There was a pause. Phil looked up and smiled.

"What does it sound like?" asked the Captain, with a shade of doubt in his voice.

"Sounds to me like a Sunday-school teacher taking his class through a new catechism."

The Captain fumbled hurriedly for his keys.

"There's something wrong in there."

He opened the door and sprang in.

Ben Cameron was sitting on top of the two toughs, knocking their heads together as they repeated each chorus.

"Walk in, gentlemen. The show is going on now—the animals are doing beautifully," said Ben.

The Captain muttered an oath. Phil suddenly grasped him by the throat, hurled him against the wall, and snatched the keys from his hand.

"Now open your mouth, you white-livered cur, and inside of twenty-four hours I'll have you behind the bars. I have all the evidence I need. I'm an ex-officer of the United States Army, of the fighting corps—not the vulture division. This is my friend. Accompany us to the street and strike your charges from the record."

The coward did as he was ordered, and Ben hurried back to Piedmont with a friend toward whom he began to feel closer than a brother.

When Elsie heard the full story of the outrage, she bore herself toward Ben with unusual tenderness, and yet he knew that the event had driven their lives farther apart. He felt instinctively the cold silent eye of her father, and his pride stiffened under it. The girl had never considered the possibility of a marriage without her father's blessing. Ben Cameron was too proud to ask it. He began to fear that the differences between her father and his people reached to the deepest sources of life.

Phil found himself a hero at the Cameron House. Margaret said little, but her bearing spoke in deeper language than words. He felt it would be mean to take advantage of her gratitude.

But he was quick to respond to the motherly tenderness of Mrs. Cameron. In the groups of neighbours who gathered in the evenings to discuss with the doctor the hopes, fears, and sorrows of the people, Phil was a charmed listener to the most brilliant conversations he had ever heard. It seemed the normal expression of their lives. He had never before seen people come together to talk to one another after this fashion. More and more the simplicity, dignity, patience, courtesy, and sympathy of these people in their bearing toward one another impressed him. More and more he grew to like them.

Marion went out of her way to express her open admiration for Phil and tease him about Margaret. The Rev. Hugh McAlpin was monopolising her on the Wednesday following his return from Columbia and Phil sought Marion for sympathy.

"What will you give me if I tease you about Margaret right before her?" she asked.

He blushed furiously.

"Don't you dare such a thing on peril of your life!"

"You know you like to be teased about her," she cried, her blue eyes dancing with fun.

"With such a pretty little friend to do the teasing all by ourselves, perhaps——"

"You'll never get her unless you have more spunk."

"Then I'll find consolation with you."

"No, I mean to marry young."

"And your ideal of life?"

"To fill the world with flowers, laughter, and music—especially my own home—and never do a thing I can make my husband do for me! How do you like it?"

"I think it very sweet," Phil answered soberly.

At noon on the following Friday, the Piedmont *Eagle* appeared with an editorial signed by Dr. Cameron, denouncing in the fine language of the old school the arrest of Ben as "despotism and the usurpation of authority."

At three o'clock, Captain Gilbert, in command of the troops stationed in the village, marched a squad of soldiers to the newspaper office. One of them carried a sledge-hammer. In ten minutes he demolished the office, heaped the type and their splintered cases on top of the battered press in the middle of the street, and set fire to the pile.

On the court-house door he nailed this proclamation:

"*To the People of Ulster County:*

"The censures of the press, directed against the servants of the people, may be endured; but the military force in command of this district are not the servants of the people of South Carolina. WE ARE YOUR MASTERS. The impertinence of newspaper comment on the military will not be brooked UNDER ANY CIRCUMSTANCES WHATEVER.

"G. C. GILBERT,
"Captain in Command."

Not content with this display of power, he determined to make an example of Dr. Cameron, as the leader of public opinion in the county.

He ordered a squad of his negro troops to arrest him immediately and take him to Columbia for obstructing the execution of the Reconstruction Acts. He placed the squad under command of Gus, whom he promoted to be a corporal, with instructions to wait until the doctor was inside his house, boldly enter it and arrest him.

When Gus marched his black janizaries into the house, no one was in the office. Margaret had gone for a ride with Phil, and Ben had strolled with Elsie to Lover's Leap, unconscious of the excitement in town.

Dr. Cameron himself had heard nothing of it, having just reached home from a visit to a country patient.

Gus stationed his men at each door, and with another

trooper walked straight into Mrs. Cameron's bedroom, where the doctor was resting on a lounge.

Had an imp of perdition suddenly sprung through the floor, the master of the house of Cameron would not have been more enraged or surprised.

A sudden leap, as the spring of a panther, and he stood before his former slave, his slender frame erect, his face a livid spot in its snow-white hair, his brilliant eyes flashing with fury.

Gus suddenly lost control of his knees.

His old master transfixed him with his eyes, and in a voice, whose tones gripped him by the throat, said:

"How dare you?"

The gun fell from the negro's hand, and he dropped to the floor on his face.

His companion uttered a yell and sprang through the door, rallying the men as he went:

"Fall back! Fall back! He's killed Gus! Shot him dead wid his eye. He's conjured him! Git de whole army quick."

They fled to the Commandant.

Gilbert ordered the negroes to their tents and led his whole company of white regulars to the hotel, arrested Dr. Cameron, and rescued his fainting trooper, who had been revived and placed under a tree on the lawn.

The little Captain had a wicked look on his face. He refused to allow the doctor a moment's delay to leave instructions for his wife, who had gone to visit a neighbour. He was placed in the guard-house, and a detail of twenty soldiers stationed around it.

The arrest was made so quickly, not a dozen people in town had heard of it. As fast as it was known, people poured into the house, one by one, to express their sympathy. But a greater surprise awaited them.

Within thirty minutes after he had been placed in prison, a Lieutenant entered, accompanied by a soldier and a negro blacksmith who carried in his hand two big chains with shackles on each end.

The doctor gazed at the intruders a moment with incredulity, and then, as the enormity of the outrage dawned on him, he flushed and drew himself erect, his face livid and rigid.

He clutched his throat with his slender fingers, slowly recovered himself, glanced at the shackles in the black hands and then at the young Lieutenant's face, and said slowly, with heaving breast:

"My God! Have you been sent to place these irons on me?"

"Such are my orders, sir," replied the officer, motioning to the negro smith to approach. He stepped forward, unlocked the padlock and prepared the fetters to be placed on his arms and legs. These fetters were of enormous weight, made of iron rods three-quarters of an inch thick and connected together by chains of like weight.

"This is monstrous!" groaned the doctor, with choking agony, glancing helplessly about the bare cell for some weapon with which to defend himself.

Suddenly, looking the Lieutenant in the face, he said:

"I demand, sir, to see your commanding officer. He

cannot pretend that these shackles are needed to hold a weak unarmed man in prison, guarded by two hundred soldiers?"

"It is useless. I have his orders direct."

"But I must see him. No such outrage has ever been recorded in the history of the American people. I appeal to the Magna Charta rights of every man who speaks the English tongue—no man shall be arrested or imprisoned or deprived of his own household, or of his liberties, unless by the legal judgment of his peers or by the law of the land!"

"The bayonet is your only law. My orders admit of no delay. For your own sake, I advise you to submit. As a soldier, Dr. Cameron, you know I must execute orders."

"These are not the orders of a soldier!" shouted the prisoner, enraged beyond all control. "They are orders for a jailer, a hangman, a scullion—no soldier who wears the sword of a civilised nation can take such orders. The war is over; the South is conquered; I have no country save America. For the honour of the flag, for which I once poured out my blood on the heights of Buena Vista, I protest against this shame!"

The Lieutenant fell back a moment before the burst of his anger.

"Kill me! Kill me!" he went on, passionately throwing his arms wide open and exposing his breast. "Kill— I am in your power. I have no desire to live under such conditions. Kill, but you must not inflict on me and on my people this insult worse than death!"

"Do your duty, blacksmith," said the officer, turning his back and walking toward the door.

The negro advanced with the chains cautiously, and attempted to snap one of the shackles on the doctor's right arm.

With sudden maniac frenzy, Dr. Cameron seized the negro by the throat, hurled him to the floor, and backed against the wall.

The Lieutenant approached and remonstrated:

"Why compel me to add the indignity of personal violence? You must submit."

"I am your prisoner," fiercely retorted the doctor. "I have been a soldier in the armies of America, and I know how to die. Kill me, and my last breath will be a blessing. But while I have life to resist, for myself and for my people, this thing shall not be done!"

The Lieutenant called a sergeant and a file of soldiers, and the sergeant stepped forward to seize the prisoner.

Dr. Cameron sprang on him with the ferocity of a tiger, seized his musket, and attempted to wrench it from his grasp.

The men closed in on him. A short passionate fight, and the slender, proud, gray-haired man lay panting on the floor.

Four powerful assailants held his hands and feet, and the negro smith, with a grin, secured the rivet on the right ankle and turned the key in the padlock on the left.

As he drove the rivet into the shackle on his left arm, a spurt of bruised blood from the old Mexican War wound stained the iron.

Dr. Cameron lay for a moment in a stupor. At length he slowly rose. The clank of the heavy chains seemed to choke him with horror. He sank on the floor, covering his face with his hands and groaned:

"The shame! The shame! O God, that I might have died! My poor, poor wife!"

Captain Gilbert entered and said with a sneer:

"I will take you now to see your wife and friends if you would like to call before setting out for Columbia."

The doctor paid no attention to him.

"Will you follow me while I lead you through this town, to show them their chief has fallen, or will you force me to drag you?"

Receiving no answer, he roughly drew the doctor to his feet, held him by the arm, and led him thus in half-unconscious stupor through the principal street, followed by a drove of negroes. He ordered a squad of troops to meet him at the depot. Not a white man appeared on the streets. When one saw the sight and heard the clank of those chains, there was a sudden tightening of the lip, a clinched fist, and an averted face.

When they approached the hotel, Mrs. Cameron ran to meet him, her face white as death.

In silence she kissed his lips, kissed each shackle on his wrists, took her handkerchief and wiped the bruised blood from the old wound on his arm the iron had opened afresh, and then with a look, beneath which the Captain shrank, she said in low tones:

"Do your work quickly. You have but a few moments to get out of this town with your prisoner. I have sent a friend to hold my son. If he comes before you go, he will kill you on sight as he would a mad dog."

With a sneer, the Captain passed the hotel and led the doctor, still in half-unconscious stupor, toward the depot down past his old slave-quarters. He had given his negroes who remained faithful each a cabin and a lot.

They looked on in awed silence as the Captain proclaimed:

"Fellow citizens, you are the equal of any white man who walks the ground. The white man's day is done. Your turn has come."

As he passed Jake's cabin, the doctor's faithful man stepped suddenly in front of him, looking at the Captain out of the corners of his eyes, and asked:

"Is I yo' equal?"

"Yes."

"Des lak any white man?"

"Exactly."

The negro's fist suddenly shot into Gilbert's nose with the crack of a sledge-hammer, laying him stunned on the pavement.

"Den take dat f'um yo' equal, d—m you!" he cried, bending over his prostrate figure. "I'll show you how to treat my ole marster, you low-down slue-footed devil!"

The stirring little drama roused the doctor, and he turned to his servant with his old-time courtesy, and said:

"Thank you, Jake."

"Come in here, Marse Richard; I knock dem things off'n you in er minute, 'en I get you outen dis town in er jiffy."

"No, Jake, that is not my way; bring this gentleman some water, and then my horse and buggy. You can take me to the depot. This officer can follow with his men." And he did.

CHAPTER V

FORTY ACRES AND A MULE

WHEN Phil returned with Margaret, he drove, at Mrs. Cameron's request, to find Ben, brought him with all speed to the hotel, took him to his room, and locked the door before he told him the news. After an hour's blind rage, he agreed to obey his father's positive orders to keep away from the Captain until his return, and to attempt no violence against the authorities. Phil undertook to manage the case in Columbia, and spent three days in collecting his evidence before leaving.

Swifter feet had anticipated him. Two days after the arrival of Dr. Cameron at the fort in Columbia, a dust-stained, tired negro was ushered into the presence of General Howle.

He looked about timidly and laughed loudly.

"Well, my man, what's the trouble? You seem to have walked all the way, and laugh as if you were glad of it."

"I 'spec' I is, sah," said Jake, sidling up confidentially.

"Well?" said Howle, good-humouredly.

Jake's voice dropped to a whisper.

"I hears you got my ole marster, Dr. Cameron, in dis place."

"Yes. What do you know against him?"

235

"Nuttin', sah. I dis hurry 'long down ter take his place, so's you kin sen' him back home. He's erbleeged ter go. Dey's er pow'ful lot er sick folks up dar in de county can't git 'long widout him, en er pow'ful lot er well ones gwiner be raisin' de debbel 'bout dis. You can hol' me, sah. Des tell my ole marster when ter be yere, en he sho' come."

Jake paused and bowed low.

"Yessah, hit's des lak I tell you. Fuddermo', I 'spec' I'se de man what done de damages. I 'spec' I bus' de Capt'n's nose so 'taint gwine be no mo' good to 'im."

Howle questioned Jake as to the whole affair, asked him a hundred questions about the condition of the county, the position of Dr. Cameron, and the possible effect of this event on the temper of the people.

The affair had already given him a bad hour. The news of this shackling of one of the most prominent men in the state had spread like wildfire, and had caused the first deep growl of anger from the people. He saw that it was a senseless piece of stupidity. The election was rapidly approaching. He was master of the state, and the less friction the better. His mind was made up instantly. He released Dr. Cameron with an apology, and returned with him and Jake for a personal inspection of the affairs of Ulster county.

In a thirty-minutes' interview with Captain Gilbert, Howle gave him more pain than his broken nose.

"And why did you nail up the doors of that Presbyterian church?" he asked, suavely.

"Because McAlpin, the young cub who preaches there,

dared come to this camp and insult me about the arrest
of old Cameron."

"I suppose you issued an order silencing him from the
ministry?"

"I did, and told him I'd shackle him if he opened his
mouth again."

"Good. The throne of Russia needn't worry about a
worthy successor. Any further ecclesiastical orders?"

"None, except the oaths I've prescribed for them before they shall preach again."

"Fine! These Scotch Covenanters will feel at home
with you."

"Well, I've made them bite the dust—and they know
who's runnin' this town, and don't you forget it."

"No doubt. Yet we may have too much of even a
good thing. The League is here to run this county.
The business of the military is to keep still and back them
when they need it."

"We've the strongest council here to be found in any
county in this section," said Gilbert with pride.

"Just so. The League meets once a week. We have
promised them the land of their masters and equal social
and political rights. Their members go armed to these
meetings and drill on Saturdays in the public square.
The white man is afraid to interfere lest his house or
barn take fire. A negro prisoner in the dock needs only
to make the sign to be acquitted. Not a negro will dare
to vote against us. Their women are formed into societies,
sworn to leave their husbands and refuse to marry any
man who dares our anger. The negro churches have

pledged themselves to expel him from their membership. What more do you want?"

"There's another side to it," protested the Captain.
"Since the League has taken in the negroes, every Union
white man has dropped it like a hot iron, except the lone
scalawag or carpet-bagger who expects an office. In the
church, the social circle, in business or pleasure, these
men are lepers. How can a human being stand it? I've
tried to grind this hellish spirit in the dirt under my
heel, and unless you can do it they'll beat you in the
long run! You've got to have some Southern white
men or you're lost."

"I'll risk it with a hundred thousand negro majority,"
said Howle with a sneer. "The fun will just begin then.
In the meantime, I'll have you ease up on this county's
government. I've brought that man back who knocked
you down. Let him alone. I've pardoned him. The
less said about this affair, the better."

As the day of the election under the new régime of
Reconstruction drew near, the negroes were excited by
rumours of the coming great events. Every man was to
receive forty acres of land for his vote, and the enthusiastic speakers and teachers had made the dream a resistless
one by declaring that the Government would throw in a
mule with the forty acres. Some who had hesitated
about the forty acres of land, remembering that it must be
worked, couldn't resist the idea of owning a mule.

The Freedman's Bureau reaped a harvest in $2 mar-
riage fees from negroes who were urged thus to make

their children heirs of landed estates stocked with
mules.

Every stranger who appeared in the village was regarded
with awe as a possible surveyor sent from Washington to
run the lines of these forty-acre plots.

And in due time the surveyors appeared. Uncle Aleck,
who now devoted his entire time to organising the League,
and drinking whiskey which the dues he collected made
easy, was walking back to Piedmont from a League meeting in the country, dreaming of this promised land.

He lifted his eyes from the dusty way and saw before
him two surveyors with their arms full of line stakes
painted red, white, and blue. They were well-dressed
Yankees—he could not be mistaken. Not a doubt disturbed his mind. The kingdom of heaven was at hand!

He bowed low and cried:

"Praise de Lawd! De messengers is come! I'se
waited long, but I sees 'em now wid my own eyes!"

"You can bet your life on that, old pard," said the
spokesman of the pair. "We go two and two, just as the
apostles did in the olden times. We have only a few left.
The boys are hurrying to get their homes. All you've got
to do is to drive one of these red, white, and blue stakes
down at each corner of the forty acres of land you want,
and every rebel in the infernal regions can't pull it up."

"Hear dat now!"

"Just like I tell you. When this stake goes into the
ground, it's like planting a thousand cannon at each
corner."

"En will the Lawd's messengers come wid me right

now to de bend er de creek whar I done pick out my
forty acres?"

"We will, if you have the needful for the ceremony.
The fee for the surveyor is small—only two dollars for
each stake. We have no time to linger with foolish
virgins who have no oil in their lamps. The bride-
groom has come. They who have no oil must remain
in outer darkness." The speaker had evidently been
a preacher in the North, and his sacred accent sealed his
authority with the old negro, who had been an exhorter
himself.

Aleck felt in his pocket the jingle of twenty gold dollars,
the initiation fees of the week's harvest of the League. He
drew them, counted out eight, and took his four stakes.
The surveyors kindly showed him how to drive them down
firmly to the first stripe of blue. When they had stepped
off a square of about forty acres of the Lenoir farm, including the richest piece of bottom land on the creek, which
Aleck's children under his wife's direction were working
for Mrs. Lenoir, and the four stakes were planted, old
Aleck shouted:

"Glory ter God!"

"Now," said the foremost surveyor, "you want a deed
—a deed in fee simple with the big seal of the Government
on it, and you're fixed for life. The deed you can take to
the court-house and make the clerk record it."

The man drew from his pocket an official-looking paper,
with a red circular seal pasted on its face.

Uncle Aleck's eyes danced.

"Is dat de deed?"

"It will be if I write your name on it and describe the land."

"En what's de fee fer dat?"

"Only twelve dollars; you can take it now or wait until we come again. There's no particular hurry about this. The wise man, though, leaves nothing for to-morrow that he can carry with him to-day."

"I takes de deed right now, gemmen," said Aleck, eagerly counting out the remaining twelve dollars. "Fix 'im up for me."

The surveyor squatted in the field and carefully wrote the document.

They went on their way rejoicing, and old Aleck hurried into Piedmont with the consciousness of lordship of the soil. He held himself so proudly that it seemed to straighten some of the crook out of his bow legs.

He marched up to the hotel where Margaret sat reading and Marion was on the steps playing with a setter.

"Why, Uncle Aleck!" Marion exclaimed, "I haven't seen you in a long time."

Aleck drew himself to his full height—at least, as full as his bow legs would permit, and said gruffly:

"Miss Ma'ian, I axes you to stop callin' me 'uncle'; my name is Mr. Alexander Lenoir——"

"Until Aunt Cindy gets after you," laughed the girl. "Then it's much shorter than that, Uncle Aleck."

He shuffled his feet and looked out at the square unconcernedly.

"Yaas'm, dat's what fetch me here now. I comes ter tell yer Ma ter tell dat 'oman Cindy ter take her chillun off my farm. I gwine 'low no mo' rent-payin' ter nobody off'n my lan'!"

"Your land, Uncle Aleck? When did you get it?" asked Marion, placing her cheek against the setter.

"De Gubment gim it ter me to-day," he replied, fumbling in his pocket and pulling out the document. "You kin read it all dar yo'sef."

He handed Marion the paper, and Margaret hurried down and read it over her shoulder.

Both girls broke into screams of laughter.

Aleck looked up sharply.

"Do you know what's written on this paper, Uncle Aleck?" Margaret asked.

"Cose I do. Dat's de deed ter my farm er forty acres in de bend er de creek, whar I done stuck off wid de red, white, an' blue sticks de Gubment gimme."

"I'll read it to you," said Margaret.

"Wait a minute," interrupted Marion. "I want Aunt Cindy to hear it—she's here to see Mama in the kitchen now."

She ran for Uncle Aleck's spouse. Aunt Cindy walked around the house and stood by the steps, eyeing her erstwhile lord with contempt.

"Got yer deed, is yer, ter stop me payin' my missy her rent fum de lan' my chillun wucks? Yu'se er smart boy, you is—let's hear de deed!"

Aleck edged away a little, and said with a bow:

"Dar's de paper wid de big mark er de Gubment."

Aunt Cindy sniffed the air contemptuously.

"What is it, honey?" she asked of Margaret.

Margaret read in mock solemnity the mystic writing on the deed:

" *To Whom It May Concern:*

"As Moses lifted up the brazen serpent in the wilderness for the enlightenment of the people, even so have I lifted twenty shining plunks out of this benighted nigger!   Selah!"

As Uncle Aleck walked away with Aunt Cindy shouting in derision, "Dar, now!   Dar, now!" the bow in his legs seemed to have sprung a sharper curve.

CHAPTER VI

A Whisper in the Crowd

THE excitement which preceeded the first Reconstruction election in the South paralysed the industries of the country. When demagogues poured down from the North and began their raving before crowds of ignorant negroes, the plow stopped in the furrow, the hoe was dropped, and the millenium was at hand.

Negro tenants, working under contracts issued by the Freedman's Bureau, stopped work, and rode their landlords' mules and horses around the county, following these orators.

The loss to the cotton crop alone from the abandonment of the growing plant was estimated at over $60,000,000.

The one thing that saved the situation from despair was the large grain and forage crops of the previous season which thrifty farmers had stored in their barns. So important was the barn and its precious contents that Dr. Cameron hired Jake to sleep in his.

This immense barn, which was situated at the foot of the hill some two hundred yards behind the house, had become a favourite haunt of Marion and Hugh. She had made a pet of the beautiful thoroughbred mare which had belonged to Ben during the war. Marion went every day to give her an apple or lump of sugar, or carry her a bunch of clover. The mare would follow her about like a cat.

Another attraction at the barn for them was Becky Sharpe, Ben's setter. She came to Marion one morning wagging her tail, seized her dress, and led her into an empty stall, where beneath the trough lay sleeping snugly ten little white-and-black spotted puppies.

The girl had never seen such a sight before and went into ecstasies. Becky wagged her tail with pride at her compliments. Every morning she would pull her gently into the stall just to hear her talk and laugh and pet her babies.

Whatever election day meant to the men, to Marion it was one of unalloyed happiness: she was to ride horse-back alone and dance at her first ball. Ben had taught her to ride, and told her she could take Queen to Lover's Leap and back alone. Trembling with joy, her beautiful face wreathed in smiles, she led the mare to the pond in the edge of the lot and watched her drink its pure spring water.

When he helped her to mount in front of the hotel under her mother's gaze, and saw her ride out of the gate, with the exquisite lines of her little figure melting into the graceful lines of the mare's glistening form, he exclaimed:

"I declare, I don't know which is the prettier, Marion or Queen!"

"I know," was the mother's soft answer.

"They are both thoroughbreds," said Ben, watching them admiringly.

"Wait till you see her to-night in her first ball-dress," whispered Mrs. Lenoir.

At noon Ben and Phil strolled to the polling-place to watch the progress of the first election under Negro rule. The Square was jammed with shouting, jostling, perspiring negroes, men, women, and children. The day was warm, and the African odour was supreme even in the open air.

A crowd of two hundred were packed around a peddler's box. There were two of them—one crying the wares, and the other wrapping and delivering the goods. They were selling a new patent poison for rats.

"I've only a few more bottles left now, gentlemen," he shouted, "and the polls will close at sundown. A great day for our brother in black. Two years of army rations from the Freedman's Bureau, with old army clothes thrown in, and now the ballot—the priceless glory of American citizenship. But better still the very land is to be taken from these proud aristocrats and given to the poor down-trodden black man. Forty acres and a mule—think of it! Provided, mind you— that you have a bottle of my wonder-worker to kill the rats and save your corn for the mule. No man can have the mule unless he has corn; and no man can have corn if he has rats — and only a few bottles left——"

"Gimme one," yelled a negro.

"Forty acres and a mule, your old masters to work your land and pay his rent in corn, while you sit back in the shade and see him sweat."

"Gimme er bottle and two er dem pictures!" bawled another candidate for a mule.

The peddler handed him the bottle and the pictures and threw a handful of his labels among the crowd. These labels happened to be just the size of the ballots, having on them the picture of a dead rat lying on his back, and, above, the emblem of death, the cross-bones and skull.

"Forty acres and a mule for every black man—why was I ever born white? I never had no luck, nohow!"

Phil and Ben passed on nearer the polling-place, around which stood a cordon of soldiers with a line of negro voters two hundred yards in length extending back into the crowd.

The negro Leagues came in armed battallions and voted in droves, carrying their muskets in their hands. Less than a dozen white men were to be seen about the place.

The negroes, under the drill of the League and the Freedman's Bureau, protected by the bayonet, were voting to enfranchise themselves, disfranchise their former masters, ratify a new constitution, and elect a legislature to do their will. Old Aleck was a candidate for the House, chief poll-holder, and seemed to be in charge of the movements of the voters outside the booth as well as inside. He appeared to be omnipresent, and his self-importance was a sight Phil had never dreamed. He could not keep his eyes off him.

"By George, Cameron, he's a wonder!" he laughed.

Aleck had suppressed as far as possible the story of the painted stakes and the deed, after sending out warnings to the brethren to beware of two enticing strangers. The surveyors had reaped a rich harvest and passed on. Aleck

made up his mind to go to Columbia, make the laws himself, and never again trust a white man from the North or
South. The agent of the Freedman's Bureau at Piedmont tried to choke him off the ticket. The League
backed him to a man. He could neither read nor write,
but before he took to whiskey he had made a specialty of
revival exhortation, and his mouth was the most effective
thing about him. In this campaign he was an orator of
no mean powers. He knew what he wanted, and he
knew what his people wanted, and he put the thing in
words so plain that a wayfaring man, though a fool,
couldn't make any mistake about it.

As he bustled past, forming a battalion of his brethren
in line to march to the polls, Phil followed his every movement with amused interest.

Besides being so bow-legged that his walk was a moving
joke, he was so striking a negro in his personal appearance, he seemed to the young Northerner almost a distinct type of man.

His head was small and seemed mashed on the sides
until it bulged into a double lobe behind. Even his ears,
which he had pierced and hung with red earbobs, seemed
to have been crushed flat to the side of his head. His
kinked hair was wrapped in little hard rolls close to the
skull and bound tightly with dirty thread. His receding
forehead was high and indicated a cunning intelligence.
His nose was broad and crushed flat against his face.
His jaws were strong and angular, mouth wide, and lips
thick, curling back from rows of solid teeth set obliquely
in their blue gums. The one perfect thing about him

was the size and setting of his mouth—he was a born African orator, undoubtedly descended from a long line of savage spell-binders, whose eloquence in the palaver houses of the jungle had made them native leaders. His thin spindle-shanks supported an oblong, protruding stomach, resembling an elderly monkey's, which seemed so heavy it swayed his back to carry it.

The animal vivacity of his small eyes and the flexibility of his eyebrows, which he worked up and down rapidly with every change of countenance, expressed his eager desires.

He had laid aside his new shoes, which hurt him, and went barefooted to facilitate his movements on the great occasion. His heels projected and his foot was so flat that what should have been the hollow of it made a hole in the dirt where he left his track.

He was already mellow with liquor, and was dressed in an old army uniform and cap, with two horse-pistols buckled around his waist. On a strap hanging from his shoulder were strung a half-dozen tin canteens filled with whiskey.

A disturbance in the line of voters caused the young men to move forward to see what it meant.

Two negro troopers had pulled Jake out of the line, and were dragging him toward old Aleck.

The election judge straightened himself up with great dignity:

"What wuz de rapscallion doin'?"

"In de line, tryin' ter vote."

"Fetch 'im befo' de judgment bar," said Aleck, taking a drink from one of his canteens.

The troopers brought Jake before the judge.

"'Tryin' ter vote, is yer?'"

"''Lowed I would."

"You hear 'bout de great sassieties de Gubment's fomentin' in dis country?'"

"Yas, I hear erbout 'em."

"Is yer er member er de Union League?'"

"Na-sah. I'd rudder steal by myself. I doan' lak too many in de party!'"

"En yer ain't er No'f Ca'liny gemmen, is yer—yer ain't er member er de 'Red Strings'?'"

"Na-sah, I come when I'se called—dey doan' hatter put er string on me—ner er block, ner er collar, ner er chain, ner er muzzle——'"

"Will yer 'splain ter dis cote——" railed Aleck.

"What cote? Dat ole army cote?" Jake laughed in loud peals that rang over the square.

Aleck recovered his dignity and demanded angrily:

"Does yer belong ter de Heroes ob Americky?'"

"Na-sah. I ain't burnt nobody's house ner barn yet, ner hamstrung no stock, ner waylaid nobody atter night —honey, I ain't fit ter jine. Heroes ob Americky! Is you er hero?'"

"Ef yer doan' b'long ter no s'iety," said Aleck with judicial deliberation, "what is you?'"

"Des er ole-fashun all-wool-en-er-yard-wide nigger dat stan's by his ole marster 'cause he's his bes' frien', stays at home, en tends ter his own business."

"En yer pay no 'tenshun ter de orders I sent yer ter jine de League?'"

"Na-sah. I ain't er takin' orders f'um er skeer-crow."

Aleck ignored his insolence, secure in his power.

"You doan b'long ter no sassiety, what yer git in dat line ter vote for?"

"Ain't I er nigger?"

"But yer ain't de right kin' er nigger. 'Res' dat man fer 'sturbin' de peace."

They put Jake in jail, persuaded his wife to leave him, and expelled him from the Baptist Church, all within the week.

As the troopers led Jake to prison, a young negro apparently about fifteen years old approached Aleck, holding in his hand one of the peddler's rat labels, which had gotten well distributed among the crowd. A group of negro boys followed him with these rat labels in their hands, studying them intently.

"Look at dis ticket, Uncle Aleck," said the leader.

"Mr. Alexander Lenoir, sah—is I yo' uncle, nigger?"

The youth walled his eyes angrily.

"Den doan' you call me er nigger!"

"Who yer talkin' to, sah? You kin fling yer sass at white folks, but, honey, yuse er projeckin' wid death now!"

"I ain't er nigger—I'se er gemman, I is," was the sullen answer.

"How ole is you?" asked Aleck in milder tones.

"Me mudder say sixteen—but de Buro man say I'se twenty-one yistiddy, de day 'fo' 'lection."

"Is you voted to-day?"

"Yessah; vote in all de boxes 'cept'n dis one. Look at dat ticket. Is dat de straight ticket?"

Aleck, who couldn't read the twelve-inch letters of his favourite bar-room sign, took the rat label and examined it critically.

"What ail it?" he asked at length.

The boy pointed at the picture of the rat.

"What dat rat doin', lyin' dar on his back, wid his heels cocked up in de air—'pear ter me lak a rat otter be standin' on his feet?"

Aleck reëxamined it carefully, and then smiled benignly on the youth.

"De ignance er dese folks. What ud yer do widout er man lak me enjued wid de sperit en de power ter splain tings?"

"You sho' got de sperits," said the boy, impudently touching a canteen.

Aleck ignored the remark and looked at the rat label smilingly.

"Ain't we er votin', ter-day, on de Constertooshun what's ter take de ballot away f'um de white folks en gib all de power ter de cullud gemmen—I axes yer dat?"

The boy stuck his thumbs under his arms and walled his eyes.

"Yessah!"

"Den dat means de ratification ob de Constertooshun!"

Phil laughed, followed, and watched them fold their tickets, get in line, and vote the rat labels.

Ben turned toward a white man with gray beard, who stood watching the crowd.

He was a pious member of the Presbyterian church, but his face didn't have a pious expression to-day. He had been refused the right to vote because he had aided the Confederacy by nursing one of his wounded boys.

He touched his hat politely to Ben.

"What do you think of it, Colonel Cameron?" he asked with a touch of scorn.

"What's your opinion, Mr. McAllister?"

"Well, Colonel, I've been a member of the church for over forty years. I'm not a cussin' man—but there's a sight I never expected to live to see. I've been a faithful citizen of this state for fifty years. I can't vote, and a nigger is to be elected to-day to represent me in the Legislature. Neither you, Colonel, nor your father are good enough to vote. Every nigger in this county sixteen years old and up voted to-day—I ain't a cussin' man, and I don't say it as a cuss-word, but all I've got to say is, IF there BE such a thing as a d—d shame—that's it!"

"Mr. McAllister, the recording angel wouldn't have made a mark had you said it without the 'IF.'"

"God knows what this country's comin' to—I don't," said the old man, bitterly. "I'm afraid to let my wife and daughter go out of the house, or stay in it, without somebody with them."

Ben leaned closer and whispered, as Phil approached:

"Come to my office to-night at ten o'clock; I want to see you on some important business."

The old man seized his hand eagerly.

"Shall I bring the boys?"

Ben smiled.

"No I've seen them some time ago."

CHAPTER VII

By the Light of a Torch

O N the night of the election, Mrs. Lenoir gave a ball at the hotel in honour of Marion's entrance into society. She was only in her sixteenth year, yet older than her mother when mistress of her own household. The only ambition the mother cherished was that she might win the love of an honest man and build for herself a beautiful home on the site of the cottage covered with trailing roses. In this home-dream for Marion she found a great sustaining joy to which nothing in the life of man answers.

The ball had its political significance which the military martinet who commanded the post understood. It was the way the people of Piedmont expressed to him and the world their contempt for the farce of an election he had conducted, and their indifference as to the result he would celebrate with many guns before midnight.

The young people of the town were out in force. Marion was a universal favourite. The grace, charm, and tender beauty of the Southern girl of sixteen were combined in her with a gentle and unselfish disposition. Amid poverty that was pitiful, unconscious of its limitations, her thoughts were always of others, and she was the one human being everybody had agreed to love. In the vil-

lage in which she lived, wealth counted for naught. She
belonged to the aristocracy of poetry, beauty, and
intrinsic worth, and her people knew no other.

As she stood in the long dining-room, dressed in her
first ball costume of white organdy and lace, the little
plump shoulders peeping through its meshes, she was the
picture of happiness. A half-dozen boys hung on every
word as the utterance of an oracle. She waved gently
an old ivory fan with white down on its edges in a
way the charm of which is the secret birthright of every
Southern girl.

Now and then she glanced at the door for some one
who had not yet appeared.

Phil paid his tribute to her with genuine feeling, and
Marion repaid him by whispering:

"Margaret's dressed to kill—all in soft azure blue—
her rosy cheeks, black hair, and eyes never shone as
they do to-night. She doesn't dance on account of her
Sunday-school—it's all for you."

Phil blushed and smiled.

"The preacher won't be here?"

"Our rector will."

"He's a nice old gentleman. I'm fond of him. Miss
Marion, your mother is a genius. I hope she can plan
these little affairs oftener."

It was half-past ten o'clock when Ben Cameron entered
the room with Elsie a little ruffled at his delay over imaginary business at his office. Ben answered her criticisms
with a strange elation. She had felt a secret between
them and resented it.

At Mrs. Lenoir's special request, he had put on his full
uniform of a Confederate Colonel in honour of Marion
and the poem her father had written of one of his gallant
charges. He had not worn it since he fell that day in
Phil's arms.

No one in the room had ever seen him in this Colonel's
uniform. Its yellow sash with the gold fringe and tassels
was faded and there were two bullet holes in the coat. A
murmur of applause from the boys, sighs and exclamations
from the girls swept the room as he took Marion's hand,
bowed and kissed it. Her blue eyes danced and smiled
on him with frank admiration.

"Ben, you're the handsomest thing I've ever seen!"
she said, softly.

"Thanks. I thought you had a mirror. I'll send you
one," he answered, slipping his arm around her and glid-
ing away to the strains of a waltz. The girl's hand trembled as she placed it on his shoulder, her cheeks were
flushed, and her eyes had a wistful dreamy look in their
depths.

When Ben rejoined Elsie and they strolled on the lawn,
the military commandant suddenly confronted them with
a squad of soldiers.

"I'll trouble you for those buttons and shoulder-straps,"
said the Captain.

Elsie's amber eyes began to spit fire. Ben stood still
and smiled.

"What do you mean?" she asked.

"That I will not be insulted by the wearing of this
uniform to-day."

"I dare you to touch it, coward, poltroon!" cried the girl, her plump little figure bristling in front of her lover.

Ben laid his hand on her arm and gently drew her back to his side: "He has the power to do this. It is a technical violation of law to wear them. I have surrendered. I am a gentleman and I have been a soldier. He can have his tribute. I've promised my father to offer no violence to the military authority of the United States."

He stepped forward, and the officer cut the buttons from his coat and ripped the straps from his shoulders.

While the performance was going on, Ben quietly said:

"General Grant at Appomattox, with the instincts of a great soldier, gave our men his spare horses and ordered that Confederate officers retain their side-arms. The General is evidently not in touch with this force."

"No; I'm in command in this county," said the Captain.

"Evidently."

When he had gone, Elsie's eyes were dim. They strolled under the shadow of the great oak and stood in silence, listening to the music within and the distant murmur of the falls.

"Why is it, sweetheart, that a girl will persist in admiring brass buttons?" Ben asked, softly.

She raised her lips to his for a kiss and answered:

"Because a soldier's business is to die for his country."

As Ben led her back into the ball-room and surrendered her to a friend for a dance, the first gun pealed its note of victory from the square in the celebration of the triumph of the African slave over his white master.

Ben strolled out in the street to hear the news.

The Constitution had been ratified by an enormous majority, and a Legislature elected composed of 101 negroes and 23 white men. Silas Lynch had been elected Lieutenant-Governor, a negro Secretary of State, a negro Treasurer, and a negro Justice of the Supreme Court.

When Bizzel, the wizzen-faced agent of the Freedman's Bureau, made this announcement from the court house steps, pandemonium broke loose. An incessant rattle of musketry began in which ball cartridges were used, the missiles whistling over the town in every direction. Yet within half an hour the square was deserted and a strange quiet followed the storm.

Old Aleck staggered by the hotel, his drunkenness having reached the religious stage.

"Behold, a curiosity, gentlemen," cried Ben to a group of boys who had gathered, "a voter is come among us—in fact, he is the people, the king, our representative elect, the Honourable Alexander Lenoir, of the county of Ulster!"

"Gemmens, de Lawd's bin good ter me," said Aleck, weeping copiously.

"They say the rat labels were in a majority in this precinct—how was that?" asked Ben.

"Yessah—dat what de scornful say—dem dat sets in de seat o' de scornful, but de Lawd er Hosts He fetch em low. Mistah Bissel de Buro man count all dem rat votes right, sah—dey couldn't fool him—he know what dey mean—he count 'em all for me an' de ratification."

"Sure-pop!" said Ben; "if you can't ratify with a rat, I'd like to know why?"

"Dat's what I tells 'em, sah."

"Of course," said Ben, good-humouredly. "The voice of the people is the voice of God—rats or no rats—if you know how to count."

As old Aleck staggered away, the sudden crash of a volley of musketry echoed in the distance.

"What's that?" asked Ben, listening intently. The sound was unmistakable to a soldier's ear—that volley from a hundred rifles at a single word of command. It was followed by a shot on a hill in the distance, and then by a faint echo, farther still. Ben listened a few moments and turned into the lawn of the hotel. The music suddenly stopped, the tramp of feet echoed on the porch, a woman screamed, and from the rear of the house came the cry:

"Fire! Fire!"

Almost at the same moment an immense sheet of flame shot skyward from the big barn.

"My God!" groaned Ben. "Jake's in jail, to-night, and they've set the barn on fire. It's worth more than the house."

The crowd rushed down the hill to the blazing building, Marion's fleet figure in its flying white dress leading the crowd.

The lowing of the cows and the wild neighing of the horses rang above the roar of the flames.

Before Ben could reach the spot Marion had opened every stall. Two cows leaped out to safety, but not a horse would move from its stall, and each moment wilder and more pitiful grew their death-cries.

Marion rushed to Ben, her eyes dilated, her face as white as the dress she wore.

"Oh, Ben, Queen won't come out! What shall I do?"

"You can do nothing, child. A horse won't come out of a burning stable unless he's blindfolded. They'll all be burned to death."

"Oh! no!" the girl cried in agony.

"They'd trample you to death if you tried to get them out. It can't be helped. It's too late."

As Ben looked back at the gathering crowd, Marion suddenly snatched a horse-blanket, lying at the door, ran with the speed of a deer to the pond, plunged in, sprang out, and sped back to the open door of Queen's stall, through which her shrill cry could be heard above the others.

As the girl ran toward the burning building, her thin white dress clinging close to her exquisite form, she looked like the marble figure of a sylph by the hand of some great master into which God had suddenly breathed the breath of life.

As they saw her purpose, a cry of horror rose from the crowd, her mother's scream loud above the rest.

Ben rushed to catch her, shouting:

"Marion! Marion! She'll trample you to death!"

He was too late. She leaped into the stall. The crowd held their breath. There was a moment of awful suspense, and the mare sprang through the open door with the little white figure clinging to her mane and holding the blanket over her head.

A cheer rang above the roar of the flames. The girl

did not loose her hold until her beautiful pet was led to a place of safety, while she clung to her neck and laughed and cried for joy. First her mother, then Margaret, Mrs. Cameron, and Elsie took her in their arms.

As Ben approached the group, Elsie whispered to him: "Kiss her!"

Ben took her hand, his eyes full of unshed tears, and said:

"The bravest deed a woman ever did—you're a heroine, Marion!"

Before she knew it, he stooped and kissed her.

She was very still for a moment, smiled, trembled from head to foot, blushed scarlet, took her mother by the hand, and without a word hurried to the house.

Poor Becky was whining among the excited crowd and sought in vain for Marion. At last she got Margaret's attention, caught her dress in her teeth and led her to a corner of the lot, where she had laid side by side her puppies, smothered to death. She stood and looked at them with her tail drooping, the picture of despair. Margaret burst into tears and called Ben.

He bent and put his arm around the setter's neck and stroked her head with his hand. Looking up at his sister, he said:

"Don't tell Marion of this. She can't stand any more to-night."

The crowd had all dispersed, and the flames had died down for want of fuel. The odour of roasting flesh, pungent and acrid, still lingered a sharp reminder of the tragedy.

Ben stood on the back porch, talking in low tones to his father.

"Will you join us now, sir? We need the name and influence of men of your standing."

"My boy, two wrongs never make a right. It's better to endure awhile. The sober common sense of the Nation will yet save us. We must appeal to it."

"Eight more fires were seen from town to-night."

"You only guess their origin."

"I know their origin. It was done by the League at a signal as a celebration of the election and a threat of terror to the county. One of our men concealed a faithful negro under the floor of the school-house and heard the plot hatched. We expected it a month ago—but hoped they had given it up."

"Even so, my boy, a secret society such as you have planned means a conspiracy that may bring exile or death. I hate lawlessness and disorder. We have had enough of it. Your clan means ultimately martial law. At least we will get rid of these soldiers by this election. They have done their worst to me, but we may save others by patience."

"It's the only way, sir. The next step will be a black hand on a white woman's throat!"

The doctor frowned. "Let us hope for the best. Your clan is the last act of desperation."

"But if everything else fail, and this creeping horror becomes a fact—then what?"

"My boy, we will pray that God may never let us live to see the day!"

CHAPTER VIII

THE RIOT IN THE MASTER'S HALL

A LARMED at the possible growth of the secret clan into which Ben had urged him to enter, Dr. Cameron determined to press for relief from oppression by an open appeal to the conscience of the Nation.

He called a meeting of conservative leaders in a Taxpayers' Convention at Columbia. His position as a leader had been made supreme by the indignities he had suffered, and he felt sure of his ability to accomplish results. Every county in the state was represented by its best men in this gathering at the Capital.

The day he undertook to present his memorial to the Legislature was one he never forgot. The streets were crowded with negroes who had come to town to hear Lynch, the Lieutenant-Governor, speak in a mass-meeting. Negro policemen swung their clubs in his face as he pressed through the insolent throng up the street to the stately marble Capitol. At the door a black, greasy trooper stopped him to parley. Every decently dressed white man was regarded a spy.

As he passed inside the doors of the House of Representatives, the rush of foul air staggered him. The reek of vile cigars and stale whiskey, mingled with the odour of perspiring negroes, was overwhelming. He paused and gasped for breath.

The space behind the seats of the members was strewn with corks, broken glass, stale crusts, greasy pieces of paper, and picked bones. The hall was packed with negroes, smoking, chewing, jabbering, pushing, perspiring.

A carpet-bagger at his elbow was explaining to an old darkey from down east why his forty acres and a mule hadn't come.

On the other side of him a big negro bawled:

"Dat's all right! De cullud man on top!"

The doctor surveyed the hall in dismay. At first not a white member was visible. The galleries were packed with negroes. The Speaker presiding was a negro, the Clerk a negro, the doorkeepers negroes, the little pages all coal-black negroes, the Chaplain a negro. The negro party consisted of one hundred and one—ninety-four blacks and seven scallawags, who claimed to be white. The remains of Aryan civilisation were represented by twenty-three white men from the Scotch-Irish hill counties.

The doctor had served three terms as the member from Ulster in this hall in the old days, and its appearance now was beyond any conceivable depth of degradation.

The ninety-four Africans, constituting almost its solid membership, were a motley crew. Every negro type was there, from the genteel butler to the clodhopper from the cotton and rice fields. Some had on second-hand seedy frock-coats their old masters had given them before the war, glossy and threadbare. Old stovepipe hats, of every style in vogue since Noah came out of the ark, were placed conspicuously on the desks or cocked on the backs of the heads of the honourable members. Some wore the coarse clothes of the field, stained with red mud.

Old Aleck, he noted, had a red woolen comforter wound round his neck in place of a shirt or collar. He had tried to go barefooted, but the Speaker had issued a rule that members should come shod. He was easing his feet by placing his brogans under the desk, wearing only his red socks.

Each member had his name painted in enormous gold letters on his desk, and had placed beside it a sixty-dollar French imported spittoon. Even the Congress of the United States, under the inspiration of Oakes Ames and Speaker Colfax, could only afford one of domestic make, which cost a dollar.

The uproar was deafening. From four to six negroes were trying to speak at the same time. Aleck's majestic mouth with blue gums and projecting teeth led the chorus, as he ambled down the aisle, his bow-legs flying their red-sock ensigns.

The Speaker singled him out—his voice was something which simply could not be ignored—rapped and yelled:

"De gemman from Ulster set down!"

Aleck turned crestfallen and resumed his seat, throwing his big flat feet in their red woollens up on his desk and hiding his face behind their enormous spread.

He had barely settled in his chair before a new idea flashed through his head and up he jumped again:

"Mistah Speaker!" he bawled.

"Orda da!" yelled another.

"Knock 'im in de head!"

"Seddown, nigger!"

The Speaker pointed his gavel at Aleck and threatened him laughingly:

"Ef de gemman from Ulster doan set down I gwine call 'im ter orda!"

Uncle Aleck greeted this threat with a wild guffaw, which the whole House about him joined in heartily. They laughed like so many hens cackling—when one started the others would follow.

The most of them were munching peanuts, and the crush of hulls under heavy feet added a subnote to the confusion like the crackle of a prairie fire.

The ambition of each negro seemed to be to speak at least a half-dozen times on each question, saying the same thing every time.

No man was allowed to talk five minutes without an interruption which brought on another and another until the speaker was drowned in a storm of contending yells. Their struggles to get the floor with bawlings, bellowings, and contortions, and the senseless rap of the Speaker's gavel, were something appalling.

On this scene, through fetid smoke and animal roar, looked down from the walls, in marble bas-relief, the still white faces of Robert Hayne and George McDuffie, through whose veins flowed the blood of Scottish kings, while over it brooded in solemn wonder the face of John Laurens, whose diplomatic genius at the court of France won millions of gold for our tottering cause, and sent a

French fleet and army into the Chesapeake to entrap Cornwallis at Yorktown.

The little group of twenty-three white men, the descendants of these spirits, to whom Dr. Cameron had brought his memorial, presented a pathetic spectacle. Most of them were old men, who sat in grim silence with nothing to do or say as they watched the rising black tide, their dignity, reserve, and decorum at once the wonder and the shame of the modern world.

At least they knew that the minstrel farce being enacted on that floor was a tragedy as deep and dark as was ever woven of the blood and tears of a conquered people. Beneath those loud guffaws they could hear the death-rattle in the throat of their beloved state, barbarism strangling civilisation by brute force.

For all the stupid uproar, the black leaders of this mob knew what they wanted. One of them was speaking now, the leader of the House, the Honourable Napoleon Whipper.

Dr. Cameron had taken his seat in the little group of white members in one corner of the chamber, beside an old friend from an adjoining county whom he had known in better days.

"Now listen," said his friend. "When Whipper talks he always says something."

"Mr. Speaker, I move you, sir, in view of the arduous duties which our presiding officer has performed this week for the State, that he be allowed one thousand dollars extra pay."

The motion was put without debate and carried.

The speaker then called Whipper to the Chair and made the same motion, to give the Leader of the House an extra thousand dollars for the performance of his heavy duties.

It was carried.

"What does that mean?" asked the doctor.

"Very simple; Whipper and the Speaker adjourned the House yesterday afternoon to attend a horse race. They lost a thousand dollars each betting on the wrong horse. They are recuperating after the strain. They are booked for judges of the Supreme Court when they finish this job. The negro mass-meeting to-night is to indorse their names for the Supreme Bench.

"Is it possible!" the doctor exclaimed.

When Whipper resumed his place at his desk, the introduction of bills began. One after another were sent to the Speaker's desk, a measure to disarm the whites and equip with modern rifles a Negro militia of 80,000 men; to make the uniform of Confederate gray the garb of convicts in South Carolina, with the sign of rank to signify the degree of crime; to prevent any person calling another a "nigger"; to require men to remove their hats in the presence of all officers, civil or military, and all disfranchised men to remove their hats in the presence of voters; to force whites and blacks to attend the same schools and open the State University to negroes; to permit the intermarriage of whites and blacks; and to inforce social equality.

Whipper made a brief speech on the last measure:

"Before I am through, I mean that it shall be known that Napoleon Whipper is as good as any man in South

Carolina. Don't tell me that I am not on an equality with any man God ever made."

Dr. Cameron turned pale, and trembling with excitement, asked his friend:

"Can that man pass such measures, and the Governor sign them?"

"He can pass anything he wishes. The Governor is his creature—a dirty little scalawag who tore the Union flag from Fort Sumter, trampled it in the dust, and helped raise the flag of the Confederacy over it. Now he is backed by the Government at Washington. He won his election by dancing at negro balls and the purchase of delegates. His salary as Governor is $3,500 a year, and he spends over $40,000. Comment is unnecessary. This Legislature has stolen millions of dollars, and already bankrupted the treasury. The day Howle was elected to the Senate of the United States, every negro on the floor had his roll of bills and some of them counted it out on their desks. In your day the annual cost of the State government was $400,000. This year it is $2,000,000. These thieves steal daily. They don't deny it. They simply dare you to prove it. The writing-paper on the desks cost $16,000. These clocks on the wall $600 each, and every little Radical newspaper in the state has been subsidised in sums varying from $1,000 to $7,000. Each member is allowed to draw for mileage, per diem, and "sundries." God only knows what the bill for "sundries" will aggregate by the end of the session."

"I couldn't conceive of this!" exclaimed the doctor.

"I've only given you a hint. We are a conquered race.

The iron hand of Fate is on us. We can only wait for the shadows to deepen into night. President Grant appears to be a babe in the woods. Schuyler Colfax, the Vice-president, and Belknap, the Secretary of War, are in the saddle in Washington. I hear things are happening there that are quite interesting. Besides, Congress now can give little relief. The real law-making power in America is the State Legislature. The State law-maker enters into the holy of holies of our daily life. Once more we are a sovereign State—a sovereign Negro State."

"I fear my mission is futile," said the doctor.

"It's ridiculous—I'll call for you to-night and take you to hear Lynch, our Lieutenant Governor. He is a remarkable man. Our negro Supreme Court Judge will preside——"

Uncle Aleck, who had suddenly spied Dr. Cameron, broke in with a laughing welcome:

"I 'clar ter goodness, Dr. Cammun, I didn't know you wuz here, sah. I sho' glad ter see you. I axes yer ter come across de street ter my room; I got sumfin' pow'ful pertickler ter say ter you."

The doctor followed Aleck out of the Hall and across the street to his room in a little boarding-house. His door was locked, and the windows darkened by blinds. Instead of opening the blinds, he lighted a lamp.

"Ob cose, Dr. Cammun, you say nuffin 'bout what I gwine tell you?"

"Certainly not, Aleck."

The room was full of drygoods boxes. The space under

the bed was packed, and they were piled to the ceiling around the walls.

"Why, what's all this, Aleck?"

The member from Ulster chuckled.·

"Dr. Cammun, yu'se been er pow'ful good frien' ter me—gimme medicine lots er times, en I hain't nebber paid you nuttin'. I'se sho' come inter de kingdom now, en I wants ter pay my respects ter you, sah. Des look ober dat paper, en mark what you wants, en I hab 'em sont home fur you."

The member from Ulster handed his physician a printed list of more than five hundred articles of merchandise. The doctor read it over with amazement.

"I don't understand it, Aleck. Do you own a store?"

"Na-sah, but we git all we wants fum mos' eny ob 'em. Dem's 'sundries,' sah, dat de gubment gibs de members. We des orda what we needs. No trouble 'tall, sah. De men what got de goods come roun' en beg us ter take 'em."

The doctor smiled in spite of the tragedy back of the joke.

"Let's see some of the goods, Aleck—are they first class?"

"Yessah; de bes' goin'. I show you."

He pulled out a number of boxes and bundles, exhibiting carpets, door-mats, hassocks, dog-collars, cow-bells, oil-cloths, velvets, mosquito-nets, damask, Irish linen, billiard outfits, towels, blankets, flannels, quilts, women's hoods, hats, ribbons, pins, needles, scissors, dumb-bells, skates, crape, skirt braids, tooth-brushes, face-powder, hooks and eyes, skirts, bustles, chignons, garters, artificial busts, chemises, parasols, watches, jewelry, diamond earrings, ivory-handled knives and forks, pistols and guns, and a Webster's Dictionary.

"Got lots mo' in dem boxes nailed up dar—yessah, hit's no use er lettin' good tings go by yer when you kin des put out yer han' en stop 'em! Some er de members ordered horses en carriages, but I tuk er par er fine mules wid harness en two buggies en er wagin. Dey 'roun at de libry stable, sah."

The doctor thanked Aleck for his friendly feeling, but told him it was, of course, impossible for him at this time, being only a taxpayer and neither a voter nor a member of the Legislature, to share in his supply of "sundries."

He went to the warehouse that night with his friend to hear Lynch, wondering if his mind were capable of receiving another shock.

This meeting had been called to indorse the candidacy, for Justice of the Supreme Court, of Napoleon Whipper, the Leader of the House, the notorious negro thief and gambler, and William Pitt Moses, an ex-convict, his confederate in crime. They had been unanimously chosen for the positions by a secret caucus of the ninety-four negro members of the House. This addition to the Court, with the negro already a member, would give a majority to the black man on the last Tribunal of Appeal.

The few white men of the party who had any sense of decency were in open revolt at this atrocity. But their influence was on the wane. The carpet-bagger shaped the first Convention and got the first plums of office. Now the Negro was in the saddle, and he meant to stay. There were not enough white men in the Legislature to force a roll-call on a division of the House. This meeting was an open defiance of all palefaces inside or outside party lines.

Every inch of space in the big cotton warehouse was jammed—a black living cloud, pungent and piercing.

The distinguished Lieutenant-Governor, Silas Lynch, had not yet arrived, but the negro Justice of the Supreme Court, Pinchback, was in his seat as the presiding officer.

Dr. Cameron watched the movements of the black judge, already notorious for the sale of his opinions, with a sense of sickening horror. This man was but yesterday a slave, his father a medicine-man in an African jungle who decided the guilt or innocence of the accused by the test of administering poison. If the poison killed the man, he was guilty; if he survived, he was innocent. For four thousand years his land had stood a solid bulwark of unbroken barbarism. Out of its darkness he had been thrust upon the seat of judgment of the laws of the proudest and highest type of man evolved in time. It seemed a hideous dream.

His thoughts were interrupted by a shout. It came spontaneous and tremendous in its genuine feeling. The magnificent figure of Lynch, their idol, appeared walking down the aisle escorted by the little scalawag who was the Governor.

He took his seat on the platform with the easy assurance of conscious power. His broad shoulders, superb head, and gleaming jungle-eyes held every man in the audience before he had spoken a word.

In the first masterful tones of his voice the doctor's keen intelligence caught the ring of his savage metal and felt the shock of his powerful personality—a personality which had thrown to the winds every mask, whose sole aim of life was sensual, whose only fears were of physical pain and death, who could worship a snake and sacrifice a human being.

His playful introduction showed him a child of Mystery, moved by Voices and inspired by a Fetish. His face was full of good humour, and his whole figure rippled with sleek animal vivacity. For the moment, life was a comedy and a masquerade teeming with whims, fancies, ecstasies and superstitions.

He held the surging crowd in the hollow of his hand. They yelled, laughed, howled, or wept as he willed.

Now he painted in burning words the imaginary horrors of slavery until the tears rolled down his cheeks and he wept at the sound of his own voice. Every dusky hearer burst into tears and moans.

He stopped, suddenly brushed the tears from his eyes, sprang to the edge of the platform, threw both arms above his head and shouted:

"Hosannah to the Lord God Almighty for Emancipation!"

Instantly five thousand negroes, as one man, were on their feet, shouting and screaming. Their shouts rose in unison, swelled into a thunder peal, and died away as one voice.

Dead silence followed, and every eye was again riveted on Lynch. For two hours the doctor sat transfixed, listening and watching him sway the vast audience with hypnotic power.

There was not one note of hesitation or of doubt. It was the challenge of race against race to mortal combat. His closing words again swept every negro from his seat and melted every voice into a single frenzied shout:

"Within five years," he cried, "the intelligence and the wealth of this mighty state will be transferred to the Negro race. Lift up your heads. The world is yours. Take it. Here and now I serve notice on every white man who breathes that I am as good as he is. I demand, and I am going to have, the privilege of going to see him in his house or his hotel, eating with him and sleeping with him, and when I see fit, to take his daughter in marriage!"

As the doctor emerged from the stifling crowd with his friend, he drew a deep breath of fresh air, took from his pocket his conservative memorial, picked it into little bits, and scattered them along the street as he walked in silence back to his hotel.

CHAPTER IX

AT LOVER'S LEAP

IN spite of the pitiful collapse of old Stoneman under his stroke of paralysis, his children still saw the unconquered soul shining in his colourless eyes. They had both been on the point of confessing their love-affairs to him and joining the inevitable struggle when he was stricken. They knew only too well that he would not consent to a dual alliance with the Camerons under the conditions of fierce hatreds and violence into which the state had drifted. They were too high-minded to consider a violation of his wishes while thus helpless, with his strange eyes following them about in childlike eagerness. His weakness was mightier than his iron will.

So, for eighteen months, while he slowly groped out of mental twilight, each had waited—Elsie with a tender faith struggling with despair, and Phil in a torture of uncertainty and fear.

In the meantime, the young Northerner had become as radical in his sympathies with the Southern people as his father had ever been against them. This power of assimilation has always been a mark of Southern genius. The sight of the Black Hand on their throats now roused his righteous indignation. The patience with which they endured was to him amazing. The Southerner he had found to be the last man on earth to become a revolutionist. All his traits were against it. His genius for command, the deep sense of duty and honour, his hospitality, his deathless love of home, his supreme constancy and sense of civic unity, all combined to make him ultraconservative. He began now to see that it was reverence for authority as expressed in the Constitution under which slavery was established which made Secession inevitable.

Besides, the laziness and incapacity of the Negro had been more than he could endure. With no ties of tradition or habits of life to bind him, he simply refused to tolerate them. In this feeling Elsie had grown early to sympathise. She discharged Aunt Cindy for feeding her children from the kitchen, and brought a cook and house girl from the North, while Phil would employ only white men in any capacity.

In the desolation of Negro rule, the Cameron farm had become worthless. The taxes had more than absorbed the income, and the place was only kept from execution by the indomitable energy of Mrs. Cameron, who made the hotel pay enough to carry the interest on a mortgage which was increasing from season to season.

The doctor's practise was with him a divine calling. He never sent bills to his patients. They paid something if they had it. Now they had nothing.

Ben's law practice was large for his age and experience, but his clients had no money.

While the Camerons were growing, each day, poorer, Phil was becoming rich. His genius, skill, and enterprise had been quick to see the possibilities of the water-

power. The old Eagle cotton mills had been burned
during the war. Phil organised the Eagle & Phœnix Company, interested Northern capitalists, bought the falls,
and erected two great mills, the dim hum of whose
spindles added a new note to the river's music. Eager,
swift, modest, his head full of ideas, his heart full of
faith, he had pressed forward to success.

As the old Commoner's mind began to clear, and his
recovery was sure, Phil determined to press his suit for
Margaret's hand to an issue.

Ben had dropped a hint of an interview of the Rev.
Hugh McAlpin with Dr. Cameron, which had thrown
Phil into a cold sweat.

He hurried to the hotel to ask Margaret to drive with
him that afternoon. He would stop at Lover's Leap and
settle the question.

He met the preacher, just emerging from the door,
calm, handsome, serious, and Margaret by his side. The
dark-haired beauty seemed strangely serene. What
could it mean? His heart was in his throat. Was he
too late? Wreathed in smiles when the preacher had
gone, the girl's face was a riddle he could not solve.

To his joy, she consented to go.

As he left in his trim little buggy for the hotel, he
stooped and kissed Elsie, whispering:

"Make an offering on the altar of love for me, Sis!"

"You're too slow. The prayers of all the saints will
not save you!" she replied with a laugh, throwing him a
kiss as he disappeared in the dust.

As they drove through the great forest on the cliffs, overlooking the river, the Southern world seemed lit with new splendour to-day for the Northerner. His heart beat with a strange courage. The odour of the pines, their sighing music, the subtone of the falls below, the subtle life-giving perfume of the fullness of summer, the splendour of the sun gleaming through the deep foliage, and the sweet sensuous air, all seemed incarnate in the calm lovely face and gracious figure beside him.

They took their seat on the old rustic built against the beech, which was the last tree on the brink of the cliff. A hundred feet below flowed the river, rippling softly along a narrow strip of sand which its current had thrown against the rocks. The ledge of towering granite formed a cave eighty feet in depth at the water's edge. From this projecting wall, tradition said a young Indian princess once leaped with her lover, fleeing from the wrath of a cruel father who had separated them. The cave below was inaccessible from above, being reached by a narrow footpath along the river's edge when entered a mile down-stream.

The view from the seat, under the beech, was one of marvellous beauty. For miles, the broad river rolled in calm shining glory seaward, its banks fringed with cane and trees, while fields of corn and cotton spread in waving green toward the distant hills and blue mountains of the west.

Every tree on this cliff was cut with the initials of generations of lovers from Piedmont.

They sat in silence for awhile. Margaret idly playing

with a flower she had picked by the pathway, and Phil watching her devoutly.

The Southern sun had tinged her face the reddish warm hue of ripened fruit, doubly radiant by contrast with her wealth of dark-brown hair. The lustrous glance of her eyes, half veiled by their long lashes, and the graceful, careless pose of her stately figure held him enraptured. Her dress of airy, azure blue, so becoming to her dark beauty, gave Phil the impression of the eiderdown feathers of some rare bird of the tropics. He felt that if he dared to touch her she might lift her wings and sail over the cliff into the sky and forget to light again at his side.

"I am going to ask a very bold and impertinent question, Miss Margaret," Phil said with resolution. "May I?"

Margaret smiled incredulously.

"I'll risk your impertinence, and decide as to its boldness."

"Tell me, please, what that preacher said to you to-day."

Margaret looked away, unable to suppress the merriment that played about her eyes and mouth.

"Will you never breathe it to a soul, if I do?"

"Never."

"Honest Injun, here on the sacred altar of the princess?"

"On my honour."

"Then I'll tell you," she said, biting her lips to keep back a laugh. "Mr. McAlpin is very handsome and eloquent. I have always thought him the best preacher we have ever had in Piedmont——"

"Yes, I know," Phil interrupted with a frown.

"He is very pious," she went on evenly, "and seeks Divine guidance in prayer in everything he does. He called this morning to see me, and I was playing for him in the little music-room off the parlour, when he suddenly closed the door and said:

"'Miss Margaret, I am going to take, this morning, the most important step of my life——'

"Of course, I hadn't the remotest idea what he meant——

"'Will you join me in a word of prayer?' he asked, and knelt right down. I was accustomed, of course, to kneel with him in family worship at his pastoral calls, and so from habit I slipped to one knee by the piano-stool, wondering what on earth he was about. When he prayed with fervour for the Lord to bless the great love with which he hoped to hallow my life—I giggled. It broke up the meeting. He rose and asked me to marry him. I told him the Lord hadn't revealed it to me——"

Phil seized her hand and held it firmly. The smile died from the girl's face, her hand trembled, and the rose-tint on her cheeks flamed to scarlet.

"Margaret, my own, I love you," he cried with joy. "You could have told that story only to the one man whom you love—is it not true?"

"Yes. I've loved you always," said the low sweet voice.

"Always?" asked Phil through a tear.

"Before I saw you, when they told me you were as Ben's

twin brother, my heart began to sing at the sound of your name——"

"Call it," he whispered.

"Phil, my sweetheart!" she said with a laugh.

"How tender and homelike the music of your voice! The world has never seen the match of your gracious Southern womanhood! Snow-bound in the North, I dreamed, as a child, of this world of eternal sunshine. And now every memory and dream I've found in you."

"And you won't be disappointed in my simple ideal that finds its all within a home?"

"No. I love the old-fashioned dream of the South. Maybe you have enchanted me, but I love these green hills and mountains, these rivers musical with cascade and fall, these solemn forests—but for the Black Curse, the South would be to-day the garden of the world!"

"And you will help our people lift this curse?" softly asked the girl, nestling closer to his side.

"Yes, dearest, thy people shall be mine! Had I a thousand wrongs to cherish, I'd forgive them all for your sake. I'll help you build here a new South on all that's good and noble in the old, until its dead fields blossom again, its harbours bristle with ships, and the hum of a thousand industries make music in every valley. I'd sing to you in burning verse if I could, but it is not my way. I have been awkward and slow in love, perhaps— but I'll be swift in your service. I dream to make dead stones and wood live and breathe for you, of victories wrung from Nature that are yours. My poems will be deeds, my

flowers the hard-earned wealth that has a soul, which I
shall lay at your feet."

"Who said my lover was dumb?" she sighed, with a
twinkle in her shining eyes. "You must introduce me
to your father soon. He must like me as my father does
you, or our dream can never come true."

A pain gripped Phil's heart, but he answered, bravely:
"I will. He can't help loving you."

They stood on the rustic seat to carve their initials
within a circle, high on the old beechwood book of love.

"May I write it out in full—Margaret Cameron—
Philip Stoneman?" he asked.

"No—only the initials now—the full names when you've
seen my father and I've seen yours. Jeannie Campbell
and Henry Lenoir were once written thus in full, and
many a lover has looked at that circle and prayed for happiness like theirs. You can see there a new one cut over
the old, the bark has filled, and written on the fresh page
is 'Marion Lenoir' with the blank below for her lover's
name."

Phil looked at the freshly cut circle and laughed:
"I wonder if Marion or her mother did that?"

"Her mother, of course."

"I wonder whose will be the lucky name some day
within it?" said Phil, musingly, as he finished his own.

CHAPTER X

A Night Hawk

WHEN the old Commoner's private physician had gone and his mind had fully cleared, he would sit for hours in the sunshine of the vine-clad porch, asking Elsie of the village, its life, and its people. He smiled good-naturedly at her eager sympathy for their sufferings as at the enthusiasm of a child who could not understand. He had come possessed by a great idea—events must submit to it. Her assurance that the poverty and losses of the people were far in excess of the worst they had known during the war was too absurd even to secure his attention.

He had refused to know any of the people, ignoring the existence of Elsie's callers. But he had fallen in love with Marion from the moment he had seen her. The cold eye of the old fox-hunter kindled with the fire of his forgotten youth at the sight of this beautiful girl, seated on the glistening back of the mare she had saved from death.

As she rode through the village, every boy lifted his hat as to passing royalty, and no one, old or young, could allow her to pass without a cry of admiration. Her exquisite figure had developed into the full tropic splendour of Southern girlhood.

She had rejected three proposals from ardent lovers, on one of whom her mother had quite set her heart. A great fear had grown in Mrs. Lenoir's mind lest she were in love with Ben Cameron. She slipped her arm around her one day and timidly asked her.

A faint flush tinged Marion's face up to the roots of her delicate blonde hair, and she answered, with a quick laugh:

"Mama, how silly you are! You know I've always been in love with Ben—since I can first remember. I know he is in love with Elsie Stoneman. I am too young, the world too beautiful, and life too sweet to grieve over my first baby love. I expect to dance with him at his wedding, then meet my fate and build my own nest."

Old Stoneman begged that she come every day to see him. He never tired praising her to Elsie. As she walked gracefully up to the house one afternoon, holding Hugh by the hand, he said to Elsie:

"Next to you, my dear, she is the most charming creature I ever saw. Her tenderness for everything that needs help touches the heart of an old lame man in a very soft spot."

"I've never seen any one who could resist her," Elsie answered. "Her gloves may be worn, her feet clad in old shoes, yet she is always neat, graceful, dainty, and serene. No wonder her mother worships her."

Sam Ross, her simple friend, had stopped at the gate, and looked over into the lawn as if afraid to come in.

When Marion saw Sam, she turned back to the gate to invite him in. The keeper of the poor, a vicious-looking negro, suddenly confronted him, and he shrank in terror close to the girl's side.

"What you doin' here, sah?" the black keeper railed. "Ain't I done tole you 'bout runnin' away?"

"You let him alone," Marion cried.

The negro pushed her roughly from his side and knocked Sam down. The girl screamed for help, and old Stoneman hobbled down the steps, following Elsie.

When they reached the gate, Marion was bending over the prostrate form.

"Oh, my, my, I believe he's killed him!" she wailed.

"Run for the doctor, sonny, quick," Stoneman said to Hugh. The boy darted away and brought Dr. Cameron.

"How dare you strike that man, you devil?" thundered the old statesman.

"'Case I tole 'im ter stay home en do de wuk I put 'im at, en he all de time runnin' off here ter git sumfin' ter eat. I gwine frail de life outen 'im, ef he doan min' me."

"Well, you make tracks back to the Poor House. I'll attend to this man, and I'll have you arrested for this before night," said Stoneman, with a scowl.

The black keeper laughed as he left.

"Not 'less you'se er bigger man dan Gubner Silas Lynch, you won't!"

When Dr. Cameron had restored Sam, and dressed the wound on his head where he had struck a stone in falling, Stoneman insisted that the boy be put to bed.

Turning to Dr. Cameron, he asked:

"Why should they put a brute like this in charge of the poor?"

"That's a large question, sir, at this time," said the doctor, politely, "and now that you have asked it, I have some things I've been longing for an opportunity to say to you."

"Be seated, sir," the old Commoner answered, "I shall be glad to hear them."

Elsie's heart leaped with joy over the possible outcome of this appeal, and she left the room with a smile for the doctor.

"First, allow me," said the Southerner, pleasantly, "to express my sorrow at your long illness, and my pleasure at seeing you so well. Your children have won the love of all our people and have had our deepest sympathy in your illness."

Stoneman muttered an inaudible reply, and the doctor went on:

"Your question brings up, at once, the problem of the misery and degradation into which our country has sunk under Negro rule——"

Stoneman smiled coldly and interrupted:

"Of course, you understand my position in politics, Doctor Cameron—I am a Radical Republican."

"So much the better," was the response. "I have been longing for months to get your ear. Your word will be all the more powerful if raised in our behalf. The Negro is the master of our state, county, city, and town governments. Every school, college, hospital, asylum, and poorhouse is his prey. What you have seen is but a sample.

Negro insolence grows beyond endurance. Their women are taught to insult their old mistresses and mock their poverty as they pass in their old, faded dresses. Yesterday a black driver struck a white child of six with his whip, and when the mother protested, she was arrested by a negro policeman, taken before a negro magistrate, and fined $10 for 'insulting a freedman.'"

Stoneman frowned: "Such things must be very exceptional."

"They are every-day occurrences and cease to excite comment. Lynch, the Lieutenant-Governor, who has bought a summer home here, is urging this campaign of insult with deliberate purpose——"

The old man shook his head. "I can't think the Lieutenant-Governor guilty of such petty villainy."

"Our school commissioner," the doctor continued, "is a negro who can neither read nor write. The black grand jury last week discharged a negro for stealing cattle and indicted the owner for false imprisonment. No such rate of taxation was ever imposed on a civilised people. A tithe of it cost Great Britain her colonies. There are 5,000 homes in this county—2,900 of them are advertised for sale by the sheriff to meet his tax bills. This house will be sold next court day——"

Stoneman looked up sharply. "Sold for taxes?"

"Yes; with the farm which has always been Mrs. Lenoir's support. In part her loss came from the cotton tax. Congress, in addition to the desolation of war, and the ruin of Black rule, has wrung from the cotton farmers of the South a tax of $67,000,000. Every dollar of this money bears the stain of the blood of starving people. They are ready to give up, or to spring some desperate scheme of resistance——"

The old man lifted his massive head and his great jaws came together with a snap:

"Resistance to the authority of the National Government?"

"No; resistance to the travesty of government and the mockery of civilisation under which we are being throttled! The bayonet is now in the hands of a brutal Negro militia. The tyranny of military martinets was child's play to this. As I answered your call this morning, I was stopped and turned back in the street by the drill of a company of negroes under the command of a vicious scoundrel named Gus who was my former slave. He is the captain of this company. Eighty thousand armed Negro troops, answerable to no authority save the savage instincts of their officers, terrorise the state. Every white company has been disarmed and disbanded by our scalawag Governor. I tell you, sir, we are walking on the crust of a volcano!——"

Old Stoneman scowled, as the doctor rose and walked nervously to the window and back.

"An appeal from you to the conscience of the North might save us," he went on, eagerly. "Black hordes of former slaves, with the intelligence of children and the instincts of savages, armed with modern rifles, parade daily in front of their unarmed former masters. A white man has no right a negro need respect. The children of the breed of men who speak the tongue of Burns and Shakespeare, Drake and Raleigh, have been disarmed and made subject to the black spawn of an African jungle! Can human flesh endure it? When Goth and Vandal barbarians overran Rome, the Negro was the slave of the Roman Empire. The savages of the North blew out the light of Ancient Civilisation, but in all the dark ages which followed they never dreamed the leprous infamy of raising a black slave to rule over his former master! No people in the history of the world have ever before been so basely betrayed, so wantonly humiliated and degraded!"

Stoneman lifted his head in amazement at the burst of passionate intensity with which the Southerner poured out his protest.

"For a Russian to rule a Pole," he went on, "a Turk to rule a Greek, or an Austrian to dominate an Italian, is hard enough, but for a thick-lipped, flat-nosed, spindle-shanked negro, exuding his nauseating animal odour, to shout in derision over the hearths and homes of white men and women is an atrocity too monstrous for belief. Our people are yet dazed by its horror. My God! when they realise its meaning, whose arm will be strong enough to hold them?"

"I should think the South was sufficiently amused with resistance to authority," interrupted Stoneman.

"Even so. Yet there is a moral force at the bottom of every living race of men. The sense of right, the feeling of racial destiny—these are unconquered and unconquerable forces. Every man in South Carolina to-day is glad that slavery is dead. The war was not too great a price for us to pay for the lifting of its curse. And now to ask a Southerner to be the slave of a slave——"

"And yet, Doctor," said Stoneman, coolly, "manhood suffrage is the one eternal thing fixed in the nature of Democracy. It is inevitable."

"At the price of racial life? Never!" said the Southerner, with fiery emphasis. "This Republic is great, not by reason of the amount of dirt we possess, the size of our census roll, or our voting register—we are great because of the genius of the race of pioneer white freemen who settled this continent, dared the might of kings, and made a wilderness the home of Freedom. Our future depends on the purity of this racial stock. The grant of the ballot to these millions of semi-savages and the riot of debauchery which has followed are crimes against human progress."

"Yet may we not train him?" asked Stoneman.

"To a point, yes, and then sink to his level if you walk as his equal in physical contact with him. His race is not an infant; it is a degenerate—older than yours in time. At last we are face to face with the man whom slavery concealed with its rags. Suffrage is but the new paper cloak with which the Demagogue has sought to hide the issue. Can we assimilate the Negro? The very question is pollution. In Hayti no white man can own land. Black dukes and marquises drive over them and swear at them for getting under their wheels. Is civilisation a patent cloak with which law-tinkers can wrap an animal and make him a king?"

"But the negro must be protected by the ballot," protested the statesman. "The humblest man must have the opportunity to rise. The real issue is Democracy."

"The issue, sir, is Civilisation! Not whether a negro

shall be protected, but whether Society is worth saving from barbarism."

"The statesman can educate," put in the Commoner.

The doctor cleared his throat with a quick little nervous cough he was in the habit of giving when deeply moved.

"Education, sir, is the development of that which *is*. Since the dawn of history the Negro has owned the Continent of Africa—rich beyond the dream of poet's fancy, crunching acres of diamonds beneath his bare black feet. Yet he never picked one up from the dust until a white man showed to him its glittering light. His land swarmed with powerful and docile animals, yet he never dreamed a harness, cart, or sled. A hunter by necessity, he never made an axe, spear or arrow-head worth preserving beyond the moment of its use. He lived as an ox, content to graze for an hour. In a land of stone and timber he never sawed a foot of lumber, carved a block, or built a house save of broken sticks and mud. With league on league of ocean strand and miles of inland seas, for four thousand years he watched their surface ripple under the wind, heard the thunder of the surf on his beach, the howl of the storm over his head, gazed on the dim blue horizon calling him to worlds that lie beyond, and yet he never dreamed a sail! He lived as his fathers lived—stole his food, worked his wife, sold his children, ate his brother, content to drink, sing, dance, and sport as the ape!

"And this creature, half-child, half-animal, the sport of impulse, whim and conceit, 'pleased with a rattle, tickled with a straw,' a being who, left to his will, roams at night and sleeps in the day, whose speech knows no word of love, whose passions, once aroused, are as the fury of the tiger—they have set this thing to rule over the Southern people——"

The doctor sprang to his feet, his face livid, his eyes blazing with emotion. "Merciful God—it surpasses human belief!"

He sank exhausted in his chair, and, extending his hand in an eloquent gesture, continued:

"Surely, surely, sir, the people of the North are not mad? We can yet appeal to the conscience and the brain of our brethren of a common race?"

Stoneman was silent as if stunned. Deep down in his strange soul he was drunk with the joy of a triumphant vengeance he had carried locked in the depths of his being, yet the intensity of this man's suffering for a people's cause surprised and distressed him as all individual pain hurt him.

Dr. Cameron rose, stung by his silence, and the consciousness of the hostility with which Stoneman had wrapped himself.

"Pardon my apparent rudeness, Doctor," he said, at length, extending his hand. "The violence of your feeling stunned me for the moment. I'm obliged to you for speaking. I like a plain-spoken man. I am sorry to learn of the stupidity of the former military commandant in this town——"

"My personal wrongs, sir," the doctor broke in, "are nothing!"

"I am sorry, too, about these individual cases of suffering. They are the necessary incidents of a great upheaval.

But may it not all come out right in the end? After the Dark Ages, day broke at last. We have the printing press, railroad and telegraph—a revolution in human affairs. We may do in years what it took ages to do in the past. May not the Black man speedily emerge? Who knows? An appeal to the North will be a waste of breath. This experiment is going to be made. It is written in the book of Fate. But I like you. Come to see me again."

Dr. Cameron left with a heavy heart. He had grown a great hope in this long-wished-for appeal to Stoneman. It had come to his ears that the old man, who had dwelt as one dead in their village, was a power.

It was ten o'clock before the doctor walked slowly back to the hotel. As he passed the armory of the black militia, they were still drilling under the command of Gus. The windows were open, through which came the steady tramp of heavy feet and the cry of "Hep! Hep! Hep!" from the Captain's thick cracked lips. The full-dress officer's uniform, with its gold epaulets, yellow stripes, and glistening sword, only accentuated the coarse bestiality of Gus. His huge jaws seemed to hide completely the gold braid on his collar.

The doctor watched, with a shudder, his black bloated face covered with perspiration and the huge hand gripping his sword.

They suddenly halted in double ranks and Gus yelled: "Odah, arms!"

The butts of their rifles crashed to the floor with precision, and they were allowed to break ranks for a brief rest.

They sang "John Brown's Body," and as its echoes died away a big negro swung his rifle in a circle over his head, shouting:

"Here's your regulator for white trash! En dey's nine hundred ob 'em in dis county!"

"Yas, Lawd!" howled another.

"We got 'em down now en we keep 'em dar, chile!" bawled another.

The doctor passed on slowly to the hotel. The night was dark, the streets were without lights under their present rulers, and the stars were hidden with swift-flying clouds which threatened a storm. As he passed under the boughs of an oak in front of his house, a voice above him whispered:

"A message for you, sir."

Had the wings of a spirit suddenly brushed his cheek, he would not have been more startled.

"Who are you?" he asked, with a slight tremor.

"A Night Hawk of the Invisible Empire, with a message from the Grand Dragon of the Realm," was the low answer, as he thrust a note in the doctor's hand. "I will wait for your answer."

The doctor fumbled to his office on the corner of the lawn, struck a match, and read:

"A great Scotch-Irish leader of the South from Memphis is here to-night and wishes to see you. If you will meet General Forrest, I will bring him to the hotel in fifteen minutes. Burn this. Ben."

The doctor walked quickly back to the spot where he had heard the voice, and said:

"I'll see him with pleasure."

The invisible messenger wheeled his horse, and in a moment the echo of his muffled hoofs had died away in the distance.

CHAPTER XI

The Beat of a Sparrow's Wing

D R. CAMERON'S appeal had left the old Commoner unshaken in his idea. There could be but one side to any question with such a man, and that was his side. He would stand by his own men too. He believed in his own forces. The bayonet was essential to his revolutionary programme—hence the hand which held it could do no wrong. Wrongs were accidents which might occur under any system.

Yet in no way did he display the strange contradictions of his character so plainly as in his inability to hate the individual who stood for the idea he was fighting with maniac fury. He liked Dr. Cameron instantly, though he had come to do a crime that would send him into beggared exile.

Individual suffering he could not endure. In this the doctor's appeal had startling results.

He sent for Mrs. Lenoir and Marion.

"I understand, Madam," he said, gravely, "that your house and farm are to be sold for taxes?"

"Yes, sir; we've given it up this time. Nothing can be done," was the hopeless answer.

"Would you consider an offer of twenty dollars an acre?"

"Nobody would be fool enough to offer it. You can buy all the land in the county for a dollar an acre. It's not worth anything."

"I disagree with you," said Stoneman, cheerfully. "I am looking far ahead. I would like to make an experiment here with Pennsylvania methods on this land. I'll give you ten thousand dollars cash for your five hundred acres if you will take it."

"You don't mean it?" Mrs. Lenoir gasped, choking back the tears.

"Certainly. You can at once return to your home, I'll take another house, and invest your money for you in good Northern securities."

The mother burst into sobs, unable to speak, while Marion threw her arms impulsively around the old man's neck and kissed him.

His cold eyes were warmed with the first tear they had shed in years.

He moved the next day to the Ross estate, which he rented, had Sam brought back to the home of his childhood in charge of a good-natured white attendant, and installed in one of the little cottages on the lawn. He ordered Lynch to arrest the keeper of the poor, and hold him on a charge of assault with intent to kill, awaiting the action of the Grand Jury. The Lieutenant-Governor received this order with sullen anger—yet he saw to its execution. He was not quite ready for a break with the man who had made him.

Astonished at his new humour, Phil and Elsie hastened to confess to him their love-affairs and ask his approval of their choice. His reply was cautious, yet he did not refuse his consent. He advised them to wait a few months, allow him time to know the young people, and get his bearings on the conditions of Southern society. His mood of tenderness was a startling revelation to them of the depth and intensity of his love.

When Mrs. Lenoir returned with Marion to her vine-clad home, she spent the first day of perfect joy since the death of her lover-husband. The deed had not yet been made for the transfer of the farm, but it was only a question of legal formality. She was to receive the money in the form of interest-bearing securities and deliver the title on the following morning.

Arm in arm, mother and daughter visited again each hallowed spot, with the sweet sense of ownership. The place was in perfect order. Its flowers were in gorgeous bloom, its walks clean and neat, the fences painted, and the gates swung on new hinges.

They stood with their arms about one another, watching the sun sink behind the mountains, with tears of gratitude and hope stirring their souls.

Ben Cameron strode through the gate, and they hurried to meet him, with cries of joy.

"Just dropped in a minute to see if you are snug for the night?" he said.

"Of course, snug and so happy, we've been hugging one another for hours," said the mother. "Oh, Ben, the clouds have lifted at last!"

"Has Aunt Cindy come yet?" he asked.

"No, but she'll be here in the morning to get breakfast. We don't want anything to eat," she answered.

"Then I'll come out when I'm through my business,
to-night, and sleep in the house to keep you company."

"Nonsense," said the mother, "we couldn't think of
putting you to the trouble. We've spent many a night
here alone."

"But not in the past two years," he said, with a frown.

"We're not afraid," Marion said, with a smile. "Besides, we'd keep you awake all night with our laughter and
foolishness, rummaging through the house."

"You'd better let me," Ben protested.

"No," said the mother, "we'll be happier to-night alone
with only God's eye to see how perfectly silly we can be.
Come and take supper with us to-morrow night. Bring
Elsie and her guitar—I don't like the banjo—and we'll
have a little love-feast with music in the moonlight."

"Yes, do that," cried Marion. "I know we owe this
good luck to her. I want to tell her how much I love her
for it."

"Well, if you insist on staying alone," said Ben, reluctantly, "I'll bring Miss Elsie to-morrow, but I don't
like your being here without Aunt Cindy to-night."

"Oh, we're all right!" laughed Marion, "but what I
want to know is what you are doing out so late every
night since you've come home, and where you were gone
for the past week?"

"Important business," he answered, soberly.

"Business—I expect!" she cried. "Look here, Ben

Cameron, have you another girl somewhere, you're flirting with?"

"Yes," he answered, slowly, coming closer and his voice dropping to a whisper, "and her name is Death."

"Why, Ben!" Marion gasped, placing her trembling hand unconsciously on his arm, a faint flush mantling her cheek and leaving it white.

"What do you mean?" asked the mother in low tones.

"Nothing that I can explain. I only wish to warn you both never to ask me such questions before any one."

"Forgive me," said Marion, with a tremor. "I didn't think it serious."

Ben pressed the little warm hand, watching her mouth quiver with a smile that was half a sigh, as he answered:

"You know I'd trust either of you with my life, but I can't be too careful."

"We'll remember, Sir Knight," said the mother. "Don't forget, then, to-morrow—and spend the evening with us. I wish I had one of Marion's new dresses done. Poor child, she has never had a decent dress in her life before. You know I never look at my pretty baby grown to such a beautiful womanhood without hearing Henry say over and over again—'Beauty is a sign of the soul—the body is the soul!'"

"Well, I've my doubts about your improving her with a fine dress," he replied, thoughtfully. "I don't believe that more beautifully dressed women ever walked the earth than our girls of the South who came out of the war clad in the pathos of poverty, smiling bravely through the shadows, bearing themselves as queens though they wore the dress of the shepherdess."

"I'm almost tempted to kiss you for that, as you once took advantage of me!" said Marion with enthusiasm.

The moon had risen and a whippoorwill was chanting his weird song on the lawn as Ben left them leaning on the gate.

It was past midnight before they finished the last touches in restoring their nest to its old homelike appearance and sat down happy and tired in the room in which Marion was born, brooding and dreaming and talking over the future.

The mother was hanging on the words of her daughter, all the baffled love of the dead poet husband, her griefs and poverty consumed in the glowing joy of new hopes. Her love for this child was now a triumphant passion, which had melted her own being into the object of worship, until the soul of the daughter was superimposed on the mother's as the magnetised by the magnetiser.

"And you'll never keep a secret from me, dear?" she asked of Marion.

"Never."

"You'll tell me all your love-affairs?" she asked, softly, as she drew the shining blonde head down on her shoulders.

"Faithfully."

"You know I've been afraid sometimes you were keeping something back from me, deep down in your heart—and I'm jealous. You didn't refuse Henry Grier because you loved Ben Cameron—now, did you?"

The little head lay still before she answered:

"How many times must I tell you, Silly, that I've loved Ben since I can remember, that I will always love him, and when I meet my fate, at last, I shall boast to my children of my sweet girl romance with the Hero of Piedmont, and they shall laugh and cry with me over it——"

"What's that?" whispered the mother, leaping to her feet.

"I heard nothing," Marion answered, listening.

"I thought I heard footsteps on the porch."

"Maybe it's Ben, who decided to come anyhow," said the girl.

"But he'd knock!" whispered the mother.

The door flew open with a crash, and four black brutes leaped into the room, Gus in the lead, with a revolver in his hand, his yellow teeth grinning through his thick lips.

"Scream, now, an' I blow yer brains out," he growled.

Blanched with horror, the mother sprang before Marion with a shivering cry:

"What do you want?"

"Not you," said Gus, closing the blinds and handing a rope to another brute. "Tie de ole one ter de bedpost."

The mother screamed. A blow from a black fist in her mouth, and the rope was tied.

With the strength of despair she tore at the cords, half rising to her feet, while with mortal anguish she gasped:

"For God's sake, spare my baby! Do as you will with me, and kill me—do not touch her!"

Again the huge fist swept her to the floor.

Marion staggered against the wall, her face white, her delicate lips trembling with the chill of a fear colder than death.

"We have no money—the deed has not been delivered," she pleaded, a sudden glimmer of hope flashing in her blue eyes.

Gus stepped closer, with an ugly leer, his flat nose dilated, his sinister bead-eyes wide apart gleaming ape-like, as he laughed:

"We ain't atter money!"

The girl uttered a cry, long, tremulous, heart-rending, piteous.

A single tiger-spring, and the black claws of the beast sank into the soft white throat and she was still.

CHAPTER XII

At the Dawn of Day

IT was three o'clock before Marion regained consciousness, crawled to her mother, and crouched in dumb convulsions in her arms.

"What can we do, my darling?" the mother asked at last.

"Die!—thank God, we have the strength left!"

"Yes, my love," was the faint answer.

"No one must ever know. We will hide quickly every trace of crime. They will think we strolled to Lover's Leap and fell over the cliff, and my name will always be sweet and clean—you understand—come, we must hurry——"

With swift hands, her blue eyes shining with a strange light, the girl removed the shreds of torn clothes, bathed, and put on the dress of spotless white she wore the night Ben Cameron kissed her and called her a heroine.

The mother cleaned and swept the room, piled the torn clothes and cord in the fireplace and burned them, dressed herself as if for a walk, softly closed the doors, and hurried with her daughter along the old pathway through the moonlit woods.

At the edge of the forest she stopped and looked back

tenderly at the little home shining amid the roses, caught
their faint perfume and faltered:

"Let's go back a minute—I want to see his room, and
kiss Henry's picture again."

"No, we are going to him now—I hear him calling us
in the mists above the cliff," said the girl—"come, we
must hurry. We might go mad and fail!"

Down the dim cathedral aisles of the woods, hallowed
by tender memories, through which the poet lover and
father had taught them to walk with reverent feet and
without fear, they fled to the old meeting-place of Love.

On the brink of the precipice, the mother trembled,
paused, drew back and gasped:

"Are you not afraid, my dear?"

"No; death is sweet, now,".said the girl. "I fear only
the pity of those we love."

"Is there no other way? We might go among
strangers," pleaded the mother.

"We could not escape ourselves! The thought of life is
torture. Only those who hate me could wish that I live.
The grave will be soft and cool, the light of day a burning shame."

"Come back to the seat a moment—let me tell you my
love again," urged the mother. "Life still is dear while
I hold your hand."

As they sat in brooding anguish, floating up from the
river valley came the music of a banjo in a negro cabin,
mingled with vulgar shout and song and dance. A verse
of the ribald senseless lay of the player echoed above
the banjo's pert refrain:

> "Chicken in de bread tray, pickin' up dough;
> Granny, will your dog bite? No, chile, no!"

The mother shivered and drew Marion closer.

"Oh, dear! oh, dear! has it come to this—all my hopes of your beautiful life!"

The girl lifted her head and kissed the quivering lips.

"With what loving wonder we saw you grow," she sighed, "from a tottering babe on to the hour we watched the mystic light of maidenhood dawn in your blue eyes— and all to end in this hideous, leprous shame!—No!—No! I will not have it! It's only a horrible dream! God is not dead!"

The young mother sank to her knees and buried her face in Marion's lap in a hopeless paroxysm of grief.

The girl bent, kissed the curling hair and smoothed it with her soft hand.

A sparrow chirped in the tree above, a wren twittered in a bush, and down on the river's brink a mocking-bird softly waked his mate with a note of thrilling sweetness.

"The morning is coming, dearest; we must go," said Marion. "This shame I can never forget, nor will the world forget. Death is the only way."

They walked to the brink, and the mother's arms stole round the girl.

"Oh, my baby, my beautiful darling, life of my life, heart of my heart, soul of my soul!"

They stood for a moment, as if listening to the music of the falls, looking out over the valley faintly outlining itself in the dawn. The first far-away streaks of blue light on the mountain ranges, defining distance, slowly appeared. A fresh motionless day brooded over the world as the amorous stir of the spirit of morning rose from the moist earth of the fields below.

A bright star still shone in the sky, and the face of the mother gazed on it intently. Did the Woman-spirit, the burning focus of the fiercest desire to live and will, catch in this supreme moment the star's Divine speech before which all human passions sink into silence? Perhaps, for she smiled. The daughter answered with a smile; and then, hand in hand, they stepped from the cliff into the mists and on through the opal gates of Death.

Book IV—The Ku Klux Klan

CHAPTER I

The Hunt for the Animal

AUNT CINDY came at seven o'clock to get break-fast, and finding the house closed and no one at home, supposed Mrs. Lenoir and Marion had remained at the Cameron House for the night. She sat down on the steps, waited grumblingly an hour, and then hurried to the hotel to scold her former mistress for keeping her out so long.

Accustomed to enter familiarly, she thrust her head into the dining-room, where the family were at breakfast with a solitary guest, muttering the speech she had been rehearsing on the way:

"I lak ter know what sort er way dis—whar's Miss Jeannie?"

Ben leaped to his feet.

"Isn't she at home?"

"Been waitin' dar two hours."

"Great God!" he groaned, springing through the door and rushing to saddle the mare. As he left he called to his father: "Let no one know till I return."

At the house he could find no trace of the crime he had suspected. Every room was in perfect order. He searched the yard carefully, and under the cedar by the window he saw the barefoot tracks of a negro. The white man was never born who could make that track. The enormous heel projected backward, and in the hollow of the instep where the dirt would scarcely be touched by an Aryan was the deep wide mark of the African's flat foot. He carefully measured it, brought from an outhouse a box, and fastened it over the spot.

It might have been an ordinary chicken-thief, of course. He could not tell, but it was a fact of big import. A sudden hope flashed through his mind that they might have risen with the sun and strolled to their favourite haunt at Lover's Leap.

In two minutes he was there, gazing with hard-set eyes at Marion's hat and handkerchief lying on the shelving rock.

The mare bent her glistening neck, touched the hat with her nose, lifted her head, dilated her delicate nostrils, looked out over the cliff with her great soft half-human eyes, and whinnied gently.

Ben leaped to the ground, picked up the handkerchief and looked at the initials, "M. L.," worked in the corner. He knew what lay on the river's brink below as well as if he stood over the dead bodies. He kissed the letters of her name, crushed the handkerchief in his locked hands, and cried:

"Now, Lord God, give me strength for the service of my people!"

He hurriedly examined the ground, amazed to find no

trace of a struggle or crime. Could it be possible they had ventured too near the brink and fallen over?

He hurried to report to his father his discoveries, instructed his mother and Margaret to keep the servants quiet until the truth was known, and the two men returned along the river's brink to the foot of the cliff.

They found the bodies close to the water's edge. Marion had been killed instantly. Her fair blonde head lay in a crimson circle sharply defined in the white sand. But the mother was still warm with life. She had scarcely ceased to breathe. In one last desperate throb of love the trembling soul had dragged the dying body to the girl's side, and she had died with her head resting on the fair round neck as though she had kissed her and fallen asleep.

Father and son clasped hands and stood for a moment with uncovered heads. The doctor said at length:

"Go to the coroner at once, and see that he summons the jury *you* select and hand to him. Bring them immediately. I will examine the bodies before they arrive."

Ben took the negro coroner into his office alone, turned the key, told him of the discovery, and handed him the list of the jury.

"I'll hatter see Mr. Lynch fust, sah," he answered.

Ben placed his hand on his hip-pocket and said coldly:

"Put your cross-mark on those forms I've made out there for you, go with me immediately, and summon these men. If you dare put a negro on this jury, or open your mouth as to what has occurred in this room, I'll kill you."

The negro tremblingly did as he was commanded.

The coroner's jury reported that the mother and daughter had been killed by accidentally falling over the cliff.

In all the throng of grief-stricken friends who came to the little cottage that day, but two men knew the hell-lit secret beneath the tragedy.

When the bodies reached the home, Doctor Cameron placed Mrs. Cameron and Margaret outside to receive visitors and prevent any one from disturbing him. He took Ben into the room and locked the doors.

"My boy, I wish you to witness an experiment."

He drew from its case a powerful microscope of French make.

"What on earth are you going to do, sir?"

The doctor's brilliant eyes flashed with a mystic light as he replied:

"Find the fiend who did this crime—and then we will hang him on a gallows so high that all men from the rivers to ends of the earth shall see and feel and know the might of an unconquerable race of men."

"But there's no trace of him here."

"We shall see," said the doctor, adjusting his instrument.

"I believe that a microscope of sufficient power will reveal on the retina of these dead eyes the image of this devil as if etched there by fire. The experiment has been made successfully in France. No word or deed of man is lost. A German scholar has a memory so wonderful he can repeat whole volumes of Latin, German, and French without an error. A Russian officer has been known to repeat the roll-call of any regiment by reading

it twice. Psychologists hold that nothing is lost from the
memory of man. Impressions remain in the brain like
words written on paper in invisible ink. So I believe of
images in the eye if we can trace them early enough. If
no impression were made subsequently on the mother's
eye by the light of day, I believe the fire-etched record of
this crime can yet be traced."

Ben watched him with breathless interest.

He first examined Marion's eyes. But in the cold azure
blue of their pure depths he could find nothing.

"It's as I feared with the child," he said. "I can see
nothing. It is on the mother I rely. In the splendour
of life, at thirty-seven she was the full-blown perfection
of womanhood with every vital force at its highest tension——"

He looked long and patiently into the dead mother's
eye, rose and wiped the perspiration from his face.

"What is it, sir?" asked Ben.

Without reply, as if in a trance, he returned to the
microscope and again rose with the little quick nervous
cough he gave only in the greatest excitement, and whispered:

"Look now and tell me what you see."

Ben looked and said:

"I can see nothing."

"Your powers of vision are not trained as mine," replied
the doctor, resuming his place at the instrument.

"What do you see?" asked the younger man, bending
nervously.

"The bestial figure of a negro—his huge black hand

plainly defined—the upper part of the face is dim, as if obscured by a gray mist of dawn—but the massive jaws and lips are clear—merciful God!—yes!—it's Gus!"

The doctor leaped to his feet livid with excitement.

Ben bent again, looked long and eagerly, but could see nothing.

"I'm afraid the image is in your eye, sir, not the mother's " said Ben, sadly.

"That's possible, of course," said the doctor, "yet I don't believe it."

"I've thought of the same scoundrel and tried blood hounds on that track, but for some reason they couldn't follow it. I suspected him from the first, and especially since learning that he left for Columbia on the early morning train on pretended official business."

"Then I'm not mistaken," insisted the doctor, trembling with excitement. "Now do as I tell you. Find when he returns. Capture him, bind, gag, and carry him to your meeting-place under the cliff, and let me know."

On the afternoon of the funeral, two days later, Ben received a cypher telegram from the conductor of the train telling him that Gus was on the evening mail due at Piedmont at nine o'clock.

The papers had been filled with accounts of the accident, and an enormous crowd from the county, and many admirers of the fiery lyrics of the poet-father, had come from distant parts to honour his name. All business was suspended, and the entire white population of the village followed the bodies to their last resting-place.

As the crowds returned to their homes, no notice was

taken of a dozen men on horseback who rode out of town by different ways about dusk. At eight o'clock they met in the woods, near the first little flag-station located on McAllister's farm four miles from Piedmont, where a buggy awaited them. Two men of powerful build, who were strangers in the county, alighted from the buggy and walked along the track to board the train at the station three miles beyond and confer with the conductor.

The men, who gathered in the woods, dismounted, removed their saddles, and from the folds of the blankets took a white disguise for horse and man. In a moment it was fitted on each horse, with buckles at the throat, breast, and tail, and the saddles replaced. The white robe for the man was made in the form of an ulster overcoat with cape, the skirt extending to the top of the shoes. From the red belt at the waist were swung two revolvers which had been concealed in their pockets. On each man's breast was a scarlet circle within which shone a white cross. The same scarlet circle and cross appeared on the horse's breast, while on his flanks flamed the three red mystic letters, K. K. K. Each man wore a white cap, from the edges of which fell a piece of cloth extending to the shoulders. Beneath the visor was an opening for the eyes and lower down one for the mouth. On the front of the caps of two of the men appeared the red wings of a hawk as the ensign of rank. From the top of each cap rose eighteen inches high a single spike held erect by a twisted wire. The disguises for man and horse were made of cheap unbleached domestic and weighed less than three pounds. They were easily folded within a blanket and kept under the saddle in a crowd without discovery. It required less than two minutes to remove the saddles, place the disguises, and remount.

At the signal of a whistle, the men and horses arrayed in white and scarlet swung into double-file cavalry formation and stood awaiting orders. The moon was now shining brightly, and its light shimmering on the silent horses and men with their tall spiked caps made a picture such as the world had not seen since the Knights of the Middle Ages rode on their Holy Crusades.

As the train neared the flag-station, which was dark and unattended, the conductor approached Gus, leaned over, and said: "I've just gotten a message from the sheriff telling me to warn you to get off at this station and slip into town. There's a crowd at the depot there waiting for you and they mean trouble."

Gus trembled, and whispered:

"Den fur Gawd's sake lemme off here."

The two men who got on at the station below stepped out before the negro, and, as he alighted from the car, seized, tripped, and threw him to the ground. The engineer blew a sharp signal, and the train pulled on.

In a minute Gus was bound and gagged.

One of the men drew a whistle and blew twice. A single tremulous call like the cry of an owl answered. The swift beat of horses' feet followed, and four white-and-scarlet clansmen swept in a circle around the group.

One of the strangers turned to the horseman with red-winged ensign on his cap, saluted, and said:

"Here's your man, Night Hawk."

"Thanks, gentlemen," was the answer. "Let us know when we can be of service to your county."

The strangers sprang into their buggy and disappeared toward the North Carolina line.

The clansmen blindfolded the negro, placed him on a horse, tied his legs securely, and his arms behind him to the ring in the saddle.

The Night Hawk blew his whistle four sharp blasts, and his pickets galloped from their positions and joined him.

Again the signal rang, and his men wheeled with the precision of trained cavalrymen into column formation three abreast, and rode toward Piedmont, the single black figure tied and gagged in the centre of the white-and-scarlet squadron.

CHAPTER II

THE FIERY CROSS

THE clansmen with their prisoner skirted the village and halted in the woods on the river bank. The Night Hawk signalled for single file, and in a few minutes they stood against the cliff under Lover's Leap and saluted the chief, who sat his horse, awaiting their arrival.

Pickets were placed in each direction on the narrow path by which the spot was approached, and one was sent to stand guard on the shelving rock above.

Through the narrow crooked entrance they led Gus into the cave which had been the rendezvous of the Piedmont Den of the Klan since its formation. The meeting-place was a grand hall eighty feet deep, fifty feet wide, and more than forty feet in height, which had been carved out of the stone by the swift current of the river in ages past when its waters stood at a higher level.

To-night it was lighted by candles placed on the ledges of the walls. In the centre, on a fallen boulder, sat the Grand Cyclops of the Den, the presiding officer of the township, his rank marked by scarlet stripes on the white-cloth spike of his cap. Around him stood twenty or more clansmen in their uniform, completely disguised. One among them wore a yellow sash, trimmed in gold, about his

318

waist, and on his breast two yellow circles with red crosses interlapping, denoting his rank to be the Grand Dragon of the Realm, or Commander-in-Chief of the State.

The Cyclops rose from his seat:

"Let the Grand Turk remove his prisoner for a moment and place him in charge of the Grand Sentinel at the door, until summoned."

The officer disappeared with Gus, and the Cyclops continued:

"The Chaplain will open our Council with prayer."

Solemnly every white-shrouded figure knelt on the ground, and the voice of the Rev. Hugh McAlpin, trembling with feeling, echoed through the cave:

"Lord God of our Fathers, as in times past thy children, fleeing from the oppressor, found refuge beneath the earth until once more the sun of righteousness rose, so are we met to-night. As we wrestle with the powers of darkness now strangling our life, give to our souls to endure as seeing the invisible, and to our right arms the strength of the martyred dead of our people. Have mercy on the poor, the weak, the innocent and defenseless, and deliver us from the body of the Black Death. In a land of light and beauty and love our women are prisoners of danger and fear. While the heathen walks his native heath unharmed and unafraid, in this fair Christian Southland, our sisters, wives, and daughters dare not stroll at twilight through the streets, or step beyond the highway at noon. The terror of the twilight deepens with the darkness, and the stoutest heart grows sick with fear for the red message the morning bringeth. Forgive our sins—they are

many, but hide not thy face from us, O God, for thou
art our refuge!"

As the last echoes of the prayer lingered and died in the
vaulted roof, the clansmen rose and stood a moment in
silence.

Again the voice of the Cyclops broke the stillness:

"Brethren, we are met to-night at the request of the
Grand Dragon of the Realm, who has honoured us with
his presence, to constitute a High Court for the trial of a
case involving life. Are the Night Hawks ready to submit their evidence?"

"We are ready," came the answer.

"Then let the Grand Scribe read the objects of the
Order on which your authority rests."

The Scribe opened his Book of Record, "*The Prescript
of the Order of the Invisible Empire,*" and solemnly read:

"To the lovers of law and order, peace and justice, and
to the shades of the venerated dead, greeting:

"This is an institution of Chivalry, Humanity, Mercy,
and Patriotism: embodying in its genius and principles
all that is chivalric in conduct, noble in sentiment, generous in manhood, and patriotic in purpose: its peculiar
objects being,

"First: To protect the weak, the innocent, and the
defenseless from the indignities, wrongs and outrages of
the lawless, the violent, and the brutal; to relieve the injured and the oppressed: to succour the suffering and unfortunate, and especially the widows and the orphans of
Confederate Soldiers.

"Second: To protect and defend the Constitution of

the United States, and all the laws passed in conformity thereto, and to protect the states and the people thereof from all invasion from any source whatever.

"Third: To aid and assist in the execution of all Constitutional laws, and to protect the people from unlawful seizure, and from trial except by their peers in conformity to the laws of the land."

"The Night Hawks will produce their evidence," said the Cyclops, "and the Grand Monk will conduct the case of the people against the negro Augustus Caesar, the former slave of Dr. Richard Cameron."

Dr. Cameron advanced and removed his cap. His snow-white hair and beard, ruddy face and dark-brown brilliant eyes made a strange picture in its weird surroundings, like an ancient alchemist ready to conduct some daring experiment in the problem of life.

"I am here, brethren," he said, "to accuse the black brute about to appear of the crime of assault on a daughter of the South——"

A murmur of thrilling surprise and horror swept the crowd of white and scarlet figures as with one common impulse they moved closer.

"His feet have been measured and they exactly tally with the negro tracks found under the window of the Lenoir cottage. His flight to Columbia and return on the publication of their deaths as an accident is a confirmation of our case. I will not relate to you the scientific experiment which first fixed my suspicion of this man's guilt. My witness could not confirm it, and it might not be to you credible. But this negro is peculiarly sensitive to hypnotic influence. I propose to put him under this power to-night before you, and, if he is guilty, I can make him tell his confederates, describe and rehearse the crime itself."

The Night Hawks led Gus before Doctor Cameron, untied his hands, removed the gag, and slipped the blindfold from his head.

Under the doctor's rigid gaze the negro's knees struck together, and he collapsed into complete hypnosis, merely lifting his huge paws lamely as if to ward a blow.

They seated him on the boulder from which the Cyclops rose, and Gus stared about the cave and grinned as if in a dream seeing nothing.

The doctor recalled to him the day of the crime, and he began to talk to his three confederates, describing his plot in detail, now and then pausing and breaking into a fiendish laugh.

Old McAllister, who had three lovely daughters at home, threw off his cap, sank to his knees, and buried his face in his hands, while a dozen of the white figures crowded closer, nervously gripping the revolvers which hung from their red belts.

Doctor Cameron pushed them back and lifted his hand in warning.

The negro began to live the crime with fearful realism —the journey past the hotel to make sure the victims had gone to their home; the visit to Aunt Cindy's cabin to find her there; lying in the field waiting for the last light of the village to go out; gloating with vulgar exultation over their plot, and planning other crimes to follow its success—how they crept along the shadows of the hedge-row of the lawn to avoid the moonlight, stood under the cedar, and through the open windows watched the mother and daughter laughing and talking within——

"Min' what I tells you now—Tie de ole one, when I gib you de rope," said Gus in a whisper.

"My God!" cried the agonised voice of the figure with the double cross—"that's what the piece of burnt rope in the fireplace meant!"

Doctor Cameron again lifted his hand for silence.

Now they burst into the room, and with the light of hell in his beady, yellow-splotched eyes, Gus gripped his imaginary revolver and growled:

"Scream, an' I blow yer brains out!"

In spite of Doctor Cameron's warning, the white-robed figures jostled and pressed closer——

Gus rose to his feet and started across the cave as if to spring on the shivering figure of the girl, the clansmen with muttered groans, sobs and curses falling back as he advanced. He still wore his full Captain's uniform, its heavy epaulets flashing their gold in the unearthly light, his beastly jaws half covering the gold braid on the collar. His thick lips were drawn upward in an ugly leer and his sinister bead-eyes gleamed like a gorilla's. A single fierce leap and the black claws clutched the air slowly as if sinking into the soft white throat.

Strong men began to cry like children.

"Stop him! Stop him!" screamed a clansman, spring-ing on the negro and grinding his heel into his big thick neck. A dozen more were on him in a moment, kicking, stamping, cursing, and crying like madmen.

Doctor Cameron leaped forward and beat them off:

"Men! Men! You must not kill him in this condition!"

Some of the white figures had fallen prostrate on the ground, sobbing in a frenzy of uncontrollable emotion. Some were leaning against the walls, their faces buried in their arms.

Again old McAllister was on his knees crying over and over again:

"God have mercy on my people!"

When at length quiet was restored, the negro was revived, and again bound, blindfolded, gagged, and thrown to the ground before the Grand Cyclops.

A sudden inspiration flashed in Doctor Cameron's eyes. Turning to the figure with yellow sash and double cross he said:

"Issue your orders and despatch your courier to-night with the old Scottish rite of the Fiery Cross. It will send a thrill of inspiration to every clansman in the hills."

"Good—prepare it quickly," was the answer.

Doctor Cameron opened his medicine case, drew the silver drinking-cover from a flask, and passed out of the cave to the dark circle of blood still shining in the sand by the water's edge. He knelt and filled the cup half full of the crimson grains, and dipped it into the river. From a saddle he took the lightwood torch, returned within, and placed the cup on the boulder on which the Grand Cyclops had sat. He loosed the bundle of lightwood, took two pieces, tied them into the form of a cross, and laid it beside a lighted candle near the silver cup.

The silent figures watched his every movement. He lifted the cup and said:

"Brethren, I hold in my hand the water of your river bearing the red stain of the life of a Southern woman, a priceless sacrifice on the altar of outraged civilisation. Hear the message of your chief."

The tall figure with the yellow sash and double cross stepped before the strange altar, while the white forms of the clansmen gathered about him in a circle. He lifted his cap, and laid it on the boulder, and his men gazed on the flushed face of Ben Cameron, the Grand Dragon of the Realm.

He stood for a moment silent, erect, a smouldering fierceness in his eyes, something cruel and yet magnetic in his alert bearing.

He looked on the prostrate negro lying in his uniform at his feet, seized the cross, lighted the three upper ends and held it blazing in his hand, while, in a voice full of the fires of feeling, he said:

"Men of the South, the time for words has passed, the hour for action has struck. The Grand Turk will execute this negro to-night and fling his body on the lawn of the black Lieutenant-Governor of the state."

The Grand Turk bowed.

"I ask for the swiftest messenger of this Den who can ride till dawn."

The man whom Doctor Cameron had already chosen stepped forward:

"Carry my summons to the Grand Titan of the adjoining province in North Carolina whom you will find at Hambright. Tell him the story of this crime and what you have seen and heard. Ask him to report to me here the second night from this,. at eleven o'clock, with six Grand Giants from his adjoining counties, each accompanied by two hundred picked men. In olden times when the Chieftain of our people summoned the clan on an errand of life and death, the Fiery Cross, extinguished in sacrificial blood, was sent by swift courier from village to village. This call was never made in vain, nor will it be to-night in the new world. Here, on this spot made holy ground by the blood of those we hold dearer than life, I raise the ancient symbol of an unconquered race of men——"

High above his head in the darkness of the cave he lifted the blazing emblem——

"The Fiery Cross of old Scotland's hills! I quench its flames in the sweetest blood that ever stained the sands of Time."

He dipped its ends in the silver cup, extinguished the fire, and handed the charred symbol to the courier, who quickly disappeared.

CHAPTER III

The Parting of the Ways

THE discovery of the Captain of the African Guards lying in his full uniform in Lynch's yard sent a thrill of terror to the triumphant leagues. Across the breast of the body was pinned a scrap of paper on which was written in red ink the letters K. K. K. It was the first actual evidence of the existence of this dreaded order in Ulster county.

The First Lieutenant of the Guards assumed command and held the full company in their armory under arms day and night. Beneath his door he had found a notice which was also nailed on the court-house. It appeared in the Piedmont *Eagle* and in rapid succession in every newspaper not under Negro influence in the state. It read as follows:

"Headquarters of Realm No. 4.
"Dreadful Era, Black Epoch,
"Hideous Hour.
"General Order No. 1.

"The Negro Militia now organised in this State threatens the extinction of civilisation. They have avowed their purpose to make war upon and exterminate the Ku Klux Klan, an organisation which is now the sole guardian of Society. All negroes are hereby given forty-eight hours from the publication of this notice in their respective counties to surrender their arms at the court-house door. Those who refuse must take the consequences.

"By order of the G. D. of Realm No. 4.

"By the Grand Scribe."

The white people of Piedmont read this notice with a thrill of exultant joy. Men walked the streets with an erect bearing which said without words:

"Stand out of the way."

For the first time since the dawn of Black Rule negroes began to yield to white men and women the right of way on the streets.

On the day following, the old Commoner sent for Phil.

"What is the latest news?" he asked.

"The town is in a fever of excitement—not over the discovery in Lynch's yard—but over the blacker rumour that Marion and her mother committed suicide to conceal an assault by this fiend."

"A trumped-up lie," said the old man emphatically

"It's true, sir. I'll take Doctor Cameron's word for it."

"You have just come from the Camerons?"

"Yes."

"Let it be your last visit. The Camerons are on the road to the gallows, father and son. Lynch informs me that the murder committed last night, and the insolent notice nailed on the court-house door, could have come only from their brain. They are the hereditary leaders of these people. They alone would have had the audacity to fling this crime into the teeth of the world and threaten worse. We are face to face with Southern barbarism. Every man now to his own standard! The house of Stoneman can have no part with midnight assassins."

"Nor with black barbarians, father. It is a question of who possesses the right of life and death over the citizen, the organised virtue of the community, or its organised crime. You have mistaken for death the patience of a generous people. We call ourselves the champions of liberty. Yet for less than they have suffered, kings have lost their heads and empires perished before the wrath of freemen."

"My boy, this is not a question for argument between us," said the father with stern emphasis. "This conspiracy of terror and assassination threatens to shatter my work to atoms. The election on which turns the destiny of Congress, and the success or failure of my life, is but a few weeks away. Unless this foul conspiracy is crushed, I am ruined, and the Nation falls again beneath the heel of a slaveholders' oligarchy."

"Your nightmare of a slaveholders' oligarchy does not disturb me."

"At least you will have the decency to break your affair with Margaret Cameron pending the issue of my struggle of life and death with her father and brother?"

"Never."

"Then I will do it for you."

"I warn you, sir," Phil cried, with anger, "that if it comes to an issue of race against race, I am a white man. The ghastly tragedy of the condition of society here is something for which the people of the South are no longer responsible——"

"I'll take the responsibility!" growled the old cynic.

"Don't ask me to share it," said the younger man, emphatically.

The father winced, his lips trembled, and he answered brokenly:

"My boy, this is the bitterest hour of my life that has had little to make it sweet. To hear such words from you is more than I can bear. I am an old man now—my sands are nearly run. But two human beings love me, and I love but two. On you and your sister I have lavished all the treasures of a maimed and strangled soul—and it has come to this! Read the notice which one of your friends thrust into the window of my bedroom last night."

He handed Phil a piece of paper on which was written:

"The old club-footed beast who has sneaked into our town, pretending to search for health, in reality the leader of the infernal Union League, will be given forty-eight hours to vacate the house and rid this community of his presence.
"K. K. K."

"Are you an officer of the Union League?" Phil asked in surprise.

"I am its soul."

"How could a Southerner discover this, if your own children didn't know it?"

"By their spies who have joined the League."

"And do the rank and file know the Black Pope at the head of the order?"

"No, but high officials do."

"Does Lynch?"

"Certainly."

"Then he is the scoundrel who placed that note in your

room. It is a clumsy attempt to forge an order of the Klan. The white man does not live in this town capable of that act. I know these people."

"My boy, you are bewitched by the smiles of a woman to deny your own flesh and blood."

"Nonsense, father—you are possessed by an idea which has become an insane mania——"

"Will you respect my wishes?" the old man broke in, angrily.

"I will not," was the clear answer. Phil turned and left the room, and the old man's massive head sank on his breast in helpless baffled rage and grief.

He was more successful in his appeal to Elsie. He convinced her of the genuineness of the threat against him. The brutal reference to his lameness roused the girl's soul. When the old man, crushed by Phil's desertion, broke down the last reserve of his strange cold nature, tore his wounded heart open to her, cried in agony over his deformity, his lameness, and the anguish with which he saw the threatened ruin of his life-work, she threw her arms around his neck in a flood of tears and cried:

"Hush, father, I will not desert you. I will never leave you, or wed without your blessing. If I find that my lover was in any way responsible for this insult, I'll tear his image out of my heart and never speak his name again!"

She wrote a note to Ben, asking him to meet her at sundown on horseback at Lover's Leap.

Ben was elated at the unexpected request. He was hungry for an hour with his sweetheart, whom he had not seen save for a moment since the storm of excitement broke following the discovery of the crime.

He hastened through his work of ordering the movement of the Klan for the night, and determined to surprise Elsie by meeting her in his uniform of a Grand Dragon

Secure in her loyalty, he would deliberately thus put his life in her hands. Using the water of a brook in the woods for a mirror, he adjusted his yellow sash and pushed the two revolvers back under the cape out of sight, saying to himself with a laugh:

"Betray me? Well, if she does, life would not be worth the living!"

When Elsie had recovered from the first shock of surprise at the white horse and rider waiting for her under the shadows of the old beech, her surprise gave way to grief at the certainty of his guilt, and the greatness of his love in thus placing his life without a question in her hands.

He tied the horses in the woods, and they sat down on the rustic.

He removed his helmet cap, threw back the white cape showing the scarlet lining, and the two golden circles with their flaming crosses on his breast, with boyish pride. The costume was becoming to his slender graceful figure, and he knew it.

"You see, sweetheart, I hold high rank in the Empire," he whispered.

From beneath his cape he drew a long bundle which he unrolled. It was a triangular flag of brilliant yellow edged in scarlet. In the centre of the yellow ground was the figure of a huge black dragon with fiery red eyes and tongue. Around it was a Latin motto worked in scarlet: "*quod semper, quod ubique, quod ab omnibus*"—what always, what everywhere, what by all has been held to be true. "The battle-flag of the Klan," he said; "the standard of the Grand Dragon."

Elsie seized his hand and kissed it, unable to speak.

"Why so serious to-night?"

"Do you love me very much?" she answered.

"Greater love hath no man than this, that he lay his fife at the feet of his beloved," he responded, tenderly.

"Yes, yes; I know—and that is why you are breaking my heart. When first I met you—it seems now ages and ages ago—I was a vain, self-willed, pert little thing——"

"It's not so. I took you for an angel—you were one. You are one to-night."

"Now," she went on slowly, "in what I have lived through you I have grown into an impassioned, serious, self-disciplined, bewildered woman. Your perfect trust to-night is the sweetest revelation that can come to a woman's soul and yet it brings to me unspeakable pain——"

"For what?"

"You are guilty of murder."

Ben's figure stiffened.

"The judge who pronounces sentence of death on a criminal outlawed by civilised society is not usually called a murderer, my dear."

"And by whose authority are you a judge?"

"By authority of the sovereign people who created the State of South Carolina. The criminals who claim to be our officers are usurpers placed there by the subversion of law."

"Won't you give this all up for my sake?" she pleaded. "Believe me, you are in great danger."

"Not so great as is the danger of my sister and mother and my sweetheart—it is a man's place to face danger," he gravely answered.

"This violence can only lead to your ruin and shame——"

"I am fighting the battle of a race on whose fate hangs the future of the South and the Nation. My ruin and shame will be of small account if they are saved," was the even answer.

"Come, my dear," she pleaded, tenderly, "you know that I have weighed the treasures of music and art and given them all for one clasp of your hand, one throb of your heart against mine. I should call you cruel did I not know you are infinitely tender. This is the only thing I have ever asked you to do for me——"

"Desert my people! You must not ask of me this infamy, if you love me," he cried.

"But, listen; this is wrong—this wild vengeance is a crime you are doing, however great the provocation. We cannot continue to love one another if you do this. Listen: I love you better than father, mother, life or career—all my dreams I've lost in you. I've lived through eternity to-day with my father——"

"You know me guiltless of the vulgar threat against him——"

"Yes, and yet you are the leader of desperate men who might have done it. As I fought this battle to-day, I've lost you, lost myself, and sunk down to the depths of despair, and at the end rang the one weak cry of a woman's heart for her lover! Your frown can darken the brightest sky. For your sake I can give up all save the sense of right. I'll walk by your side in life—lead you gently and tenderly along the way of my dreams if I can, but if you go your way, it shall be mine; and I shall still be glad because you are there! See how humble I am—only you must not commit crime!"

"Come, sweetheart, you must not use that word," he protested, with a touch of wounded pride.

"You are a conspirator——"

"I am a revolutionist."

"You are committing murder!"

"I am waging war."

Elsie leaped to her feet in a sudden rush of anger and extended her hand:

"Good-bye. I shall not see you again. I do not know you. You are still a stranger to me."

He held her hand firmly.

"We must not part in anger," he said slowly. "I have grave work to do before the day dawns. We may not see each other again."

She led her horse to the seat quickly and without waiting for his assistance sprang into the saddle.

"Do you not fear my betrayal of your secret?" she asked.

He rode to her side, bent close, and whispered:

"It's as safe as if locked in the heart of God."

A little sob caught her voice, yet she said slowly in firm tones:

"If another crime is committed in this county by your Klan, we will never see each other again."

He escorted her to the edge of the town without a word, pressed her hand in silence, wheeled his horse, and disappeared on the road to the North Carolina line.

CHAPTER IV

THE BANNER OF THE DRAGON

BEN CAMERON rode rapidly to the rendezvous of the pickets who were to meet the coming squadrons.

He returned home and ate a hearty meal. As he emerged from the dining-room, Phil seized him by the arm and led him under the big oak on the lawn:

"Cameron, old boy, I'm in a lot of trouble. I've had a quarrel with my father, and your sister has broken me all up by returning my ring. I want a little excitement to ease my nerves. From Elsie's incoherent talk I judge you are in danger. If there's going to be a fight, let me in."

Ben took his hand:

"You're the kind of a man I'd like to have for a brother, and I'll help you in love—but as for war—it's not your fight. We don't need help."

At ten o'clock Ben met the local Den at their rendezvous under the cliff, to prepare for the events of the night.

The forty members present were drawn up before him in double rank of twenty each.

"Brethren," he said to them, solemnly, "I have called you to-night to take a step from which there can be no retreat. We are going to make a daring experiment of the utmost importance. If there is a faint heart among you, now is the time to retire——"

"We are with you!" cried the men.

"There are laws of our race, old before this Republic was born in the souls of white freemen. The fiat of fools has repealed on paper these laws. Your fathers who created this Nation were first Conspirators, then Revolutionists, now Patriots and Saints. I need to-night ten volunteers to lead the coming clansmen over this county and disarm every negro in it. The men from North Carolina cannot be recognised. Each of you must run this risk. Your absence from home to-night will be doubly dangerous for what will be done here at this negro armory under my command. I ask of these ten men to ride their horses until dawn, even unto death, to ride for their God, their native land, and the womanhood of the South!

"To each man who accepts this dangerous mission, I offer for your bed the earth, for your canopy the sky, for your bread stones; and when the flash of bayonets shall fling into your face from the Square the challenge of martial law, the protection I promise you—is exile, imprisonment, and death! Let the ten men who accept these terms step forward four paces."

With a single impulse the whole double line of forty white-and-scarlet figures moved quickly forward four steps!

The leader shook hands with each man, his voice throbbing with emotion as he said:

"Stand together like this, men, and armies will march and countermarch over the South in vain! We will save the life of our people."

The ten guides selected by the Grand Dragon rode forward, and each led a division of one hundred men through the ten townships of the county and successfully disarmed every negro before day without the loss of a life.

The remaining squadron of two hundred and fifty men from Hambright, accompanied by the Grand Titan in command of the Province of Western Hill Counties, were led by Ben Cameron into Piedmont as the waning moon rose between twelve and one o'clock.

They marched past Stoneman's place on the way to the negro armory, which stood on the opposite side of the street a block below.

The wild music of the beat of a thousand hoofs on the cobblestones of the street waked every sleeper. The old Commoner hobbled to his window and watched them pass, his big hands fumbling nervously, and his soul stirred to its depths.

The ghostlike shadowy columns moved slowly with the deliberate consciousness of power. The scarlet circles on their breasts could be easily seen when one turned toward the house, as could the big red letters K.K.K. on each horse's flank.

In the centre of the line waved from a gold-tipped spear the battleflag of the Klan. As they passed the bright lights burning at his gate, old Stoneman could see this standard plainly. The huge black dragon with flaming eyes and tongue seemed a living thing crawling over a scarlet-tipped yellow cloud.

At the window above stood a little figure watching that banner of the Dragon pass with aching heart.

Phil stood at another, smiling with admiration for their daring:

"By George, it stirs the blood to see it! You can't crush men of that breed!"

The watchers were not long in doubt as to what the raiders meant.

They deployed quickly around the armory. A whistle rang its shrill cry, and a volley of two hundred and fifty carbines and revolvers smashed every glass in the building. The sentinel had already given the alarm, and the drum was calling the startled negroes to their arms. They returned the volley twice, and for ten minutes were answered with the steady crack of two hundred and fifty guns. A white flag appeared at the door, and the firing ceased. The negroes laid down their arms and surrendered. All save three were allowed to go to their homes for the night and carry their wounded with them.

The three confederates in the crime of their captain were bound and led away. In a few minutes the crash of a volley told their end.

The little white figure rapped at Phil's door and placed a trembling hand on his arm:

"Phil," she said softly, "please go to the hotel and stay until you know all that has happened—until you know the full list of those killed and wounded. I'll wait. You understand?"

As he stooped and kissed her, he felt a hot tear roll down her cheek.

"Yes, little Sis, I understand," he answered.

CHAPTER V

THE REIGN OF THE KLAN

IN quick succession every county followed the example of Ulster, and the arms furnished the negroes by the state and National governments were in the hands of the Klan. The League began to collapse in a panic of terror.

A gale of chivalrous passion and high action, contagious and intoxicating, swept the white race. The moral, mental, and physical earthquake which followed the first assault on one of their daughters revealed the unity of the racial life of the people. Within the span of a week they had lived a century.

The spirit of the South "like lightning had at last leaped forth, half startled at itself, its feet upon the ashes and the rags," its hands tight-gripped on the throat of tyrant, thug, and thief.

It was the resistless movement of a race, not of any man or leader of men. The secret weapon with which they struck was the most terrible and efficient in human history—these pale hosts of white-and-scarlet horsemen! They struck shrouded in a mantle of darkness and terror. They struck where the power of resistance was weakest and the blow least suspected. Discovery or retaliation was impossible. Not a single disguise was ever pene-

341

trated. All was planned and ordered as by destiny. The accused was tried by secret tribunal, sentenced without a hearing, executed in the dead of night without warning, mercy, or appeal. The movements of the Klan were like clockwork, without a word, save the whistle of the Night Hawk, the crack of his revolver, and the hoof-beat of swift horses moving like figures in a dream, and vanishing in mists and shadows.

The old club-footed Puritan, in his mad scheme of vengeance and party power, had overlooked the Covenanter, the backbone of the South. This man had just begun to fight! His race had defied the Crown of Great Britain a hundred years from the caves and wilds of Scotland and Ireland, taught the English people how to slay a king and build a commonwealth, and, driven into exile into the wilderness of America, led our Revolution, peopled the hills of the South, and conquered the West.

As the young German patriots of 1812 had organised the great struggle for their liberties under the noses of the garrisons of Napoleon, so Ben Cameron had met the leaders of his race in Nashville, Tennessee, within the picket lines of thirty-five thousand hostile troops, and in the ruins of an old homestead discussed and adopted the ritual of the Invisible Empire.

Within a few months this Empire overspread a territory larger than modern Europe. In the approaching election it was reaching out its daring white hands to tear the fruits of victory from twenty million victorious conquerors.

The triumph at which they aimed was one of incredible

grandeur. They had risen to snatch power out of defeat and death. Under their clan - leadership the Southern people had suddenly developed the courage of the lion, the cunning of the fox, and the deathless faith of religious enthusiasts.

Society was fused in the white heat of one sublime thought and beat with the pulse of the single will of the Grand Wizard of the Klan at Memphis.

Women and children had eyes and saw not, ears and heard not. Over four hundred thousand disguises for men and horses were made by the women of the South, and not one secret ever passed their lips!

With magnificent audacity, infinite patience, and remorseless zeal, a conquered people were struggling to turn his own weapon against their conqueror, and beat his brains out with the bludgeon he had placed in the hands of their former slaves.

Behind the tragedy of Reconstruction stood the remarkable man whose iron will alone had driven these terrible measures through the chaos of passion, corruption, and bewilderment which followed the first assassination of an American President. As he leaned on his window in this village of the South and watched in speechless rage the struggle at that negro armory, he felt for the first time the foundations sinking beneath his feet. As he saw the black cowards surrender in terror, noted the indifference and cool defiance with which those white horsemen rode and shot, he knew that he had collided with the ultimate force which his whole scheme had overlooked.

He turned on his big club foot from the window, clinched his fist, and muttered:

"But I'll hang that man for this deed if it's the last act of my life!"

The morning brought dismay to the negro, the carpet-bagger, and the scalawag of Ulster. A peculiar freak of weather in the early morning added to their terror. The sun rose clear and bright except for a slight fog that floated from the river valley, increasing the roar of the falls. About nine o'clock, a huge black shadow suddenly rushed over Piedmont from the west, and in a moment the town was shrouded in twilight. The cries of birds were hushed, and chickens went to roost as in a total eclipse of the sun. Knots of people gathered on the streets and gazed uneasily at the threatening skies. Hundreds of negroes began to sing and shout and pray, while sensible people feared a cyclone or cloud-burst. A furious downpour of rain was swiftly followed by sunshine, and the negroes rose from their knees, shouting with joy to find the end of the world had after all been postponed.

But that the end of their brief reign in a white man's land had come, but few of them doubted. The events of the night were sufficiently eloquent. The movement of the clouds in sympathy was unnecessary.

Old Stoneman sent for Lynch, and found he had fled to Columbia. He sent for the only lawyer in town whom the Lieutenant-Governor had told him could be trusted.

The lawyer was polite, but his refusal to undertake the prosecution of any alleged member of the Klan was emphatic.

"I'm a sinful man, sir," he said with a smile. "Besides, I prefer to live, on general principles."

"I'll pay you well," urged the old man, "and if you secure the conviction of Ben Cameron, the man we believe to be the head of this Klan, I'll give you ten thousand dollars."

The lawyer was whittling on a piece of pine meditatively.

"That's a big lot of money in these hard times. I'd like to own it, but I'm afraid it wouldn't be good at the bank on the other side. I prefer the green fields of South Carolina to those of Eden. My harp isn't in tune."

Stoneman snorted in disgust:

"Will you ask the Mayor to call to see me at once?"

"We ain't got none," was the laconic answer.

"What do you mean?"

"Haven't you heard what happened to his Honour last night?"

"No."

"The Klan called to see him," went on the lawyer with a quizzical look, "at 3 A. M. Rather early for a visit of state. They gave him forty-nine lashes on his bare back, and persuaded him that the climate of Piedmont didn't agree with him. His Honour, Mayor Bizzel, left this morning with his negro wife and brood of mulatto children for his home, the slums of Cleveland, Ohio. We are deprived of his illustrious example, and he may not be a wiser man than when he came, but he's a much sadder one."

Stoneman dismissed the even-tempered member of the

bar, and wired Lynch to return immediately to Piedmont. He determined to conduct the prosecution of Ben Cameron in person. With the aid of the Lieutenant-Governor he succeeded in finding a man who would dare to swear out a warrant against him.

As a preliminary skirmish he was charged with a violation of the statutory laws of the United States relating to Reconstruction and arraigned before a Commissioner.

Against Elsie's agonising protest, old Stoneman appeared at the court-house to conduct the prosecution.

In the absence of the United States Marshal, the warrant had been placed in the hands of the sheriff, returnable at ten o'clock on the morning fixed for the trial. The new Sheriff of Ulster was no less a personage than Uncle Aleck, who had resigned his seat in the House to accept the more profitable one of High Sheriff of the County.

There was a long delay in beginning the trial. At 10:30, not a single witness summoned had appeared, nor had the prisoner seen fit to honour the court with his presence.

Old Stoneman sat fumbling his hands in nervous sullen rage, while Phil looked on with amusement.

"Send for the sheriff," he growled to the Commissioner.

In a moment Aleck appeared bowing humbly and politely to every white man he passed. He bent half way to the floor before the Commissioner and said:

"Marse Ben be here in er minute, sah. He's er eatin' his breakfus'. I run erlong erhead."

Stoneman's face was a thundercloud as he scrambled to his feet and glared at Aleck:

"*Marse* Ben? Did you say *Marse* Ben? Who's he?"
Aleck bowed low again.

"De young Colonel, sah—Marse Ben Cameron."

"And you the sheriff of this county trotted along in front to make the way smooth for your prisoner?"

"Yessah!"

"Is that the way you escort prisoners before a court?"

"Dem kin' er prisoners—yessah."

"Why didn't you walk beside him?"

Aleck grinned from ear to ear and bowed very low:

"He say sumfin' to me, sah!"

"And what did he say?"

Aleck shook his head and laughed:

"I hates ter insinuate ter de cote, sah!"

"What did he say to you!" thundered Stoneman.

"He say — he say — ef I walk 'longside er him — he knock hell outen me, sah!"

"Indeed."

"Yessah, en I 'spec' he would," said Aleck, insinuatingly. "La, he's a gemman, sah, he is! He tell me he come right on. He be here sho'."

Stoneman whispered to Lynch, turned with a look of contempt to Aleck, and said:

"Mr. Sheriff, you interest me. Will you be kind enough to explain to this court what has happened to you lately to so miraculously change your manners?"

Aleck glanced around the room nervously.

"I seed sumfin'—a vision, sah!"

"A vision? Are you given to visions?"

"Na-sah. Dis yere wuz er sho' 'nuff vision! I wuz er feelin' bad all day yistiddy. Soon in de mawnin', ez I wuz gwine 'long de road, I see a big black bird er settin' on de fence. He flop his wings, look right at me en say, 'Corpse! Corpse! Corpse!'"—Aleck's voice dropped to a whisper—"'en las' night de Ku Kluxes come ter see me, sah!"

Stoneman lifted his beetling brows.

"That's interesting. We are searching for information on that subject."

"Yessah! Dey wuz Sperits, ridin' white hosses wid flowin' white robes, en big blood-red eyes! De hosses wuz twenty feet high, en some er de Sperits wuz higher dan dis cote-house! Dey wuz all bal' headed, 'cept right on de top whar dere wuz er straight blaze er fire shot up in de air ten foot high!"

"What did they say to you?"

"Dey say dat ef I didn't design de sheriff's office, go back ter farmin' en behave myself, dey had er job waitin' fer me in hell, sah. En shos' you born dey wuz right from dar!"

"Of course!" sneered the old Commoner.

"Yessah! Hit's des lak I tell yer. One ob 'em makes me fetch 'im er drink er water. I carry two bucketsful ter 'im 'fo' I git done, en I swar ter God he drink it all right dar 'fo' my eyes! He say hit wuz pow'ful dry down below, sah! En den I feel sumfin' bus' loose inside er me, en I disremember all dat come ter pass! I made er jump fer de ribber bank, en de next I knowed I wuz er pullin' fur de odder sho'. I'se er pow'ful good swimmer, sah, but I nebber git ercross er creek befo' ez quick es I got ober de ribber las' night."

"And you think of going back to farming?"

"I done begin plowin' dis mornin', marster!"

"*Don't* you call me marster!" yelled the old man. "Are you the sheriff of this county?"

Aleck laughed loudly.

"Na-sah! Dat's er joke! I ain't nuttin' but er plain nigger—I wants peace, judge."

"Evidently we need a new sheriff."

"Dat's what I tell 'em, sah, dis mornin'—en I des flings mysef on de ignance er de cote!"

Phil laughed aloud, and his father's colourless eyes began to spit cold poison.

"About what time do you think your master, Colonel Cameron, will honour us with his presence?" he asked Aleck.

Again the sheriff bowed.

"He's er comin' right now, lak I tole yer—he's er gemman, sah."

Ben walked briskly into the room and confronted the Commissioner.

Without apparently noticing his presence, Stoneman said:

"In the absence of witnesses we accept the discharge of this warrant, pending developments."

Ben turned on his heel, pressed Phil's hand as he passed through the crowd, and disappeared.

The old Commoner drove to the telegraph office and sent a message of more than a thousand words to the

White House, a copy of which the operator delivered to
Ben Cameron within an hour.

President Grant next morning issued a proclamation
declaring the nine Scotch-Irish hill counties of South
Carolina in a state of insurrection, ordered an army corps
of five thousand men to report there for duty, pending
the further necessity of martial law and the suspension
of the writ of *Habeas Corpus.*

CHAPTER VI

THE COUNTER STROKE

FROM the hour he had watched the capture of the armory old Stoneman felt in the air a current against him which was electric, as if the dead had heard the cry of the clansmen's greeting, risen and rallied to their pale ranks.

The daring campaign these men were waging took his breath. They were going not only to defeat his delegation to Congress, but send their own to take their seats, reinforced by the enormous power of a suppressed Negro vote. The blow was so sublime in its audacity, he laughed in secret admiration while he raved and cursed.

The army corps took possession of the hill counties, quartering from five to six hundred regulars at each court-house; but the mischief was done. The state was on fire. The eighty thousand rifles with which the negroes had been armed were now in the hands of their foes. A white rifle-club was organised in every town, village, and hamlet. They attended the public meetings with their guns, drilled in front of the speakers' stands, yelled, hooted, hissed, cursed, and jeered at the orators who dared to champion or apologise for Negro rule. At night the hoof-beat of squadrons of pale horsemen and the crack of their revolvers struck terror to the heart of every negro, carpet-bagger, and scalawag.

There was a momentary lull in the excitement, which Stoneman mistook for fear, at the appearance of the troops. He had the Governor appoint a white sheriff, a young scalawag from the mountains who was a noted moonshiner and desperado. He arrested over a hundred leading men in the county, charged them with complicity in the killing of the three members of the African Guard, and instructed the judge and clerk of the court to refuse bail and commit them to jail under military guard.

To his amazement, the prisoners came into Piedmont armed and mounted. They paid no attention to the deputy sheriffs who were supposed to have them in charge. They deliberately formed in line under Ben Cameron's direction and he led them in a parade through the streets.

The five hundred United States regulars who were camped on the river bank were Westerners. Ben led his squadron of armed prisoners in front of this camp and took them through the evolutions of cavalry with the precision of veterans. The soldiers dropped their games and gathered, laughing, to watch them. The drill ended with a double-rank charge at the river embankment. When they drew every horse on his haunches on the brink, firing a volley with a single crash, a wild cheer broke from the soldiers, and the officers rushed from their tents.

Ben wheeled his men, galloped in front of the camp, drew them up at dress parade, and saluted. A low word of command from a trooper, and the Westerners quickly

formed in ranks, returned the salute, and cheered. The
officers rushed up, cursing, and drove the men back to
their tents.

The horsemen laughed, fired a volley in the air, cheered,
and galloped back to the court-house. The court was
glad to get rid of them. There was no question raised
over technicalities in making out bail-bonds. The clerk
wrote the names of imaginary bondsmen as fast as his pen
could fly, while the perspiration stood in beads on his red
forehead.

Another telegram from old Stoneman to the White
House, and the Writ of *Habeas Corpus* was suspended
and Martial Law proclaimed.

Enraged beyond measure at the salute from the troops,
he had two companies of negro regulars sent from Columbia, and they camped in the Court-House Square.

He determined to make a desperate effort to crush the
fierce spirit before which his forces were being driven like
chaff. He induced Bizzel to return from Cleveland with
his negro wife and children. He was escorted to the City
Hall and reinstalled as Mayor by the full force of seven
hundred troops, and a negro guard placed around his
house. Stoneman had Lynch run an excursion from the
Black Belt, and brought a thousand negroes to attend a
final rally at Piedmont. He placarded the town with
posters on which were printed the Civil Rights Bill
and the proclamation of the President declaring
Martial Law.

Ben watched this day dawn with nervous dread. He
had passed a sleepless night, riding in person to every

Den of the Klan and issuing positive orders that no white man should come to Piedmont.

A clash with the authority of the United States he had avoided from the first as a matter of principle. It was essential to his success that his men should commit no act of desperation which would imperil his plans. Above all, he wished to avoid a clash with old Stoneman personally.

The arrival of the big excursion was the signal for a revival of negro insolence which had been planned. The men brought from the Eastern part of the state were selected for the purpose. They marched over the town yelling and singing. A crowd of them, half drunk, formed themselves three abreast and rushed the sidewalks, pushing every white man, woman, and child into the street.

They met Phil on his way to the hotel and pushed him into the gutter. He said nothing, crossed the street, bought a revolver, loaded it and put it in his pocket. He was not popular with the negroes, and he had been shot at twice on his way from the mills at night. The whole affair of this rally, over which his father meant to preside, filled him with disgust, and he was in an ugly mood.

Lynch's speech was bold, bitter, and incendiary, and at its close the drunken negro troopers from the local garrison began to slouch through the streets, two and two, looking for trouble.

At the close of the speaking, Stoneman called the officer in command of these troops, and said:

"Major, I wish this rally to-day to be a proclamation

of the supremacy of law, and the enforcement of the
equality of every man under law. Your troops are entitled to the rights of white men. I understand the hotel
table has been free to-day to the soldiers from the camp
on the river. They are returning the courtesy extended
to the criminals who drilled before them. Send two of
your black troops down for dinner and see that it is served.
I wish an example for the state."

"It will be a dangerous performance, sir," the major
protested.

The old Commoner furrowed his brow.

"Have you been instructed to act under my orders?"

"I have, sir," said the officer, saluting.

"Then do as I tell you," snapped Stoneman.

Ben Cameron had kept indoors all day, and dined with
fifty of the Western troopers whom he had identified as
leading in the friendly demonstration to his men. Margaret, who had been busy with Mrs. Cameron entertain-
ing these soldiers, was seated in the dining-room alone
eating her dinner, while Phil waited impatiently in the
parlour.

The guests had all gone when two big negro troopers,
fighting drunk, walked into the hotel. They went to
the water-cooler and drank ostentatiously, thrusting
their thick lips coated with filth far into the cocoanut
dipper, while a dirty hand grasped its surface.

They pushed the dining-room door open and suddenly
flopped down beside Margaret.

She attempted to rise, and cried in rage:

"How dare you, black brutes?"

One of them threw his arm around her chair, thrust his face into hers, and said with a laugh:

"Don't hurry, my beauty; stay and take dinner wid us!"

Margaret again attempted to rise, and screamed, as Phil rushed into the room with drawn revolver. One of the negroes fired at him, missed, and the next moment dropped dead with a bullet through his heart.

The other leaped across the table and through the open window.

Margaret turned, confronting both Phil and Ben with revolvers in their hands, and fainted.

Ben hurried Phil out the back door and persuaded him to fly.

"Man, you must go! We must not have a riot here to-day. There's no telling what will happen. A disturbance now, and my men will swarm into town to-night. For God's sake go, until things are quiet!"

"But I tell you I'll face it. I'm not afraid," said Phil quietly.

"No, but I am," urged Ben. "These two hundred negroes are armed and drunk. Their officers may not be able to control them, and they may lay their hands on you—go—go!—go!—you must go! The train is due in fifteen minutes."

He half lifted him on a horse tied behind the hotel, leaped on another, galloped to the flag-station two miles out of town, and put him on the north-bound train.

"Stay in Charlotte until I wire for you," was Ben's parting injunction.

He turned his horse's head for McAllister's, sent the

two boys with all speed to the Cyclops of each of the ten township Dens with positive orders to disregard all wild rumours from Piedmont and keep every man out of town for two days.

As he rode back he met a squad of mounted white regulars, who arrested him. The trooper's companion had sworn positively that he was the man who killed the negro.

Within thirty minutes he was tried by drum-head court martial and sentenced to be shot.

CHAPTER VII

THE SNARE OF THE FOWLER

SWEET was the secret joy of old Stoneman over the fate of Ben Cameron. His death sentence would strike terror to his party, and his prompt execution, on the morning of the election but two days off, would turn the tide, save the state, and rescue his daughter from a hated alliance.

He determined to bar the last way of escape. He knew the Klan would attempt a rescue, and stop at no means fair or foul short of civil war. Afraid of the loyalty of the white battalions quartered in Piedmont, he determined to leave immediately for Spartanburg, order an exchange of garrisons, and, when the death warrant was returned from headquarters, place its execution in the hands of a stranger, to whom appeal would be vain. He knew such an officer in the Spartanburg post, a man of fierce, vindictive nature, once court martialed for cruelty, who hated every Southern white man with mortal venom. He would put him in command of the death-watch.

He hired a fast team and drove across the county with all speed, doubly anxious to get out of town before Elsie discovered the tragedy and appealed to him for mercy. Her tears and agony would be more than he could endure. She would stay indoors on account of the crowds, and he would not be missed until evening, when safely beyond her reach.

When Phil arrived at Charlotte he found an immense crowd at the bulletin board in front of the *Observer* office reading the account of the Piedmont tragedy. To his horror he learned of the arrest, trial, and sentence of Ben for the deed which he had done.

He rushed to the office of the Division Superintendent of the Piedmont Air Line Railroad, revealed his identity, told him the true story of the tragedy, and begged for a special to carry him back. The Superintendent, who was a clansman, not only agreed, but within an hour had the special ready and two cars filled with stern-looking men to accompany him. Phil asked no questions. He knew what it meant. The train stopped at Gastonia and King's Mountain and took on a hundred more men.

The special pulled into Piedmont at dusk. Phil ran to the Commandant and asked for an interview with Ben alone.

"For what purpose, sir?" the officer asked.

Phil resorted to a ruse, knowing the Commandant to be unaware of any difference of opinion between him and his father.

"I hold a commission to obtain a confession from the prisoner which may save his life by destroying the Ku Klux Klan."

He was admitted at once and the guard ordered to withdraw until the interview ended.

Phil took Ben Cameron's place, exchanging hat and

coat, and wrote a note to his father, telling in detail the truth, and asked for his immediate interference.

"Deliver that, and I'll be out of here in two hours," he said, as he placed the note in Ben's hand.

"I'll go straight to the house," was the quick reply.

The exchange of the Southerner's slouch hat and Prince Albert for Phil's derby and short coat completely fooled the guard in the dim light. The men were as much alike as twins except the shade of difference in the colour of their hair. He passed the sentinel without a challenge, and walked rapidly toward Stoneman's house.

On the way he was astonished to meet five hundred soldiers just arrived on a special from Spartanburg. Amazed at the unexpected movement, he turned and followed them back to the jail.

They halted in front of the building he had just vacated, and their commander handed an official document to the officer in charge. The guard was changed and a cordon of soldiers encircled the prison.

The Piedmont garrison had received notice by wire to move to Spartanburg, and Ben heard the beat of their drums already marching to board the special.

He pressed forward and asked an interview with the Captain in command.

The answer came with a brutal oath:

"I have been warned against all the tricks and lies this town can hatch. The commander of the death-watch will permit no interview, receive no visitors, hear no appeal, and allow no communication with the prisoner until after the execution. You can announce this to whom it may concern."

"But you've got the wrong man. You have no right to execute him," said Ben, excitedly.

"I'll risk it," he answered, with a sneer.

"Great God!" Ben cried, beneath his breath. "The old fool has entrapped his son in the net he spread for me!"

CHAPTER VIII

A Ride for a Life

WHEN Ben Cameron failed to find either Elsie or her father at home, he hurried to the hotel, walking under the shadows of the trees to avoid recognition, though his resemblance to Phil would have enabled him to pass in his hat and coat unchallenged by any save the keenest observers.

He found his mother's bedroom door ajar and saw Elsie within sobbing in her arms. He paused, watched, and listened.

Never had he seen his mother so beautiful—her face calm, intelligent and vital, crowned with a halo of gray. She stood, flushed and dignified, softly smoothing the golden hair of the sobbing girl whom she had learned to love as her daughter. Her whole being reflected the years of homage she had inspired in husband, children, and neighbours. What a woman! She had made war inevitable, fought it to the bitter end; and in the despair of a Negro reign of terror, still the prophetess and high priestess of a people, serene, undismayed and defiant, she had fitted the uniform of a Grand Dragon on her last son, and sewed in secret day and night to equip his men. And through it all she was without affectation, her sweet motherly ways, gentle manner and bearing always resistless to those who came within her influence.

362

"If he dies," cried the tearful voice, "I shall never forgive myself for not surrendering without reserve and fighting his battles with him!"

"He is not dead yet," was the mother's firm answer. "Doctor Cameron is on Queen's back. Your lover's men will be riding to-night—these young dare-devil Knights of the South, with their life in their hands, a song on their lips, and the scorn of death in their souls!"

"Then I'll ride with them," cried the girl, suddenly lifting her head.

Ben stepped into the room, and with a cry of joy Elsie sprang into his arms. The mother stood silent until their lips met in the long tender kiss of the last surrender of perfect love.

"How did you escape so soon?" she asked quietly, while Elsie's head still lay on his breast.

"Phil shot the brute, and I rushed him out of town. He heard the news, returned on the special, took my place, and sent me for his father. The guard has been changed, and it's impossible to see him, or communicate with the new Commandant——"

Elsie started and turned pale.

"And father has hidden to avoid me—merciful God— if Phil is executed——"

"He isn't dead yet, either," said Ben, slipping his arm around her. "But we must save him without a clash or a drop of bloodshed, if possible. The fate of our people may hang on this. A battle with United States troops now might mean ruin for the South——

"But you will save him?" Elsie pleaded, looking into his face.

"Yes—or I'll go down with him," was the steady answer.

"Where is Margaret?" he asked.

"Gone to McAllister's with a message from your father," Mrs. Cameron replied.

"Tell her when she returns to keep a steady nerve. I'll save Phil. Send her to find her father. Tell him to hold five hundred men ready for action in the woods by the river and the rest in reserve two miles out of town——"

"May I go with her?" Elsie asked, eagerly.

"No. I may need you," he said. "I am going to find the old statesman now, if I have to drag the bottomless pit. Wait here until I return."

Ben reached the telegraph office unobserved, called the operator at Columbia, and got the Grand Giant of the county into the office. Within an hour he learned that the death-warrant had been received and approved. It would be returned by a messenger to Piedmont on the morning train. He learned also that any appeal for a stay must be made through the Honourable Austin Stoneman, the secret representative of the Government clothed with this special power. The execution had been ordered the day of the election, to prevent the concentration of any large force bent on rescue.

"The old fox!" Ben muttered.

From the Grand Giant at Spartanburg he learned, after a delay of three hours, that Stoneman had left with a boy in a buggy, which he had hired for three days, and refused to tell his destination. He promised to follow and locate him as quickly as possible.

It was the afternoon on the day following, during the progress of the election, before Ben received the message from Spartanburg that Stoneman had been found at the Old Red Tavern where the roads crossed from Piedmont to Hambright. It was only twelve miles away, just over the line on the North Carolina side.

He walked with Margaret to the block where Queen stood saddled, watching with pride the quiet air of self-control with which she bore herself.

"Now, my sister, you know the way to the tavern. Ride for your sweetheart's life. Bring the old man here by five o'clock, and we'll save Phil without a fight. Keep your nerve. The Commandant knows a regiment of mine is lying in the woods, and he's trying to slip out of town with his prisoner. I'll stand by my men ready for a battle at a moment's notice, but for God's sake get here in time to prevent it."

She stooped from the saddle, pressed her brother's hand, kissed him, and galloped swiftly over the old Way of Romance she knew so well.

On reaching the tavern, the landlord rudely denied that any such man was there, and left her standing dazed and struggling to keep back the tears.

A boy of eight, with big wide friendly eyes, slipped into the room, looked up into her face tenderly, and said:

"He's the biggest liar in North Carolina. The old man's right upstairs in the room over your head. Come on; I'll show you."

Margaret snatched the child in her arms and kissed him.

She knocked in vain for ten minutes. At last she heard his voice within:

"Go away from that door!"

"I'm from Piedmont, sir," cried Margaret, "with an important message from the Commandant for you."

"Yes; I saw you come. I will not see you. I know everything, and I will hear no appeal."

"But you can not know of the exchange of men"— pleaded the girl.

"I tell you I know all about it. I will not interfere——"

"But you could not be so cruel——"

"The majesty of the law must be vindicated. The judge who consents to the execution of a murderer is not cruel. He is showing mercy to Society. Go, now; I will not hear you."

In vain Margaret knocked, begged, pleaded, and sobbed.

At last, in a fit of desperation, as she saw the sun sinking lower and the precious minutes flying, she hurled her magnificent figure against the door and smashed the cheap lock which held it.

The old man sat at the other side of the room, looking out of the window, with his massive jaws locked in rage. The girl staggered to his side, knelt by his chair, placed her trembling hand on his arm, and begged:

"For the love of Jesus, have mercy! Come with me quickly!"

With a growl of anger, he said:

"No!"

"It was a mad impulse, in my defense as well as his own."

"Impulse, yes! But back of it lay banked the fires of cruelty and race hatred! The Nation can not live with such barbarism rotting its heart out."

"But this is war, sir,—a war of races, and this an accident of war—besides, his life had been attempted by them twice before."

"So I've heard, and yet the Negro always happens to be the victim——"

Margaret leaped to her feet and glared at the old man for a moment in uncontrollable anger.

"Are you a fiend?" she fairly shrieked.

Old Stoneman merely pursed his lips.

The girl came a step closer, and extended her hand again in mute appeal.

"No, I was foolish. You are not cruel. I have heard of a hundred acts of charity you have done among our poor. Come, this is horrible! It is impossible! You can not consent to the death of your son——"

Stoneman looked up sharply:

"Thank God, he hasn't married my daughter yet——"

"Your daughter!" gasped Margaret. "I've told you it was Phil who killed the negro! He took Ben's place just before the guards were exchanged——"

"Phil!—Phil?" shrieked the old man, staggering to his club foot and stumbling toward Margaret with dilated eyes and whitening face; "My boy—Phil?—why—why, are you crazy?—Phil? Did you say—*Phil?*"

"Yes. Ben persuaded him to go to Charlotte until

the excitement passed to avoid trouble.—Come, come, sir, we must be quick! We may be too late!"

She seized and pulled him toward the door.

"Yes. Yes, we must hurry," he said in a laboured whisper, looking around dazed. "You will show me the way, my child—you love him—yes, we will go quickly—quickly! my boy—my boy!"

Margaret called the landlord, and while they hitched Queen to the buggy, the old man stood helplessly wringing and fumbling his big ugly hands, muttering incoherently, and tugging at his collar as though about to suffocate.

As they dashed away, old Stoneman laid a trembling hand on Margaret's arm.

"Your horse is a good one, my child?"

"Yes; the one Marion saved—the finest in the county."

"And you know the way?"

"Every foot of it. Phil and I have driven it often."

"Yes, yes—you love him," he sighed, pressing her hand.

Through the long reckless drive, as the mare flew over the rough hills, every nerve and muscle of her fine body at its utmost tension, the father sat silent. He braced his club foot against the iron bar of the dashboard and gripped the sides of the buggy to steady his feeble body. Margaret leaned forward intently watching the road to avoid an accident. The old man's strange colourless eyes stared straight in front, wide open, and seeing nothing, as if the soul had already fled through them into eternity.

CHAPTER IX

"Vengeance Is Mine"

IT was dark long before Margaret and Stoneman reached Piedmont. A mile out of town a horse neighed in the woods, and, tired as she was, Queen threw her head high and answered the call.

The old man did not notice it, but Margaret knew a squadron of white-and-scarlet horsemen stood in those woods, and her heart gave a bound of joy.

As they passed the Presbyterian church, she saw through the open window her father standing at his Elder's seat leading in prayer. They were holding a watch service, asking God for victory in the eventful struggle of the day.

Margaret attempted to drive straight to the jail, and a sentinel stopped them.

"I am Stoneman, sir—the real commander of these troops," said the old man, with authority.

"Orders is orders, and I don't take 'em from you," was the answer.

"Then tell your commander that Mr. Stoneman has just arrived from Spartanburg and asks to see him at the hotel immediately."

He hobbled into the parlour and waited in agony while

369

Margaret tied the mare. Ben, her mother and father, and every servant were gone.

In a few moments the second officer hurried to Stoneman, saluted, and said:

"We've pulled it off in good shape, sir. They've tried to fool us with a dozen tricks, and a whole regiment has been lying in wait for us all day. But at dark the Captain outwitted them, took his prisoner with a squad of picked cavalry, and escaped their pickets. They've been gone an hour, and ought to be back with the body——"

Old Stoneman sprang on him with the sudden fury of a madman, clutching at his throat.

"If you've killed my son," he gasped—"go—go! Follow them with a swift messenger and stop them! It's a mistake—you're killing the wrong man—you're killing my boy—quick—my God, quick—don't stand there staring at me!"

The officer rushed to obey his order, as Margaret entered.

The old man seized her arm, and said with laboured breath:

"Your father, my child, ask him to come to me quickly."

Margaret hurried to the church, and an usher called the doctor to the door.

He read the question trembling on the girl's lips.

"Nothing has happened yet, my daughter. Your brother has held a regiment of his men in readiness every moment of the day."

"Mr. Stoneman is at the hotel and asks to see you immediately," she whispered.

"God grant he may prevent bloodshed," said the father. "Go inside and stay with your mother."

When Doctor Cameron entered the parlour, Stoneman hobbled painfully to meet him, his face ashen, and his breath rattling in his throat as if his soul were being strangled.

"You are my enemy, Doctor," he said, taking his hand, "but you are a pious man. I have been called an infidel—I am only a wilful sinner—I have slain my own son, unless God Almighty, who can raise the dead, shall save him! You are the man at whom I aimed the blow that has fallen on my head. I wish to confess to you and set myself right before God. He may hear my cry, and have mercy on me."

He gasped for breath, sank into his seat, looked around, and said:

"Will you close the door?"

The doctor complied with his request and returned.

"We all wear masks, Doctor," began the trembling voice. "Beneath lie the secrets of love and hate from which actions move. My will alone forged the chains of Negro rule. Three forces moved me—party success, a vicious woman, and the quenchless desire for personal vengeance. When I first fell a victim to the wiles of the yellow vampire who kept my house, I dreamed of lifting her to my level. And when I felt myself sinking into the black abyss of animalism, I, whose soul had learned the pathway of the stars and held high converse with the great spirits of the ages——"

He paused, looked up in terror, and whispered:

"What's that noise? Isn't it the distant beat of horses' hoofs?"

"No," said the doctor, listening; "it's the roar of the falls we hear, from a sudden change of the wind."

"I'm done now," Stoneman went on, slowly fumbling his hands. "My life has been a failure. The dice of God are always loaded."

His great head drooped lower, and he continued:

"Mightiest of all was my motive of revenge. Fierce business and political feuds wrecked my iron-mills. I shouldered their vast debts, and paid the last mortgage of a hundred thousand dollars the week before Lee invaded my state. I stood on the hill in the darkness, cried, raved, cursed, while I watched his troops lay those mills in ashes. Then and there I swore that I'd live until I ground the South beneath my heel! When I got back to my house, they had buried a Confederate soldier in the field. I dug his body up, carted it to the woods, and threw it into a ditch——"

The hand of the white-haired Southerner suddenly gripped old Stoneman's throat—and then relaxed. His head sank on his breast, and he cried in anguish:

"God be merciful to me a sinner! Would I, too, seek revenge!"

Stoneman looked at the doctor, dazed by his sudden onslaught and collapse.

"Yes, he was somebody's boy down here," he went on, "who was loved perhaps even as I love—I don't blame you. See, in the inside pocket next to my heart I carry the pictures of Phil and Elsie taken from babyhood up, all set in a little book. They don't know this—nor does the world dream I've been so soft-hearted——"

He drew a miniature album from his pocket and fumbled it aimlessly:

"You know Phil was my first-born——"

His voice broke, and he looked at the doctor helplessly.

The Southerner slipped his arm around the old man's shoulders and began a tender and reverent prayer.

The sudden thunder of a squad of cavalry with clanking sabres swept by the hotel toward the jail.

Stoneman scrambled to his feet, staggered, and caught a chair.

"It's no use," he groaned, "—they've come with his body—I'm slipping down—the lights are going out—I haven't a friend! It's dark and cold—I'm alone, and lost—God—has—hidden—His—face—from—me!"

Voices were heard without, and the tramp of heavy feet on the steps.

Stoneman clutched the doctor's arm in agony:

"Stop them!—Stop them! Don't let them bring him in here!"

He sank limp into the chair and stared at the door as it swung open and Phil walked in, with Ben and Elsie by his side in full clansman disguise.

The old man leaped to his feet and gasped:

"The Klan!—The Klan! No? Yes! It's true—glory to God, they've saved my boy!—Phil—Phil!"

"How did you rescue him?" Doctor Cameron asked Ben.

"Had a squadron lying in wait on every road that led

from town. The Captain thought a thousand men were on him, and surrendered without a shot."

At twelve o'clock, Ben stood at the gate with Elsie.

"Your fate hangs in the balance of this election to-night," she said. "I'll share it with you, success or failure, life or death."

"Success, not failure," he answered, firmly. "The Grand Dragons of six states have already wired victory. Look at our lights on the mountains! They are ablaze —range on range our signals gleam until the Fiery Cross is lost among the stars!"

"What does it mean?" she whispered.

"That I am a successful revolutionist—that Civilisation has been saved, and the South redeemed from shame."

The End